Frank's
500

THE **THRILLER** FILM GUIDE
Alan Frank

Frank's 500

HE **THRILLER** FILM GUIDE

Alan Frank

B.T. Batsford Ltd • London

ACKNOWLEDGEMENTS

My thanks to Channel 4 Television, Richard Parsons, Laszlo Svaty-Pramen, Gary Parfitt, Warren Sherman, Hayden Williams, to my patient and helpful editor, Richard Reynolds, a.k.a. crippled newsboy Billy Batson, and to the sadly long-ago-demolished Playhouse Cinema in Nairobi where it all began.

First published 1997

© Alan Frank 1997

Printed by Butler & Tanner, Frome, Somerset

For the publishers

B.T. Batsford Ltd
583 Fulham Road
London SW6 5BY

A CIP catalogue record for this book is available from The British Library.

ISBN 7134 2728 0

CONTENTS

To Gilly, who thrills me.

INTRODUCTION

Westerns, musicals, horror and science fiction movies are easy to recognize, but thrillers are not as amenable to absolute definition, since they can and do embrace selections from such genre staples as mystery, murder, mayhem, intrigue, suspense and shock.

There are no empirical parameters that uneqivocally brand thriller movies, but they do possess one common component, and this is the major criterion I have used to select the films for this book. It seems obvious that the prime purpose of thrillers is that they should thrill, or at least make the pulse race a little faster for most moviegoers.

Inevitably though, as with all genres, there is little real consensus as to what constitues a 'good' thriller, apart, that is, from those truly devout and blinkered *auteur* obsessives whose heroes can do no wrong even when, embarrassingly, they do.

Frank's 500 is patently not intended to be a definitive guide. My choices are strictly personal, arbitary (it would need several large volumes to cover so wide a genre properly), undoubtedly biased, and culled, Leone-style, from the good, the bad and the ugly. If the latter predominate, it is simply because the majority of movies fit snugly into the categories of bad and downright hideous, and my selection unashamedly reflects this. I can't see that it is possible to recognize, let alone rate, great films unless you have seen sufficient cinematic dreck to provide you with a basic critical perspective. In addition, many 'minor' movies prove to be considerably more entertaining than more lauded/expensive/over-promoted pictures.

I also believe it is facile and ultimately counterproductive to follow critical fads slavishly and hail hollow heroes unreservedly, since today's Tarantinos far too frequently become yesterday's forgotten failures and find themselves relegated to sad footnotes in film history. Not that I have excluded the usual cult suspects from an eclectic criminal line-up that is rather more the product of many hours happily misspent in the cinema than a momument to cinecultural orthodoxy. However, I should stress that not *all* the blood in these pages belongs in the films – some of it is the result of my unfortunate tendency to take a chainsaw to sacred cows.

Alan Frank
London 1997

THE ACCUSED

(US 1949)

pc Paramount. p Hal B Wallis. d William Dieterle. w Ketti Frings, (uncredited) Leonard Spigelgass, Barre Lyndon, Jonathan Latimer, Allen Rivkin, Charles Schnee, from the novel *Be Still My Love* by June Truesdell. ph Milton Krasner. B&W. ad Hans Dreier, Earl Hedrick. m Victor Young. 101 mins

Cast: Loretta Young (Wilma Tuttle), Robert Cummings (Warren Ford), Wendell Corey (Lt Ted Dorgan), Sam Jaffe (Dr Rompley), Douglas Dick (Bill Perry), Suzanne Delbert (Susan Duval), Sara Allgood (Mrs Connor), Mickey Knox (Jack Hunter), George Spaulding (Dean Rhodes), Ann Doran (Miss Rice)

A repressed professor of psychology accidentally kills the student who tries to seduce her, and a detective sets out to prove the man was murdered.

The plotting is slipshod, the direction tepid, there is little suspense since it is obvious that Loretta Young is never in real peril from the law, and the so-called psychologist is strictly for the naive.

'The story does not ring true, and there are too many unnecessary red herrings to make for clarity.'
Monthly Film Bulletin

ACROSS 110TH STREET

(US 1972)

pc Film Guarantors. exec p Anthony Quinn, Barry Shear. p Fouad Said, Ralph Serpe. d Barry Shear. w Luther Davis, from the novel by Wally Ferris. ph Jack Priestley. Colour. ad Perry Watkins. m J J Johnson. 102 mins

Cast: Antony Quinn (Capt. Frank Mattelli), Yaphet Kotto (Det. Lt Pope). Anthony Franciosa (Nick D'Salvio), Paul Benjamin (Jim Harris), Ed Bernard (Joe Logart), Richard Ward (Doc Johnson), Antonio Fargas (Henry J Jackson), Norma Donaldson (Gloria Roberts), Gilbert Lewis (Shevvy), Nat Polen (Lt Reilly)

Three blacks disguised as policemen rob a Harlem bank and trigger off violence involving the Mafia, blacks and the police.

Barry Shear's direction is slick and efficient and almost disguises the fact that the film is simply meretricious and violent, with exploitative racial overtones. Visceral, certainly, but lacking in intellectual content.

'The violence is so continuous and the death rate so high that one's sensibilities have become bloated long before the hostile black cop and the revengeful white cop die hand in hand on the rooftops.'
Morning Star

AFTER THE THIN MAN

(US 1936)

pc MGM. p Hunt Stromberg. d W S Van Dyke. w Frances Goodrich, Albert Hackett. ph Oliver T Marsh. B&W. m Herbert Stothart, Edward Ward. 110 mins

Cast: William Powell (Nick Charles), Myrna Loy (Nora Charles), Elissa Landi (Salma Landis), James Stewart (David Graham), Joseph Calleia (Dancer). Jessie Ralph (Aunt Katherine Forrest), Alan Marshall (Robert Landis), Sam Levene (Lt Abrams), George Zucco (Dr Adolph Kammer)

Husband-and-wife sleuths Nick and Nora Charles unmask a killer in San Francisco.

Pleasing sequel to *The Thin Man* (*q.v.*): the leads are as much fun as before, and the thriller element just sufficient to showcase their engaging relationship.

'If *After the Thin Man* is not quite the delight *The Thin Man* was, it is, at the very least, one of the most urbane comedies of the season.'
The New York Times

AL CAPONE
(US 1959)

pc Allied Artists. A Burrows-Ackerman Production. p John H Burrows, Leonard J Ackerman. d Richard Wilson. w Marvin Wald, Henry Greenberg. ph Lucien Ballard. B&W. ad Hilyard Brown. sfx Dave Koehler. m David Raksin. 105 mins

Cast: Rod Steiger (Al Capone), Fay Spain (Maureen Flannery), Murvyn Vye (Bugs Moran), Nehemiah Persoff (Johnny Torrio), Martin Balsam (Keely), James Gregory (Schaeffer), Joe De Santis (Big Jim Colosimo), Lewis Charles (Hymie Weiss), Robert Gist (O'Bannion), Louis Quinn (Joe Lorenzo)

Fictionalized biopic of Capone, tracing his career from his arrival in Chicago in the twenties, his rise to power and his eventual conviction for income tax evasion which led to his being jailed in Alcatraz.

Competent, if hardly informative, throwback to the typical Warner Bros. gangster pictures of the thirties, with a nice eye for period detail and a typically over-the-top performance by Steiger.

'If we have to have gangster films, this is obviously the one.'
The Star

THE ALPHABET MURDERS
(US 1965)

pc MGM. p Lawrence P Bachman. assoc p Ben Arbeid. d Frank Tashlin. w David Pursall, Jack Seddon, from the novel *The ABC Murders* by Agatha Christie. ph Desmond Dickinson. B&W. ad Bill Andrews. m Ron Goodwin. 90 mins

Cast: Tony Randall (Hercule Poirot), Anita Ekberg (Amanda Beatrice Cross), Robert Morley (Hastings), Maurice Denham (Insp. Japp), Guy Rolfe (Duncan Doncaster), Sheila Allen (Lady Diane), James Villiers (Franklin), Julian Glover (Don Fortune), Clive Morton ('K'), Austin Trevor (Judson)

Belgian detective Hercule Poirot comes to London and solves a series of puzzling murders in which the victims are linked alphabetically.

The star is miscast, the screenplay is no better, and the ill-chosen director makes them seem even worse, so that the poorly-judged blend of unfunny 'humour' and mystery falls fatally flat.

'It is hard to combine comedy and murder and keep both viable and Tashlin does a good job.'
The Hollywood Reporter

AMSTERDAM KILL
(GB 1968)

pc Trio Films/Group W. exec p William Gell, Howard Barnes. p George Willoughby. d Gerry O'Hara. w Edmund Ward, from the novel

Love in Amsterdam by Nicolas Freeling. ph Gerry Fisher. Colour. ad Terry Pritchard. m Patrick John Scott. 91 mins

Cast: Wolfgang Kieling (Insp. Van Der Valk), William Marlowe (Martin Ray), Catherine Von Schell (Sophie Ray), Pamela Ann Davy (Elsa De Charnoy), Josef Dubin-Behrman (Eric De Charnoy), Lo Van Hensbergen (Magistrate), Will Van Selst (Policeman), Erik Plooyer (Baron), Guido De Moor (Piet Ulbricht)

A thriller writer is charged with killing his former mistress in Amsterdam, but a police inspector is not sure they have the right man.

Neat, unpretentious murder mystery, with Amsterdam locations adding interest.

'Well made, workmanlike thriller, given an attractively bitter flavour by Edmund Ward's acidic dialogue ... satisfying fare for addicts.'
The Daily Cinema

THE AMSTERDAM KILL
(HONG KONG 1977)

pc Golden Harvest/Fantastic Films SA. exec p Raymond Chow. p André Morgan. d Robert Clouse. w Robert Clouse, Gregory Teifer. st Gregory Teifer. ph Alan Hume. Colour. Panavision. ad John Blezzard, K S Chen. sfx Gene Grigg. m Hal Schaeffer. 93 mins

Cast: Robert Mitchum (Quinlan), Bradford Dillman (Odums), Richard Egan (Ridgeway), Leslie Nielsen (Riley Knight), Keye Luke (Chung Wei), George Chung (Jimmy Wong), Chen Hsing (Assassin), Stephen Leung (rn

Leung Kerlung) (Insp. Paul Fox)

A discredited American narcotics agent becomes an intermediary for an Amsterdam-based Chinese drug dealer, smashes the operation and clears his name.
East meets West, but who cares? Certainly, judging by their lacklustre performances, the cast doesn't.

'Hardly different from the most routine and impoverished TV movie.'
Screen International

AND SOON THE DARKNESS
(GB 1970)
pc Associated British Productions. p Albert Fennell, Brian Clemens. d Robert Fuest. w Brian Clemens, Terry Nation. ph Ian Wilson. Colour. ad Phillip Harrison. m Laurie Johnson. 99 mins

Cast: Pamela Franklin (Jane), Michele Dotrice (Cathy), Sandor Eles (Paul), John Nettleton (Gendarme), Clare Kelly (Schoolmistress), Hans-Maria Pravda (Madame Lassal), John Franklyn (Old Man), Claude Bertrand (Lassal), Jean Carmet (Renier)

When a young English girl vanishes on a cycling holiday in France, her companion, aware there is a sex killer on the loose, elists a man to help find her.
Occasionally suspenseful but mostly risibly bad, with a low budget and even lower aspirations.

'*And Soon the Darkness*, which makes use of many Hitchcockian techniques, is thin in comparison.'
Films and Filming

THE ANDERSON TAPES
(US 1971)
pc Robert M Weitman Productions. p Robert M Weitman. assoc p George Justin. d Sidney Lumet. w Frank R Pierson, from the novel by Lawrence Sanders. ph Arthur J Ornitz. Colour. Panavision. pd Benjamin J Kasazkow. ad Philip Rosenberg. m Quincy Jones. 99 mins

Cast: Sean Connery (Duke Anderson), Dyan Cannon (Ingrid Everleigh), Martin Balsam (Tommy Haskins), Ralph Meeker (Capt. Delaney), Alan King (Pat Angelo), Christopher Walken (The Kid), Val Avery ('Socks' Parelli), Dick Williams (Spencer), Garrett Morris (Everson), Margaret Hamilton (Mrs Kaler)

A former convict recruits a gang to rob an entire Manhattan apartment block, unaware that his plans have been accidentally monitored and taped.
Ingeniously plotted with above-average direction, a suspenseful climax and good performances.

'Faced with a highly professional cast, taut, well written, beautifully cast, brilliantly photographed, skilfully edited, splendidly acted thriller like *The Anderson Tapes* there is very little for a critic to say except "Go and see it."'
The Observer

ARREST BULLDOG DRUMMOND
(US 1939)
pc Paramount. p Stuart Walker. d James Hogan. w Stuart Palmer. from the novel *The Final Count* by 'Sapper' (rn H C McNeile). ph Ted Tetzlaff. B&W. ad Hans Dreier, Franz Bachelin.

md Boris Morros. 60 mins

Cast: John Howard (Hugh 'Bulldog' Drummond), Heather Angel (Phyllis Clavering), H B Warner (Col. Neilson), Reginald Denny (Algy Longworth), E E Clive (Tenny), Jean Fenwick (Lady Beryl Ledyard), Zeffie Tilbury (Aunt Meg), George Zucco (Rolf Anderson), Leonard Mudie (Richard Gannett), John Sutton (Insp. Tredinnis)

Bulldog Drummond clears his name by unmasking the real villain when he is accused of stealing a deadly ray machine.
Howard's final fling as Paramount's Bulldog Drummond is a tired affair, with only Zucco's pebble-lensed villain to recommend it. Those who bothered to see it through to the end saw Drummond finally marry.

'Quite a lark, especially if you've a mind to boo the hero and cheer the villains.'
The New York Times

THE ASPHALT JUNGLE
(US 1950)
pc MGM. p Arthur Hornblow Jr. d John Huston. w John Huston, Ben Maddow, from the novel by W R Burnett. ph Harold Rosson. B&W. ad Cedric Gibbons, Randall Duell. m Miklos Rosza. 112 mins

Cast: Sterling Hayden (Dix Handley), Louis Calhern (Alonzo D Emmerich), Jean Hagen (Moll Conovan), James Whitmore (Gus Minissi), Sam Jaffe (Doc Riedenschneider), John McIntire (Police Commissioner Hardy), Marc Lawrence (Cobby), Barry Kelly (Lt

Dietrich), Marilyn Monroe (Angela Phinlay), Anthony Caruso (Louis Ciavelli), Brad Dexter (Bob Brannon)

A man leaves jail and recruits a gang of criminals to carry out a million-dollar jewel heist.

Bleak, archetypal heist-and-its-aftermath movie with exemplary direction by Huston (Oscar-nominated for screenplay and direction) and concerned as much with character as with the mechanics of the crime itself. The performances are uniformly good, and the film is notable, in retrospect, for Marilyn Monroe's first major performance – as Louis Calhern's mistress. Remade (indifferently) as *The Badlanders* (1958), *Cairo* (1963) and *Cool Breeze* (1972).

'Even with its shortcomings, the picture succeeds to a remarkable extent in understanding its criminals, and creating a kind of perverse sympathy for them without condoning their crimes. To have accomplished that within a story which is also a taut and exciting thriller, lifts *The Asphalt Jungle* high above the run of melodramas that do not score half as well on targets much easier to hit.'
Time

'Full of nasty, ugly people doing nasty things. I wouldn't walk across the room to see a thing like that.'
MGM chief Louis B Mayer

ASSASSINS

(US 1995)

pc Silver Pictures. In association with Donner/Shuler-Donner Productions. p Richard Donner, Joel Silver, Bruce Evans, Raynold Gideon, Andrew Lazar, Jim van Wyck. co-p Richard Solomon, Alexander Collett, Dan Cracchiolo. assoc p J Mills Goodloe, Ryse A Reiutlinger, Cynthia L Neber, Tony Munafo, Karyn Fileds, Julie Durk. d Richard Donner. w Andy Wachowski, Larry Wachowski, Brian Hegeland. st Andy Wachowski, Larry Wachowski. ph Vilmos Zsigmond. 2nd unit ph Gary Holt. aerial ph Frank Holgate. Colour. ed Richard Marks, Lawrence Jordan, Lori C Ingle. pd Tom Sanders. sup ad Daniel T Dorrance. ad Nathan Crowley, Steven Arnold, Leticia Stella. sc Conrad Palmisano, Dick Hancock. m Mark Mancina. add m Don Harper, John van Tongeren, Christopher Ward, Jeff Rona. 133 mins

Cast: Sylvester Stallone (Robert Rath), Antonio Banderas (Miguel Bain), Julianne Moore (Electra), Anatoly Davydov (Nikolai), Muse Watson (Ketcham), Stephen Kahan (Alan Branch), Kelly Rowan (Jennifer), Reed Diamond (Bob), Kai Wulff (Remy), Kerry Staisky, James Douglas Haskins, David 'Shark' Fralick (Buyers)

A hitman sets out to kill his rival so as to establish himself as the best in the business.

Over-complex, mindless mayhem hokum with more producers than sense and far better direction than the material deserves, and a performance of such awe-inspiring awfulness from Banderas that he makes Stallone resemble Olivier at his peak.

'Expensive, brainless tosh and it goes on for far too long.'
Daily Star

ASSASSINS

BAD BOYS

(US 1995)

pc Columbia. exec p Bruce S Pustin, Lucas Foster. p Don Simpson, Jerry Bruckheimer. d Michael Bay. 2nd unit d Ken Bates. w Michael Barrie, Jim Mulholland, Doug Richardson. st George Gallo. ph Howard Atherton. 2nd unit ph Peter Lyons Collister. Colour. ed Christian Wagner. pd John Vallone. ad Peter Politanoff. sfx co-ord Richard Lee Jones. sc Ken Bates. m Mark Mancina, Nick Glennie Smith, Christopher Ward. 118 mins

Cast: Martin Lawrence (Marcus Burnett), Will Smith (Mike Lowry), Tea Leoni (Julie Mott), Tcheky Karyo (Fouchat), Theresa Randle (Theresa Burnett), Marg Helgenberger (Alison Sinclair), Hector Serrano (Det. Sanchez), Julio Oscar Hecheso (Det. Ruiz), Michael Imperioli (Jojo), Joe Pantoliano (Capt. Howard), Saviero Guerra (Chet the Doorman), Anna Thompson (Francine)

Two black Miami narcotics cops sort out a ruthless European criminal who steals millions of dollars worth of drugs from the police.

All slick surface sheen and shallow excitement, a typical Simpson-Bruckheimer production in fact, designed to provide fast-moving, fast-food-style visceral thrills without engaging the intellect for even an MTV moment.

'The plot is sheer nonsense. As always, though, the action is loud, the explosions impressive enough for any Saturday-night pyromaniac. Trouble is, the boys themselves aren't quite bad enough to hold the interest.'
The Daily Telegraph

'Part way through this noisy, brainless, clichéd but undoubtedly exciting action thriller, somebody pauses long enough to say "This is bullshit!" With which critical sentiment I heartily agree.'
Video Home Entertainment

THE BAD SEED

(US 1956)

pc A Mervyn LeRoy Production. p, d Mervyn LeRoy. w John Lee Mahin, from the play by Maxwell Anderson & the novel by William March. ph Hal Rosson. B&W. ad John Beckman. m Alex North. 128 mins

Cast: Patty McCormack (Rhoda), Nancy Kelly (Christine), Henry Jones (Le Roy), Eileen Heckart (Mrs Daigle), Evelyn Varden (Monica), William Hopper (Kenneth), Paul Fix (Bravo), Jesse White (Emory), Gage Clark (Tasker), Joan Croyden (Miss Fern), Frank Caidy (Mr Daigle)

An eight-year-old girl is a conscienceless murderer and survives her mother's attempt to kill her.

Macabre and spellbinding (although highly suspect in its interpretation of genetics – the girl's mother turns out to be the daughter of a notorious killer whose own lethal career started young), it's tautly claustrophobic up to the attempt on the girl's life: then contemporary censorship sets in, there's a risible climax in which the girl is killed by a fortuitous lightning bolt, followed by a ludicrous 'curtain call' in which the actors take their

Left: **BAD BOYS**
Above: **THE BAD SEED**

Rosenberg. sfx Conrad Brink. tech adv Eddie Egan. m J J Jackson. 116 mins

Cast: Robert Duvall (Eddie Egan), Verna Bloom (Maureen), Henry Darrow (Sweet William), Eddie Egan (Scanlon), Felipe Luciano (Ruben), Tina Cristiana (Mrs Caputo), Marina Durell (Rita Garcia), Chico Martinez (Frankie Diaz), Joe Duval (Ferrer), Louis Cosentino (Gigi Caputo)

After being suspended from the force following the death of a suspect, police detective Eddie Egan investigates the murder of his former partner.

Glossy, tough, brutal and basically B-feature thriller based on the exploits of NYPD cop Eddie Egan (of *The French Connection* fame) who was the technical adviser and appears as Scanlon. Efficient but hardly holding, with a dubious line in morality: the slow-paced direction isn't much help either.

bows and McCormack's screen mother puts her over her knee and soundly spanks her. The performances are uniformly excellent, and McCormack (reprising her Broadway role along with Heckart and Jones) genuinely chilling. She, Heckart and Kelly were Oscar-nominated.

'A truly classic chiller: the stuff nightmares are made of.'
New York Post

'Brilliant acting and production, a grim, thought-provoking "X" certificate thriller which will hold you throughout.'
Picture Show

BADGE 373
(US 1973)
pc Paramount. p, d Howard W Koch. assoc p Lawrence Appelbaum. 2nd unit d Michael D Moore. w Pete Hamill, based on the exploits of Eddie Egan. ph Arthur J Ornitz. Colour. ad Philip

BASIC INSTINCT

BASIC INSTINCT

(US 1992)

pc Carolco/Studio Canal. exec p Mario Kassar. p Alan Marshall. assoc p William S Beasley, Louis D'Esposito. d Paul Verhoeven. 2nd unit d M James Arnett. w Joe Eszterhas. ph Jan De Bont. 2nd unit ph Michael Ferris. aerial ph Stan McClain. Colour. Panavision. ed Frank J Urioste. pd Terence Marsh. ad Mark Billerman. visual sfx Rob Bottin. sc M James Arnett, Charles Picerni. m Jerry Goldsmith. 128 mins

Cast: Michael Douglas (Det. Nick Curran), Sharon Stone (Catherine Tramell), George Dzundza (Gus), Jeanne Tripplehorn (Dr Beth Garner), Denis Arndt (Lt Walker), Leilani Sarelle (Roxy), Bruce A Young (Andrews), Chelcie Ross (Capt. Talcott), Dorothy Malone (Hazel Dobkins), Wayne Knight (John Correli), Daniel Von Bargen (Lt Nilsen), Stephen Tobolowsky (Dr Lamott)

A none-too-stable San Francisco police detective investigating the slaying of a rock star falls for the beautiful nymphomaniac and bisexual prime suspect.

The notorious scene of Stone crossing her legs, without benefit of underwear, for the benefit of the detectives who are interrogating her simply underlines the basic sleaziness of a glossy 'erotic thriller' whose liberal nudity and simulated sex scenes are depressingly unerotic and whose thrills are laid on with little motivation or logic. Laughable rather than lurid, with a memorably dreadful performance by Douglas, who appears to be more concerned with concealing his genitalia than with attempting to act. Eszterhas's overwrought screenplay, for which he was reportedly paid $3 million, manages to offend gays, heterosexuals and those who are not in the market for glossy soft-core porn. Pure trash, but Verhoeven's stylish direction makes it seductively watchable and, inevitably, it was a hit.

BASIC INSTINCT

'It's one of those movies you hate yourself for liking. It's soft-porn. It's anti-gay. It's gratuitously violent. And they're the good points!

The dialogue often resembles a chat between a brain transplant patient and his pet goldfish. But it is an ingenious, sizzling thriller that will have you guessing the outcome until the final nail-biting frame – and that's a rarity.'
The Sun

BEAR ISLAND

(CANADA/GB 1979)
pc Selkirk Films/Bear Island Films. For Columbia. In association with the Canadian Film Development Corporation. p Peter Snell. assoc p Bill Hill. d Don Sharp. 2nd unit d, sc Vic Armstrong. w David Butler, Don Sharp, (uncredited) Tony Williamson, Paul Wheeler, from the novel by Alistair MacLean. add material Murray Smith. ph Alan Hume. 2nd unit ph Derek V Browne, Keith Woods. underwater ph Arthur Wooster. aerial ph Donald Morgan. Colour. Panavision. pd Harry Pottle. ad Kenneth Ryan, Peter Childs. sfx sup Roy Whybrow. sfx David Harris, Thomas Clark, Paul Whybrow. m Robert Farnon. 118 mins

Cast: Donald Sutherland (Frank Lansing), Vanessa Redgrave (Hedi Lindquist), Richard Widmark (Prof. Otto Gerran), Christopher Lee (Pro. Lechinski), Barbara Parkins (Judith Riben), Lloyd Bridges (Smithy), Lawrence Dane (Paul Hartman), Patricia Collins (Inge Van Zipper)

A killer reduces the numbers of a United Nations meteorological team working on an isolated arctic island.

Preposterous, poorly-produced farrago of murder, mystery and intrigue whose understandably embarrassed-looking international cast sleepwalk through the motions with minimal conviction and a bewildering array of unlikely accents. Its one arcane pleasure is watching one-time Dracula Christopher Lee having a blood transfusion.

'When Don Sharp's direction isn't frozen stiff, he brings a modest excitement to the pursuit scenes, but it is awfully hard to work onself up into a state of concern over the fate of these unbelievable characters.'
Films Illustrated

THE BEAST OF THE CITY

(US 1932)
pc MGM. d Charles Brabin. w John L Mahin, from a story by W R Burnett. ph Norbert Brodine. B&W. ed Anne Bauchens. 74 mins

Cast: Walter Huston (Capt. John Fitzpatrick), Jean Harlow (Daisy Stevens), Wallace Ford (Ed Fitzpatrick), Jean Hersholt (Sam Belmonte), Dorothy Peterson (Mary Fitzpatrick), Tully Marshall (Michaels), John Miljan (DA), Emmett Corrigan (Chief of Police), Warner Richmond (Tom), J Carrol Naish (Cholo), Mickey Rooney (Mickey Fitzpatrick)

An ambitious policeman has problems bringing a racketeer to book.

Competent gangster melodrama with a violent resolution.

'Endowed with vitality and realism,

the various characters being exceptionally true to life.'
The New York Times

BENEFIT OF THE DOUBT

(US/GERMANY 1993)
pc Benefit Productions/Cine Vox International (Los Angeles)/Cine Vox Filmproduktion (Munich). A Monument Pictures production. exec p Bob Weinstein, Harvey Weinstein. p Michael Spielberg, Brad M Gilbert. co-p Dieter Geissler. d Jonathan Heap. w Jeffrey Polman, Christopher Keyser. st Michael Lieber. ph Johnny E Jensen. Colour. ed Sharyn L Ross. pd Marina Kieser. ad David Seth Lazan. sc Rob King. m Hummie Mann. 91 mins

Cast: Donald Sutherland (Frank Braswell), Amy Irving (Karen Braswell), Rider Strong (Pete Braswell), Christopher McDonald (Dan), Graham Greene (Sheriff Calhoun), Theodore Bikel (Gideon Lee), Gisela Kovach (Suzanna), Ferdinand Mayne (Mueller), Julie Hasel (Young Karen), Don Collier (Charlie)

A man paroled after 22 years in jail for the murder of his wife seeks revenge against his daughter, who gave evidence against him when she was eleven.

Inept, by-numbers moviemaking whose numbers add up to a tedious collation of clichés overwhelmed by yet another serving of overripe ham from Sutherland.

'The director is Jonathan Heap, the film, a heap of something else.'
The Daily Telegraph

BEYOND A REASONABLE DOUBT

(US 1956)
pc RKO. A Bert Friedlob Production.
p Bert Friedlob. d Fritz Lang. w
Douglas Morrow. ph William Snyder.
B&W. RKO-Scope. ed Gene Fowler Jr.
ad Carroll Clark. m Herschel Burke
Gilbert. 80 mins

Cast: Dana Andrews (Tom Garrett),
Joan Fontaine (Susan Spencer), Sidney
Blackmer (Austin Spencer), Philip
Bourneuf (Thompson), Shepperd
Strudwick (Wilson), Arthur Franz
(Hale), Edward Binns (Lt Kennedy),
Robin Raymond (Terry), Barbara
Nichols (Sally), William Leicester
(Charlie Miller)

A newspaperman's scheme to frame
himself for murder to prove an
innocent man can be tried and
convicted on purely circumstantial
evidence goes wrong and he finds
himself facing execution.

Lang's (inevitably) overrated final
American film is a low-budget, low-
voltage affair with a contrived
screenplay, lacklustre direction and a
'surprise' ending whose sole surprise is
that anyone would have the gall to try
and foist it on an audience.

'If you can swallow such arrant
disregard for the law, you may find
this a fairly intriguing and brain-teasing
mystery film.'
The New York Times

BEYOND THIS PLACE

(GB 1959)
(US: WEB OF EVIDENCE)
pc A Georgefield Production presented
by George Minter. p Maxwell Setton,
John R Sloan. d Jack Cardiff. w
Kenneth Taylor. adap Kenneth Hyde,
from the novel by A J Cronin. ph
Wilkie Cooper. B&W. ad Kent Adam.
m Douglas Gamley. 90 mins

Cast: Van Johnson (Paul Mathry), Vera
Miles (Lena Anderson), Emlyn
Williams (Enoch Oswald), Bernard
Lee (Patrick Mathry), Jean Kent
(Louise Burt), Moultrie Kelsall (Chief
Insp. Dale), Leo McKern (McEvoy),
Ralph Truman (Sir Matthew Sprott
QC), Geoffrey Keen (Prison Governor)

A man comes to Britain from America
to investigate his father's death in
World War Two, finds him alive and in
prison for murder, and sets out to
prove his innocence.

Sincerity of intention is not
enough: pallid in all departments.

'This emerges as a third-rate film, on
which music has been plastered with
the usual insensitivity.'
Films and Filming

BIG BAD MAMA

(US 1974)
pc Santa Cruz. p Roger Corman. assoc
p Jon Davison. d Steve Carver. w
William Norton, Frances Doel. ph
Bruce Logan. Colour. ed Tina Hirsch.
sfx Roger George. m David Grisman.
83 mins

Cast: Angie Dickinson (Wilma
McClatchie), William Shatner (William
J Baxter), Tom Skerritt (Fred Diller),
Susan Bennett (Billie Jean McClatchie),
Robbie Lee (Polly McClatchie), Noble
Willingham (Uncle Barney), Dick
Miller (Bonney), Tom Signorelli
(Dodds), Royal Dano (Rev. Johnson)

In 1932 Texas, a lusty widow and her
two daughters become bank robbers.

Brisk, enjoyably-executed, violent
and sexy Corman exploiter.

'Pretty good entertainment, lowdown
and rambunctious, thanks to Angie
Dickinson, William Shatner and Tom
Skerritt, and, above all, Steve Carver's
admirable and resourceful direction.'
Los Angeles Times

THE BIG CLOCK

(US 1948)
pc Paramount. p Richard Maibaum. d
John Farrow. w Jonathan Latimer. adap
Harold Goldman, from the novel by
Kenneth Fearing. ph John F Seitz. sfx
ph Gordon Jennings. process ph
Farciot Edouart. B&W. ad Hans
Dreier, Roland Anderson, Albert
Nozaki. m Victor Young. song *The Big
Clock* by Jay Livingston, Ray Evans.
93 mins

Cast: Ray Milland (George Stroud),
Charles Laughton (Earl Janoth),
Maureen O'Sullivan (Georgette
Stroud), George Macready (Steve
Hagen), Rita Johnson (Pauline Delos),
Elsa Lanchester (Louise Patterson),
Harold Vermilyea (Don Kalusmeyer),
Dan Tobin (Roy Cordette), Henry
Morgan (Bill Womack)

A megalomaniac publisher murders
his mistress and orders one of his
editors to track down the man he saw
leaving her apartment so that he can
frame him. Fortuitously, the editor
turns out to be the man in question.

Undernourished, over-convoluted
and overrated *film noir* with good
performances by Laughton, Milland,
Macready and Lanchester in a cameo

as an eccentric artist, and moody cinematography. Considerably reworked as *No Way Out* (1987 q.v.)

'Heavy but exciting, and the tension is held at high pitch throughout.'
CEA Film Report

THE BIG EASY
(US 1986)
pc Kings Road Entertainment. exec p Mort Engelberg. p Stephen Friedman. d Jim McBride. w Daniel Petrie Jr, Jack Baran. ph Affonso Beato. Colour. ed Mia Goldman. sfx co-ord William Purcell, Gregory C Landerer. sc Richard Diamond Farnsworth. m Brad Fiedel. 108 mins

Cast: Dennis Quaid (Remy McSwain), Ellen Barkin (Anne Osborne), Ned Beatty (Jack Kellom), John Goodman (Det. André DeSoto), Lisa Jane Persky (Det. McCabe), Ebbe Roe Smith (Det. Ed Dodge), Charles Ludlam (Lamar Permental), Grace Zabriskie (Mama), Tom O'Brien (Bobby McSwain), Judge James Garrison (Judge Jim Garrison), Marc Lawrence (Vince 'The Cannon' DiMotti), Carol Sutton (Kudge Raskov), David Petijean (Uncle Sos), Gailard Sartain (Chef Paul)

A New Orleans detective clashes with a special prosecutor assigned to investigate police corruption until romance and homicide intervene.

Stylish blend of sharply-characterized crime thriller and sex drama decorated by attractive leads and well-used New Orleans locations. Pity about the ending, though.

'One of the richest American films of the year. It also happens to be a

BIG HEAT

great thriller.'
Chicago Sun-Times

THE BIG HEAT
(US 1953)
pc Columbia. p Robert Arthur. d Fritz Lang. w Sydney Boehm, from the novel by William P McGivern. ph Charles Lang. B&W. ad Robert Peterson. md Mischa Bakaleinikoff. m Daniele Amfiteatrof. 90 mins.
Cast: Glenn Ford (Dave Bannion), Gloria Grahame (Debby Marsh), Jocelyn Brando (Katie Bannion), Alexander Scourby (Mike Lagana), Lee Marvin (Vince Stone), Jeanette Nolan (Bertha Duncan), Peter Whitney (Tierney), Willis Bouchey (Lt Wilkes), Robert Burton (Gus Burke), Carolyn Jones (Doris)

A policeman investigating the suicide of a fellow officer uncovers underworld connections and is warned off by his superiors and the dead man's wife.

Tough and sadistic for its time, now best remembered for the scene in which Lee Marvin throws boiling coffee in Gloria Grahame's face and her later retaliation in kind. Competently, if anonymously, written and directed.

'It is neither bad or good. Fritz Lang is no longer Fritz Lang. We have known this for several years. There is no more symbolism in the works which the creator of *Metropolis* fashions and even less expressionism.'
Le Figaro

'The main impression left by the film is of violence employed arbitrarily, mechanically and in the long run pointlessly.'
Monthly Film Bulletin

THE BIG SHOT
(US 1942)
pc WB. p Walter MacEwen. d Lewis Seiler. w Bertram Millhauser, Abem

Finkel, Daniel Fuchs. ph Sid Hickox. B&W. ad John Hughes. m Adolph Deutsch. 82 mins

Cast: Humphrey Bogart (Duke Berne), Irene Manning (Lorna Fleming), Richard Travis (George Anderson), Susan Peters (Ruth Carter), Stanley Ridges (Martin Fleming), Minor Watson (Warden Booth), Chick Chandler (Dancer), Joseph Downing (Frenchy), Howard da Silva (Sandor), Murray Alper (Quinto)

A wrongly-imprisoned one-time public enemy breaks out and, after a brief idyll with a girl, is killed when he gives himself up to save a fellow crook.

Bogart gives it his best shot, but the film remains resolutely routine.

'There are several strong dramatic situations and the action is brisk and exciting.'
CEA Film Report

THE BIG SLEEP

(US 1946)
pc WB-First National. p, d Howard Hawks. w William Faulkner, Leigh Brackett, Jules Furthman, from the novel by Raymond Chandler. ph Sid Hickox. B&W. ed Christian Nyby. ad Carl Jules Wyel. m Max Steiner. sfx Roy Davison, Warren E Lynch, William McGann, Robert Burks,

Willard Van Enger. 114 mins

Cast: Humphrey Bogart (Philip Marlowe), Lauren Bacall (Vivian Rutledge), John Ridgely (Eddie Mars), Martha Vickers (Carmen Sternwood), Dorothy Malone (Bookshop assistant), Peggy Knudsen (Mrs Eddie Mars), Regis Toomey (Bernie Ohls), Charles Waldron (Gen. Sternwood), Charles D Brown (Norris), Bob Steele (Canino), Elisha Cook Jr (Harry Jones), Louis Jean Heydt (Joe Brody)

Private eye Philip Marlowe is caught up in murder and mayhem when he is hired by a millionaire to rescue his

THE BIG SLEEP (US 1946)

nymphomaniac daughter from a blackmailer.

Other actors have played Chandler's celebrated private eye, among them Dick Powell, Robert Montgomery, James Garner, Elliott Gould and Robert Mitchum (twice), but Bogart remains the definitive Marlowe – tough, unimpeachable and laconically witty, notably in his scenes with Bacall, with whom he had made *To Have and Have Not* in 1945, also directed by Hawks, and to whom he was now married. It hardly matters that the complicated plot frequently makes no sense (reportedly the screenwriters, Hawks and the stars were unable to work out what was happening during filming and, allegedly, Chandler was unable to help either) since *The Big Sleep* is supremely atmospheric, vividly-written, stylish in every department and as near a genre masterpiece as makes no difference. The plot is the least important element in the mix, as triumphantly demonstrated by the dire 1978 Michael Winner remake (q.v.).

'A highly complicated tale that rivets attention to the screen for almost two tight hours.'
Motion Picture Herald

'A violent, smoky cocktail shaken together from most of the printable misdemeanours and some that aren't – one of those Raymond Chandler Specials which puts you, along with the cast, into a state of semi-amnesia through which tough action and reaction drum with something of the nonsensical solace of hard rain on a tin roof.'
The Nation

'By no means easy to follow, but even so, many big thrills emerge from its haze ... its secret lies in its swiftness of surface action, its ability to create surprise after surprise. A Bogart beanfeast – or perhaps bloodbath is a more appropriate term.'
Kine Weekly

THE BIG SLEEP (GB 1978)

'Neither the author, the writer, nor myself knew who killed who.'
Howard Hawks

THE BIG SLEEP

(GB 1978)

pc Winkast. An Elliott Kastner-Jerry Blick production. d Michael Winner. p Elliott Kastner, Michael Winner. assoc p Bernard Williams. w Michael Winner, from the novel by Raymond Chandler. ph Robert Paynter. Colour. sup ed Freddie Wilson. pd Harry Pottle. ad John Graysmark. m Jerry Fielding. song *Won't Someone Dance With Me* by Lynsey de Paul, performed by Diana Quick. 99 mins

Cast: Robert Mitchum (Philip Marlowe), Sarah Miles (Charlotte Regan), Richard Boone (Lash Canino), Candy Clark (Camilla Sternwood), Joan Collins (Angel Lozelle), Edward Fox (Joe Brody), John Mills (Insp. Jim Carson), James Stewart (Gen. Sternwood), Oliver Reed (Eddie Mars), Harry Andrews (Vincent Norris), Colin Blakely (Harry Jones), Richard Todd (Commander Barker), Diana Quick (Mona Mars), James Donald (Insp. Gregory), John Justin (Arthur Gwynn Geiger)

Expatriate American private eye Philip Marlowe finds himself enmeshed in intrigue, mystery and murder when he sets out to scare off a blackmailer.

Worthless remake of the 1946 Hawks-Bogart classic (q.v.), with the action pointlessly transposed to England and with Marlowe driving a Mercedes. Mitchum is too old for the part, and looks it, the screenplay is explicit without being interesting, and Winner (whose name appeared some seven times on the synopsis issued by the picture's British distributors) directs without style. Unaesthetic and anaesthetic.

'What a botch *The Big Sleep* is. The result is a movie that lurches unsteadily from scene to scene. *The Big Sleep* is just another snooze.'
Time

'The pace is so slow that the picture is in danger of being booked for loitering with intent.'
Daily Mirror

THE BIG STEAL

(US 1949)

pc RKO. p Jack J Gross. d Don Siegel. w Geoffrey Homes, Gerald Drayson Adams, from the story *The Road To Carmichael's* by Richard Wormser. ph Harry J Wild. B&W. ad Albert D'Agostino, Ralph Berger. m Leigh Harline. 71 mins

Cast: Robert Mitchum (Duke), Jane Greer (Joan), William Bendix (Blake), Patric Knowles (Fliske), Ramon Novarro (Col. Ortega), Don Alvarado (Lt Ruiz), John Qualen (Seton), Pascal Garcia Pena (Manuel)

An army lieutenant is framed for a payroll theft and, with a woman in tow, pursues the real perpetrator in Mexico while a fellow officer comes after him.

Siegel's subsequent elevation to *auteur* status gives this effective but essentially minor chase thriller rather more value than it really deserves. Well-photographed Mexican locations add impact.

'Acting and direction are excellent and the presentation is bright.'
CEA Film Report

THE BIGGEST BUNDLE OF THEM ALL

(US 1967)

pc MGM. A Shaftel-Stewart Production. p, st Josef Shaftel. d Ken Annakin. w Josef Shaftel, Sy Salkowitz. ph Piero Portalupi. Colour. Panavision. ad Arrigo Equini. m Riz Ortolani. 105 mins

Cast: Robert Wagner (Harry Price), Raquel Welch (Juliana), Godfrey Cambridge (Benjamin Brownstead), Vittorio De Sica (Cesari Celli), Edward G Robinson (Prof. Samuels), Davy Kaye (Davy Collins), Francesco Mule (Antonio Tozzi), Victor Spinetti (Capt. Giglio), Yvonne Sanson (Teresa)

When amateur crooks kidnap a deported American gangster living in Italy and nobody will pay a ransom, he takes command and plans a £5 million robbery.
Pointless sixties crime caper notable only for De Sica's hammy performance and the mildly interesting question as to why Robinson bothered with it.

'Begins like one of those really bad movies that are unintentionally funny. Then it becomes clear that it intends to be funny and isn't.'
The New York Times

BILLION DOLLAR BRAIN

(GB 1967)

pc Lowndes Productions. exec p André de Toth. p Harry Saltzman. d Ken Russell. w John McGrath, from the novel by Len Deighton. ph Billy Williams. Colour. Panavision. pd Syd Cain. ad Bert Davey. m Richard Rodney Bennett. 111 mins

Cast: Michael Caine (Harry Palmer), Karl Malden (Leo Newbegin), Françoise Dorleac (Anya), Oscar Homolka (Col. Stock), Ed Begley (Gen. Midwinter), Guy Doleman (Col. Ross), Vladek Sheybal (Dr Eiwort), Milo Sperber (Basil), Mark Elwes (Birkinshaw), Stanley Caine (GPO Delivery Boy)

A British secret agent is sent to Scandinavia, where he becomes involved with a megalomaniac Texas oil billionaire planning world domination.

Caine is dull and sluggish, and director Russell mistakes visual and editing pyrotechnics for storytelling, resulting in an incomprehensible farrago that fails to entertain and which ended the Harry Palmer cinema features that began in 1965 with *The Ipcress File*. Caine returned to the role even less auspiciously in the nineties in dismal, made-for-television movies.

'Must have been composed by a computer ... the machine went haywire and produced as bewildering a piece of cinema as I have ever seen.'
The Observer

THE BISHOP MURDER CASE
(US 1930)
pc MGM. d Nick Grinde, David Burton. w Lenore J Coffee, from a story by S S Van Dine. ph Roy Overbaugh. B&W. ed William Le Vanway. ad Cedric Gibbons. 91 mins

Cast: Basil Rathbone (Philo Vance), Leila Hyams (Belle Dillard), Roland Young (Sigurd Arnesson), Alec B Francis (Prof. Bertrand Dillard), George Marion (Adolph Drukker), Zelda Sears (Mrs Otto Drukker),

Carroll Nye (John E Sprigg), James Donlan (Ernest Heath), Bodil Rosing (Grete Menzel), Charles Quartermaine (John Pardee)

Amateur sleuth Philo Vance solves a series of murders 'announced' by nursery rhymes.

Rathbone, replacing William Powell in the third Philo Vance film, does a smooth enough job (later finding his private detective screen niche as Sherlock Holmes). The plot is interesting if rather over-literary, but the pace is slow.

'Plenty of thrills.'
Photoplay

BLACK EYE
(US 1973)
pc Pat Rooney Productions. A Jerry Buss presentation. exec p Jack Reeves. p Pat Rooney. assoc p Larry Noble. d Jack Arnold. w Mark Haggard, Jim Martin, from the novel *Murder on the Wild Side* by Jeff Hacks. ph Ralph Woolsey. Colour. ad Chuck Pierce, John Rozman. m Mort Garson. 98 mins

Cast: Fred Williamson (Shep Stone), Rosemary Forsyth (Miss Francis), Teresa Graves (Cynthia), Floy Dean (Diane Davis), Richard Anderson (Raymond Dole), Cyril Delevanti (Talbot), Richard X Slattery (Bill Bowen), Larry Mann (Rev. Avery), Bret Morrison (Max Majors), Belinda Balaski (Mary)

A former policeman, suspended from the force for killing the drug pusher responsible for his sister's death, becomes a private eye and

investigates a series of drug-related killings in Venice, California.

Brisk blaxploitation actioner with pacy direction by Arnold, and one of the better examples of its genre.

'It's a gem ... fast moving and irreverent ... the screenplay is witty and, for once, intentionally so.'
Women's Wear Daily

BLACKMAIL
(GB 1929)
pc British International. d John Maxwell. d Alfred Hitchcock. w Alfred Hitchcock, Benn W Levy, Charles Bennett. dial Benn W Levy, from the play by Charles Bennett. ph Jack Cox. B&W. ed Emile de Ruelle. ad Norman Arnold, Wilfred Arnold. m Campbell and Connelly, Hubert Bath, Henry Stafford. 78 mins

Cast: Anny Ondra (Alice White), John Longden (Insp. Frank Webber), Sara Allgood (Mrs White), Charles Paton (Mr White), Donald Calthrop (Tracy), Cyril Ritchard (Artist) Hannah Jones (Landlady), Harvey Braban (Chief Inspector), Phyllis Monkman (Charlady)
When a young woman kills a would-be rapist, her policeman boyfriend conceals her guilt but the couple fall victim to a blackmailer.

Britain's first major sound film shows Hitchcock in imaginative control of the new medium. It was shot as a silent picture, but with the advent of sound it was decided it should become a part-talkie, silent apart from the last reel. However, Hitchcock prevailed upon the producers to revamp the film, and was given *carte blanche* to re-shoot several scenes. German star Ondra spoke little

English: because no technique for post-synchronization existed, Joan Barry spoke her lines on the set while the star mimed the dialogue.

Hitchock's mastery is particularly evident in the breakfast-table sequence, where the word 'knife' is highlighted on the soundtrack, causing Ondra to become increasingly hysterical with each repetition. The director makes his customary appearance, being pestered by a small boy on a train.

Seen now, *Blackmail* inveitably appears primitive, but the trademark Hitchcock touches are there. (Future director Michael Powell was a stills photographer, while Ronald Neame, who went on to become a noted cinematographer and then a director, was the clapper boy.)

'*Blackmail* should please everybody – the highbrows because it is intelligent and sensible drama unspoiled by blatant absurdities and the lowbrows because it is a thrilling film packed throughout with excitement and incident.'
The Bystander

'This is a considerable achievement, and compares favourably with the best American "talkies" ... the story is interesting and holding, and has been brilliantly directed ... the illusion that the actors are actually talking is convincing.'
CEA Film Report

'Not just a talker, but a motion picture that talks. Alfred J Hitchcock has solved the problem of making a picture which does not lose any film technique and gains effect from dialogue. Silent, it would be an unusu-ally good film; as it is, it comes near to being a landmark.'
Variety

BLIND ALLEY

(US 1939)
pc Columbia. p Fred Kohlmar. d Charles Vidor. w Philip MacDonald, Michael Blankfort, from the play by James Warwick. ph Lucien Ballard. B&W. ed Otto Meyer. md Morris W Stoloff. 68 mins

Cast: Chester Morris (Hal Wilson), Ralph Bellamy (Dr Shelley), Ann Dvorak (Mary), Joan Perry (Linda Curtis), Melville Cooper (George Curtis), Rose Stradner (Doris Shelby), Ann Doran (Agnes), Marc Lawrence (Buck), Stanley Brown (Fred Landis), Scotty Beckett (Davy Shelby), Grady Sutton (Holmes)

An escaped killer holds a professor of psychology and his family hostage, and is subjected to healing psychoanalyis.

A fascinating early attempt to blend psychology and crime that doesn't outstay its welcome. Remade on a larger scale in 1947 as *The Dark Past.*

'Survive a sticky ten minutes and you have a thriller of quite unusual merit.'
The Spectator

BLIND DATE

(GB 1959)
(US: CHANCE MEETING)
pc Independent Artists. A Julian Wintle-Leslie Parkyn Production. p David Deutsch. d Joseph Losey. w Ben Barzman, Millard Lampell, from the novel by Leigh Howard. ph Christopher Challis. B&W. ad Edward Carrick. m Richard Rodney Bennett. 95 mins

Cast: Hardy Kruger (Jan Van Rooyen), Stanley Baker (Insp. Morgan), Micheline Presle (Jacqueline Cousteau), Robert Flemyng (Sir Brian Lewis), Gordon Jackson (Police Sergeant), John Van Eyssen (Insp. Westover), Jack McGowran (Postman), David Markam (Sir Howard Fenton), Lee Montague (Farrow)

A Dutch artist living in London is framed for the murder of his mistress.

The dialogue is often intelligent and pointed, Stanley Baker's truculent policeman with a chip on his shoulder about the old-boy network in the police force is entertaining, but the screenplay is unnecessarily complex and unconvincing, and Losey's direction is mannered and self-conscious.

'Its pretensions reached beyond the ingenuity of its plot ... the fascinating parts don't add up to a fascinating movie.'
Picturegoer`

BLIND TERROR

(US 1971)
(US: SEE NO EVIL)
pc Filmways/Genesis. p Martin Ransohoff, Leslie Linder. assoc p Basil Appleby. d Richard Fleischer. w Brian Clemens. ph Gerry Fisher. Colour. ad John Howell. m Elmer Bernstein. 89 mins
Cast: Mia Farrow (Sarah), Robin Bailey (George Rexton), Dorothy Alison (Betty Rexton), Diane Grayson (Sandy Rexton), Norman Eshley (Steve Reding), Brian Rawlinson (Barker), Christopher Matthews (Frost), Paul Nicholas (Jack Osgood), Michael Elphick (Gypsy Tom), Barrie Houghton (Gypsy Jack)

A woman returns home after being blinded in an accident and is terrorized by a homicidal maniac.

Efficient but undistinguished B-picture masquerading as a first feature, with Fleischer's by-the-book direction emphasizing Farrow's inherent blandness and underlining the frequent clichés in Brian Clemens's TV-movie-style screenplay.

'So clumsily structured, so full of inconsequences and improbabilities, so ineptly written and sad to say so thoughtlessly directed as to lose all the impact.'
Financial Times

BLINK
(US 1994)
pc New Line. exec p Robert Shaye, Sara Risher. p, 2nd unit d David Blocker. d Michael Apted. w Dana Stevens. ph Dante Spinotti. Colour. Scope. ed Rick Shaine. pd Dan Bishop. ad Jefferson Sage. sfx Sam Barkan. m Brad Fiedel. 106 mins

Cast: Madeleine Stowe (Emma Brody), Aidan Quinn (Det. John Hallstrom), Laurie Metcalf (Candice), James Remar (Dr Thomas Ridgely), Peter Friendman (Dr Ryan Pierce), Bruce A Young (Lt Mitchell), Matt Roth (Officer Crowe), Paul Dillon (Neal Booker), Michael P Byrne (Barry), Anthony Cannata (Ned)

A young woman, her sight restored after 20 years, suffers from 'ocular flashbacks' in which blurred images only become clear the next day, and is stalked by the serial killer she has glimpsed and she alone can identify.

Despite a far-fetched, not to say daft premise, a feisty performance from

Stowe and stylish direction creates a surprising amount of suspense.

'A gripping story with a unique conceit ... laced with a wry sense of humour that thrillers of this ilk seldom aspire to.'
What's On in London

BLOOD RELATIVES
(CANADA/FRANCE 1977)
(FRANCE: LES LIENS DE SANG)
pc Classic Film Industries/Cinévidéo/Filmel. exec p Julian Melzak. p Denis Héroux, Eugene Lepecier. assoc p Claude Léger. d Claude Chabrol. w Claude Chabrol, Sydney Banks, from the novel by Ed McBain (rn Evan Hunter). ph Jean Rabier. Colour. ed. Yves Langlois. pd Anne Pritchard. m Howard Blake. m (French version) Pierre Jansen. 95 mins

Cast: Donald Sutherland (Steve Carella), Aude Landry (Patricia Lowrery), Lisa Langlois (Muriel), Laurent Malet (Andy Lowery), Stéphan Audran (Mrs Lowery), Donald Pleasence (Doniac), David Hemmings (Jack Armstrong), Walter Massey (Mr Lowery), Micheline Lanctot (Mrs Carella), Ian Ireland (Klinger)

A detective investigates the brutal rape and murder of a young girl in Montreal.

Ed McBain's '87th Precinct' thrillers are strong on plot, characterization, humour and detailed police procedure. Chabrol, gaining nothing by transposing the setting from New York to Montreal and casting a glum, uncharismatic Sutherland in the lead, comes up with

a thriller whose complexities are matched only by the general tedium of the proceedings.

'You can certainly tell it's a film by Chabrol: but somehow the familiar ground has disappeared from under his feet.'
The Guardian

BLOODY MAMA
(US 1969)
pc AIP. exec p Samuel Z Arkoff, James H Nicholson. p, d Roger Corman. co-p Norman T Herman. w Robert Thom. st Robert Thom, Don Peters. ph John A Alonzo. Colour. sfx A D Flowers. m Don Randi. title song Don Randi, Guy Hemric, Bob Silver. 90 mins

Cast: Shelley Winters (Kate 'Ma' Barker), Pat Hingle (Sam Adams Pendlebury), Don Stroud (Herman Barker), Diane Varsi (Mona Gibson), Bruce Dern (Kevin Dirkman), Clint Kimbrough (Arthur Barker), Robert De Niro (Lloyd Barker), Robert Walden (Fred Barker) Alex Nicol (George Barker)

'Ma' Barker and her brood of psychopathic sons terrorize the American southland during the thirties.

Vigorous, very violent biopic with scant regard for facts and motivated by highly suspect psychology. Zestfully directed by Corman, the climactic shootout is brilliantly staged, and Winters gives a bravura, vulgar performance. De Niro is mannered and unmemorable.

'If not an overwhelming experience, at least the film is a small pleasure I

BLOODY MAMA

would urge you not to miss.'
The Times

'What I can't understand is how critics who are supposed to know a bit more than the commonest man can discuss such a movie as anything but a shrewd commercial exercise.'
Newsweek

BLOWN AWAY

(US 1994)
pc Trilogy Entertainment Group. For MGM. exec p Lloyd Segan. p John

Watson, Richard Lewis, Pen Densham. co-p Dean O'Brien. d Stephen Hopkins. w Joe Battner, John Rice. st Joe Battner, John Rice, M Jay Roach. ph Peter Levy. visual fx p Dana Bickel. Colour. ed Timothy Welburn. pd John Graysmark. ad Steve Cooper, Lawrence A Hubbs. sfx co-ord Clay Pinney. sc Vince Deadrick Jr. m Alan Silvestri. 121 mins

Cast: Jeff Bridges (Jimmy Dove), Tommy Lee Jones (Ryan Gaerity), Lloyd Bridges (Max O'Bannon), Forest Whitaker (Anthony Franklin), Suzy

Amis (Kate), Stephi Lineburg (Lizzy), Caitlin Clarke (Rita), John Finn (Capt. Roarke), Chris De Oni (Cortez), Loyd Catlett (Bama), Lucinda West (Nancy)

A psychotic Irish terrorist escapes from a Northern Ireland prison and goes to Boston to wreak explosive vengeance on his former 'pupil', who has reformed and is now a member of the police bomb squad.

The characters are ciphers, the politics suspect and exploitative, the writing, direction and acting barely achieve competence, and the noisy, impressively-staged pyrotechnics simply serve to illuminate the essential empty cynicism of the enterprise.

'In fact, you're less likely to be Blown Away than Browned Off. Shame.'
Empire

THE BLUE DAHLIA

(US 1946)

pc Paramount. p John Houseman. d George Marshall. w Raymond Chandler. ph Lionel Lindon, process ph Farciot Edouart. B&W. ad Hans Dreier, Walter Tyler. m Victor Young. 98 mins

Cast: Alan Ladd (Johnny Morrison), Veronica Lake (Joyce Harwood), William Bendix (Buzz Wanchek), Howard da Silva (Eddie Harwood), Doris Dowling (Helen Morrison), Tom Powers (Capt. Hendrickson), Hugh Beaumont (George Copeland), Howard Freeman (Corelli), Don Costello (Leo), Will Wright (Dad Newell)

A recently-discharged World War Two veteran returns home to find his wife had been unfaithful, and becomes the prime suspect when she is subsequently murdered.

Entertaining, well-written murder mystery with no-nonsense direction and appropriate acting.

'As neatly stylized and synchronized, and as uninterested in moral excitement as a good ballet; it knows its own weight and size perfectly and carries them gracefully and without self-importance; it is, barring occasional victories and noble accidents, about as good a movie as can be expected from the big factories.'
The Nation

'Better check your blood pressure at the door ... because Raymond Chandler has written the year's fastest suspense-filled mystery of murder in full bloom!'
Press advertisement

THE BLUE GARDENIA

(US 1953)

pc Blue Gardenia Productions. p Alex Gottlieb. d Fritz Lang. w Charles Hoffman, from the short story *Gardenia* by Vera Caspary. ph Nicholas Musuraca. B&W. ad Daniel Hall. sfx Willis Cook. m Raoul Kraushaar. song *The Blue Gardenia* by Bob Russell, Lester Lee, sung by Nat 'King' Cole. 90 mins

Cast: Anne Baxter (Norah Larkin), Richard Conte (Casey Mayo), Ann Sothern (Crystal Carpenter), Raymond Burr (Harry Prebble), Jeff Donnell (Sally Ellis), Richard Erdman (Al), George Reecs (Police Capt. Haynes), Ruth Storey (Rose Miller), Ray Walker (Homer), Nat 'King' Cole (Himself)

A woman hits a would-be seducer with a poker, passes out and wakes the next morning to find him dead. While she believes herself guilty of murder, a reporter proves her innocence and finds the real killer.

Unremarkable thriller, of note only because of Lang – although his direction is nothing to write home about and the identity of the killer is obvious.

'It is difficult to accept the evidence of the credits that this nondescript and far from exciting thriller was directed by Fritz Lang.'
Monthly Film Bulletin

THE BLUE LAMP

(GB 1949)

pc Ealing. A Michael Balcon Production. assoc p Michael Relph. d Basil Dearden. 2nd unit d, add dial Alexander Mackendrick. w T E B Clarke. st Jan Read, Ted Willis. ph Gordon Dines. 2nd unit ph Lionel Banes. B&W. ad Jim Morahan. m Ernest Irving. 84 mins

Cast: Jack Warner (PC George Dixon), Jimmy Hanley (PC Andy Mitchell), Robert Flemyng (Sgt Roberts), Bernard Lee (Divisional Det. Insp. Cherry), Meredith Edwards (PC Hughes), Dirk Bogarde (Tom Riley), Patric Doonan (Spud), Peggy Evans (Diana Lewis), Gladys Henson (Mrs Dixon), Dora Bryan (Maisie)

London police track down the killer of a police constable.

Seminal Ealing thriller whose rampant sentimentality and cosiness sit uneasily alongside semi-documentary direction and well-used London locations. Most of the characterization is clichéd, although Bogarde gives his portrait of a killer an occasional depth not evident in the screenplay or in the efficient but anonymous direction.

PC Dixon, killed off in the film, was raised from the dead like Dracula by writer Ted Willis and turned into a super-saccharine series that ran on British television for some 200 episodes from 1955 to 1976 but whose attitudes remained firmly in the 1950s, with Warner resolutely resisting any temptation to make his character credible.

'Unavoidably challenges comparison with Hollywood in style and verismili-

tude; it must be said that comparison on all major counts is unfavourable.'
Monthly Film Bulletin

'A soundly made crime thriller which would not be creating much of a stir if it were American.'
Punch

BODY HEAT
(US 1981)
pc The Ladd Company. p Fred T Gallo. assoc p Robert Grand. d, w Lawrence Kasdan. ph Richard H Kline. Colour. pd Bill Kenney. sfx Howard Jensen, Hal Bigger. m John Barry. 113 mins

Cast: William Hurt (Ned Racine), Kathleen Turner (Matty Walker), Richard Crenna (Edmund Walker), Ted Danson (Peter Lowenstein), J A Preston (Oscar Grace), Mickey Rourke (Teddy Lewis), Kim Zimmer (Mary Ann Simpson), Jane Hallaren (Stella), Lanna Saunders (Roz Kraft), Michael Ryan (Miles Hardin)

The wife of a wealthy businessman lures her lawyer lover into helping her kill her husband – but their would-be perfect murder plan goes wrong.

Kasdan made a memorable directorial debut with a carefully-crafted homage to 1940s *film noir*. His plot (although not credited as such) is a virtual reworking of *Double Indemnity* (q.v.) with an ingenious twist ending. Acting, direction and cinematography are meticulous.

'It *is* hugely enjoyable. The pace is fast; the subtleties are almost but not quite thrown away. Kasdan does what all good film-makers do. He creates a

THE BLUE LAMP

BODY HEAT

THE BODYGUARD

world and gives it life. He also has a
fine respect for actors.'
Daily Mail

THE BODYGUARD

(US 1992)
pc WB. A Tig production in
association with Kasdan Pictures. p
Lawrence Kasdan, Jim Wilson, Kevin
Costner. d Mick Jackson. w Lawrence
Kasdan. ph Andrew Dunn. Colour. ed
Richard A Harris. assoc ed Donn
Cambern. pd Geoffrey Beecroft. ad W.
Ladd Skinner. sfx co-ord Burt Dalton.
sc Norman L Howell. m Alan Silvestri.
chor Sean Cheesman. 129 mins

Cast: Kevin Costner (Frank Farmer),
Whitney Houston (Rachel Marron),
Gary Kemp (Sy Spector), Bill Cobbs
(Devaney), Ralph Waite (Herb
Farmer), Tomas Arana (Portman),
Michele Lamar Richards (Nicki), Mike
Starr (Tony), Christopher Birt
(Henry), Debbie Reynolds (Herself),
Robert Wuhl (Oscar Host), Tony
Pierce (Dan), DeVaughan Nixon
(Fletcher), Joe Urla (Minella)

A bodyguard falls for the actress-singer
he has been hired to protect from a
would be-killer.

The flat, ten-year-old screenplay
(written with Steve McQueen in mind)
that should have remained at the
bottom of Kasdan's reject pile, and no
discernible chemistry between
Houston (who cannot act) and
Costner (who appears not to want to)
defeat the director and the audience,
who are more likely to side with the
killer than the intended victim.

'A formulaic and ruinously long thriller
that might have been more fun if its

BONNIE AND CLYDE

absurdities had been played as high camp.'
The New Yorker

'All as daft as a cartload of monkeys and about as deep as a toddler's pad-dling pool.'
Today

BONNIE AND CLYDE

(US 1967)
pc Tatira/Hiller/WB. p Warren Beatty.
d Arthur Penn. w David Newman,
Robert Benton. add dial Robert
Towne. ph Burnett Guffey. Colour. ad
Dean Tavoularis. sfx Danny Lee. m

Charles Strouse. background m Lester
Flatt, Earl Scruggs. cos Theadora Van
Runkle. 111 mins

Cast: Warren Beatty (Clyde Barrow),
Faye Dunaway (Bonnie Parker), Gene
Hackman (Buck Barrow), Michael J
Pollard (C W Moss), Estelle Parsons
(Blanche), Denver Pyle (Frank
Hamer), Gene Wilder (Eugene
Grizzard), Evans Evans (Velma Davis),
Dub Taylor (Moss), Ken Mayer
(Sheriff Smoot)

Bonnie Parker and Clyde Barrow embark
on an orgy of robbery and murder in the

American south-west in the early thirties.

Stylish, highly-influential gangster
movie which was a critical and box-office
success. The violence (notably the climax
in which Bonnie and Clyde are gunned
down in a bloody hail of bullets) was
notable for the time. The screenplay,
which whitewashed the protagonists,
presenting them – against the facts – as a
latter-day Robin Hood and Maid
Marian, spawned a series of films whose
hoodlum protagonists were depicted as
folk heroes. Almost inevitably, the film,
and especially Penn's direction, were
critically overrated. Penn, abetted by
Guffey's Oscar-winning cinematography,

prettified the subject and often reduced the narrative to a black comic-strip. Beatty and Dunaway (the latter giving her best screen performance) are good but shallow, Hackman contributes strong support, and Parsons won the Best Supporting Actress Oscar.

Seen today, the film is slick, glossy and often meretricious, but its evocation of Depression America is impressive.

'A film from which we shall date reputation and innovations in American cinema. It cries out to be seen ... the most significant American film to come from America since *On the Waterfront*. Like that film *Bonnie and Clyde* is made by people who are one hundred per cent certain of what they are aiming for.'
Evening Standard

'Killings and the backdrop of the Depression are scarely material for a bundle of laughs.'
Variety

'Unusual, and even fascinating, in its depiction of the reactions to the crime wave by people who had no reason to love banks, and of the sheer seeming normality of the way of life of the criminal. But will the picture do well because of its more probing aspects, or because of the vivid violence with which it is filled? Warner Brothers, I am sure, knows the answer.'
Saturday Review

BOOMERANG!

(US 1947)
pc 20th Century Fox. p Louis De Rochement. d Elia Kazan. w Richard Murphy. Based on the *Reader's Digest* article by Anthony Abbott (rn Fulton

Oursler) ph Norbert Brodine. B&W. ad James Basevi, Chester Gore. sfx Fred Sersen. m David Buttolph. 86 mins

Cast: Dana Andrews (Henry L Harvey), Jane Wyatt (Mrs Harvey), Lee J Cobb (Chief Robinson), Cara Williams (Irene Nelson), Arthur Kennedy (John Waldron), Sam Levene (Woods), Robert Keith (McCreery), Taylor Holmes (Wade), Lester Lonergan (Cary), Lewis Leverett (Whitney), Karl Malden (Lt White)

A State's Attorney fights to prove the innocence of a vagrant accused of murdering an elderly clergyman. He succeeds, but the real killer is never found.

Influential semi-documentary thriller, based on a real-life unsolved murder in Bridgeport, Connecticut, and produced by Louis De Rochement who brought the techniques of his seminal *March of Time* series impressively to bear on feature-film-making. Kazan filmed entirely on location mostly in and around Stamford, Connecticut, and did an exemplary job. Andrews gave one of his best performances and was ably supported, notably by Cobb.

'An excellent movie of its kind – and its kind is very good and rare indeed.'
Time

'Never tries to get beyond the very good best that journalistic artists can do, but on that level it is a triumph, a perfect job, and I very much hope a springboard for many more films of its kind.'
The Nation

BORSALINO

(FRANCE/ITALY 1970)
pc Adele Productions/Marianne/Mars Film. p Alain Delon. d Jacques Deray. w Jean-Claude Carriere, Claude Sautet, Jacques Deray, Jean Cau, from the book *Bandits à Marseille* by Eugene Soccomare. ph Jean-Jacques Tarbes. Colour. m Claude Billing. cos Jacques Fonteray. 126 mins

Cast: Jean-Paul Belmondo (Capella), Alain Delon (Siffredi), Michel Bouquet (Rinaldi), Catherine Rouvel (Lola), Françoise Christophe (Madame Escarguel), Corinne Marchand (Madame Rinaldi), Julien Guiomar (Boccace), Arnoldo Foa (Marello), Nicole Calfan (Ginette), Mario David (Mario)

Two gangsters rise to the top in the Marseilles underworld in the thirties.

Sumptuously mounted mock-Hollywood with vivid period detail but, in spite of its blend of violence and humour, essentially dull.

'The period sets suggest that at any moment Gene Kelly will come on with *Slaughter on Tenth Avenue*. The screenplay is credited to four writers and goes to prove the old dictum that four writers usually make a film four times worse rather than four times better.'
The Observer

BOXCAR BERTHA

(US 1972)
pc AIP. p Roger Corman. assoc p Julie Corman. d Martin Scorsese. w Joyce H Corrington, John William Corrington. Based on characters in *Sister of the Road*, the autobiography of

Boxcar Bertha Thompson, as told to Dr Ben L Reitman. ph John Stephens. Colour. m Gib Guilbeau, Thad Maxwell. cos Bob Modes. 92 mins

Cast: Barbara Hershey (Boxcar Bertha), David Carradine (Big Bill Shelley), Barry Primus (Rake Brown), Bernie Casey (Von Morton), John Carradine (H Buckram Sartoris), Victor Argo, David R Osterhout (The McIvers), Ann Morrell (Tillie Stone), Graham Pratt (Emeric Pressburger), Mariane Dole (Mrs Mailler)

In Depression America, a young woman, a drifter and a black join forces to carry out a series of train robberies and bank hold-ups.

Violent reworking of the theme of *Bonnie and Clyde* for the seventies, with convincingly recreated thirties period atmosphere and a strong performance from Hershey. Scorsese's direction is vigorous, and once more demonstrates producer Roger Corman's ability to pick fledgling talent: the direction more than compensates for the meretriciously fictionalized screenplay.

'A weirdly interesting movie, and not really the sleazy exploitation film the ads promise ... Scorsese has gone for mood and atmosphere more than for action, and his violence is always blunt and unpleasant – never liberating and exhilarating, as the New Violence is supposed to be.'
Chicago Sun-Times

'Roger really let me do what I wanted within the time schedule and the condition that every fifteen pages there had to be some nudity in the script.'
Martin Scorsese

BRANNIGAN
(GB 1975)
pc Wellborn. For UA. exec p Michael Wayne. p Jules Levy, Arthur Gardner. d Douglas Hickox. w Christopher Trumbo, Michael Butler, William P McGivern, William Norton. st Christopher Trumbo, Michael Butler. ph Gerry Fisher. Colour. Panavision. ad Ted Marshall, sfx Roy Whybrow. sc Peter Brayham. m Dominic Frontiere. 111 mins

Cast: John Wayne (Lt Jim Brannigan), Richard Attenborough (Commander Sir Charles Swann), Judy Geeson (Det. Sgt Jennifer Thatcher), Mel Ferrer (Mel Fields), John Vernon (John Larkin), Daniel Pilon (Gorman), John Stride (Insp. Traven), James Booth (Charlie), Del Henney (Drexel), Lesley-Ann Down (Luana)

A Chicago policeman arrives in London to pick up a gangster for extradition, and has to hunt for him when he is kidnapped.

Zestful *Coogan's Bluff* clone showcasing Wayne and London, both of whom get ample opportunities to show off. Nothing original, but it succeeds in providing fast-moving, thick-ear entertainment, with Wayne towering over his co-stars (literally, in his scenes with Attenborough).

'British director Douglas Hickox has welded unpromising material into a thoroughly efficient action thriller for younger audiences.'
Films and Filming

THE BRASHER DOUBLOON
(US 1947) (GB: THE HIGH WINDOW)

pc 20th Century Fox. p Robert Bassler. d John Brahm. w Dorothy Hannah. adap Dorothy Bennett, Leonard Praskins, from the novel *The High Window* by Raymond Chandler. ph Lloyd Ahern. sfx ph Fred Sersen. B&W. ad James Basevi, Richard Irvine. m David Buttolph. 72 mins

Cast: George Montgomery (Philip Marlowe), Nancy Guild (Merle Davis), Conrad Janis (Leslie Murdock), Roy Roberts (Lt Breeze), Fritz Kortner (Vannier), Florence Bates (Mrs Murdock), Marvin Miller (Blaire), Houseley Stevenson (Morningstar), Bob Adler (Sgt Spangler), Paul Maxey (Coroner)

Los Angeles private eye Philip Marlowe is caught up in robbery, blackmail and murder when he is hired to find a valuable stolen coin.

Low-budget, low-aim Chandler with a colourless Marlowe and an over-intricate plot. Director Brahm does well with his thin material, though, and Kortner is a satisfying villain.

'As is too often usual, the story line here is complicated and the who-does-what-when-and-why is sometimes lost, but there is action aplenty, some nicely done humour, the necessary amount of love interest and a melodramtic climax that blend into sure-fire entertainment.'
Motion Picture Herald

BREAKHEART PASS
(US 1975)
pc EK Corporation. exec p Elliott Kastner. p Jerry Gershwin. d Tom Gries. 2nd unit d, stunt arr Yakima Canutt. w Alistair MacLean. ph Lucien

allard. 2nd unit ph Robert McBride. process ph William Suhr, Don Hansard Jr. Colour. pd Johannes Larsen. ad Herbert S Deverill, Richard Gilbert Clayton. sfx A D Flowers, Gerald Endler. Logan Frazee Jr. m Jerry Goldsmith. 94 mins

Cast: Charles Bronson (Charles Deakin), Ben Johnson (Nathan Pearce), Jill Ireland (Marcia Scoville), Richard Crenna (Governor Fairchild), Charles Durning (Frank O'Brien), Roy Jensen (Banlon), Casey Tibbs (Jackson), Joe Kapp (Henry), Archie Moore (Carlos), Ed Lauter (Maj. Claremont)

A killer strikes on board a train travelling across the American West in 1873.

A murder mystery masquerading as a Western, whose illogical screenplay and poor direction don't help to alleviate the general air of lethargy: only some effective second unit action occasionally raises minor interest. By the end we know whodunnit, but never find out why anyone bothered to make the film.

'A dandy suspense melodrama – fast-paced and breath-bating, with a slam-bang conclusion.'
American Way

BRIGHTON ROCK
(GB 1947) (US: YOUNG SCARFACE)
pc ABPC/Boulting Brothers. p Roy Boulting. assoc p Peter de Sarigny. d John Boulting. w Graham Greene, Terence Rattigan, from the novel by Graham Greene. ph Harry Waxman. B&W. ad John Howell. m Hans May. 92 mins

BRIGHTON ROCK

Cast: Richard Attenborough (Pinkie Brown), Hermione Baddeley (Ida Arnold), William Hartnell (Dallow), Carol Marsh (Rose), Harcourt Williams (Prewitt), Wylie Watson (Spicer), Nigel Stock (Cubbitt), Alan Wheatley (Fred Hale), George Carney (Phil Corkery), Charles Goldner (Colleoni), Reginald Purdell (Frank)

A teenage racecourse hoodlum commits murder and then marries a waitress in order to provide himself with an alibi, but his scheme fails.

While it dilutes the force of Greene's novel, it remains a powerful if overrated thriller, with location filming vividly evoking the seedy Brighton milieu. Attenborough as the young razor-wielding thug gives arguably his best performance.

'That the production and direction by the Boulting Brothers is first rate goes almost without saying. But what is particularly striking in this brilliant and horrible English piece is its handling of background.'
The Sunday Times

'What will a person untutored as to the book, and Graham Greene's preoccupation with cosmic evil, make of these characters? They come from nowhere to flit motiveless before us.'
News Chronicle

BROTHER ORCHID
(US 1940)
pc WB-First National. exec p Hal B Wallis. assoc p Mark Hellinger. d Lloyd Bacon. w Earl Baldwin, from the *Collier's Magazine* story by Richard Connell. ph Tony Gaudio. B&W. ad Max Parker. sfx Byron Haskin, Willard Van Enger, Edwin DuPar. montages Don Siegel, Robert Burks. m Heinz Roemheld. 91 mins

Cast: Edward G Robinson (Little John Sarto), Ann Sothern (Flo Addams), Humphrey Bogart (Jack Buck), Ralph Bellamy (Clarence Fletcher), Donald Crisp (Brother Superior), Allen Jenkins (Willie 'The Knife' Carson), Cecil Kellaway (Brother Goodwin), Charles D Brown (Brother Wren), Joseph Crehan (Brother MacEwen)

A gangster who goes to Europe seeking 'culture' returns to find he has been deposed as gang leader, is almost killed, and takes refuge in a monastery, where he discovers his true vocation.

Enjoyable comic reworking by Warner Bros of their 'traditional' gangster pictures, with a stand-out performance by Robinson, whose transition from racketeer to orchid-growing monk is a delight.

'The story is funnier than the treatment given it, I would say, but even so, the production keeps to a high level of entertaining nonsense and is frequently hilarious.'
New York Herald-Tribune

A BULLET FOR JOEY
(US 1955)
pc Bischoff-Diamond. p Samuel Bischoff, David Diamond. d Lewis Allen. w Geoffrey Holmes, A I Bezzerides. st James Benson Nablo. ph Harry Neuman. B&W. ad Jack Okey. m Harry Sukman. 85 mins

Cast: Edward G Robinson (Insp. Paul Leduc), George Raft (Joe Victor), Audrey Totter (Joyce Geary), George Dolenz (Carl Maklin), Peter Hanson (Fred), Peter Van Eyck (Eric Hartman), Karen Verne (Mrs Hartman), Ralph Smiley (Paola), Sally Blane (Marie), Steven Geray (Garcia), Joseph Vitale (Nick)

A Canadian policeman investigates murders connected with a nuclear scientist working in Montreal.

Routine spy thriller, with Robinson and Raft going through their familiar paces with little evident enthusiasm.

'Needlessly complicated espionage story, which makes unexciting use of the standard ingredients.'
Monthly Film Bulletin

BULLETS OR BALLOTS
(US 1936)
pc First National-WB. assoc p Louis F Edelman. d William Keighley. w Seton I Miller. st Martin Mooney, Seton I Miller. ph Hal Mohr. B&W. ad Carl Jules Weyl. sfx Fred Jackman, Fred Jackman Jr, Warren E Lynch. m Heinz Roemheld. 81 mins

Cast: Edward G Robinson (Johnny Blake), Joan Blondell (Lee Morgan), Barton MacLane (Al Kruger), Humphrey Bogart (Nick 'Bugs' Fenner), Frank McHugh (Herman), Joseph King (Capt. Dan McLaren), Richard Purcell (Ed Driscoll), George E Stone (Wires), Louise Beavers (Nelli LaFleur), Frank Faylen (Gatley)

A New York strong-arm squad detective goes undercover to bring a big-time racketeer to book.

Slick and hard-hitting exposé of the sleazy symbiosis of crime and politics, with a snappy screenplay. Keighley's fast-paced direction ensures not a minute of the relatively short running time is wasted.

'Considered simply as a gangster melodrama, it is a satisfying piece of work with as much vigorous story-telling, deftly managed thrills and fights and cunningly built-up suspense as anyone could wish for.'
Film Weekly

BULLITT
(US 1968)

pc Solar. exec p Robert E Relyea. p Philip D'Antoni. d Peter Yates. w Alan R Trustman, Harry Kleiner, from the novel *Mute Witness* by Robert L Pike. ph William A Fraker. Colour. ad Albert Brenner. sfx Sass Bedig. m Lalo Schiffrin. 114 mins

Cast: Steve McQueen (Frank Bullitt), Robert Vaughn (Walter Chalmers), Jacqueline Bisset (Cathy), Don Gordon Delgetti), Robert Duvall (Weissberg), Simon Oakland (Capt. Bennet), Norman Fell (Capt. Baker), Carl Reindel (Stanton), Felice Orlandi Renick), Pat Renella (Johnny Ross)

Mob assassins slay an underworld witness being protected by a San Francisco police lieutenant, who suppresses news of the hit while he goes after the killers.

Pacy thriller that moves its complex story along at breakneck speed under Peter Yates's expert direction, making superb use of San Francisco locations, particularly during the seminal eleven-minute car chase – still one of the most exciting ever filmed (although sharp-eyed viewers may notice the cars lose more hub caps during the chase than they started with).

Yates triumphantly proved to be one of the very few British directors to make a seamless transition to Hollywood, and the stunts (McQueen did his own driving, rejecting the use of process photography) are exemplary.

'A thriller that creeps up and makes you jump out of your skin.'
Daily Sketch

'Efficiently made and extremely well-edited but basically uninteresting.'
The New Yorker

'In short, it's the thriller of the year.'
The Guardian

THE BURGLAR
(US 1957)

pc Columbia. p Louis W Kellman. d Paul Wendkos. w David Goodie, from his novel. ph Don Malkames. B&W. ad Jim Leonard. m Sol Kaplan. 90 mins

Cast: Dan Duryea (Nat Harbin), Jayne Mansfield (Gladden), Martha Vickers (Delia), Peter Capell (Baylock), Mickey Shaughnessy (Dohmer), Wendell Phillips (Police Captain), Phoebe Mackay (Sister Sara), Stewart Bradley (Charley), Richard Emery (Child Harbin), Andrea McLaughlin (Child Gladden)

A burglar and his female accomplice steal a diamond necklace and are trailed by a crooked policeman who wants the loot for himself.

Wendkos's first film as director is self-consciously arty (as though he hoped to review it himself) but occasionally interesting. Remade as *The Burglars* (1971).

'An unusual and intriguing thriller which is cleverly presented and contains a good measure of both suspense and action, the whole moving at a brisk pace so that the attention is gripped throughout.'
CEA Film Report

C

CALL NORTHSIDE 777/ CALLING NORTHSIDE 777

(US 1948)

pc 20th Century Fox. p Otto Lang. d Henry Hathaway. w Jerome Cady, Jay Dratler. adap Leonard Hoffman, Quentin Reynolds. Based on articles in the *Chicago Tribune* by James P McGuire. ph Joe MacDonald. B&W. ad Lyle Wheeler, Mark-Lee Kirk. sfx Fred Sersen. md Alfred Newman. 111 mins

Cast: James Stewart (McNeal), Richard Conte (Frank Wiecek), Lee J Cobb (Brian Kelly), Helen Walker (Laura McNeal), Betty Garde (Wanda Skutnik), Kasia Orazewski (Tillie Wiecek), Joanne de Bergh (Helen Wiecek-Rayska), Howard Smith (Palmer), Moroni Olsen (Parole Board Chairman), John McIntire (Sam Faxon)

A woman works scrubbing floors for eleven years to save enough money to advertise in a newspaper personal column that she will pay $5,000 for evidence to clear her wrongly-jailed son. A dogged reporter turns detective to expose the miscarriage of justice.

Hathaway's impeccable documentary-style direction and pacing and vivid use of Chicago locations (unusual in the still largely studio-bound movies of the period) add impact to this fact-based suspenser. Stewart is particularly effective in a typical newspaperman turned sleuth role, and the film marks a significant advance in his post-war career and helped consolidate his stardom.

'The documentary angles of this revealing page in the annals of crime and its detection are emphasized by authentic Chicago and prison backgrounds, taut direction and first-rate all-round portrayals.'
Today's Cinema

'A rather dogged but otherwise competent fact-fiction movie; good camera work on the Chicago slums; intelligent use of natural sound. Next to *Boomerang!* the best, so far, of its kind.'
The Nation

CALLAN

(GB 1974)

pc Magnum Films. p Derek Horne. assoc p Harry Benn. d Don Sharp. w James Mitchell, from his novel *A Red File for Callan*. ph Ernest Steward. Colour. ad John Clark. sfx John Richardson. m William Josephs. solo harmonica Tommy Reilly. 106 mins

Cast: Edward Woodward (Callan), Eric Porter (Hunter), Carl Mohner (Schneider), Catherine Schell (Jenny), Peter Egan (Mears), Russell Hunter (Lonely), Kenneth Griffith (Waterman), Veronica Lang (Liz), Michael da Costa (Greek), Dave Prowse (Arthur), Don Henderson (George), Clifford Rose (Snell)

A former secret agent is offered reinstatement if he will kill a German businessman in London.

One of the few film spin-offs from a television series to make a satisfactory transition to the big screen, due in large measure to Mitchell's taut, laconic screenplay, Woodward's ideally in-character performance and Sharp's efficient, if styleless, direction.

'It has a sharp neat plot and a good deal more feeling for character than is usual in such exercises in violence.'
The Sunday Times

CANDIDATO PER UN ASSASSINO/UN SUDARIO A LA MEDIDA

(ITALY/SPAIN 1969) (US, GB:

CANDIDATE FOR A KILLING)
pc Aica Cinematografica/Fisa Films. p
Stanley Abrams. d Jose Maria Elorietta.
. (English-language version) Sidney
Pink. w Giancinto Solito, Aurelio
Lopez Monis. w (English-language
version) John Nelson. st Aurelio Lopes
Monis. add dial John and Bob Lowell.
h Miguel Mila. Colour. ad Wolfgang
Burman. m Bill Conti. 95 mins

Cast: John Richardson (Nicholas
Warfield), Anita Ekberg (Jacqueline),
Margaret Lee (Kina Lund), Fernando
Rey (Marcus August): with Polo
Pendani, Maria Martin, Giuseppe
Pertilo, Fernando Hilbeck, Dante
Cleri, David Hiller

A hitchhiker in the South of France
accepts $5,000 to impersonate a
European businessman and discovers
he is the target for a killer.

  Banal Eurotosh, of interest only to
those who wonder what happened to
former sex symbol Anita Ekberg, who
would probably be happy to forget this
ill-made anaesthetic.

'Although memory tells me that a
great deal happens in this story, it
happens so slowly and most of the
characters enunciate their words so
deliberately that it didn't seem so
at the time.'
CinemaTV Today

CAPE FEAR

(US 1962)
pc Melville-Talbot. p Sy Bartlett. d J
Lee Thompson. w James R Webb, from
the novel *The Executioners* by John D
MacDonald. ph Sam Leavitt. B&W. ad
Alexander Golitzen, Robert Boyle. m
Bernard Herrmann. 105 mins

Cast: Gregory Peck (Sam Bowden),
Robert Mitchum (Sam Cady), Polly
Bergen (Peggy), Lori Martin (Nancy),
Martin Balsam (Chief Dutton), Jack

Kruschen (Grafton), Telly Savalas
(Sievers), Barrie Chase (Diane), Paul
Comi (Garner), Page Slattery (Deputy
Kersek), Edward Platt (Judge), Will
Wright (Dr Peasall)

A sadistic, psychopathic ex-convict
terrorizes a lawyer and his family in
revenge for his conviction.

  Thompson's direction is often
thumpingly obvious (like the near-
to-parody musical score), but this is
far and away his best Hollywood
work and he racks up considerable
suspense thanks to Mitchum's
enjoyably larger-than-life
characterization of the psychopath
and Leavitt's atmospheric
cinematography. It's no masterpiece,
but seems like one in comparison
with the ludicrous and laughably
overwrought 1991 Scorsese-De Niro
remake (q.v.).

'Not a pretty film, but a riveting one.'
Daily Herald

'The tension mounts quickly with the
tempo constantly accelerating to
keep the audience on an even
sharper edge.'
Saturday Review

CAPE FEAR

(US 1991)
pc Universal. exec p Kathleen
Kennedy, Frank Marshall. p Barbara
De Fina. d Martin Scorsese. w Wesley
Strick, from a screenplay by James R
Webb and the novel *The Executioners*
by John D MacDonald. ph Freddie
Francis. 2nd unit ph Burns Shoot.
underwater ph Pete Romano. Colour.
Panavision. ed Thelma Schoonmaker.
pd Henry Bumstead. ad Jack Taylor Jr.

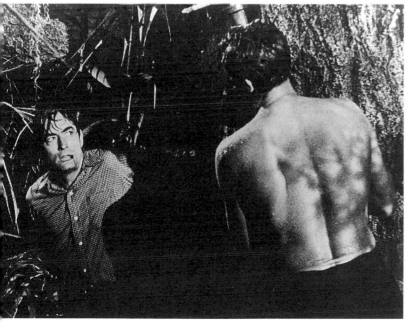

CAPE FEAR

sfx co-ord J B Jones. sc Moby John Griffin. m Bernard Herrmann. adap/arr Elmer Bernstein. 126 mins

Cast: Robert De Niro (Max Cady), Nick Nolte (Sam Bowden), Jessica Lange (Leigh Bowden), Juliette Lewis (Danielle Bowden), Joe Don Baker (Claude Kersek), Robert Mitchum (Lt Elgart), Gregory Peck (Lee Heller), Martin Balsam (Judge), Illeana Douglas (Lori Davis), Fred Dalton Thompson (Tom Broadbent), Zully Montero (Graciella)

A psychopath jailed for rape and battery embarks on a reign of terror against the lawyer who put him inside and his family.

Overwrought, over-inflated, over-directed and redundant remake of J Lee Thompson's 1962 thriller (q.v.). De Niro is embarrassingly over-the-top as the tattooed comic-book psycho, the film becomes progressively more ludicrous, and the would-be horrific climax is risible. The presence of original stars Mitchum, Peck and Balsam in minor roles only serves to underline the innate hysteria of Scorsese's derivative direction. Francis's cinematography is a minor redeeming feature.

'The greatest horror in *Cape Fear* is the death of imagination brought about by its suffocating reliance on pastiche.'
Sight and Sound

'A disgrace, an ugly, incoherent, dishonest piece of work.'
The New Yorker

'What's puzzling at this stage of his career is the way Scorsese could set his sights so low.'
Washington Post

CAPONE
(US 1975)
pc Santa Fe Productions. p Roger Corman. assoc p John Broderick. d Steve Carver. w Howard Browne. ph Vilis Lapenieks. Colour. ad Ward Preston. sfx Roger George. sc Charles Picerni. m Davis Grisman. add m Rudy Cipolla. 101 mins

Cast: Ben Gazzara (Al Capone), Susan Blakely (Iris Crawford), Harry Guardino (Johnny Torrio), John Cassavetes (Frankie Vale), Sylvester Stallone (Frank Nitti), Peter Malone (Jake Guzik), Frank Campanella (Big Jim Colosimo), Royal Dano (Anton Cermak), Dick Miller (Joe Pryor), John Davis Chandler (Hymie Weiss)

Al Capone biopic.

Violent without being particularly interesting. A dull and mannered performance by Gazzara in the title role doesn't help either.

'Inevitably, the cast follows a well-trodden path and there can be no surprises in the development of the plot.'
CinemaTV Today

'Steve Carver directed the film and did a good job. Gazzara was very good as Capone.'
Producer Roger Corman

CASINO
(US 1995)
pc Universal/Syalis D.A./Legende Enterprises Present a De Fina/Cappa Production. p Barbara de Fina. assoc p Joseph Reidy. d Martin Scorsese. w Nicholas Pileggi, Martin Scorsese, from a book by Nicholas Pileggi. ph Robert Richardson. 2nd unit ph Tom Sigel, Philip Pfeiffer. Colour. ed Thelma Schoonmaker. pd Dante Ferretti, ad Jack G Taylor Jr. visual fx sup Craig Barron. sc Doug Coleman, Daniel W Barringer. m cons Robbie Robertson. titles Elaine Bass, Saul Bass. 178 mins

Cast: Robert De Niro (Sam 'Ace' Rothstein), Sharon Stone (Ginger McKenna), Joe Pesci (Nicky Santoro), James Woods (Lester Diamond), Don Rickles (Billy Sherbert), Alan King (Andy Stone), Kevin Pollack (Philip Green), L Q Jones (Pat Webb), Dick Smothers (Senator), Frank Vincent (Frank Marino), John Bloom (Don Ward), Pasquale Cajano (Remo Gaggi), Melissa Prophet (Jennifer Santoro)

A Jewish mobster operates a Las Vegas casino for the Mafia.

An expensive, graphically violent, foul-mouthed riff on *Goodfellas*, whose flaccid screenplay gives the impression of being an unedited first draft and which gets direction to match. De Niro sleepwalks through his role as the least likely Jewish gangster since Warren Beatty played Bugsy Siegel, while Pesci, reprising his foul-mouthed psycho from *Goodfellas*, achieves the near-impossible by making the character even more loathsome. Only Stone emerges with some credit from a largely pointless fiasco, whose minimal interest derives from documentary-style sequences showing how gamblers are parted from their cash.

'Scorsese's appetite for foul language, machismo and violence have never

been more questionable than here. Scenes of torture are portrayed with pornographic relish. The movie is as morally myopic as *Bugsy*, and far more brutal. It's also quite boring.'
Daily Mail

'A mess. At three hours long, it's a boring mess, too, and a sad waste of money, time and talent.'
Daily Star

T AND MOUSE

(GB 1958)
pc Anvil Films. p, d, w Paul Rotha, from the novel by Michael Halliday (rn John Creasey). ph Wolfgang Suschitsky. B&W. ad Tony Inglis. 79 mins

Cast: Lee Patterson (Rod Fenner), Ann Sears (Ann Coltby), Hilton Edwards (William Scruby), Victor Maddern (Det. Supt. Harding), George Rose (Second-hand Clothes Dealer), Roddy McMillan (Mr Pomeroy), Diana Fawcett (Mrs Pomeroy)

An American Army deserter holds a young woman captive while he searches for a cache of stolen gems.

Minor suspenser, of some interest because of the involvement of noted documentary film-maker Rotha.

'The point of the film is the degree of achievement within an essentially modest framework.'
Sight and Sound

CAUSE FOR ALARM

(US 1951)
pc MGM. p Tom Lewis. d Tay Garnett. w Mel Dinelli, Tom Lewis, from an unpublished story by Larry Marcus. ph Joseph Ruttenberg. B&W.

ad Cedric Gibbons, Arthur Lonergan. m André Previn. 74 mins

Cast: Loretta Young (Ellen Jones), Barry Sullivan (George Jones), Bruce Cowling (Dr Ranney Grahame), Margalo Gilmore (Mrs Edwards), Brady Mora (Hoppy Billy), Irving Bacon (Postman), Georgia Backus (Mrs Warren), Don Haggerty (Mr Russell), Art Baker (Superintendent), Richard Anderson (Sailor)

A jealous husband tries to frame his wife for murder.

Efficient enough, with the confined setting of a suburban home potentiating the suspense, although Garnett's static direction tends to vitiate the overall effect.

'Intensely dramatic, packed with suspense, acted and directed with subtlety.'
Picture Show

CHARADE

(US 1963)
pc Stanley Donen Productions. p, d Stanley Donen. assoc p James Ware. w Peter Stone. st Peter Stone, Mark Behm. ph Charles Lang Jr. Colour. ad Jean D'Eaubonne. m Henry Mancini. title song Henry Mancini, Johnny Mercer. 113 mins

Cast: Cary Grant (Peter Joshua), Audrey Hepburn (Reggie Lambert), Walter Matthau (Hamilton Bartholomew), James Coburn (Tex Penthollow), George Kennedy (Herman Scobie), Ned Glass (Leopold Gideon), Jacques Marin (Insp. Grandpierre), Paul Bonifas (Felix), Dominique Minot (Sylvie Gaudet)

A young, recently-widowed American in Paris finds herself in danger from three men who are after a fortune hidden by her murdered husband.

Slick, glossy pseudo-Hitchcock with a deft script and chic direction that turns Paris into a co-star. The stars – notably Grant, who acts his age as the ambivalent hero-villain – are in good form.

'It is certainly one of the smoothest and most winning pieces of sheer entertainment to come our way for a very long time.'
The Times

'This most enjoyable film is full of holes but it keeps on its feet and it keeps moving.'
Daily Express

CHARLEY VARRICK

(US 1973)
pc Universal. exec p Jennings Lang. p, d Don Siegel. w Howard Rodman, Dean Reisner, from the novel *The Looters* by John Reese. ph Michael Butler. Colour. ad Fernando Carrere. flying sequences Frank Tallman. m Lalo Schifrin. 111 mins

Cast: Walter Matthau (Charley Varrick), Joe Don Baker (Molly), Felicia Farr (Sybil Ford), Andy Robinson (Harman Sullivan), John Vernon (Maynard Boyle), Sheree North (Jewell Everett), Norman Fell (Mr Garfinkle), Benson Fong (Honest John), Woodrow Parfrey (Howard Young), William Schallert (Sheriff Bill Norton)

A minor-league crook ends up with a hired killer on his trail after robbing a

CHARADE

small New Mexico bank which turns out to be used by the Mafia.

Fast-moving and violent, with an enjoyable streak of sardonic humour and well-cast minor characters. Baker is icily memorable as the hitman, and while it loses momentum in the second half, crisp editing and Siegel's direction (for once, apparently, not with an eye to his *auteur* status) carries it through to an improbable but exciting airfield climax.

'Bright touches of comedy, its suspense is skilfully built and the script has ingenious twists and much crisp dialogue.'
San Francisco Chronicle

'The best crime thriller since *The French Connection*. When gifted people who take this kind of film making seriously get the right material to be serious about, they make very good trifles. Which this is.'
New Republic

CHASE A CROOKED SHADOW
(GB 1957)
pc Associated Dragon Films. p Douglas Fairbanks Jr. d Michael Anderson. w David Osborn, Charles Sinclair. ph Erwin Hillier. B&W. ad Paul Sheriff. m Matyas Seiber. 87 mins

Cast: Richard Todd (Ward), Anne Baxter (Kimberley), Herbert Lom (Vargas), Alexander Knox (Chandler Bridson), Faith Brook (Mrs Whitman), Alan Tilvern (Carlos), Thelma D'Aguiar (Maria)

A man invades an heiress's Costa Brava home claiming to be her brother (who was killed in a car accident) and she is

unable to make anyone believe he is an imposter.

The theme is hardly pristine, but an excellent screenplay (despite some obvious flaws) and Anderson's self-conscious direction rack up admirable suspense.

'Dracula, Frankenstein's Monster, "things" from outer space ... they're kid's stuff. This taut spine-chiller has them beaten in every way.'
Picturegoer

CHINATOWN
(US 1974)
pc Long Road Productions. A Paramount-Penthouse presentation. p Robert Evans. assoc p CO Erickson. d Roman Polanski. w Robert Towne. ph John A Alonzo. Colour. pd Richard Sylbert. ad W Stewart Campbell. sfx Logan Frazee. m Jerry Goldsmith. 131 mins

Cast: Jack Nicholson (J J Gittes), Faye Dunaway (Evelyn Mulwray), John Huston (Noah Cross), Perry Lopez (Escobar), John Hillerman (Yelburton), Darrell Zwerling (Hollis Mulwray), Diane Ladd (Ida Session), Roy Jenson (Mulvihill), Roman Polanski (Man with Knife), Dick Bakalyan (Loach)

In 1937 Los Angeles, a private detective hired by a mysterious woman to find out if her husband is being unfaithful is drawn into a complex web of corruption, murder and incest.

Overrated: despite Towne's clever, multilayered screenplay and competent direction by Polanski, there is considerably less here than meets the eye. It does establish the period well, but Nicholson lacks the kind of charisma

Bogart had, so that one is left admiring plot twists and individual sequences rather than the film as a whole.

It was nominated for the Best Picture Oscar, and there were nominations for Nicholson, Polanski, cinematographer John A Alonzo, composer Jerry Goldsmith and Towne. In the event, only Towne received an Academy Award.

Nicholson directed the inept 1990 sequel, *The Two Jakes*.

'A cogently low-key thriller in which action and even suspense take a back seat to atmosphere.'
Esquire

'Someone once said of Richard Strauss' *Salome* that it was composed of bits and pieces of fecal matter: the same is true of director Roman Polanski's *Chinatown*; quickly, however, we must add both are extraordinarily successful *tours de force*.'
Films in Review

'If *Chinatown* were shorter and less consciously paradigmatic, it would be a good sinister thriller. But Towne and Polanski are insufficiently innocent.'
The New Republic

CLEAR AND PRESENT DANGER
(US 1994)
pc Paramount. p Mace Neufeld, Robert Rehne. co-p Ralph S Singleton. assoc p Lis Kern. d Philip Noyce. 2nd unit d David R Ellis, Craig Hosking. w Donald Stewart, Steven Zaillian, John Milius, from the novel by Tom Clancy. ph Donald McAlpine. 2nd unit ph Michael A Benson. pd Terence Marsh. ad William Cruse, Fernando Ramirez.

sfx co-ord Joe Lombardi, Phil Lombardi, Phil Fravel, Laurencio Cordero. sfx Robert G Willard. sc Dirk Ziker. m James Horner. 141 mins

Cast: Harrison Ford (Jack Ryan), Willem Dafoe (Clark), Anne Archer (Cathy Ryan), Joaquim de Almeida (Felix Cortez), Henry Czerny (Robert Ritter), Harris Yulin (James Cutter), Donald Moffat (President Bennett), Miguel Sandoval (Ernesto Escobedo), Benjamin Bratt (Capt. Ramirez), Raymond Cruz (Chavez), Dean Jones (Judge Moore), Thora Birch (Sally Ryan), Hope Lange (Senator Mayo), James Earl Jones (Admiral Grover)

A CIA agent tangles with a Colombian drugs cartel and uncovers high-level corruption in the White House.

Over-plotted to the point of constipation, with a wooden performance by Ford, whose dogged dullness makes the secondary characters seem far more interesting than they really are. The director tries hard, but his job is basically that of expensive embalmer.

'Hollywood is staggering into a realm of banal movie-making that never ceases to surprise. Just when you think you've seen the worst, they manage to pull off another coup. *Clear and Present Danger* is not just a bad movie, its gives B movies a bad name.'
Morning Star

CLEOPATRA JONES
(US 1973)
pc WB. p William Tennant, Max Julien. d Jack Starrett. w Max Julien, Sheldon Keller. st Max Julien. ph David Walsh. Colour. Panavision. ad

Peter Wooley. Hapkido karate master Bong Soo Han. m J J Johnson. add m Carl Brandt, Joe Simon. song *The Theme From Cleopatra Jones* by Joe Simon, sung by Joe Simon, Millie Jackson. 89 mins

Cast: Tamara Dobson (Cleopatra Jones), Bernie Casey (Reuben), Brenda Sykes (Tiffany), Antonio Fargas (Doodlebug), Shelley Winters (Mommy), Bill McKinney (Officer Purdey), Dan Frazer (Det. Crawford), Stafford Morgan (Sgt Kert), Mike Warren (Andy), Albert Popwell (Matthew), Caro Kenyatta (Melvyn Johnson)

A black US secret agent brings a Los Angeles narcotics syndicate to book.

With its karate-kicking superheroine and lively pace, packed with comic-strip violence and action and featuring a truly grotesque (even by her later standards) performance by Winters, it emerges as one of the better blaxploitation pictures of the seventies.

'The movie is funky and fun, and as the dude in the nightclub says, if you don't dig it you've got a hole in the soul.'
Washington Star-News

'Hampers the cause of racial entente more effectively than any work since *Uncle Tom's Cabin*.'
Monthly Film Bulletin

CLEOPATRA JONES AND THE CASINO OF GOLD
(US/HONG KONG 1975)
pc WB/Shaw Brothers. p William Tennant, Run Run Shaw. d Chuck Bail. w William Tennant, based on characters created by Max Julien. ph

Alan Hume. Colour. Panavision. ad Johnson Tsao. sfx Nobby Clark, Milt Rice. Chinese fighting instructors Tang Chia, Yuen Shien Yan. m Dominic Frontiere. song *Playin' With Fire* by Dominic Frontiere, Kenny Kerner, Richie Wise. 95 mins

Cast: Tamara Dobson (Cleopatra Jones), Stella Stevens (Dragon Lady), Tanny (Mi Ling), Norman Fell (Stanley Nagel), Albert Popwell (Mathew Johnson), Caro Kenyatta (Melvyn Johnson), Chan Sen (Soo Da Chen), Christopher Hunt (Mendez), Lin Chen Chi (Madalyna), Eddy Donno (Morgan)

Black US agent Cleopatra Jones teams up with a Chinese private detective in Hong Kong to smash the narcotics operation run by the sinister Dragon Lady.

Simple-minded sequel with simple-minded stunts and mayhem, and Dobson creating a vacuum when called upon to act, or even in repose. But the action is briskly staged by Hollywood stunt coordinator Bail, here turning his hand to direction.

'This one is wild ... an incredible variety of action.'
Chicago Sun-Times

THE COLLECTOR
(US/GB 1965)
pc The Collector Company. p Jud Kinberg, John Kohn. d William Wyler. 2nd unit d Robert Zwink. w Stanley Mann, John Kohn, from the novel by John Fowles. ph Robert L Surtees, Robert Krasker. 2nd unit ph Norman Warwick. Colour. ad John Stoll. m Maurice Jarre. 120 mins

Cast: Terence Stamp (Freddie Clegg), Samantha Eggar (Miranda Grey), Mona Washbourne (Aunt Annie), Maurice Dallimore (The Neighbour)

An unbalanced young man comes into money and kidnaps the girl he worships from afar.

Over-long, tepid and short on suspense, embalmed rather than directed by Wyler, and burdened with Stamp and Eggar, who are woefully inadequate. Not worth collecting.

Incomprehensibly, Wyler, the screenplay and Eggar all received Oscar nominations.

'Tolerably tense little war of nerves, but directed and written without much edge.'
Sight and Sound

COLOR OF NIGHT
(US 1994)

pc Cinergi. exec p Andrew G Vajna. p David Matalon, Buzz Feitshans. co-p David Willis, Caroline Zozzora. d Richard Rush. w Matthew Chapman, Billy Ray. st Billy Ray. ph Dietrich Lohmann. 2nd unit p John Connor, George Mooradian. underwater ph Pete Romano. Colour. ed Jack Hofstra. pd James L Schoppe. ad Jack Mahoney. sfx co-ord Terry King. sfx Gerry Elmendorf, Peter Albiez. m Dominic Frontiere. 121 mins

Cast: Bruce Willis (Dr Bill Capa), Jane March (Rose), Scott Bakula (Dr Bob Moore), Ruben Blades (Martinez), Lesley Ann Warren (Sondra Dorio), Lance Henricksen (Buck), Brad Dourif (Clark), Kevin J O'Connor (Casey), Andrew Lowery (Dale), Eriq La Salle (Anderson), Jeff Corey (Ashland), Kathleen Wilhoite (Michelle), Shirley Knight (Edith Niedelmeyer)

A traumatized New York psychoanalyst goes to Los Angeles and joins a friend's therapy group. When the friend is murdered, he turns detective to find the killer.

An alleged 'erotic thriller' that is less erotic than congealed Ovaltine, in spite of liberal helpings of the naked Ms March and flashes of Willis's flaccid penis, and whose few thrills are neutralized by the preposterous plot and even more preposterous performances. The final nail in the coffin of Rush as *auteur*.

'Rush has clearly made a comedy-thriller, but it can be hard telling which is which.'
Independent on Sunday

'As Hitchcock would have said, it's only a movie – and one he wouldn't have made.'
Variety

COMA
(US 1977)

pc MGM. p Martin Erlichman. d, w Michael Crichton, from the novel by Robin Cook (in Michael Crichton). ph Victor J Kemper. Jefferson Institute ph Gerald Hirschfeld. Colour. pd Albert Brenner. sfx Joe Day, Ernie Smith. m Jerry Goldsmith. 113 mins

Cast: Genevieve Bujold (Dr Susan Wheeler), Michael Douglas (Dr Mark Bellows), Elizabeth Ashley (Mrs Emerson), Rip Torn (Dr George), Richard Widmark (Dr George A Harris), Lois Chiles (Nancy Greenly), Harry Rhodes (Dr Morelind), Gary Barton (Computer Operator), Tom Selleck (Sean Murphy)

A woman doctor discovers patients in a big-city hospital are being killed and their organs sold for transplantation.

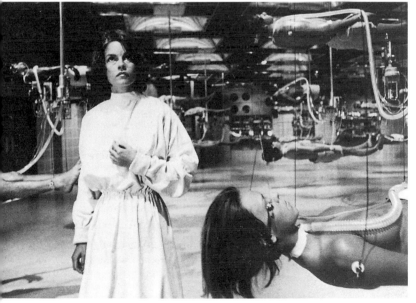

COMA

Stark suspense with seat-wetting tension. Writer-director Crichton qualified as a doctor before becoming a moviemaker, and combines knowledge of medicine and skilled cinematic scaremongering to create one of the most consistently enjoyable genre films of the seventies.

'The most cunningly crafted thriller of the year. It is an exercise in audience manipulation worthy of the Steven Spielberg of *Close Encounters* and *Jaws*.'
The Sunday Times

COMPULSION
(US 1959)
pc Darryl F Zanuck. p Richard D Zanuck. d Richard Fleischer. w Richard Murphy, from the novel by Meyer Levin. ph William C Mellor. B&W. CinemaScope. ad Lyle R Wheeler, Mark-Lee Kirk. m Lionel Newman. 103 mins

Cast: Dean Stockwell (Judd Steiner), Bradford Dillman (Artie Strauss), E G Marshall (Horn), Orson Welles (Jonathan Wilk), Diane Varsi (Ruth Evans), Martin Milner (Sid), Richard Anderson (Max), Robert Simon (Lt Johnson), Edward Binns (Tom Daly), Robert Burton (Mr Straus), Wilton Graff (Mr Steiner)

Believing they can commit the perfect crime, two wealthy students from upper-class families murder a young boy for kicks in twenties Chicago.
Based, like *Rope* (q.v.), on the infamous Leopold-Loeb case, it skirts delicately around the homosexuality of the protagonists (extremely well played by Stockwell and Dillman) but still

emerges as riveting and suspenseful in spite of Fleischer's stolid direction and unwieldy use of CinemaScope. Welles gives a bravura performance as the defence counsel: the character was based on Clarence Darrow.

'Shockingly good, in the best possible way ... can hardly be faulted – down to the playing of the tiniest supporting part. The treatment is serious, understated and unsensational ... Welles, ridding himself of characteristic mannerisms, rises magnificently to the occasion and gives the most impressive performance of his career – NOT excepting *Citizen Kane*.'
Picturegoer

CONFESSIONS OF A NAZI SPY
(US 1939)
pc WB-First National. assoc p Robert Lord. d Anatole Litvak. w Milton Krims, John Wexley, from material gathered by Leon G Turrou. ph Sol Polito. B&W. ed Owen Marks. m Max Steiner. 110 mins

Cast: Edward G Robinson (Ed Renard), Francis Lederer (Schneider), George Sanders (Schlager), Paul Lukas (Dr Kassel), Henry O'Neill (DA Kellogg), Lya Lys (Erika Wolff), Grace Stafford (Mrs Schneider), James Stephenson (Scotland Yard Man), Sig Rumann (Krogman), Fred Tozere (Phillips), Dorothy Tree (Hilda), Joe Swayer (Renz), Celia Sibelius (Mrs Kassel), Hans von Twardowsky (Wildebrandt)

A G-Man goes after Nazis planning to kidnap an American Air Force general.
The film, based on a real-life 1937 spy trial of Nazi sympathizers and

organizers, caused an outcry in America because of its assertion that espionage directed from Berlin was tied up with the German–American bunds in the US. Litvak's documentary-style direction added to the impact.

'Like a real monolith among cardboard foothills. Confessions of a Nazi Spy looms large above the dozens of phon spy pictures of the last decade.'
Daily Worker

THE CONVERSATION
(US 1974)
pc Coppola Company/Paramount. A Directors Company Presentation. p Francis Ford Coppola, Fred Roose. assoc p Mona Skaga. d, w Francis Ford Coppola. ph Bill Butler. Colour. pd Dean Tavoularis. m David Shire. 113 mins

Cast: Gene Hackman (Harry Caul), John Cazale (Stan), Allen Garfield (Bernie Moran), Frederic Forrest (Mark), Cindy Williams (Ann), Michael Higgins (Paul), Elizabeth MacRae (Meredith), Teri Garr (Amy), Harrison Ford (Martin Stett), Mark Wheeler (Receptionist), Robert Duvall (The Director)

A surveillance expert accidentally stumbles on a sinister stew of power politics and murder in San Francisco.
Over-long, over-complex and overrated thriller that rapidly vanishes up its own paranoid intricacies.

'The icy fascination soon succumbs to two forms of excess. One is Coppola's infatuation with the technical aspects of his subject, which drenches us with

ever splashier aural effects, closely combines with scarcely less frantic visual hocus-pocus. The other is a mystery story that thickens into even greater contrivance, improbability and opacity.'
Esquire

CONVICTED
(US 1950)

pc Columbia. p Jerry Bresler. d Henry Levin. w William Bowers, Fred Niblo Jr, Seton I Miller, from the play *The Criminal Code* by Martin Flavin. ph Burnett Guffey. B&W. ad Carl Anderson. m George Duning. 91 mins

Cast: Glenn Ford (Joe Hufford), Broderick Crawford (George Knowland), Millard Mitchell (Malloby), Dorothy Malone (Kay Knowland), Carl Benton Reid (Capt. Douglas), Frank Faylen (Ponti), Will Geer (Mapes), Martha Stewart (Bertie Williams), Henry O'Neill (Detective Dorn), Ed Begley (Mackay)

A man unjustly jailed for murder refuses to name the killer of the informer who foils an attempted escape, and is finally paroled.

The contrived plot and lacklustre direction fail to add up to much, and the romantic interest is both dull and unbelievable. A remake of *The Criminal Code* (1932).

'You need to be in a tolerant mood to get the best out of *Convicted*.'
Picturegoer

COOGAN'S BLUFF
(US 1968)

pc Universal. exec p Richard E Lyons. p, d Donald Siegel. assoc p Irving

Leonard. w Herman Miller, Dean Riesner, Howard Rodman. st Herman Miller. ph Bud Thackery. Colour. ad Alexander Golitzen, Robert C MacKichan. m Lalo Schifrin. 94 mins

Cast: Clint Eastwood (Walt Coogan), Lee J Cobb (Det. Lt McElroy), Susan Clark (Julie), Tisha Sterling (Linny Raven), Don Stroud (Ringerman), Betty Field (Mrs Ringerman), Tom Tully (Sheriff McCrea), Melodie Johnson (Millie), James Edwards (Jackson), Rudy Diaz (Running Bear), Marjorie Bennett (Mrs Fowler)

An Arizona Deputy Sheriff uses unorthodox methods to recapture an escaped killer in New York.

Eastwood's first film with Siegel is well-written, briskly-directed, with good action and laced with enjoyably laconic humour. It was the 'inspiration' for Dennis Weaver's seventies television series *McCloud*.

'A fast-moving thriller; well worth dropping in on; and giving out a sharp sense of time and place without straining belief at every turn.'
The Daily Telegraph

'A sharp little number which spits out wisecracks as frequently as broken teeth and balances its hot violence with a nice line in cool sex.'
The Sun

COPS AND ROBBERS
(US 1973)

pc E K Corp. p Elliott Kastner, assoc p George Papas. d Aram Avakian. w Donald E Westlake. ph David L Quaid. Colour. ad Gene Rudolf. m Michel Legrand. 89 mins

Cast: Cliff Osmond (Tom), Joe Bologna (Joe), Dick Ward (Paul Jones), Shepperd Strudwick (Mr Eastpoole), Ellen Holly (Mrs Wells), John P Ryan (Patsy O'Neil/Pasquale Aniello), Nino Ruggieri (Mr Joe), Gayle Gorman (Mary), Lucie Martin (Grace), Joseph Spinell (Marty), Dolph Sweet (George)

Two New York policemen pull off a $1 million robbery on Wall Street.

Agreeable crime caper, combining excitement and comedy with a smart screenplay and good direction.

'Laced with melodrama and suspense, generally well-produced and told with certain realism.'
Variety

COPYCAT
(US 1995)

pc Monarchy Enterprises/Regency Entertainment. exec p Michael Nathanson, John Fiedler. p Arnon Milchan, Marek Tarlov. co-p Joe Carracciolo Jr. d Jon Amiel. w Ann Biderman, David Madsen. ph Laszlo Kovacs. add ph Tony Pierce-Roberts. Colour. ed Alan Helm, Jim Clark. pd Jim Clay. ad Chris Seagers. sfx co-ord R Bruce Steinheimer. sc Tim A Davison, John C Meier. m Christopher Young. 123 mins

Cast: Sigourney Weaver (Helen Hudson), Holly Hunter (M J Monahan), Dermot Mulroney (Ruben Goetz), William McNamara (Peter Foley), Harry Connick Jr (Daryll Lee Cullum), J E Freeman (Lt Quin), Will Patton (Nicoletti), John Rothman (Andy), Shannon O'Hurley (Susan Schiffer), Bob Greene (Pachulski), Tony Haney (Kerby), Danny Kovacs

COPYCAT

(Kostas), Tahmus Rounds (Landis)
A criminologist and expert on serial
killers becomes an agoraphobe after
almost being slain by one of her
subjects and is pressured by a Los
Angeles policewoman to help trap a
serial murderer whose *modus operandi*
is to 'copy' celebrated homicides.

More repulsive than gripping,
with bludgeoning direction, a script
that veers between gloating sadism
and unintentional comedy, and
motivations on the level of a high-
school psychology primer that reduce
a moderately interesting premise to
the level of glossy, expensively-
produced exploitation. Amiel seems

more interested in avoiding showing
the considerable difference in height
between his two leading ladies than in
any other aspect of the film. He even
manages to rob an apparently surefire
climax of most of its suspense.

'As unoriginal and unprepossessing
as its killer, a dreary farrago of all
the old themes – such as the killer's
gruesome fallacy that murder can
be an art.'
The Daily Telegraph

THE CRIMINAL
1960) (US: THE CONCRETE
JUNGLE)

pc Merton Park Studios. p Jack
Greenwood. assoc p J P O'Connolly.
d Joseph Losey. w Alun Owen. st
Jimmy Sangster. ph Robert Krasker.
B&W. ad Scott McGregor. m Johnny
Dankworth. 97 mins

Cast: Stanley Baker (Johnny
Mannion), Sam Wanamaker (Mike
Carter), Margit Saad (Suzanne),
Patrick Magee (Chief Warder
Barrows), Noel Willman (Prison
Governor), Gregoire Aslan (Frank
Saffron), Jill Bennett (Maggie),
Kenneth J Warren (Cobber), Nigel
Green (Ted), Kenneth Cope (Kelly),
Patrick Wymark (Sol)

A convict is sprung from prison by associates who want him to lead them to hidden loot from a racetrack robbery.

Tough British thriller that tries, with some success, to ape its American exemplars, but somewhat unsure as to whether it is providing a grim picture of prison life, thrills, or mordant social comment. Over-melodramatic, with gritty dialogue, not particularly good direction and better acting than it deserves.

'A story which the average onlooker may find difficult to follow. The very viciousness of the action, however, makes the narrative interesting for the addict who likes the going to be tough.'
CEA Film Report

THE CRIMSON KIMONO
(US 1959)
pc Globe Enterprises. p, d, w Sam Fuller. ph Sam Leavitt. B&W. ad William F. Flannery, Robert Boyle. m Harry Sukman. 82 mins

Cast: Victoria Shaw (Christine Downes), Glenn Corbett (Det. Sgt Charlie Bancroft), James Shigeta (Det. Joe Kojaku), Anna Lee (Mac), Paul Dubov (Casale), Jaclyne Greene (Roma), Neyle Morrow (Hansel), Gloria Pall (Sugar Torch), Barbara Hayden (Mother), George Yoshinaga (Willy Hidaka)

Two Los Angeles police detectives investigate the murder of a stripper.

Location filming in Los Angeles's Little Tokyo district adds some passing interest but, apart from those firmly wedded to the *auteur* theory and to preserving Fuller's position in the pantheon of great directors, the movie meanders and loses its grip early on.

'The mystery melodrama part of the film gets lost during the complicated romance and the racial tolerance plea is cheapened by its inclusion in a film of otherwise straight action.'
Variety

CRISS CROSS
(US 1949)
pc Universal. p Michael Drake. d Robert Siodmak. w Daniel Fuchs, from the novel by Don Tracy. ph Franz Planer. B&W. ad Bernard Herzbrun, Boris Leven. sfx David S Horsley. m Miklos Rozsa. 87 mins

Cast: Burt Lancaster (Steve Thompson), Yvonne De Carlo (Anna), Dan Duryea (Slim Dundee), Stephen McNally (Pete Ramirez), Richard Long (Slade Thompson), Esy Morales (Orchestra leader), Tom Pedi (Vincent), Percy Helton (Frank), Alan Napier (Finchley), Griff Barnett (Pop), Tony Curtis (Gigolo)

A man has an affair with his former wife, now married to a criminal, and she persuades him to take part in an armoured car robbery that ends in double-crosses and death.

The taut screenplay, assured direction, Franz Planer's appropriately low-key cinematography and strong contributions by Lancaster and Duryea should have added up to something better than this disappointment. Tony Curtis made his screen debut.

'You are not likely to feel much sympathy for any of the characters ... and it's long odds that before you reach the story's end you will be confused about what exactly they are thinking of each other, too.'
Picturegoer

CROSSPLOT
(GB 1969)
pc Tribune Productions. p Robert S Baker. assoc p Johnny Goodman. d Alvin Rakoff. w, st Leigh Vance. add scenes & dial John Kruse. ph Brendan J Stafford. Colour. ad Ivan King. m Stanley Black. 96 mins

Cast: Roger Moore (Gary Fenn), Martha Hyer (Jo Grinling), Claudie Lange (Marla Kogash), Alexis Kanner (Tarquin), Francis Matthews (Ruddock), Bernard Lee (Chilmore), Derek Francis (Sir Charles Moberley), Ursula Howells (Maggi Thwaites), Veronica Carlson (Dinah), Dudley Sutton (Warren)

A London executive is caught up in a plot to assassinate a visiting African statesman.

Empty mock-Hitchcock, given a passable gloss but utterly unmemorable.

'Spritely bang-bang, kiss-kiss, chase-chase thriller closely related to *The Saint* and his television stable companions. Acceptable double-bill material for average audiences.'
Kine Weekly

CRUISING
(US 1980)
pc Lorimar. In association with CIP-Europäische Treuhand AG. p Jerry Weintraub. assoc p Burtt Harris. d, w William Friedkin, from the novel by

Gerald Walker. ph James Contner. Colour. pd Bruce Weintraub. ad Edward Pisoni. m Jack Nitzsche. 106 mins

Cast: Al Pacino (Steve Burns), Paul Sorvino (Capt. Edison), Karen Allen (Nancy), Richard Cox (Stuart Richards), Don Scardino (Ted Bailey), Joe Spinell (Patrolman DiSimone), Jay Avacone (Skip Lee), Randy Jurgensen (Detective Lefransky), Allan Miller (Chief of Detectives), Barton Heyman (Dr Rifkin)

A policeman goes undercover, posing as a homosexual, to track down a killer whose victims come from New York's gay cruising district.

Crass, embarassingly inept attempt to graft a routine murder mystery onto a homosexual milieu. Tedious and unconvincing, it simply served – justifiably – to outrage gay sensibilities without providing much in the way of entertainment by way of compensation.

'Has plenty to offend on its flashy, kinky surface, but inside it's quite dull.'
Sight and Sound

CRY OF THE CITY
(US 1948)
pc 20th Century Fox. p Sol Siegel. d Robert Siodmak. w Richard Murphy, from the novel *The Chair for Martin Rome* by Henry Edward Helseth. ph Lloyd Ahern. sfx ph Fred Sersen. B&W. ad Lyle Wheeler, Albert Hogsett. m Alfred Newman. 96 mins

Cast: Victor Mature (Lt Candella), Richard Conte (Martin Rome), Fred Clark (Lt Collins), Shelley Winters (Brenda), Betty Garde (Mrs Pruett), Berry Kroeger (Niles), Tommy Cook (Tony), Debra Paget (Teena Riconti), Hope Emerson (Rose Given), Roland Winters (Ledbetter), Walter Baldwin (Orvy)

Two boys end up on opposite sides of the law, and the honest cop is forced to hunt down his erstwhile friend who has become a ruthless killer.

A time-hallowed story is given a reasonable new gloss by Sidomak, who is particularly able to bring the minor characters – memorably Hope Emerson as a masseuse and Berry Kroeger's corrupt attorney – to life. Not, however, as good as its devotees claim.

'Hackneyed though the storyline may be, it is a thriller executed with some considerable style – the style being *film noir*. *Film noir*, for those who don't understand French, is the mood brought to the brutal and seamy recesses of the American criminal mind by German expressionist émigrés such as Siodmak, in this case, and Fritz Lang.'
New Musical Express

CRY TERROR
(US 1958)
pc A Virginia and Andrew Stone Production. p, ed Virginia Stone. d, w Andrew L Stone. ph Walter Strenge. B&W. m Howard Jackson. 96 mins

Cast: James Mason (Jim Molner), Rod Steiger (Paul Hoplin), Inger Stevens (Joan Molner), Neville Brand (Steve), Angie Dickinson (Kelly), Kenneth Tobey (Frank Cole), Jack Klugman (Vince), Jack Kruschen (Charles Pope), Carleton Young (Robert Adams), Barney Phillips (Pringe), Harland Warde (Operative No.1)

A criminal forces an old army friend to help him extort $500,000 from an airline.

Stone piles on so many cliff-hanging incidents that it is only after seeing the film that one realizes the sheer improbability of it all. Direction is suspenseful, New York locations are used well, and Steiger's portrait of villainy is so over-the-top one half expects him to self-destruct.

'Though not very original, it is all rather exciting and keeps you on the edge of your seat.'
News Chronicle

DADDY'S GONE A-HUNTING

(US 1969)
pc Red Lion Productions. p, d Mark Robson. w Larry Cohen, Lorenzo Semple Jr. ph Ernest Laszlo. Colour. ad James Sullivan. m John Williams. title song John Williams, Dory Previn. 108 mins

Cast: Carol White (Cathy Palmer), Paul Burke (Jack Byrnes), Scott Hylands (Kenneth Daly), Mala Powers (Meg Stone), Rachel Ames (Dr Parkington's Nurse), Barry Cahill (FBI Agent Crossley), Matilda Calnan (Ilsa), Andrea King (Brenda Frazier), Gene Lyons (Dr Blanker), James Sikking (FBI Agent Menchell)

A young English girl goes to San Francisco and has an abortion after an affair. When she marries a politician, her former lover terrorizes her.

The heady (for the period) mixture of eroticism, perverse psychopathy and suspense is about as subtle as a guillotine, but the film, notably its vertiginous, skyscraper-set climax, is unnervingly tense.

'It is complete rubbish but may make your feet ache for a while.'
The Observer

'All quite loathsome.'
The Sunday Times

A DANDY IN ASPIC

(GB 1968)
pc Columbia. p, d Anthony Mann. d (uncredited) Laurence Harvey. assoc p Leslie Gilliat. w Derek Marlowe, from his novel. ph Christopher Challis. Colour. Panavision. ad Carmen Dillon. m Quincy Jones. 107 mins

Cast: Laurence Harvey (Eberlin), Tom Courtenay (Gatiss), Mia Farrow (Caroline), Lionel Stander (Sobakevich), Harry Andrews (Fraser), Peter Cook (Prentiss), Per Oscarsson (Pavel), Barbara Murray (Heather Vogler), Norman Bird (Copperfield), John Bird (Henderson), Michael Trubshawe (Flowers)

A Russian double agent is ordered by British Intelligence to eliminate the killer of three British spies – but his target is himself.

Negligible, tedious espionage thriller that finally disappears up its own convolutions without a trace. Harvey and Farrow are woefully inadequate, and the rest of the cast is wasted. Harvey completed the film after Mann's death: he shouldn't have bothered.

'Basically, of course, it is routing hokum featuring the fashionable anti-hero spy.'
The Daily Cinema

DANGER WITHIN

(GB 1958) (US: BREAKOUT)
pc A Colin Lesslie Production. p Colin Lesslie. d Don Chaffey. w Bryan Forbes, Frank Harvey, from the novel by Michael Gilbert. ph Arthur Grant. B&W. ad Ray Simm. m Francis Chagrin. 101 mins

Cast: Richard Todd (Lt Col. Baird), Bernard Lee (Lt Col. Huxley), Michael Wilding (Maj. Marquand), Richard Attenborough (Capt. 'Bunter' Phillips), Dennis Price (Capt. Callender), Donald Houston (Capt. Byfold), William Franklyn (Capt. Long), Vincent Ball (Capt. Foster) Peter Arne (Capitano Benucci)

British officers planning an escape from a World War Two Italian prisoner-of-war camp in northern Italy discover a traitor in their midst.

Ingenious combination of whodunnit and POW drama with a satisfying denouement. For once, casting familiar British faces works to the film's advantage.

'A smooth blend of understated excitement and sly humour. the film is a thoroughly expert thriller, efficiently acted by its admirably professional cast.'
Picturegoer

DANGEROUS CROSSING
(US 1953)
pc 20th Century Fox. p Robert Bassler. d Joseph M Newman. w Leo Townsend, from a story by John Dickson Carr. ph Joseph LaShelle. B&W. ad Lyle Wheeler, Maurice Ransford. m Lionel Newman. 76 mins

Cast: Jeanne Crain (Ruth Bowman), Michael Rennie (Dr Paul Manning), Casey Adams (Jim Logan), Carl Betz (John Bowman), Mary Anderson (Stewardess), Marjorie Hoshelle (Kay Prentiss), Willis Bouchey (Capt. Peters), Gayne Whitman (Purser), Yvonne Peattie (Nurse), Antony Joschim (Steward)

A newlywed's husband vanishes on board an Atlantic liner and she cannot convince anyone that he ever existed. The whole affair turns out to be a plot to kill her.

Even at 76 minutes, this tepid variation on *So Long at the Fair* is over-long.

'It's a slow-moving, verbose affair, which, while getting "curiouser and curiouser", just doesn't take root.'
Picturegoer

THE DARK PAST
(US 1949)
pc Columbia. p Buddy Adler. d Rudolph Maté. w Philip MacDonald, Michael Blankfort, Albert Duffy. adap Marvin Wald, Oscar Saul, from the play *Blind Alley* by James Warwick. ph Joseph Walker. B&W. ad Gary Odell. m George Duning. 74 mins

Cast: William Holden (Al Walker), Nina Foch (Betty), Lee J Cobb (Dr Andrew Collins), Adele Jergens (Laura Stevens), Stephen Dunne (Owen Talbot), Lois Maxwell (Ruth Collins), Berry Kroeger (Mike), Steven Geray (Prof. Fred Linder), Wilton Graff (Frank Stevens), Robert Osterloh (Pete), Ellen Corby (Agnes)

A psychiatrist held captive with his family by criminal in a lakeside cabin psychoanalyses their leader to win their freedom.

The Desperate Hours meets Sigmund Freud in a reasonably tense, psychologically facile remake of *Blind Alley* (1939). Holden is colourless as the gang leader with an Oedipus complex, but Cobb and Foch seize their dramatic opportunities and make the most of them.

'The idea that adult crime would be drastically reduced if juvenile delinquents were treated by psychiatry has been made into an absorbing thriller.'
New York Sunday Mirror Magazine

THE DARK WIND
(US 1991)
pc Carolco/North Face Motion Picture Company. exec p Robert Redford, Bonni Lee. p Patrick Markey. co-p Richard Erdman. assoc p Allen Alsobrook, Steve Foley. d Errol Morris. 2nd unit d Steve Perry. w Neal Jimenez, Eric Bergren, Mark Horowitz, from the novel by Tony Hillerman. ph Stefan Czapsky. 2nd unit ph Phil Carr-Foster, Peter R Norman. Colour. ed Susan Crutcher, Freeman Davis. pd Ted Bafaloukos. ad John Krenz Reinhart Jr. sc Dan Bradley. m Michel Colombier. 111 mins

Cast: Lou Diamond Phillips (Officer Jim Chee), Gary Farmer (Cowboy Albert Dashee), Fred Ward (Lt Joe Leaphorn), Guy Boyd (Agent Johnson), John Karlen (Jake West), Jane Loranger (Gail Pauling), Gary Basaraba (Larry), Blake Clark (Ben Gaines), Faye B Tso (Fannie Musket), Michele Thrush (Shirley Topaha)

A Navajo policeman investigates murder and drug-running on an Arizona reservation.

Part-Native American Phillips is competent but hardly charismatic, and while director Morris makes good use of his experience in documentary filmmaking to give his first feature convincing visual impact, the lack of dramatic momentum becomes increasingly hard to bear.

'The complete lack of any action amid the interviews and the prowling for clues makes the near two-hour running time occasionally seem like something akin to a painful tribal initiation rite.'
Empire

DEAD HEAT ON A MERRY-GO-ROUND

(US 1966)
pc DeHaven-Girard. For Columbia. p Carter DeHaven. d, w Bernard Girard. ph Lionel Lindon. Colour. ad Walter M Simonds. m Stu Phillips. 104 mins

Cast: James Coburn (Eli Kotch), Camilla Sparv (Inger Knudson), Aldo Ray (Eddie Hart), Nina Wayne (Frieda Schmid), Robert Webber (Milo Stewart), Rose Marie (Margaret Kirby), Todd Armstrong (Alfred Morgan), Marian Moses (Dr Marion Hague), Michael Strong (Paul Feng), Severn Darden (Miles Fisher)

A paroled crook plans to rob the bank at Los Angeles International Airport during the arrival of the Russian premier.

Lighthearted crime caper, carried by brisk direction and Coburn's charm as a confidence trickster with a way with ladies and a talent for impersonation. Harrison Ford made his screen debut in an unmemorable bit part.

'Fast and frantic fun ... the thriller element doesn't emerge until the latter half but when it does the tension builds admirably.'
The Daily Cinema

DEADLIER THAN THE MALE

(GB 1966)
pc Sydney Box/Bruce Newberry. p Betty E Box. d Ralph Thomas. w Jimmy Sangster, David Osborn, Liz Charles-Williams. ph Ernest Steward. Colour. Scope. ad Alex Vetchinsky. sfx Kit West. m Malcolm Lockyer. title song John Franz, Scott Engel, sung by The Walker Brothers. 101 mins

Cast: Richard Johnson (Hugh Drummond), Elke Sommer (Irma Eckman), Sylva Koscina (Penelope), Nigel Green (Carl Petersen), Steve Carlson (Robert Drummond), Suzanna Leigh (Grace), Zia Mohyeddin (King Fedra), Virginia North (Brenda), Justine Lord (Miss Ashenden), Leonard Rossiter (Bridgenorth)

Bulldog Drummond comes up against two lethal female assassins when he investigates the murder of men associated with a Middle East oil company.

An unwise attempt to resurrect and refashion Sapper's gentleman crimefighter for the sixties as a pallid James Bond clone. Johnson tries hard (and reprised the role in 1969 in *Some Girls Do*, q.v.) but is roundly defeated by a cliché-ridden script and dull direction.

'The usual mixture of indifferently blended lethal gadget, continental settings and poison-ivy girls. When the formula is as starkly exposed as this it all looks as dead as a dodo.'
The Sunday Times

DEADLY IS THE FEMALE/GUN CRAZY

(US 1950)
pc King Brothers. p Frank and Maurice King. d Joseph H Lewis. w McKinlay Cantor, Millard Kaufman, from Kantor's story *Gun Crazy*. ph Russell Harlan. B&W. pd Gordon Wiles. m Victor Young. 87 mins

Cast: Peggy Cummins (Annie Laurie Starr), John Dall (Bart Tare), Berry Kroeger (Packett), Morris Karnovsky (Judge Willoughby), Anabel Shaw (Ruby Tare), Harry Lewis (Clyde Boston), Nedrick Young (Dave Allister), Trevor Bardette (Sheriff

DEADLY IS THE FEMALE/GUN CRAZY

Boston), Mickey Little (Bart, aged 7), Rusty Tamblyn (Bart, aged 14)

A gun-obsessed World War Two veteran and a circus sharpshooter join forces and embark on a spree of robbery and murder.

Stylishly and briskly (in the second half, at least) directed by the ever-efficient Lewis, the story has strong affinities with *Bonnie and Clyde* (1967, q.v.), and in many ways – notably because of its lack of pretension and good leading performances – it is as enjoyable. Mercifully, it's considerably shorter. Now a victim of cult status.

'After a slow beginning, generates considerable excitement ... it's not a pleasant story, nor is the telling.'
Variety

'Compulsive genre cinema, wearing its low budget and Freudian motifs with almost equal disdain; it simply knocks spots off senile imitations like *Bonnie and Clyde*.'
Time Out

DEATH ON THE NILE
(GB 1978)
pc Mersham. For EMI. p John Brabourne, Richard Goodwin. assoc p Norton Knatchbull. d John Guillermin. w Anthony Shaffer, from the novel by Agatha Christie. ph Jack Cardiff. 2nd unit ph John Cardiff. Colour. pd Peter Murton. ad Brian Ackland-Snow, Terry Ackland-Snow. sfx Nobby Clark. m Nino Rota. 140 mins

Cast: Peter Ustinov (Hercule Poirot), Jane Birkin (Louise Bourget), Lois Chiles (Linnet Ridgeway), Bette Davis (Mrs Van Schuyler), Mia Farrow

(Jacqueline de Bellfort), Jon Finch (Mr Ferguson), Olivia Hussey (Rosalie Otterbourne), George Kennedy (Andrew Pennington), Angela Lansbury (Salome Otterbourne), David Niven (Col. Race), Maggie Smith (Miss Bowers), Jack Warden (Dr Ludwig Besser)

Belgian sleuth Hercule Poirot solves murders on board a Nile cruise steamer.

Handsomely-mounted – not to say handsomely-embalmed – whodunnit, whose story is faithful to the Christie original but whose bland telling is so over-long and so overloaded with stars, all of them determined to do their party pieces or die in the attempt (some do), that it finally sinks into unmemorability. Ustinov's Poirot is all Ustinov and no Christie.

'It is one way and another a cast iron box office concoction – totally predictable both in appeal and construction, about as exciting as a tractor, but reliable as hell at successfully ploughing the well-worn Christie furrow.'
The Guardian

DEATH WISH
(US 1974)
pc Dino De Laurentiis Corporation. For Paramount. p Hal Landers, Bobby Roberts, Michael Winner. d Michael Winner. w Wendell Mayes, from the novel by Brian Garfield. ph Arthur J Ornitz. Colour. pd Robert Grundlach. m Herbie Hancock. 94 mins

Cast: Charles Bronson (Paul Kersey), Hope Lange (Joanna Kersey), Vincent Gardenia (Insp. Frank Ochon), Steven Keats (Jack Toby), William Redfield

(Sam Kreutzer), Stuart Margolin (Aimes Jainchill), Stephen Elliott (Police Commissioner), Kathleen Tolan (Carol Toby), Fred Scollay (District Attorney)

A mild-mannered, liberal New Yorker turns vigilante killer after his wife and daughter are savagely raped by muggers.

Initial controversy over its killer-as-hero protagonist helped it towards huge commercial success. An undoubtedly riveting piece of cleverly-contrived audience manipulation that disembowels Garfield's novel in favour of sheer visceral exploitation. Characterization is painfully obvious, Bronson is impassive as usual and, as so often with Winner, slickness is all and the violence is crude, excessive and gratuitous.

Winner and Bronson returned to the scene of the crime in 1981, with *Death Wish II* (q.v.) in order to boost their sagging careers, and again in 1984 with *Death Wish III*. Bronson, unable to leave ill alone, made *Death Wish IV* in 1985 and *Death Wish V* in 1994.

'So cleverly constructed as entertainment that it bounces liberal challenges off its political back like a duck shaking raindrops. Even the most militant liberals are applauding like kids at a Saturday afternoon Punch and Judy show ... a powerful, explosive audience-identification movie that is probably going to make millions because it stimulates our latent sadism with some truly startling moments of voyeurism ... a complex and startlingly original film that will anger and provoke, but its most important

questions are the ones it raises about
ourselves.'
New York Daily News

'Poisonous incitement to do-it-yourself
law enforcement is the vulgar exploitation hook on which *Death Wish* is awk-
wardly hung.'
Variety

DEATH WISH II

(US 1981)
pc Golan-Globus/Landers-Roberts. For
City Films. exec p Hal Landers, Bobby
Roberts. p Menahem Golan, Yoram
Globus. d Michael Winner. w David
Engelbach. Based on characters created
by Brian Garfield. ph Richard H
Kline, Tom Del Ruth. Colour. pd
William Hiney. sfx Kenneth Pepiot. m
Jimmy Page. 95 mins

Cast: Charles Bronson (Paul Kersey),
Jill Ireland (Geri Nichols), Vincent
Gardenia (Frank Ochoa), J D Cannon
(New York District Attorney),
Anthony Franciosa (Los Angeles Police
Commissioner), Ben Frank (Lt
Mankiewicz), Robin Sherwood (Carol
Kersey), Silvana Gillardo (Rosario),
Robert F Lyons (Fred McKenzie)

Paul Kersey, now relocated to Los
Angeles, returns to his homicidal
vigilante role when his housekeeper is
raped and murdered and his teenage
daughter is abducted by five young
thugs.

Presumably it made a profit:
otherwise, a dire, totally redundant
sequel with a bad screenplay, poor
direction and dismal performances.

'Less a sequel than a remake. If the
earlier film was not graced by any subtlety of either staging or argument,
this one rapidly succumbs to such glib
and galumphing over-emphasis as to
sacrifice credibility on any level. The
acting is uniformly wooden, but in Jill
Ireland's case positively catatonic.'
Monthly Film Bulletin

THE DESPERATE HOURS

(US 1955)
pc Paramount. p, d William Wyler.
assoc p Robert Wyler. w Joseph Hayes,
from his novel and play. ph Lee
Garmes. B&W. VistaVision. ad Hal
Pereira, Joseph MacMillan Johnson. sfx
Farciot Edouart, John P Fulton. m
Gail Kubik. 112 mins

Cast: Humphrey Bogart (Glenn
Griffin), Fredric March (Dan Hilliard),
Arthur Kennedy (Jesse Bard), Martha
Scott (Eleanor Hilliard), Dewey
Martin (Hal Griffin), Gig Young
(Chuck), Mary Murphy (Cindy
Hilliard), Robert Middleton (Sam
Kobish), Richard Eyer (Ralphie
Hilliard), Whit Bissell (Carson)

DEATH WISH II

Three escaped convicts hold a family hostage in their suburban home. Bogart, whose role is strongly reminiscent of his first archetypal gangster role in *The Petrified Forest* (1936), was really too old (and knew it), but nevertheless turns in a memorable portrayal. The film, in spite of Wyler's often stagey direction and March's inevitable dullness, is tense, claustrophobic and gripping. The crass 1990 remake isn't.

'A thriller that jabs so shrewdly and sharply at sensibility that the moviegoer's eye might feel that it has not so much been entertained as used for a pin cushion. But for melodrama fans, it may prove one of the most pleasurably frustrating evenings ever spent in a movie house.'
Time

THE DETECTIVE
(US 1968)
pc Arcola/Millfield. p Aaron Rosenberg. d Gordon Douglas. w Abby Mann, from the novel by Roderick Thorpe. ph Joseph Biroc. sfx ph L B Abbott, Art Cruikshank. Colour. Panavision. ad Jack Martin Smith, William Creber. m Jerry Goldsmith. 114 mins

Cast: Frank Sinatra (Joe Leland), Lee Remick (Karen Leland), Jacqueline Bisset (Norma MacIver), Ralph Meeker (Lt Curran), Jack Klugman (Lt Dave Schoenstein), Horace McMahon (Chief Tom Farrell), Lloyd Bochner (Dr Wendell Roberts), William Windom (Colin MacIver), Tony Musante (Felix Tesla), Robert Duvall (Det. Mickey Nestor), Sugar Ray Robinson (Officer Kelly)

A New York policeman with personal problems investigates the messy murder of a young homosexual, and later realizes he has sent an innocent man to his execution.

Abby Mann's dialogue is unusually strong for the time, Douglas's direction is rather better than his usually efficiently anonymous work: the result is a remarkably effective thriller that makes valid points about then current attitudes towards homosexuality within the framework of a hard-boiled whodunnit.

'Yes, teeth-grating, eye-offending as *The Detective* is for much of its length, it must be admitted that Gordon Douglas does have something of a flair for catching the more raffish aspects of city life, the look of a precinct station, routine details of crime detection.'
Saturday Review

DIAL M FOR MURDER
(US 1953)
pc WB. An Alfred Hitchcock Production. p, d Alfred Hitchcock. w Frederick Knott, from his play. ph Robert Burks. Colour. ad Edward Carrere. m Dimitri Tiomkin. 105 mins

Cast: Ray Milland (Tony Wendice), Grace Kelly (Margot Wendice), Robert Cummings (Mark Halliday), John Williams (Insp. Halliday), Anthony Dawson (Capt. Swan Lesgate), Leo Britt (Narrator), Patrick Allen (Pearson), George Leigh (Williams), George Alderson (Detective), Robin Hughes (Police Sergeant)

A man arranges for his wealthy wife to be killed, but his complex scheme goes badly wrong.

Painfully stagebound but still tense, due more to Knott's clever screenplay and construction than to Hitchcock's largely uninspired, seemingly uninterested, direction. Only John Williams's wry performance as an urbane policeman has any real spark, and Kelly is barely adequate. Filmed in 3-D but mostly shown flat, it gains little from being seen in three dimensions apart from minor novelty value.

'The best film of the week but not vintage Hitchcock.'
Reynolds News

'Offers the prolific Hitchcock little more than an opportunity to carpenter a neat piece of filmed theatre – an opportunity which perhaps satisfied the master a little more than it does us.'
Monthly Film Bulletin

'How creative of Hitch not to be seduced by the more obvious three-dimensional clichés on offer.'
Reynolds News

DIAMONDS ARE FOREVER
(GB 1971)
pc Eon/Danjaq. p Harry Saltzman, Albert R Broccoli. assoc p Stanley Sopel. d Guy Hamilton. w Richard Maibaum, Tom Mankiewicz, from the novel by Ian Fleming. ph Ted Moore. 2nd unit ph Harold Wellman. sfx ph Albert Whitlock, Wally Veevers. Colour. Panavision. pd Ken Adam. ad Jack Maxted, Bill Kenney. sfx Leslie Hillman, Whitey McMahon. stunt arr Bob Simmons, Paul Baxley. m John Barry. title song John Barry, Don Black, sung by

DIE HARD

Shirley Bassey. titles Maurice Binder.
120 mins

Cast: Sean Connery (James Bond), Jill
St John (Tiffany Case), Charles Gray
(Blofeld), Lana Wood (Plenty O'Toole),
Jimmy Dean (Willard Whyte), Bruce
Cabot (Saxby), Putter Smith (Mr
Kidd), Bruce Glover (Mr Wint),
Bernard Lee ('M'), Lois Maxwell (Miss
Moneypenny), Desmond Llewellyn
('Q'), Norman Burton (Leiter)

Bond follows smuggled diamonds from
South Africa to Amsterdam to the US
and uncovers super-villain Blofeld's plan
for world domination.

Connery's return as 007 after the
disastrous attempt to animate George
Lazenby as Bond in *On Her Majesty's
Secret Service* (1969, q.v.) revitalized a
series whose formula of flip humour,
outrageous sets and gadgets, amazing
stunts and fast-paced action was more
like forties serials than Fleming, and all
the better for it. The set-pieces (an
exciting car chase, a skyscraper ascent
and Bond's obligatory brush with death
in a crematorium) come off well under
Hamilton's expert direction, and
compensate for an overall lack of real
suspense. The Bond girls, romantic
and homicidal alike, are as glamorous
as ever.

'Boy, if this movie isn't a boon to every
tired businessman in creation then
nothing is or can be.'
Village Voice

'This James Bond thriller is a downright
imbecile intrigue – but it is cretinism
with style and style is forever.'
Newsweek

DIE HARD
(US 1988)
pc 20th Century Fox. A Gordon
Company/Silver Pictures production.
exec p Charles Gordon. p Lawrence
Gordon, Joel Silver. assoc p, 2nd unit d
Beau E L Marks. d John McTiernan.

DIE HARD

w Jeb Stuart, Steven E de Souza, from the novel *Nothing Lasts Forever* by Roderick Thorp. ph Jan De Bont. Colour. visual sfx Richard Edlund. Panavision. ed Frank J Urioste, John F Link. pd Jackson DeGovia. ad John R Jensen. sfx co-ord Al DiSarro. sc Charles Picerni. m Michael Kamen. 131 mins

Cast: Bruce Willis (John McClane), Alan Rickman (Hans Gruber), Bonnie Bedelia (Holly Gennaro McClane), Alexander Godunov (Karl), Reginald Veljohnson (Sgt Al Powell), Paul Gleason (Dwayne T Robinson), De'voreaux White (Argyle), William Atherton (Thornburg), Hart Bochner (Ellis), James Shigeta (Takagi), Robert Davi (Big Johnson), Grand L Bush (Little Johnson)

A lone New York policeman rescues his estranged wife and other hostages held by terrorists on the 30th floor of a Los Angeles skyscraper office block on Christmas Eve while they steal $600,000 in negotiable bonds.

Slam-bang Hollywood action moviemaking at its best and most mindlessly exciting, with Willis in fine form as the singlet-wearing superhero and Alan Rickman rising so far over the top as the sneering German heavy that it comes as something of a surprise to see him actually fall to his death instead of floating away. Lashings of high-tech thrills and suspense are given high-powered direction and all the polish and expertise a huge budget and an army of the best technical experts can provide. Sequels were inevitable.

DIRTY HARRY

'Pic plays like a reworked version of Fox's Aliens, with terror lurking in the bowels of an enormous man-made structure and striking from any angle at any time. Director John McTiernan does not often play for outright shock, but atmosphere of claustrophobia and ever-present threat is eerily similar.'
Variety

'Situated somewhere between The Towering Inferno and The Poseidon Adventure, this is an inventively entertaining full-blooded all-action film mixed with a little acerbic wit and social commentary.'
Morning Star

DILLINGER

(US 1973)
pc AIP. exec p Samuel Z Arkoff, Lawrence A Gordon. p Buzz Feitshans. assoc p Robert Papazian. d, w John Milius. ph Jules Brenner. Colour. ad Trevor Williams. sfx A D Flowers, Cliff Wenger. m Barry Devorzon. 107 mins

Cast: Warren Oates (John Dillinger), Ben Johnson (Melvin Purvis), Michelle Phillips (Billie Frechette), Cloris Leachman (Anna Sagal/The Lady in Red), Harry Dean Stanton (Homer Van Meter), Steve Kanaly (Lester 'Pretty Boy' Floyd), Richard Dreyfuss (George 'Baby Face' Nelson), Geoffrey Lewis (Harry Pierpont)

Midwest FBI Chief Melvin Purvis pursues John Dillinger and his gang, finally gunning down the gangster as he leaves a cinema in Chicago in 1934.

After a career as a screenwriter, Milius made his effective, typically muscular directorial debut with a violent and bloody biopic which owes as much to myth as to reality. Oates and Johnson are excellent, and the period evocation is vivid.

'A generous measure of violence, offered without apology; in fact, with a certain relish. Milius's devotion to guns emerges in every dramatic encounter ... the gun is to banditry what blood was to Poe's Red Death, its avatar and seal ... one can forgive *Dillinger* a few longueurs for its acceptance of this particular American obsession.'
Focus on Films

DIRTY HARRY

(US 1971)
pc WB/Malpaso. exec p Robert Daley. p, d Don Siegel. assoc p, ed Carl Pingitore. w Harry Julian Fink, Rita M Fink, Dean Reisner. st Harry Julian Fink, Rita M Fink. ph Bruce Surtees. Colour. Panavision. m Lalo Schifrin. 101 mins

Cast: Clint Eastwood (Harry Callahan), Harry Guardino (Lt Bressler), Reni Santoni (Chico), John Vernon (Mayor), Andy Robinson (Killer), John Larch (Chief), John Mitchum (Dr Georgio), Mae Mercer (Mrs Russell), Lyn Edginton (Norma), Ruth Kobart (Bus Diver), Josef Sommer (Rothko), Woodrow Parfrey (Mr Jaffe)

A tough San Francicso policeman with little time for rules or authority hunts down and kills a psychopathic murderer.

Brutal, hard-edged and immensely exciting, with a mesmerizing star performance by Eastwood, who took the role after Frank Sinatra, John Wayne and Paul Newman turned it down. His portrait of iconoclastic Harry Callahan outraged liberal sensibilities and scored a massive box-office success. Said Eastwood: 'I think the appeal of the Dirty Harry-type character is that he's basically for good, and he's got a morality that's higher than society's morality. He hates bureaucracy and he thinks that the law is often wrong. If that's being called fascistic, as several critics have called it, they're full of it.' The editing is impeccable, and Siegel sensibly abandons his desire to be enthroned as an *auteur* in favour of taut, fast-moving film-making.

Eastwood reprised the role in *Magnum Force* (1973, q.v.), *The Enforcer* (1976, q.v.), *Sudden Impact* (1983) and *The Dead Pool* (1988).

'The kind of movie that brightens up Hollywood's tarnished name.'
Time

'A rip-roaring entertainment package.'
Playboy

'The pessimism of emotional atrophy and self-destructive action is all-pervasive. The result is a film that seems curiously introverted and unexplored, at once more sufficient as a thriller and less satisfying as some of Siegel's more flawed works.'
Monthly Film Bulletin

DIRTY WEEKEND

(GB 1992)
pc Scimitar Films. exec p Jim Beach. p Michael Winner, Robert Earl. d Michael Winner. w Michael Winner, Helen Zahawi, from the novel by Helen Zahawi. ph Alan Jones. Colour.

$/DOLLARS

$/DOLLARS

ed Arnold Crust (rn Michael Winner) exec ed Chris Barnes. pd Crispian Sallis. m David Fanshawe. 103 mins

Cast: Lia Williams (Bella), Rufus Sewell (Tim), Michael Cole (Norman), David McCallum (Reggie), Ian Richardson (Nimrod), Mark Burns (Mr Brown), Shaughan Seymour (Charles), Sylvia Syms (Mrs Crosby), Christopher Ryan (Small Victim), Sean Pertwee (Quiet Victim), Nicholas Hewetson (Bitter Victim), Christopher Adamson (Serial Killer), Jack Galloway (David), Neil Norman (Party Guest)

A young woman moves from London to Brighton when her lover dumps her and, after killing an obscene telephone caller, turns to multiple male murder with a will.

Winner's last film to date (happily

he appears to have become a newspaper restaurant critic) ranks extremely high among his worst movies, which is no mean feat when you consider the competition. His attempt at a sex-change version of *Death Wish* is deeply embarrassing when it isn't simply plain awful, and looks cheaply-made into the bargain. Offensive in every respect.

'Winner is an auteur in the sense he can shrink almost any subject to his Sunday-tabloid world view – even, it would seem, a hype-inflated novel of feminist revenge … the film is uniquely awful.'
Sight and Sound

$/DOLLARS

(US 1971) (GB: THE HEIST)
pc Frankovich Productions. p M J

Frankovich. d, w Richard Brooks. ph Petrus Shloemp. Colour. ed George Grenville. ad Guy Sheppard, Olaf Ivens. m Quincy Jones. 121 mins

Cast: Warren Beatty (Joe Collins), Goldie Hawn (Dawn Divine), Gert Fröbe (Mr Kessel), Robert Webber (Attorney), Scott Brady (Sarge), Artur Brauss (Candy Man), Robert Stiles (Major), Wolfgang Kieling (Granich), Robert Herron (Bodyguard), Christiane Maybach (Helga), Hans Hutter (Karl)

An American security expert installs burglar-proof protection in a Hamburg bank, and then robs it with the help of his girlfriend.

Underwritten and over-directed: a brisk chase comes too late to prevent rigor mortis.

'Parody? One wonders charitably if this had not been Mr Brooks's intention all along. Nice idea to parody the perfect crime film, but where is the wit, where is the light touch essential to such a project?'
The Daily Telegraph

DON'T BOTHER TO KNOCK
(US 1952)
pc 20th Century Fox. p Julian Blaustein. d Roy Baker. w Daniel Taradash, from the novel by Charlotte Armstrong. ph Lucien Ballard. B&W. ed George Gitten. ad Lyle Wheeler, Richard Irvine. md Lionel Newman. 76 mins

Cast: Marilyn Monroe (Nell), Richard Widmark (Jeff), Anne Bancroft (Lynn Leslie), Donna Corcoran (Bunny), Jeannie Cagney (Rochelle), Lurene

Tuttle (Mrs Jones), Jim Backus (Mr Jones), Elisha Cook Jr (Eddie), Verna Felton (Mrs Ballew), Gloria Blondell (Photographer), Willis B Bouchey (Bartender)

A young girl released from an insane asylum gets a job as a babysitter and displays both homicidal and suicidal tendencies.
Weakly-scripted and improbable: designed as a vehicle to showcase Monroe's then minimal dramatic talents, it fails even to get into first gear.

'Effective spine-chiller ... the picture is repulsively fascinating, but certainly not everybody's dish.'
Picturegoer

DOUBLE INDEMNITY

(US 1944)
pc Paramount. exec p B G De Sylva. p Joseph Sistrom. d Billy Wilder. w Billy Wilder, Raymond Chandler, from the novel by James M Cain. ph John F Seitz. process ph Farciot Edouart. B&W. ed Doane Harrison. ad Hans Dreier, Hal Pereira. m Miklos Rosza. 106 mins

Cast: Fred MacMurray (Walter Neff), Barbara Stanwyck (Phyllis Dietrichson), Edward G Robinson (Barton Keyes), Porter Hall (Mr Jackson), Jean Heather (Lola Dietrichson), Tom Powers (Mr Dietrichson), Byron Barr (Nino Zachette), Richard Gaines (Mr Norton), Fortunio Bonanova (Sam Gorlopis)

An insurance agent and his mistress conspire to murder her husband.
Archetypal forties *film noir* with a sharp, hard-boiled screenplay and exemplary playing by the principals. Stanwyck's performance is probably her best, and MacMurray is impressive, playing against his usual affable screen image. Wilder's direction is taut, cold-blooded and economical, and uses Seitz's moody monochrome cinematography to vivid dramatic effect, notably on well-chosen Los Angeles locations that exactly mirror Chandler's writings.

It is remarkably erotic for the period – Wilder makes more sexual impact with a close-up of Stanwyck's ankle chain than most contemporary gynaecologically-inclined directors are able to achieve with total nudity. Paramount excised the execution scene before release.

Nominated for Academy Awards for Best Picture, Direction, Screenplay, Actress and Musical Score, it won none, the majority going to the dangerous-to-diabetics *Going My Way*, proving – if anything – that Hollywood was not yet ready for Wilder's toughness and cynicism.

The dismal 1973 made-for-television version with Richard Crenna, Samantha Eggar (!) and Lee J Cobb, directed by Jack Smight and written by Steve Bochco, followed the original almost shot for shot, and proved there was no substitute for talent. Lawrence Kasdan's 1981 *Body Heat* (q.v.) saw no reason to stray far from *Double Indemnity*.

'It is caustic and brief and brutal and it makes its own sort of screen poetry.'
Time and Tide

'Such folks as delight in murder stories for their academic elegance alone should find this one steadily diverting ... neatly carved pieces in a variably intriguing crime game.'
The New York Times

'In many ways *Double Indemnity* is really quite a gratifying and even a good movie, essentially cheap I will grant, but smart and crisp and cruel like a whole type of American film which developed softening of the brain after the early thirties. But ... you cannot help being disappointed as well as pleased.'
The Nation

DOUBLE X

(GB 1991)
(US: DOUBLE X: THE NAME OF THE GAME)
pc String of Pearls. exec p Noel Cronin. p, d, w Shani S Grewal, based in part on the short story *Vengeance* by David Fleming. ph Dominique Grosz. Colour. ed Michael Johns. sc Terry Forrestal. m Raf Ravenscroft. 97 mins

Cast: Norman Wisdom (Arthur Clutten), William Katt (Michael Cooper), Gemma Craven (Jenny), Simon Ward (Edward Ross), Bernard Hill (Iggy Smith), Chloe Annett (Sarah), Leon Herbert (Ollie), Derren Nesbitt (Minister), Vladek Sheybal (Pawnbroker), Terry Forrestal (Swarthy Man), Steve Carlow (Detective)

The man who saves a former American policeman from a bomb in a Scottish village relates his former life of crime as an expert safecracker who finally wants out.
Slapstick comedian Wisdom unwisely returned to films after more than 20 years in an unbelievably stupid throwback to bad fifties B-features, complete with an unhappy-looking

imported American star. The actors compete to see who can give the worst performance (Hill wins by a whisker), and Grewal makes a triple mess as producer, writer and director.

'Yet again a business-incentive scheme presumably aimed at another rescue of the British film industry has led directly to the kind of movie most likely guaranteed to kill the said industry stone dead.'
Sunday Express

DR NO
(GB 1962)
pc Eon. p Harry Saltzman, Albert R Broccoli. d Terence Young. w Richard Maibaum, Johanna Harwood, Berkeley Mather, from the novel by Ian Fleming. ph Ted Moore. Colour. ed Peter Hunt. ad Ken Adam, Syd Cain. sfx Frank George. m Monty Norman. 105 mins

Cast: Sean Connery (James Bond), Ursula Andress (Honey), Joseph Wiseman (Dr No), Jack Lord (Felix Leiter), Anthony Dawson (Prof. Dent), John Kitzmiller (Quarrel), Lena Marshall (Miss Taro), Bernard Lee ('M'), Lois Maxwell (Miss Moneypenny), Eunice Gayson (Sylvia), Peter Burton (Maj. Boothroyd)

A resourceful British secret agent destroys a power-hungry megalomaniac in the Caribbean.

Empty-headed, escapist entertainment that made Connery an international star and made a fortune for its producers. The series formula was firmly established – a blend of speedy action, sex and sadism,

cliffhangers and last-minute escapes, laconic, throwaway humour, a callous disregard for violence and death, guns, girls and gimmicks, and the most indestructible hero since the heyday of the serials, set against exotic backgrounds. It proved a huge success, spawning any number of (usually) dire imitators and still-continuing sequels.

Connery may not have been the snobbish, upper-crust Bond created by Ian Fleming (who suggested Hoagy Carmichael), but he made the role uniquely his own. (Others considered were Patrick McGoohan, Richard Johnson and Roger Moore, the latter taking over from Connery in 1973 in *Live and Let Die* (q.v.), while Noel Coward passed up the opportunity to play Dr No).

Subsequent Bond adventures (happily) strayed further and further away from the not very good Fleming adventures. *Dr No* remains the most purely enjoyable in the series: in later films an often uncomfortable sense of self-consciousness and parody intruded.

'Is it possible to make a good movie out of a James Bond thriller? Fleming fans probably won't take *No* for an answer.'
Time

'*Dr No*: no, no. So inept as to be as pernicious as it might have been. Costly gloss flawed by insidious economy on girls. Superannuated Rank starlet tries to act sexy. Grotesque.'
The Spectator

'The first of the James Bond films (I trust there will be others) has the air of knowing exactly what it is up to, and that has not been common in

British thrillers since the day when Hitchcock took himself off to America.'
The Sunday Times

'*Dr No* is the headiest box office concoction of sex and sadism ever brewed in a British studio, strictly bathtub hooch but a brutally potent intoxicant for all that.'
Films and Filming

DRAGNET
(US 1954)
pc Mark VII Ltd. p Stanley Meyer. d Jack Webb. w Richard L Breen. ph Richard Colman. Colour. ed Robert M Leeds. ad Field Gray. m Walter Schumann. 89 mins

Cast: Jack Webb (Sgt Joe Friday), Ben Alexander (Officer Frank Smith), Richard Boone (Capt. Hamilton), Ann Robinson (Grace Downey), Stacy Harris (Max Troy), Virginia Gregg (Ethel Marie Starkie), Victor Perrin (Adolph Alexander), James Griffith (Jesse Quin), Georgia Ellis (Belle Davitt)

A Los Angeles policeman investigates the murder of an ex-convict.

Webb's laconic crime series *Dragnet* started on radio and successfully transferred to television, where it ran from 1951 to 1958: a second series ran from 1967 to 1969. Webb reprises his straight-faced, straight-voiced television character, and his direction (better suited to television) repeats the small-screen formula of concentrating on routine police procedure to produce a decent but dull semi-documentary thriller.

A made-for-television movie followed in 1969, and Dan Aykroyd unfunnily played Sgt Friday for laughs in the 1987 comic remake.

'Webb's first full-length film is convincing and effective – like his phenomenally popular TV shows in America. The trouble is that dramatic impact is not so good as the documentary way in which a gory murder is cleared up … the sleuthing sometimes gets a little complex.'
Picturegoer

DRESSED TO KILL
(US 1980)
pc Cinema 77. For Filmways/Warwick Associates. exec p Samuel Z Arkoff. p George Litto. assoc p Fred Caruso. p, w, d Brian De Palma. ph Ralf D Bode. Colour. Panavision. ed Jerry Greenberg. assoc ed Bill Panko. pd Gary Weist. sound fx Hastings Sound. special m-u Robert Laden. m Pino Donaggio.
104 mins

Cast: Michael Caine (Dr Robert Elliott), Angie Dickinson (Kate Miller), Nancy Allen (Liz Blake), Keith Gordon (Peter Miller), Dennis Franz (Det. Marino), David Margulies (Dr Levy), Ken Baker (Warren Lockman), Brandon Maggart (Cleveland Sam), Susanna Clem (Betty Luce), Fred Weber (Mike Miller)

A transsexual, transvestite psychiatrist embarks on a bloody killing spree.

DRESSED TO KILL

Empty, pointlessly flashy and bloody exercise in mock-Hitchcock, in which attempted homage gives way to indifferent pastiche. De Palma's undoubted technical expertise simply underlines the emotional vacuum at the centre and the basic silliness of the whole enterprise. Caine is embarrassing, Dickinson's body double gives the only adequate performance.

'Tasteless, inept, vicious and relentlessly sordid, Brian De Palma's *Dressed to Kill* is the most tedious American film I have seen this year.'
Sunday Express

'An extremely derivative *and* controversial film; but to be fair, it's also the most sheerly enjoyable horror comedy you're likely to see this year.'
Gay News

THE DRIVER

(US 1978)
pc 20th Century Fox/EMI. p Lawrence Gordon. assoc p Frank Marshall. d, w Walter Hill. ph Philip Lathrop. Colour. ed Tina Hirsch, Robert K Lambert. pd Harry Horner. ad David Ember. sfx Charley Spurgeon. sc Everett Creach. m Michael Spall. 91 mins

Cast: Ryan O'Neal (The Driver), Bruce Dern (The Detective), Isabelle Adjani (The Player), Ronee Blakley (The Connection), Matt Clark (Red Plainclothesman), Felice Orlandi (Gold Plainclothesman), Joseph Walsh (Glasses), Rudy Ramos (Teeth), Denny Macko (Exchange Man), Frank Bruno (The Kid)

A detective sets out to trap the getaway driver who is his long-time adversary.

Hill strives for *film noir* significance by creating characters known only by their occupations, but signally fails to come up with anything more than one-dimensional ciphers which his direction signally fails to flesh out. The protagonists remain shadowy: Dern tries hard but finds no depth, while O'Neal is as bland as bleached bread. The real stars are the spectacular stunts and car chases.

'Hill's objectivity ... has the cast floating about in the complexities of a plot which leaves the audience out on a limb of indifference waiting for the next car chase.'
Screen International

THE DROWNING POOL

(US 1975)
pc Coleytown Productions. For First Artists and WB. p Lawrence Turman, David Foster. d Stuart Rosenberg. w Tracy Keenan Wynn, Lorenzo Semple Jr, Walter Hill, from the novel by Ross McDonald. ph Gordon Willis. Colour. Panavision. ed John Howard. pd Paul Sylbert. ad Ed O'Donovan. sfx Chuck Gaspar, Henry Millar Sr. m Michael Small. song *Killing Me Softly With His Song* by Charles Fox, Norman Gimbel. 108 mins

Cast: Paul Newman (Lew Harper), Joanne Woodward (Iris Devereaux), Tony Franciosa (Chief Broussard), Murray Hamilton (J J Kilbourne), Gail Strickland (Mavis Kilbourne), Melanie Griffith (Schyler Devereaux), Lindsay Hayes (Gretchen), Richard Jaeckel (Lt Franks), Coral Browne (Olivia Devereaux)

A Los Angeles private eye goes to

New Orleans to investigate the blackmail of his now-married former mistress.

Over-convoluted, over-directed sequel to *Harper* (1966, q.v.), pointlessly transposing McDonald's original Los Angeles setting to New Orleans, featuring a listless and self-congratulatory performance by Newman, and pretty unconvincing into the bargain.

'The impenetrable mystery, in other words, is not particularly gripping: and the general air of pointlessness is only intensified by the sudden rush of clarification at the end.'
Monthly Film Bulletin

DU RIFIFI CHEZ LES HOMMES/RIFIFI

(FRANCE 1955)
pc Indus Films-SN/Pathé/Cinéma-Prima Film. d Jules Dassin. w René Wheeler, Jules Dassin, Auguste le Breton, from the novel by Auguste le Breton. ph Philippe Agostini. B&W. ed Roger Dwyre. ad Auguste Capelier. m Georges Auric. 113 mins

Cast: Jean Servais (Tony Le Stephanois), Carl Mohner (Jo le Suedois), Robert Manuel (Mario), Perlo Vita (rn Jules Dassin) (César), Magali Noel (Viviane), Marie Sabouret (Mado), Janine Darcy (Louise), Pierre Grasset (Louis), Robert Hossein (Remi), Marcel Lupovici (Pierre), Dominique Maurin (Tonio)
Four thieves execute the perfect robbery of a Paris jewellers, but later fall foul of a rival gang.

Taut and involving, with a classic, much-imitated thirty-minute central robbery sequence played entirely

without dialogue, otherwise, rather
glum. Dassin won the Best Director
award at the Cannes Film Festival.

'Perhaps the keenest crime film to
come from France, including Pepe Le
Moko and some of the best of Louis
Jouvet and Jean Gabin ... what makes
it vital is that Mr Dassin has already
introduced his thieves in a way that
puts you very much on their side.'
The New York Times

'The film generally is very rewarding –
and intrinsically "cinematic" – entertainment.'
Monthly Film Bulletin

THE EIGER SANCTION

(US 1975)

pc Universal/Malpaso Company. A Jennings Lang presentation. exec p Richard D Zanuck, David Brown. p Robert Daley. d Clint Eastwood. w Warren B Murphy, Hal Dresner, Rod Whitaker, from the novel by Trevanian. ph Frank Stanley. mountain sequences ph John Cleare, Jeff Schoolfield, Peter Pilafian, Pete White. Colour. Panavision. ed Ferris Webster. ad George Webb, Aurelio Crugnola. sfx Ben McMahan. m John Williams. 125 mins

Cast: Clint Eastwood (Jonathan Hemlock), George Kennedy (Ben Bowman), Vonetta McGee (Jemima Brown), Jack Cassidy (Miles Mellough), Heidi Bruhl (Anna Montaigne), Thayer David (Dragon), Reiner Schoene (Freytag), Michael Grimm (Meyer), Jean-Pierre Bernard (Montaigne), Gregory Walcott (Pope)

A former secret agent is brought out of retirement and blackmailed into terminating two men during an ascent of the north face of the Eiger.

Under-written, largely routine spy thriller, smoothly directed and with vivid mountaineering sequences at the climax, but little else to recommend it.

'A straight and definitely un-humourous treatment of a particularly silly piece of James Bond-type international espionage and assassination. The characters, plot twists and dialogue are all straight from stock.'
The Times

EL MARIACHI

(MEXICO 1992)

pc Los Hooligans. For Columbia. p, sfx Robert Rodriguez, Carlos Gallardo. assoc p Elizabeth Avellán, Carmen M De Gallardo. d, w, st, ph, ed Robert Rodriguez. Colour. add ed George Hively, Thomas Jingles, Chris Jackson. m Marc Trujillo, Alvaro Rodriguez, Juan Suarez, Cecilio Rodriguez, Eric Guthrie. 81 mins

Cast: Carlos Gallardo (El Mariachi), Consuelo Gómez (Domino), Jaime De Hoyos (Bigotón), Peter Marquardt (Mauricio/Moco), Reinol Martinez (Azul), Ramiro Gomez (Cantinero), Jesus Lopez (Viejo Clerk), Oscar Fabila (The Boy)

A mariachi musician comes to a border town and is mistaken for a hitman seeking revenge against his drug-dealer former partner. Considerable violence and bloodshed ensue.

Twenty-four-year-old Mexican-American Rodriquez made one of the most impressive debuts in years, proving himself a true *auteur* as the writer, director, cinematographer and editor of a vivid and exciting action thriller shot in two weeks for a ludicrously low $7,000 (which Rodriguez raised by working as a guinea-pig on medical research into cholesterol) on 16mm film with a hand-held camera and non-synchronous sound (Columbia paid for the blow-up to 35mm and for a Dolby soundtrack).

Sheer originality, narrative flair and inventive visual style more than compensate for rough technical edges, while sardonic, well-integrated humour and Rodriquez's editing are further considerable assets. His high-budget virtual remake is *Desperado* (1995).

'A fresh, resourceful first feature ... Spanish lingo crime meller has a verve and cheekiness that will put it over with fest and sophisticated audiences that like to latch onto hot new talent.'
Variety

By any budgetary standards, it's a fab first feature – entertaining, inventively done, and caramba-ed with action.'
Film Review

11 HARROWHOUSE
(GB 1974)

pc Harrowhouse Productions. p Elliott Kastner. assoc p Denis Holt. d Aram Avakian. 2nd unit d Anthony Squire. w Jeffrey Bloom. adap Charles Grodin, from the novel *11 Harrowhouse Street* by Gerald A Browne. ph Arthur Ibbetson. Colour. Panavision. ed Anne V Coates. ad Peter Mullin. sfx Roy Whybrow. m Michael J Lewis. songs *Long Live Love, Day After Day* by Michael J Lewis, Hal Shaper. 108 mins

Cast: Charles Grodin (Chesser), Candice Bergen (Maren), John Gielgud (Meecham), Trevor Howard (Clyde Massey), James Mason (Watts), Peter Vaughan (Colgin), Helen Cherry (Lady Bolding), Jack Watson (Miller), Jack Watling (Fitzmaurice), Cyril Shaps (Mr Wildenstein), Leon Greene (Toland)

A crooked tycoon recruits a diamond merchant to rob a gem clearing house in London.

Tedious crime caper that wastes its superior cast.

'Proves to be as stimulating as the sight of a housewife vacuum-cleaning the living room carpet.'
Daily Express

ENDLESS NIGHT
(GB 1971)

pc National Film Trustee Company/British Lion/EMI. p Leslie Gilliat. d, w Sidney Gilliat, from the novel by Agatha Christie. ph Harry Waxman. add ph Ronald Maasz. Colour. ed Thelma Connell. pd Wilfrid Shingleton. ad Fred Carter. m Bernard Herrmann. 99 mins

Cast: Hayley Mills (Ellie), Hywel Bennett (Michael), Britt Ekland (Greta), George Sanders (Lippincott), Per Oscarsson (Santonix), Peter Bowles (Reuben), Lois Maxwell (Cora), Aubrey Richards (Dr Philpott), Ann Way (Mrs Philpott), Patience Collier (Miss Townsend), Leo Genn (Psychiatrist)

An American heiress marries a chauffeur, moves into a dream house, and is targeted for murder.

A typically convoluted Christie thriller is given glossy, sub-Hitchcock treatment (complete with a poor score by Bernard Herrmann). The story creates some suspense in spite of the barely adequate leading performances and lacklustre direction.

'Has some well-organized shocks for those who haven't read Agatha Christie's thriller – and even for those who have.'
The Sunday Times

THE ENFORCER
(US 1976)

pc Malpaso. For WB. p Robert Daley. d James Fargo. w Stirling Silliphant, Dean Reisner. st Gail Hickman, S W Schurr, based on characters created by Harry Julian Fink, R M Fink. ph Charles W Short. Colour. Panavision. ed Ferris Webster, Joel Cox. ad Allen E Smith. sfx Joe Unsinn. m Jerry Fielding. 96 mins

Cast: Clint Eastwood (Insp. Harry Callahan), Harry Guardino (Lt Bressler), Bradford Dillman (Capt. McKay), John Mitchum (DiGeorgio), Tyne Daly (Kate Moore), DeVeren Bookwalter (Bobby Maxwell), John Crawford (Mayor), Samantha Doane (Wanda), Robert Hoy (Buchinski), Jocelyn Jones (Miki), M G Kelly (Father John)

Police Inspector 'Dirty Harry' Callahan is assigned a female partner when he goes after an urban terrorist group in San Francisco.

Eastwood has the laconically implacable character honed to a fine edge for his third appearance, and his performance is tough and charismatic, while future *Cagney and Lacey* star Daly does well to keep up with him. Well-staged, visceral thrills and action compensate for the formulaic storyline.

'Eastwood's third and arguably best "Dirty Harry" movie ... this time he's been presented with unprecedented humour.'
Los Angeles Times

'I never thought I'd say it, but welcome back "Dirty Harry" ... what sensitivity he has, I suspect, is largely due to Clint Eastwood's consistently spare and magnetic performance ... the film is slick, skilful, fast, unpretentious and it knows when to pull its punches.'
Daily Mail

ESCAPE FROM ALCATRAZ
(US 1979)

pc Malpaso. For Paramount. exec p Robert Daley. p, d Donald Siegel. assoc p Fritz Manes. w Robert Tuggle, from the book by J Campbell Bruce.

ph Bruce Surtees. Colour. ed Ferris Webster. pd Allen Smith. sfx Chuck Gasper. m Jerry Fielding. song *D Block Blues* by Gilbert Thomas Jr. 112 mins

Cast: Clint Eastwood (Frank Morris), Patrick McGoohan (Warden), Roberts Blossom (Chester 'Doc' Dalton), Jack Thibeau (Clarence Anglin), Fred Ward (John Anglin), Paul Benjamin (English), Larry Hankin (Charley Butts), Bruce M Fischer (Wolf), Frank Ronzio (Litmus), Fred Stuthman (Johnson), David Cryer (Wagner)

A prisoner breaks out of the supposedly escape-proof island prison of Alcatraz in 1960.

Detailed, gripping and unsensational, with a powerful, underplayed performance by Eastwood and tense direction by Siegel, who effectively reworks themes from his 1954 film *Riot in Cell Block 11* (q.v.). Here, presumably intending *Escape From Alcatraz* to be a significant entry in his canon, Siegel called himself 'Donald' instead of using his more usual (plebian) billing, 'Don'.

'A familiar enough theme but, in Donald Siegel's deft and experienced directorial hands, the old yarn emerges with considerable vigour and a gradually building tension which sets the butterflies fluttering in the pit of your stomach when you least expect it.'
Evening Standard

ESTANBUL 65/COLPO GROSSO A GALATA BRIDGE/L'HOMME D'INSTANBUL

(SPAIN/ITALY/FRANCE 1964) (US, GB: THAT MAN IN ISTANBUL)
pc Isasi Producciones/CCM/EDIC. p Nat Waschberger. d Anthony Isasi (rn Antonio Isasi-Isasmendi). w Anthony Isasi, Giovanni Simonelli, Luis Cameron, R Illa, Nat Waschberger. English dial Lewis Howard. ph Juan Gelpi. Colour. Scope. ed Juan Palleja. ad Juan Alberto. m Georges Gavarentz. 117 mins

Cast: Horst Bucholz (Tony), Silva Koscina (Kenny), Mario Adorf (Bill), Perrette Prado (Elisabeth), Klaus Kinski (Schenck), Alvaro de Luna (Bogo), Gustavo Re (Brain), Gérard Tichy (Hansi), Augustin Gonzalez (Gunther), Angel Picazo (Insp. Mallouk), Umberto Raho (Prof. Prendergast)

A female CIA agent involves a gambler in the hunt for a kidnapped American nuclear scientist.

Typical European attempt at an international feature, lighthearted and aimlessly entertaining, and taken at enough speed to skate over most of the plot lacunae.

'Contains more violent physical action, of the mindlessly anarchical sort, carried on with a bumbling delight in violence for its own sake, than we have seen since Cagney hung up his shoulder holster.'
Life

ÉTAT DE SIÈGE

(FRANCE/ITALY/WEST GERMANY 1973) (US, GB: STATE OF SIEGE)
pc Reggane/Unidis-EurInternational/Dieter Giessler Filmpproduktion. exec p Max Palevsky. p Jacques Perrin. d Costa-Gavras. w Franco Solinas, Costa-Gavras. ph

Pierre-William Glenn. 2nd unit ph Silvio Caiozzi. Colour. ed Françoise Bonet. ad Hacques d'Ovidio. m Mikis Theodorakis. 120 mins

Cast: Yves Montand (Philip Michael Santore), Renato Salvatori (Capt. Lopez), O E Hasse (Carlos Duca), Jacques Weber (Hugo), Jean-Luc Bideau (Este), Evangeline Peterson (Mrs Santore), Maurice Teynac (Minister of the Interior), Yvette Etievant (Senator), Nestor Antunes (President of the Republic)

An American CIA agent is kidnapped by left-wing guerrillas in a repressive South American state, and exposed as helping the US to overthrow the government.

Controversial, well-directed political thriller whose style tends to obscure the already not particularly clear proceedings and so patently partisan that its impact as polemic is fatally diluted.

'If you view this film as a thriller it is superb entertainment. If you see it as a comment on reality told as a thriller its morality comes into question.'
Photoplay

EVIL UNDER THE SUN

(GB 1981)
pc Mersham Productions. For Titan Productions. p John Brabourne, Richard Goodwin. assoc p Michael-John Knatchbull. d Guy Hamilton. w Anthony Shaffer, from the novel by Agatha Christie. ph Christopher Challis. 2nd unit ph Robin Browne. Colour. Panavision. ed Richard Marden. pd Elliot Scott. ad Alan Cassie. m Cole Porter, conducted & arr by John Lanchbery. cos Anthony Powell.

EXECUTIVE DECISION

17 mins
Cast: Peter Ustinov (Hercule Poirot),
Colin Blakely (Sir Horace Blatt), Jane
Birkin (Christine Redfern), Nicholas
Clay (Patrick Redfern), Maggie Smith
(Daphne Castle), Roddy McDowall
(Rex Brewster), Sylvia Miles (Myra
Gardener), James Mason (Odell
Gardener), Dennis Quilley (Kenneth
Marshall), Diana Rigg (Arlena
Marshall)

Guests are murdered at an hotel in the
Adriatic in 1938.

Lavish all-star embalming of a
Christie whodunnit, with a good cast
(although Ustinov's coy Poirot at times
resembles a non-accident-prone
Inspector Clouseau) overpowered by
expensive production values, lethargic
direction and uninvolving dialogue. As
thrilling as cold Ovaltine.

**'The only proper place for *Evil Under
the Sun* is an airplane; don't buy the
headphones – just watch the
hallucinogenic costumes through a
martini haze.'**
Voice

EXECUTIVE DECISION
(US 1996)
pc WB/Silver Pictures. exec p, 2nd
unit d Steve Perry. p Joel Silver, Jim
Thomas, John Thomas. co-p Karyn
Fields. assoc p Spencer Franklin. d
Stuart Baird. aerial unit d Craig
Hosking. w Jim Thomas, John
Thomas. ph Alex Thompson. add ph
Don Burgess. aerial ph Frank Holgate.
Colour. ed Dallas Pruett, Frank J
Urioste, Stuart Baird. pd Terence
Marsh. ad William M Cruse. visual fx
sup Peter Donen. sfx co-ord Kenneth

EXPERIMENT IN TERROR

D Pepiot. sc Dick Ziker. m Jerry Goldsmith. 132 mins

Cast: Kurt Russell (David Grant), Steven Seagal (Lt Col. Austin Travis), Halle Berry (Jean), John Leguizamo (Rat), Oliver Platt (Cahill), Joe Morton (Cappy), David Suchet (Nagi Hassan), B D Wong (Louie), Len Cariou (Secretary of Defense), Whip Hubley (Baker), Andreas Katsulas (Jaffa), Mary Ellen Trainor (Allison), Maria Maples Trump (Nancy), J T Walsh (Senator Mavros), Ingo Neuhaus (Doc), William James Jones (Catman), Nicholas Pryor (Secretary of State)

A US Special Forces commando team board a hijacked 747 airliner in mid-flight and deal with the Arab terrorists holding its passengers and the US to ransom.

Glossy, high-flying hokum directed by debutante director (and former editor) Baird with sufficient pace and suspense to compensate for much of the plot's inherent silliness, notably the mid-air invasion of the airliner.

'This "bomb-on-a-plane" action-thriller takes off smoothly, hits some terrorist turbulence at cruising altitude, and doesn't come down until the palm-sweating climax.'
Time Out

EXPERIMENT IN TERROR

EXPERIMENT IN TERROR
(US 1962) (GB: THE GRIP OF FEAR)
pc Geoffrey-Kate Productions. p, d Blake Edwards. w The Gordons, from their novel *Operation Terror*. ph Philip Lathrop. B&W. ed Patrick McCormack. ad Robert Peterson. m Henry Mancini. 123 mins

Cast: Glenn Ford (John Ripley), Lee Remick (Kelly Sherwood), Stefanie Powers (Toby Sherwood), Roy Poole (Brad), Ned Glass (Popcorn), Ross Martin (Red Lynch), Anita Loos (Lisa), Patricia Huston (Nancy), Gilbert Green (Special Agent), Clifton James (Capt. Moreno), William Bryant (Chuck)

An FBI agent hunts down the killer who abducts a bank teller's young sister to force her to help in a bank robbery.

A riveting exercise in sustained suspense with first-rate performances, notably by Martin as the asthmatic kidnapper. Edwards's direction is well-paced, and San Francisco locations are used to excellent effect. The film makes one regret Edwards's later career making obvious and overblown comedies.

It is a success, sure handed and compact, an experience in suspense in the best Hitchcock tradition, one of the shortest two hours in memory .. lifting what is basically a crime melodrama to the level of high craftsmanship with taste and imagination.'
The Hollywood Reporter

May not be great cinematic art but it is remarkably good cinematic entertainment.'
Films in Review

A standard 'boy-who-cried-wolf' story, whose director sensibly ignores the illogicalities of the screenplay and instead generates strong suspense through eclectic camera angles and clever use of Maltese locations.

'Judged purely as a thriller it is meaty and enjoyable, even if the plot won't really bear detailed examination. It is almost as full of holes as most of its numerous corpses, but that applies to most really good thrillers.'
Films and Filming

EYEWITNESS
(GB 1970)
pc Associated British Productions. exec p Irving Allen. p Paul Maslansky. d John Hough. w Ronald Harwood, from the novel by Mark Hebden. ph David Holmes. Colour. ed Geoffrey Foot. pd Herbert Westbrook. m Fairfield Parlour, Van De Graaff Generator. add m David Whitaker. 91 mins

Cast: Mark Lester (Timothy), Lionel Jeffries (Colonel), Susan George (Pippa), Tony Bonner (Tom), Jeremy Kemp (Galleria), Peter Vaughan (Paul), Peter Bowles (Victor), Betty Marsden (Madame Robiac), Anthony Stamboulieh (Tacherie), John Allison (Boutique Boy), Joseph Furst (Local Station Sergeant)

Nobody will believe an eleven-year-old boy when he claims to have witnessed the assassination of an African president on a Mediterranean island.

THE FALCON OUT WEST
(US 1944)
pc RKO. p Maurice Geraghty. d William Clemens. w Billy Jones, Morton Grant. ph Harry Wilk. B&W. ed Gene Milford. ad Albert D'Agostino, Alfred Herman. m C Bakaleinikoff, Roy Webb. 64 mins

Cast: Tom Conway (Tom Lawrence, the Falcon), Carole Gallagher (Vanessa Drake), Barbara Hale (Marion), Joan Barclay (Mrs Irwin), Cliff Clark (Insp. Donovan), Minor Watson (Caldwell), Edward Gargan (Bates), Don Douglas (Hayden), Lyle Talbot (Tex Irwin), Lee Trent (Dusty), Perc Launders (Red)

The Falcon solves the murder of a Texas millionaire in a New York nightclub.

Competent entry (the eighth in *The Falcon* series) that crams a great deal of complex plot into its short second-feature running time.

'Casting and production are excellent and the climax carries a fairly good surprise, but the picture as a whole is only moderate entertainment.'
CEA Film Report

THE FALLEN IDOL
(GB 1948)
pc London Film Productions. p David O Selznick, Carol Reed. assoc p Phil Brandon. d Carol Reed. w Graham Greene, from his short story *The Basement Room*. add dial Lesley Storm, William Templeton. ph Georges Périnal. B&W. ed Oswald Hafenrichter. ad Vincent Korda, James Sawyer. sfx W Percy Day. m William Alwyn. 95 mins

Cast: Ralph Richardson (Baines), Michele Morgan (Julie), Bobby Henrey (Felipe), Sondia Dresdel (Mrs Baines), Dennis O'Dea (Insp. Crowe), Jack Hawkins (Det. Ames), Dora Bryan (Rose), Walter Fitzgerald (Dr Fenton), Bernard Lee (Det. Hart), Karel Stepanek (Secretary), Joan Young (Mrs Barrow)

When a young boy living in a foreign embassy in London tries to protect his friend the butler, whom he believes has killed his wife, his efforts almost result in a murder charge.

Outstanding, equally effective as both character study and suspenser, Greene's screenplay superbly delineates the dramatis personae, and Reed draws memorable performances from young Henrey and especially Richardson, who was never better. A minor masterpiece.

'That young British master of the thriller, the suave and incisive Carol Reed, who has long since displayed his lofty talent for sheer excitement in *Night Train* and *Odd Man Out*, has added another cubit to his stature ... not only has he got excitement of a most sharp and urbane sort in this film, but he has also got it in one of the keenest revelations of a child we have ever had on the screen ... it is freighted with sly and salient humours, very tender understanding of humankind and some truly blood-tingling surprises that Mr Reed has directed in brilliant style.'
The New York Times

'At every turn *The Fallen Idol* is a true picture of life as seen, heard, and interpreted through the delicate senses of an artist; true in speech, behav-

our, instinct, mood and atmosphere; a very lovely heartfelt film.'
The Observer

FAREWELL, MY LOVELY
(US 1975)
pc EK Corporation/ITC. exec p Elliott Kastner, Jerry Bick. p George Pappas, Jerry Bruckheimer. d Dick Richards. w David Zelag Goodman, from the novel by Raymond Chandler. ph John A

Alonzo. Colour. ed Walter Thompson, Joel Cox. pd Dean Tavoularis. ad Angelo Graham. m David Shire. cos Tony Scarano, Sandra Berke. 95 mins

Cast: Robert Mitchum (Philip Marlowe), Charlotte Rampling (Velma/Mrs Grayle), John Ireland (Det. Lt Nulty), Sylvia Miles (Mrs Florian), Jack O'Halloran (Moose Malloy), Anthony Zerbe (Laird

Brunette), Harry Dean Stanton (Billy Rolfe), Joe Spinell (Nick), Sylvester Stallone (Jonnie)

Private detective Philip Marlowe lands up to his shoulder holster in trouble when he is hired by a former convict to find his missing girlfriend in 1941 Los Angeles.

Surprisingly good remake of *Murder, My Sweet* (1944, q.v.), with

THE FALLEN IDOL

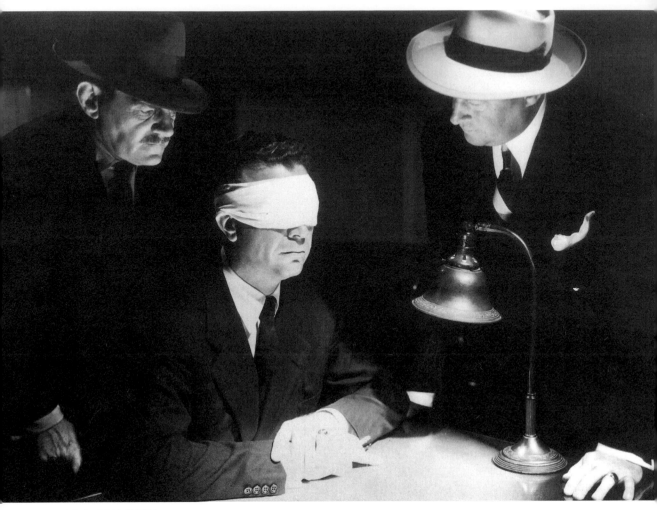

FAREWELL, MY LOVELY

direction, cinematography, production design and screenplay creating a vivid period atmosphere. Mitchum is rather too old for the role, but his laconic manner and smart handling of dialogue is convincing. Ireland is excellent as a hard-boiled cop. Rampling tries hard to suggest a *femme fatale*, but her work only results in parody.

'It's a slick, highly enjoyable tale, as taut and glossy as a chorus girl's G-string.'
Daily Mirror

'Part of the fascination with Richards' film is that it puts the private eye's encounters into an aesthetic frame-work that heightens one's sense of the genre's classic structure ... visually the style is two parts '40s lurid-novel-dustjacket to one part Edward Hopper.'
Women's Wear Daily

FATAL ATTRACTION
(US 1987)
pc Paramount. p Stanley R Jaffe, Sherry Lansing. d Adrian Lyne. w James Dearden, from his screenplay for

Diversion. ph Howard Atherton. Colour. ed Michael Kahn, Peter E Berger. pd Mel Bourne. ad Jack Blackman. sc David R Ellis. m Maurice Jarre. 120 mins

Cast: Michael Douglas (Dan Gallagher), Glenn Close (Alex Forrest), Anne Archer (Beth Gallagher), Ellen Hamilton Latzen (Ellen Gallagher), Stuart Pankin (Jimmy), Ellen Foley (Hildy), Fred Gwynne (Arthur), Meg Mundy (Joan Rogerson), Tom Brennan (Howard Rogerson), Lois Smith (Martha), Mike Nussbaum (Bob

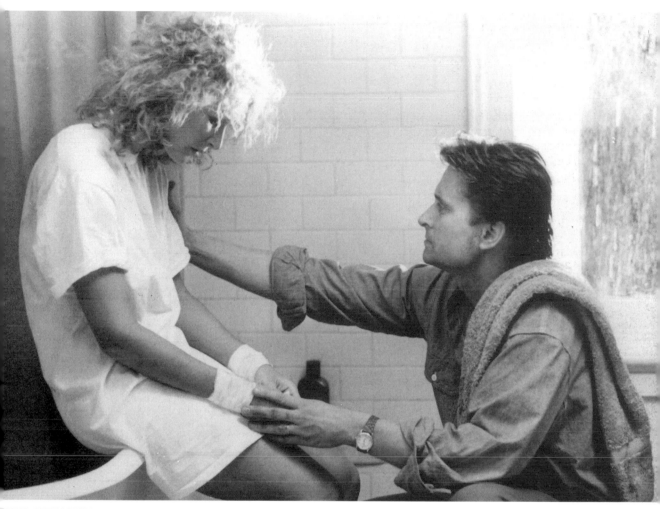

FATAL ATTRACTION

Drimmer), J J Johnston (O'Rourke), Michael Arkin (Lieutenant)

A married man enjoys what he believes is simply a two-night stand, but the woman is a psychopath ready to kill to continue their relationship.

Screenwriter Dearden deserved his Academy Award nomination. The adaptation of his 45-minute 1979 movie Diversion (which he also directed) is consistently gripping and strongly characterized, so much so that the role of the unfortunate adulterer survives another self-indulgent Douglas

performance. Close is chilling. Lyne's direction is glossy and to the point, and comes fairly near to pulling off a 'surprise' ending that comes as no surprise to anyone who has seen *Les Diaboliques* (q.v.) or, indeed, to horror fans inured to the almost inevitable last-reel return of apparently dead protagonists.

In Britain, where animals have a royal society for their protection and children do not, many considered the boiling by Close of the family pet rabbit more appalling than mere homicide.

A huge hit – graphic (for a mainstream studio feature) sex scenes obviously didn't harm its chances – and possibly the most potent warning against sexual promiscuity since the spread of herpes and AIDS. It seems almost unfair to point out that Clint Eastwood travelled the same road equally effectively in 1971 with his directorial debut Play *Misty for Me* (q.v.).

'An additional cautionary tale to those who might dare to fancy a weekend fling once in a while. The screws are tightened suspensefully ... audience

delight in being chilled by the cat-and-mouse game should make this a strong fall performer.'
Variety

'After the designer S & M of *Nine 1/2 Weeks*, Adrian Lyne here tries his hand at designer psychopathology. With its endless procession of famous New York locations ... its parading of glitzy restaurants, bars and discos, *Fatal Attraction* resembles nothing so much as a long advertisment in the Martini mould.'
Monthly Film Bulletin

'*Fatal Attraction* is a spellbinding psychological thriller that could have been a great movie if the filmmakers had not thrown character and plausibility to the winds in the last moments to give us their version of *Friday the 13th.*'
Chicago Sun-Times

FEAR IS THE KEY
(GB 1972)
pc K-L-K Productions. For Anglo-EMI/Paramount. exec p Elliott Kastner. p Alan Ladd Jr, Jay Kanter. assoc p Gavrik Losey. d Michael Tuchner. w Robert Carrington, from the novel by Alistair MacLean. ph Alex Thompson. 2nd unit ph K C Jones. Colour. Panavision. ed Ray Lovejoy. pd Sydney Caine, Maurice Carter. sfx Derek Meddings. sc Carby Loftin. m Roy Budd. 108 mins

Cast: Barry Newman (John Talbot), Suzy Kendall (Sarah Ruthven), John Vernon (Vyland), Dolph Sweet (Jablonsky), Ben Kingsley (Royale), Ray McAnnally (Ruthven), Peter Marinker (Larry), Elliott Sullivan (Jude

Mollison), Roland Brand (Deputy), Tony Anholt (FBI Agent)

A man plots elaborate revenge against the man responsible for the death of his wife, brother and young son in an aircraft crash.

Densely-plotted, exciting thriller with a rip-roaring car chase, and a lot better than the source novel. For once, stereotyped characters and storyline pay off.

'Proves to be a brisk and cleverly plotted thriller with enough narrative surprises to compel interest right up to the cliff-hanging finish.'
Monthly Film Bulletin

FINAL ANALYSIS
(US 1992)
pc WB/Roven-Cavallo Entertainment. exec p Richard Gere, Maggie Wilde. p Charles Roven, Paul Junger Witt, Anthony Thomas. co-p John Solomon. assoc p Kelley Smith. d Phil Joanu. w Wesley Strick. st Robert Berger, Wesley Strick. ph Jordan Cronenweth. Colour. ed Thom Noble, Chris Peppe. pd Dean Tavoularis. ad Angelo Graham. sfx sup Jim Fredburg. sc Jeff Smolek. m George Fenton. 124 mins

Cast: Richard Gere (Isaac Barr), Kim Basinger (Heather Evans), Uma Thurman (Diana Baylor), Eric Roberts (Jimmy Evans), Paul Guilfoyle (Mike O'Brien), Keith David (Det. Huggins), Robert Harper (Alan Lowenthal), Agustin Rodriquez (Pepe Carrero), Rita Zohar (Dr Grusin), George Murdock (Judge Costello), Shirley Prestia (DA Kaufman), Jeff Smolek (Hospital Security)

A San Francisco psychiatrist falls for a patient's married sister and becomes dangerously embroiled in murder.

Gere's psychiatrist is even more unbelievable than a ludicrous screenplay that attempts to pay homage to Hitchcock but simply goes off half-cock. As flashy as a cinema aftershave advertisement, and equally empty.

'Mainly because there are so many tic like nods to other movies – *Saboteur*, *Vertigo*, *Jagged Edge* – the film resem bles an overanxious chicken browsing in the filmic farmyard shortly before being taken off to get the chop.'
Financial Times

FIREPOWER
(GB 1979)
pc Michael Winner Ltd. For ITC. p, d Michael Winner. w Gerald Wilson. st Bill Kerby, Michael Winner. ph Rober Paynter, Dick Kratina. 2nd unit ph Richard Kline. Colour. sup ed Max Benedict. ed Arnold Crust (rn Michael Winner). pd John Stoll, John Blezard. ad Robert Gundlach. sfx Paul Stewart, Al Griswold. stunt sup Terry Leonard. m Gato Barbieri. 104 mins

Cast: Sophia Loren (Adele Tasca), James Coburn (Jerry Fanon), O J Simpson (Catlett), Eli Wallach (Sal Hyman), Anthony Franciosa ('Dr Felix'/Carl Stegner), George Grizzard (Leo Gelhorn), Vincent Gardenia (Frank Hull), Dred Stuthman (Halpin), Richard Caldicott (Calman), Victor Mature (Harold Everett)

A widow seeks vengeance against the gangster who ordered the murder of her husband.

FINAL ANALYSIS

Empty-headed, noisy time-waster: the Caribbean locations are attractive but little else, and the mind stays resolutely uninvolved. Director Winner doubles (to no great creative effect) as editor 'Arnold Crust'.

'Rip-roaring is the only kind term for this piece of cinematic opportunism which goes in one eye and out the other like the perfect piece of old-style circuit fodder.'
The Guardian

THE FIRM

(US 1993)

pc Paramount. exec p Michael Hausman, Lindsay Doran. p Sydney Pollack, Scott Rudin, John Davis. d Sydney Pollack. w David Rabe, Robert Towne, David Rayfiel, from the novel by John Grisham. ph John Seale. underwater ph Pete Romano. Colour. ed William Steinkamp, Fredric Steinkamp. pd Richard Macdonald. ad John Willett. sc Andy Armstrong. m Dave Grusin. 153 mins

Cast: Tom Cruise (Mitch McDeere), Jeanne Tripplehorn (Abby McDeere), Gene Hackman (Avery Tolar), Hal Holbrook (Oliver Lambert), Terry Kinney (Lamar Quinn), Wilford Brimley (William Devasher), Ed Harris (Wayne Tarrance), Holly Hunter (Tammy Hemphill), David Strathairn (Ray McDeere), Gary Busey (Eddie Lomax), Steven Hill (F Denton Voyles), Jerry Hardin (Royce McKnight)

A hotshot young Harvard law graduate gets a dream job with a prestigious legal firm in Memphis, only to discover it is a front for the Mafia and resignation isn't a viable option.

Grisham's best-seller has been expertly filleted and compressed and given a new ending designed to showcase Cruise as an action hero, which, given his less-than-convincing portrayal of a lawyer with a razor-sharp intellect, is eminently sensible. Pollack's smooth direction creates strong

THE FIRM

suspense and maintains a brisk pace, and fine support, notably by Hackman, Hunter and Busey, compensates for a lead who tries hard but is more pin-up than performer.

'This is a real wallow in entertainingly old-fashioned commercial candyfloss, with handsome production values and expensive locations.'
Today

'You may not remember *The Firm* a month from now, but its entertainment value is undeniable.'
Film Review

THE FIRST DEADLY SIN
(US 1980)
pc Artanis/Cinema Seven. For Filmways. exec p Frank Sinatra, Elliott Kastner. p George Pappas, Mark Shanker. assoc p Fred Caruso. d Brian G Hutton. w Mann Rubin, from the novel by Lawrence Sanders. ph Jack Priestley. Colour. ad Woody

Mackintosh. m Gordon Jenkins. 112 mins

Cast: Frank Sinatra (Edward Delaney), Faye Dunaway (Barbara Delaney), David Dukes (Daniel Blank), George Coe (Dr Bernardi), Brenda Vaccaro (Monica Gilbert), Martin Gabel (Christopher Langley), Anthony Zerbe (Capt. Broughton), James Whitmore (Dr Ferguson), Joe Spinell (Charles Lipsky)

A New York policeman on the verge of retirement goes after a psychopathic killer.

Gloomy and downbeat, and made all the more depressing by Sinatra's listless performance and by Dunaway's non-existent one as his dying wife. The ironic ending comes off poorly and unconvincingly, as though none of the protagonists or the director really cared much about what they were doing. One can only be grateful Sinatra spared us the

other six deadly sins.

'A glowering, resentful movie and remarkable only as the vehicle chosen by its star to make his screen comeback.'
The Sunday Times

FIVE AGAINST THE HOUSE
(US 1955)
pc Columbia. p Stirling Silliphant, John Barnwell. d Phil Karlson. w Stirling Silliphant, William Bowers, John Barnwell, from a story by Jack Finney. ph Leslie White. B&W. ed Jerome Thomas. ad Robert Peterson. m George Duning. 84 mins

Cast: Guy Madison (Al Mercer), Kim Novak (Kay), Brian Keith (Brick), Alvy Moore (Roy), Kerwin Matthews (Ronald), William Conrad (Erich), Jack Dimond (Frances Spieglebauer), Jean Willes (Virginia), John Zaremba (Robert Fenton), George Brand (Jack Roper), Carroll McComas (Mrs Valent)

Four college students and a nightclub singer rob a casino in Reno.

Efficient crime caper aimed at the youth market, with a well-executed robbery sequence, but marred by a flaccid climax.

'First-rate stars and superb dialogue are gambled on a mediocre plot … Bingo! They win.'
Picturegoer

'For those who think the pic offers a foolproof blueprint for larceny, it should be noted that security at Harold's is quite different now than what is shown.'
Variety

THE FLEA PIT

(GB 1934)

pc Alna Films. assoc p Jaques DeBranleur. d Ted Blaze. w Ted Blaze, from the unpublished novella by Ted Blaze & Veronica Southern. add dial (uncredited) Dornford Yates. ph Georges DuSol. B&W, plus tinted sequence. ed George Zellary. ad Woodrow Taylor. m Wol Emulov. 76 mins

Cast: Wally Patch (Kenneth Smillie), Nicole Fautrier (Mrs Van Der Kerkoff), Georges Trabant (Kremer), Paul Thorn (Dr Russell), Ian MacPherson (Insp. Jackman), Barry Flame (rn Ted Blaze) (Sgt Tickell), Ralph Grainger (Irate Customer), Stewart Tanitch (Man at Fish and Chip Shop), Gillian Girdlestone (Soignee Customer)

A demobbed soldier and ex-convict seeks refuge from the police in a disused cinema, with perplexing consequences.

Blaze's early masterpiece uses the cinematic *mise-en-scène* and gritty social realism in a way unknown elsewhere in contemporary British cinema. Blaze's apprenticeship at UFA under Erich Pommer gives this patently British story uncomfortable expressionistic edges. Sadly, his unique editing style led to the film being twice turned down by the circuit which had commissioned it, and its premiere was, bizarrely, in Stuttgart as part of a British Council event to tie in with the 1936 Olympic Games.

A truly extraordinary British picture that belies its obviously low budget with a gloss worthy of Hollywood and dialogue that owes much to both Russian and French cinema. Unique and often unfathomable.'
CEA Film Report

FLOODS OF FEAR

(GB 1958)

pc Rank. p Sydney Box. assoc p David Deutsch. d, w Charles Crichton, from the novel by John & Ward Hawkins. ph Christopher Challis. B&W. ed Peter Bezencenet. ad Cedric Dawe. m Alan Rawsthorne. 84 mins

Cast: Howard Keel (Donovan), Anne Heywood (Elizabeth), Cyril Cusack (Peebles), Harry H Corbett (Sharkey), John Crawford (Murphy), Eddie Byrne (Sheriff), John Philips (Dr Matthews), Mark Baker (Watchman), James Dyrenforth (Mayor), Jack Lester (Businessman), Peter Madden (Banker)

A man unjustly jailed for murder escapes during a torrential flood, becomes a hero, and proves his innocence.

Unpretentious B-feature directed with styleless efficiency. Keel, imported from Hollywood to provide transatlantic appeal, is rather more convincing than the made-in-Britain American settings.

'Most of the time it's as hot as a fire-cracker. The tension sizzles. And the sight of Anne Heywood in various stages of becoming undress is guaranteed to send temperatures rising in any cinema.'
Picturegoer

FOG OVER FRISCO

(US 1934)

pc First National-WB. p Henry Blanke. p sup Robert Lord. d William Dieterle. w Robert N Lee, Eugene Solow, from the story *The Five Fragments* by George Dyer. ph Tony Gaudio. B&W. ed Harold McLernon. 68 mins

Cast: Bette Davis (Arlene Bradford), Donald Woods (Tony Stirling), Margaret Lindsay (Valkyr Bradford), Lyle Talbot (Spencer Carleton), Arthur Byron (Everett Bradford), Hugh Herbert (Izzy Wright), Robert Barrat (Thorne), Douglass Dumbrille (Joshua Maynard), Irving Pichel (Jane Bellow)

A thrill-mad socialite becomes involved with gangsters and is murdered.

Forget the plot, simply enjoy the breezy acting and Dieterle's incredibly fast-paced direction, which turns it into a triumph of technique over content. (Remade in 1942 as *Spy Ship*.)

'What *Fog Over Frisco* lacks in the matter of credibility, it atones for partly by its breaktaking suspense and abundance of action.'
The New York Times

FOR YOUR EYES ONLY

(GB 1981)

pc Eon. exec p Michael G Wilson. p Albert R Broccoli. assoc p Tom Pevsner. d John Glen. 2nd unit d, ph Arthur Wooster. w Richard Maibaum, Michael G Wilson. ph Alan Hume. underwater ph Al Giddings. aerial ph James Devis. ski ph Willy Bogner. visual fx ph Paul Wilson. Colour. Panavision. ed John Grover. add ed Eric Boyd-Perkins. pd Peter Lamont. ad John Fenner, Michael Lamont, Mikes Karapiperis, Franco Fumagalli. sfx John Evans, Derek Meddings.

skating scenes staged by Brian Foley. action arr Bob Simmons. driving stunts co-ord Rémy Julienne. m Bill Conti. song *For Your Eyes Only* by Bill Conti, Michael Leeson, sung by Sheena Easton. 127 mins

Cast: Roger Moore (James Bond), Carole Bouquet (Melina Havelock), (Chaim) Topol (Columbo), Lynn-Holly Johnson (Bibi), Julian Glover (Kristatos), Cassandra Harris (Countess Lisl), Jill Bennett (Brink), Michael Gothard (Locque), John Wyman (Kriegler), Jack Hedley (Havelock), Lois Maxwell (Miss Moneypenny), Desmond Llewellyn ('Q'), Geoffrey Keen (Minister of Defence), Walter Gotell (Gen. Gogol), James Villiers (Tanner), Charles Dance (Claus)

James Bond is sent to recover a top-secret encryption device from a spy ship sunk off the Greek Albanian coast before it can fall into the wrong hands.

Former Bond-film second unit director Glen makes a confident jump to full director and stages the requisite action – notably a bravura opening sequence in which 007 drops his old enemy Blofeld down a disused factory chimney – with enjoyable vigour. The lesser reliance on gags and gadgetry is welcome, and Moore's stunt doubles are in fine form, but the absence of a notable villain and a not very charismatic supporting cast is a disadvantage.

For the first time in the series, Ian Fleming's name is omitted from the credits: given the considerable difference between his and the cinema's James Bond, he might not have been too unhappy.

'Amid the energy, excitement, and generous expenditure of sheer technical skill, it can only seem ungrateful to notice that there lurks nothing of any consequence whatever.'
Monthly Film Bulletin

'Pretty boring between the stunts, as if the director isn't interested in actors, and Broccoli forgot to commission a screenplay.'
The Observer

FOREIGN CORRESPONDENT
(US 1940)
pc UA. p Walter Wanger. d Alfred Hitchcock. w Charles Bennett, Joan Harrison. dial James Hilton, Robert Benchley. Based on *Personal History* by Vincent Sheean. ph Rudolph Maté. B&W. ed Otho Lovering, Dorothy Spencer. ad Alexander Golitzen, William Cameron Menzies. sfx Lee Zavitz. m Alfred Newman. 119 mins

Cast: Joel McCrea (Johnny Jones), Laraine Day (Carol Fisher), Herbert Marshall (Stephen Fisher), George Sanders (Scott ffolliott), Albert Basserman (Van Meer), Robert Benchley (Stebbins), Edmund Gwenn (Rowley), Eduardo Cianelli (Krug), Martin Kosleck (Tramp), Harry Davenport (Mr Powers)

An American newspaperman in Europe in 1939 to cover the impending war is caught up in a plot by Nazi spies to kidnap a Dutch diplomat carrying a secret Allied treaty.

Vintage Hitchcock with classic set pieces – a brilliantly-shot assassination in pelting rain, attemped murder on top of Westminster Cathedral, a superbly tense sequence in an isolated

Dutch windmill, an impressively-staged plane crash – compensate for the occasional longueurs. McCrea was cast after Gary Cooper rejected the role.

'The best that Hitchcock has ever done … throughout most of the film the close-packed incidents are given added urgency by the imminent presence of war.'
Documentary News Letter

'No one but Hitchcock would dare whip up a picture like this and for those of us who can take their sensationalism without batting a sceptical eye it should be high-geared entertainment.'
The New York Times

'This is real film-making, by a man who has discarded more tricks than most directors have ever known.'
The Observer

48 HRS
(US 1982)
pc Paramount. A Lawrence Gordon Production. ex p D Constantine Conte. p Lawrence Gordon, Joel Silver. d Walter Hill. w Roger Spottiswoode, Walter Hill, Larry Gross, Steven E De Souza. ph Ric Waite. Colour. ed Freeman Davies, Mark Warner, Billy Weber. pd John Vallone. sc Bennie E Dobbins. m James Horner. cartoon m W Sharples. 97 mins

Cast: Nick Nolte (Det. Jack Cates), Eddie Murphy (Reggie Hammond), Annette O'Toole (Elaine), Frank McRae (Capt. Haden), James Remar (Albert Ganz), David Patrick Kelly (Luther), Sonny Landham (Billy Bear), Brion James (Kehoe), Kerry Sherman

(Rosalie), Jonathan Banks (Algren), James Keane (Vincent)

An unorthodox San Francisco policeman springs a small-time crook from jail for 48 hours to help him track down a sadistic cop killer.

Tough, thrilling and exceedingly violent, skilfully mixing humour and action. The relationship between the white cop and his hip black ally is convincingly developed, although Murphy's trademark grin tends to become tiresome. No depth, but it keeps moving. Move away from the dire 1990 sequel *Another 48 Hrs.*

'Don't be fooled: *48 Hrs* may be as purely *entertaining* as the company accountants would have you infer, but it's also the most stylish and accomplished variation on the *Dirty Harry* maverick cop theme to date, a film which by dint of superior technique and wider imagination goes way beyond its basic brief – of simple comedy thriller – to end up in the realm of the mythic.'
New Musical Express

FOUL PLAY

(US 1978)
pc Shelburne Associates. For Paramount. A Miller-Milkis/Colin Higgins picture. p Thomas L Miller, Edward K Milkis. assoc p/p manager Peter V Herald. d, w Colin Higgins. 2nd unit d M James Arnett. ph David M Walsh. 2nd unit ph Rexford

FOUL PLAY

Metz. Colour. ed Pembroke J Herring. pd Alfred Sweeney. m Charles Fox. 116 mins

Cast: Goldie Hawn (Gloria Mundy), Chevy Chase (Tony Carlson), Burgess Meredith (Mr Hennessey), Rachel Roberts (Gerda Cresswell), Eugene Roche (Archbishop Thorncrest/Twin Brother), Dudley Moore (Stanley Tibbets), Marilyn Sokol (Stella), Brian Dennehey (Fergie), Marc Lawrence (Stiltskin)

A librarian becomes involved in a plot to assassinate the Pope during a performance of *The Mikado* in San Francisco.

Over-long but entertaining comedy-thriller, carried over the dull patches by the charm of its leads. Debuting director Higgins pays rather too liberal homage to Hitchcock, while Dudley Moore as a sexual swinger is silly and embarrassing.

'Hitchcock has done it all before, but it is still an unbeatable formula for suspense.'
Evening News

THE FOUR JUST MEN

(GB 1939) (US: THE SECRET FOUR)
pc Ealing. assoc p S C Balcon. d Walter Forde. w Roland Pertwee, Angus McPhail, Sergei Nolbandov, from the novel by Edgar Wallace. ph Ronald Neame. B&W. ed Stephen Dalby. ad Wilfred Shingleton. m Ernest Irving. 85 mins

Cast: Hugh Sinclair (Humphrey Mansfield), Griffith Jones (James Brodie), Francis L Sullivan (Leon Poiccard), Frank Lawton (Terry), Anna Lee (Ann Lodge), Basil Sydney (Frank Snell), Alan Napier (Sir Hamar Ryman), Lydia Sherwood (Myra Hastings), Roland Pertwee (Mr Hastings), Edward Chapman (B J Burrell), George Merritt (Insp. Falmouth), Garry Marsh (Bill Grant)

Four true-blue Englishmen unite to save the British Empire from foreigners and foil a plot to block the Suez Canal.

Patriotic flagwaver (first filmed as a silent picture in 1921) released at just the right time. An implausible plot is happily redeemed by plentiful action, good suspense and commendably straight-faced playing.

'The film deals with the present-day political situation and the threat to the British Empire of a certain European Power. However, clever modernised treatment and the scope of the the screen have given the subject a wider range ... there is much suspense as the melodrama unfolds.'
CEA Film Report

THE FOURTH PROTOCOL

(GB 1987)
pc Fourth Protocol Films. exec p Frederick Forsyth, Wafic Said, Michael Caine. p Timothy Burrill. d John MacKenzie. w Frederick Forsyth, from his novel. adap George Axelrod. add material Richard Burridge. ph Phil Meheux. Colour. ed Graham Walker. pd Allan Cameron. ad Tim Hutchinson. sfx sup Peter Hutchinson. sc Eddie Stacey. m Lalo Schifrin. add m Francis Shaw. 119 mins

Cast: Michael Caine (John Preston), Pierce Brosnan (Major Petrofky), Ned Beatty (Borisov), Joanna Cassidy (Irina Vassilievna), Julian Glover (Brian Harcourt-Smith), Michael Gough (Sir Bernard Hemmings), Ray McAnally (Gen. Karpov), Ian Richardson (Sir Nigel Irvine), Anton Rodgers (George Berenson), Caroline Blakiston (Angela Berenson), Betsy Brantley (Eileen McWhirter), Matt Frewer (Tom McWhirter)

A British Intelligence agent has to track down a KGB officer who intends to explode a nuclear device near a USAAF base in Britain so that America will be blamed and NATO will collapse.

Workmanlike spy thriller with solid, anonymous direction. Future 007 Brosnan is first-rate and acts Caine – who contents himself with the standard Caine performance – right off the screen.

'It is effective not simply because it's a thriller but also for long streches it simply is a very absorbing drama.'
Chicago Sun-Times

FRANTIC

(US/FRANCE 1988)
pc WB. A Mount Company production. p Thom Mount, Tim Hampton. d Roman Polanski. w Roman Polanski, Gérard Brach. ph Witold Sobocinski. 2nd unit ph Pascale Lebegue. Colour. ed Sam O'Steen. pd Pierre Guffroy. stunt arr Daniel Breton. m Ennio Morricone. 120 mins

Cast: Harrison Ford (Dr Richard Walker), Betty Buckley (Sondra Walker), Emmanuelle Seigner (Michelle), John Mahoney (Williams), Alexandra Stewart (Edie), David Huddleston (Peter), Robert Barr

(Irwin), Boll Boyer (Dédé Martin), Djiby Soumaire ('Taxi driver), Dominique Virton (Desk Clerk), Gérard Klein (Gaillard), Jacque Ciron (Hotel Manager)

An American doctor embarks on a desperate search for his kidnapped wife in Paris.

Bland and boring and remarkably slack, dominated by a bland and boring performance by Ford. Polanski's decline continues apace.

'Polanksi brings little of his customary filmmaking flair or or brilliantly perverse imagaination to bear upon *Frantic*, a thriller without much surprise, suspense or excitement.'
Variety

THE FRENCH CONNECTION
(US 1971)
pc D'Antoni Productions. In association with Schine-Moore Productions. exec p G David Schine. p Philip D'Antoni. assoc p Kenneth Utt. d William Friedkin. w Ernest Tidyman, from the book by Robin Moore. ph Owen Roizman. Colour. ed Jerry Greenberg. ad Ben Kazaskow. sfx Sass Bedig. tech cons Eddie Egan, Sonny Grosso. sc Bill Hickman. m Don Ellis. 104 mins

Cast: Gene Hackman (Jimmy 'Popeye' Doyle), Fernando Rey (Alain Charnier), Roy Scheider (Buddy Russo), Tony Lo Bianco (Sal Boca), Marcel Bozzuffi (Pierre Nicoli), Frédéric de Pasquale (Devereaux), Bill Hickman (Mulderig), Ann Rebbot (Marie Charnier), Eddie Egan (Simonson), Sonny Grosso (Klein)

Two New York policeman use unorthodox methods to track down a huge consignment of heroin brought from Marseilles hidden in a car.

Seminal, high-speed, action-packed, fact-based thriller directed in slick semi-documentary style by Friedkin, whose cleverly heightened 'realism' made vivid use of (mostly sleazy) New York locations, superbly photographed by Owen Roizman, and of Jerry Greenberg's Academy Award-winning editing. While the structure and sometimes hard-to-hear dialogue occasionally make the narrative difficult to follow, the set pieces are stunning, particularly the subsequently much-imitated car chase under the New York elevated railway.

Best Actor Oscar-winner Hackman is outstanding, Scheider earned a well-deserved Academy Award nomination. Real-life policemen Eddie Egan and Sonny Grosso, on whose exploits the film was based, served as technical consultants and also played small roles.

The French Connection won the Best Picture Academy Award and became one of the highest-grossing thrillers ever made. Inevitably, a sequel, *French Connection II* (q.v.), followed in 1975. Equally inevitably, it failed to match its predecessor.

'This thriller was made to grab your insides, and it does ... made with razor skills and a good sardonic sense of the film tradition it comes out of, it jets off from the beginning and, since in a way it's open-ended, it may still be going.'
The New Republic

'While something may be said, or rather illustrated, about violence having to be fought with violence, and something else about non co-operation or corruption in the police, the film, I

FRANTIC

think, is to be chiefly esteemed as a policer – and highly.'
The Daily Telegraph

FRENCH CONNECTION II

(US 1975) (GB: THE FRENCH CONNECTION NUMBER 2)
pc 20th Century Fox. p Robert L Rosen. d John Frankenheimer. 2nd unit d Marc Monnet. w Robert Dillon, Laurie Dillon, Alexander Jacobs. ph Claude Renoir. Colour. ed Tom Rolf. pd Jacques Saulnier. ad Gérard Viard, Georges Glon. sfx Logan Frazee. sc Hal Needham. m Don Ellis. 119 mins

Cast: Gene Hackman (Jimmy 'Popeye' Doyle), Fernando Rey (Alain Charnier), Bernard Fresson (Barthelmy), Jean-Pierre Castaldi (Raoul Diron), Charles Millot (Miletto), Cathleen Nesbitt (Mère Charnier), Pierre Collet (Old Pro), Alexander Fabro (Young Tail), Philipe Leotard (Jacques), Jacques Dynam (Insp. Genevoix)

'Popeye' Doyle, the New York policeman responsible for foiling an attempt to bring a fortune in heroin into the US (see *The French Connection*), goes to Marseilles to apprehend the criminal who masterminded the operation.

Hackman gives a bravura performance, especially in the gruelling sequence of his withdrawal from enforced heroin addiction, and there is an exciting climactic chase, but the point of view of this redundant sequel is never made clear and, having long before gone off the boil, Frankenheimer's direction is overwrought without being interesting.

'I could have put up with the obvious cashings-in on the earlier film, even the exceptionally fatuous story and routine violence. But what renders "Number 2" almost intolerable is the overpowering noise permitted by director John Frankenheimer ... perhaps the producers thought our senses would be so numbed by all this sound and fury that we wouldn't notice other weaknesses.'
Evening News

'As usual, Frankenheimer's direction plods, thuds, and hesitates at times. No-nonsense editing and evocative cinematography compensate, however.'
The Christian Science Monitor

FRENZY

(GB 1972)
pc Universal. p, d Alfred Hitchcock. w Anthony Shaffer, from the novel *Goodbye Piccadilly, Farewell Leicester Square* by Arthur La Bern. ph Gil Taylor. Colour. ed John Jympson. pd Sydney Cain. ad Robert Laing. m Ron Goodwin. 116 mins

Cast: Jon Finch (Richard Blaney), Alec McCowen (Insp. Oxford), Barry Foster (Bob Rusk), Barbara Leigh-Hunt (Brenda Blaney), Anna Massey (Barbara 'Babs' Milligan), Vivien Merchant (Mrs Oxford), Bernard Cribbins (Forsythe), Billie Whitelaw (Hetty Porter), Michael Bates (Sgt Spearman), Clive Swift (Johnny Porter)

Hitchcock's first British movie since 1950's *Stage Fright* (q.v.) marked a splendid return to form, high on suspense, gallows humour and eye-catching characters, and replete with typical directorial trademarks,

including his appearance among a crowd listening to a politician speak against pollution, interrupted by the arrival of corpse floating on the Thames. In spite of some fashionable violence and nudity, it is essentially old-fashioned in its treatment.

'A monumental joke played by a supreme expert on the gullibility of audiences. In other words, smashing entertainment.'
The Sunday Telegraph

'Smooth and shrewd and dexterous, a reminder that anyone who makes a suspense film is still an apprentice to this old master.'
Time

FROM RUSSIA WITH LOVE

(GB 1963)
pc Eon. p Harry Saltzman, Albert R Broccoli. d Terence Young. w Richard Maibaum, Johanna Harwood, from the novel by Ian Fleming. ph Ted Moore. 2nd unit ph Robert Kindred. Colour. ed Peter Hunt. ad Syd Cain. sfx John Stears, Frank George. stunt arr Peter Perkins. m John Barry, *James Bond Theme* by Monty Norman. title song Lionel Bart. titles Robert Brownjohn, Trevor Bond. 116 mins

Cast: Sean Connery (James Bond), Daniela Bianchi (Tatiana Romanova), Pedro Armendariz (Kerin Bey), Lotte Lenya (Rosa Klebb), Robert Shaw (Red Grant), Bernard Lee ('M'), Lois Maxwell (Miss Moneypenny), Eunice Gayson (Sylvia), Walter Gotell (Morzeny), Francis de Wolff (Vavra), George Pastell (Train Conductor), Nadja

FROM RUSSIA WITH LOVE

Regin (Kerim's Girl), Desmond Llewellyn (Boothroyd – 'Q') James Bond prevents SPECTRE stealing a top-secret coding machine.

The second Bond movie consolidated the success – and the formula – of *Dr No* (1962, q.v.), again decorating the less-than-credible proceedings with exotic locations, including Venice, Turkey and the Orient Express, exotic gadgetry and exotic villains, represented by Lenya's marvellously sinister Rosa Klebb, armed with a poisoned knife in her boot, and Shaw's impassive and implacable killer. Connery is more of a thug in a dinner jacket than Fleming's suave creation, and there are longueurs among the exciting highlight action. It displays the start of the creeping budgetary and aspiration inflation that was to characterize each successive 007 adventure.

'It is neither uplifting, instructive, nor life-enhancing. Neither is it great film-making. But it sure is fun.'
The Guardian

'It's hard to remember anything about the picture one hour later. Like a good Chinese dinner, you soon need another and United Artists has one in the works this very minute.'
Saturday Review

THE FUGITIVE

(US 1993)
pc WB. exec p Keith Barish, Roy
Huggins. p Arnold Kopelson. co-p
Peter MacGregor-Scott, Stephen
Brown, Nana Greenwald. d Andrew
Davis. 2nd unit d Terry J Leonard,
Mike Gray. w Jeb Stuart, David
Twohy. st David Twohy, based on
characters created by Roy Huggins. ph
Michael Chapman. 2nd unit ph Gary
H Holt, George Kohut. aerial ph
Frank M Holgate. Colour. ed Dennis
Virkler, David Finfer, Dean Goodhill,
Don Brochu, Richard Nord, Dov
Hoenig. pd Dennis Washington. ad
Maher Ahmad. visual fx sup Bill Mesa.
m James Newton Howard. 127 mins

Cast: Harrison Ford (Dr Richard
Kimble), Tommy Lee Jones (US
Marshal Samuel Gerard), Sela Ward
(Helen Kimble), Cosmo Renfro (Joe
Pantoliano), Jeroen Krabbé (Dr
Charles Nichols), Andreas Katsulas
(Sykes), Julianne Moore (Dr Anne
Eastman), Daniel Roebuck (Biggs), L
Scott Caldwell (Poole), Tom Wood
(Newman), Ron Dean (Det. Kelly),
Joseph Kosala (Det. Rosetti)

A Chicago surgeon, convicted on
circumstantial evidence of the murder
of his wife, escapes on the way to
prison and sets out to find the real,
one-armed killer.

The television series ran from 1963
to 1966, and there are times when this
overblown inflation seems even longer:
a dull performance by Ford doesn't
help, the suspense is hardly gripping
given the sure knowledge he will
triumph against all adversity, and only
someone who has never seen a film
before could fail to guess whodunit at

first sight. On the credit side, Davis
keeps the (predictable) show on the
move, there is a vividly-staged train
crash, and Best Supporting Actor
Academy Award-winner Jones is
splendid as the cynical pursuing US
Marshal who takes after Ford and takes
care of the acting chores ignored by his
quarry.

'Tommy Lee ... promptly steals the
movie by managing to ham up the
humour in a script that is otherwise
laughably predictable.'
Morning Star

'A giant toy-train entertainment with
all stops pulled out. A consummate
nail-biter that never lags.'
Variety

FUNERAL IN BERLIN

(GB 1967)
pc Lowndes. A Harry Saltzman
Production. p Charles Kasher. d Guy
Hamilton. 2nd unit d Peter Medak. w
Evan Jones, from the novel *The Berlin
Memorandum* by Len Deighton. ph
Otto Heller. Colour. Panavision. ed
John Bloom. pd Ken Adam. ad Peter
Murton. m Konrad Elfers. 102
minutes.

Cast: Michael Caine (Harry Palmer),
Eva Renzi (Samantha Steel), Paul
Hubschmid (Johnny Vulkan), Oscar
Homolka (Col Stok), Guy Doleman
(Ross), Rachel Gurney (Mrs Ross),
Hugh Burden (Hallan), Thomas
Holtzmann (Reinhart), Gunther
Meisner (Kreutzmann), Hans Schubert
(Aaron Levine)

British secret agent Harry Palmer is
sent to Berlin to confirm that a leading

Russian intelligence officer really wants
to defect to the West.

The second outing for Len
Deighton's fashionable anti-hero is a
morose – not to say funereal – affair,
with an over-complex plot that is both
difficult to follow and offers little
incentive to do so, while Hamilton's
uninteresting direction does little to
animate either Caine or the narrative.

'It emerges as flat as Michael Caine's
walk and as inscrutable as his smile.
Perhaps the smile is to suggest he
knows something we don't know – but
long before *Funeral in Berlin* is over,
it's something we don't really care to
know.'
Saturday Review

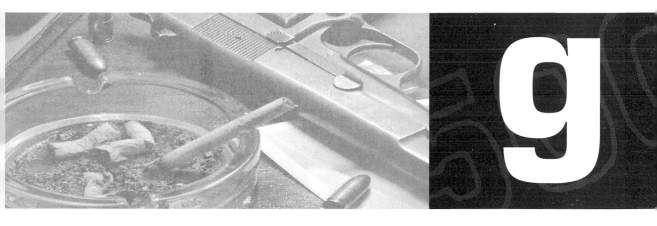

THE GANG THAT COULDN'T SHOOT STRAIGHT

(US 1971)
pc MGM. A Robert Chartoff-Irwin Winkler Production. p Irwin Winkler, Robert Chartoff. d James Goldstone. w Waldo Salt, from the novel by Jerry Breslin. ph Owen Roizman. Colour. ed Edward A Biery. ad Robert Gundlach. m Dave Grusin. 96 mins

Cast: Jerry Orbach (Salvatore 'Kid Sally' Palumbo), Leigh Taylor-Young (Angela), Jo Van Fleet (Big Momm), Lionel Stander (Baccia), Robert De Niro (Mario), Irving Selbst (Big Jelly), Herve Villechaize (Beppo), Jo Santos (Ezmon), Carmine Carido (Tony the Indian), Frank Campanella (Water Buffalo)

Internecine warfare among New York Mafiosi.

Stupid, ill-acted (especially by De Niro) attempt at a gangland comedy that is about as funny as a bullet through the kneecap.

'You don't have to be Italian to hate *The Gang That Couldn't Shoot Straight*, although that gives you a distinct edge. The movie's febrile witlessness trancends all ethnic boundaries and comes guaranteed to outrage virtually everybody.'
Time

THE GAUNTLET

(US 1977)
pc Malpaso. For WB. p Robert Daly. assoc p Fritz Manes. d Clint Eastwood. w Michael Butler, Dennis Shryack. ph Rexford Metz. Colour. Panavision. ed Ferris Webster, Joel Cox. ad Allen E Smith. sfx Chuck Gaspar. m Jerry Fielding. 109 mins

Cast: Clint Eastwood (Ben Shockley), Sondra Locke (Gus Malley), Pat Hingle (Josephson), William Prince (Blakelock), Bill McKinney (Constable), Michael Cavanaugh (Feyderspiel), Carole Cooke (Waitress), Mara Corday (Jail Matron), Douglas

THE GAUNTLET

THE GETAWAY (US 1972)

McGrath (Bookie), Fritz Manes (Helicopter Gunman)

Mafia hitmen go all-out to prevent a Phoenix policeman from delivering a key witness to give her testimony.

Unbelievable but hugely enjoyable, pacily directed by Eastwood, who also slyly sends up his tough-guy image. The action is muscular, and the pyrotechnic destruction of a large house by gunfire is particularly memorable.

'It's a plain, honest-to-goodness action thriller that's designed to appeal to a mass audience without insulting its credulity about the way things operate on the dark side of America ... I reckon, at any rate, that Chandler or Spillane would have nodded an approving head.'
Evening News

GET CARTER
(GB 1971)
pc EMI. p Michael Klinger. d, w Mike Hodges, from the novel *Jack's Return Home* by Ted Lewis. ph Wolfgang Suschitzky. Colour. ed John Trumper. pd Assheton Gorton. ad Roger King. sfx Jack Wallis. stunt d Johnny Morris. m Roy Budd. 112 mins

Cast: Michael Caine (Jack Carter),

Britt Ekland (Anna Fletcher), John Osborne (Cyril Kinnear), Ian Hendry (Eric Paice), Bryan Mosley (Cliff Brumby), Geraldine Moffatt (Glenda), Dorothy White (Margaret), Tony Beckley (Peter), Alun Armstrong (Keith), Glynn Edwards (Albert Smith), George Sewell (Con McCarty)

A London gangster goes to Newcastle to avenge the murder of his brother.

Hodges owes a stylistic debt to forties Hollywood, but pays it with a gallery of interesting characters, strong performances, and an open-eyed, unsentimental view of life in industrial Britain. Fast, violent and

THE GETAWAY (US 1994)

amoral, and one of the best-ever British thrillers.

'A cruel, vicious film even allowing for its moments of humour, but completely compelling nevertheless. I'd get Carter if I were you. He certainly got me.'
Daily Express

'So calculatedly cool and soulless and nastily erotic that it seems to belong to a new genre of virtuoso vicious-ness. What makes the movie unusual is the metallic elegance and the single-minded proficiency with which it adheres to its sadism-for-the-connoisseur formula.'
The New Yorker

THE GETAWAY
(US 1972)

pc Solar/First Artists. A Foster-Brower production. p Davis Foster, Mitchell Brower. assoc p, 2nd unit d Gordon T Dawson. d Sam Peckinpah. w Walter Hill, from the novel by Jim Thompson. ph Lucien Ballard. Colour. Todd-AO. ed Robert Wolfe. ad Ted Haworth, Angelo Graham. m Quincy Jones. 122 mins

Cast: Steve McQueen (Don McCoy), Ali McGraw (Carol McCoy), Ben Johnson (Jack Benyon), Sally Struthers (Fran Clinton), Al Lettieri (Rudy Butler), Slim Pickens (Cowboy), Richard Bright (Thief), Dub Taylor

(Laughlin), Jack Dodson (Harold Clinton), Bo Hopkins (Frank Jackson), Roy Jenson (Cully)

A former convict and his wife take the loot and make a run for Mexico after a bank robbery goes wrong.

Tense but mindless, punchily directed by Peckinpah, who indulges his trademark penchant for gratuitous violence and stages some excellent Hitchcock-style sequences, the best of which finds the fleeing couple almost being suffocated in a huge garbage crusher. McGraw shows absolutely no vestige of acting ability. Remade in 1994 (q.v.).

THE GETAWAY

(US 1994)
pc Largo/JVC. A Turman-Foster Company/John Alan Simon production. p David Foster, Lawrence Turman, John Alan Simon. assoc p Marilyn Vance. d Roger Donaldson. w Walter Hill, Amy Jones, from the novel by Jim Thompson. ph Peter Menzies Jr. 2nd unit ph Peter Levy. Colour. Scope. ed Conrad Buff. pd Joseph Nemec. ad Dan Olexiewicz. sc Glenn R Wilder. m Mark Isham. 115 mins

Cast: Alec Baldwin (Doc McCoy), Kim Basinger (Carol McCoy), Michael Madsen (Rudy Travis), James Woods (Jack Benyon), David Morse (Jim Deer Jackson), Jennifer Tilly (Fran Carvey), James Stephens (Harold Carvey), Richard Farnsworth (Slim), Philip Hoffman (Frank Hansen), Burton Gilliam (Gollie), Royce D Applegate (Gun Store Salesman), Daniel Villareal (Mendoza)

A crook sprung from a Mexican jail to execute a heist goes on the run for the border with his wife and the loot after the robbery goes badly wrong.

A remarkably good remake of the 1972 Peckinpah film (q.v.). Peckinpah may possess *auteur* status, but Donaldson has the edge on him when it comes to creating suspense sequences and staging vivid, violent set-pieces, and the casting is superior. In 1972, Steve McQueen's charisma was effectively neutralized by the non-performance of Ali McGraw. Here potent sexual chemistry between real-life husband-and-wife Baldwin and Basinger adds an exciting edge to the proceedings. Walter Hill's reworking (with Amy Jones) of his original screenplay improves on both plot and characterization, and makes the frequent double- and treble-crossings more comprehensible.

'Donaldson's version is unlikely to have the staying power of Peckinpah's, which was directed with a cobra's stealth. But when so much cinema, both lofty and trivial, emerges half-baked, you have to applaud when a film unleashes its action, sex and black comedy exactly as planned.'
The Times

THE GLASS KEY

(US 1935)
pc Paramount. p E Lloyd Sheldon. d Frank Tuttle. w Kathryn Scola, Kubec Glasmon, Harry Ruskin, from the novel by Dashiell Hammett. ph Henry Sharp. B&W. ed Hugh Bennett. 77 mins

Cast: George Raft (Ed Beaumont), Claire Dodd (Janet Henry), Edward Arnold (Paul Madvig), Rosalind Keith (Opal Madvig), Ray Milland (Taylor Henry), Robert Gleckler (Shad O'Rory), Guinn Williams (Jeff), Tammany Young (Clarkie), Harry Tyler (Henry Sloss), Charles Richman (Senator Henry), Frank McHugh (Puggy), Emma Dunn (Mom), Ann Sheridan (Nurse)

A politician's aide sets out to prove his employer is innocent of murdering the son of a political rival.

Efficient adaptation of the Hammett novel with a good cast, remade by Paramount in 1942 (q.v.).

'As murder mystery material, the story provides interesting plot situations.'
Variety

THE GLASS KEY

(US 1942)
pc Paramount. p Fred Kohlmar. d Stuart Heisler. w Jonathan Latimer, from the novel by Dashiell Hammett. ph Theodor Sparkuhl. B&W. ed Archie Marshek. ad Hans Dreier, Haldane Douglas. m Victor Young. 85 mins

Cast: Brian Donlevy (Paul Madvig), Veronica Lake (Janet Henry), Alan Ladd (Ed Beaumont), Bonita Granville (Opal Madvig), Richard Denning (Taylor Henry), Joseph Calleia (Nick Varna), William Bendix (Jeff), Frances Gifford (Nurse), Donald McBride (Farr), Margaret Hayes (Eloise Matthews), Moroni Olsen (Ralph Henry), Eddie Marr (Rusty), Arthur Loft (Clyde Matthews)

A politician's aide tangles with gangsters to prove his boss innocent of murder.

Vigorous remake, tailored to capitalize on the new-found success of Ladd and Lake, who had clicked with audiences in *This Gun For Hire* (1942, q.v.). Some reworking of the Hammett novel pays off, and the unsavoury link between crime and politics is neatly underlined.

'Recalls the ruthless gangster film, with its scenes of brutality. In spite of its sordid moments, however, it is absorbing entertainment ... there are carefully engineered twists and thrills and the interest is firmly held throughout.'
CEA Film Report

GLI INTOCCABILI

(ITALY 1968) (US, GB: MACHINE GUN McCAIN)

oc Euroatlantica Films. p Marco Vicario, Bruno Cicogna. assoc p Ascanio Cicogna. d Giuliano Montaldo. w Mino Rolli, Giuliano Montaldo. ph Erico Menczer. Colour. Techniscope. ed Franco Fraticelli. ad Flavio Mogherini. m Ennio Morricone. 115 mins

Cast: John Cassavetes (Hank McCain), Britt Ekland (Irene Tucker), Peter Falk (Charlie Adams), Gabriele Ferzetti (Don Francesco De Marco), Gena Rowlands (Rosemary Scott), Salvo Randone (Don Salvatore), Pierluigi Apra (Jack McCaine), Florinda Bolkan (Joni Adamo), Jim Morrison (Joby Cuda)

A Mafia boss springs a gangster from jail to mastermind the robbery of a luxury Las Vegas hotel.

The American stars work hard to enliven the simple-minded spaghetti gangster saga, but fail to make much progress since the plot is routine and the direction unnoticeable.

'In spite of some static intervals, this is quite a good gangster tale in the old-fashioned style.'
Kine Weekly

THE GLASS KEY

G-MEN

(US 1935)

pc WB-First National. p Lou Edelman. d William Keighley. w Seton I Miller, from the book *Public Enemy No. 1* by Gregory Rogers. ph Sol Polito. B&W. ed Jack Killifer. ad John J Hughes. md Leo Forbstein. song *You Bother Me An Awful Lot* by Sammy Fain, Irving Kahal. choreo Bobby Connolly.
85 mins

Cast: James Cagney (James 'Brick' Davis), Ann Dvorak (Jean Morgan), Margaret Lindsay (Kay McCord), Robert Armstrong (Jeff McCord), Barton MacLane (Brad Collins), Lloyd Nolan (Hugh Farrell), William Harrigan (McKay), Edawrd Pawley (Leggatt), Russell Hopton (Gerard), Noel Madison (Durfee)

A man is educated by a racketeer, becomes a lawyer and then turns G-Man to avenge the murder of a friend.

Made for $450,000 in six weeks, featuring Cagney in his best role since 1931's *Public Enemy* (q.v.), initiating a run of censorship-influenced gangster thrillers that depicted lawmen who were as tough and ruthless as their quarries, and bringing the term 'G-Man' into general currency. Taut and briskly-directed in staccato fashion.

'One long, lusty paean in homage to our federal agents. It is also a violent, sanguinary, and highly exciting film – one packed with swiftly paced action.'
Liberty Magazine

THE GODFATHER

(US 1971)

pc Alfran Productions. p Albert S Ruddy. assoc p Gray Frederickson. d Francis Ford Coppola. w Mario Puzo, Francis Ford Coppola, from the novel by Mario Puzo. ph Gordon Willis. Colour. ed William Reynolds, Peter Zinner, Marc Laub, Murray Solomon. pd Dean Tavoularis. ad Warren Clymer. sfx A D Flowers, Joe Lombardi, Sass Bedig. m Nino Rota. md Carlo Savnina. Brando's m-u Dick Smith. cos Anna Hill Johnstone. 175 mins

Cast: Marlon Brando (Don Vito Corleone), Al Pacino (Michael Corleone), James Caan (Sonny Corleone), Robert Duvall (Tom Hagen), Sterling Hayden (McCluskey), Richard Castellano (Clemenza), Richard Conte (Barzini), Diane Keaton (Kay Adams), Al Lettieri (Sollozzo), Talia Shire (Connie Rizzi), Abe Vigoda (Tessio), Al Martino (Johnny Fontane), John Cazale (Fredo Corleone)

In 1945 a Mafia don rules his gangster clan and criminal empire with an iron hand, battling rivals for control of the rackets. When he dies, his son takes over.

One of the most significant genre films ever made, and one which, on reflection, can also been seen as a triumph of hype over content and execution, and proof that with time, talent and money, filming a best-seller will attract box-office takings as surely as an open garbage can attracts flies.

Brando's subsequently much-parodied and sometimes risibly overdone portrayal of the ageing Don Vito Corleone dominates the drama, and he won, but refused to accept, his second Academy Award for Best Actor. (Richard Conte, who plays Barzini, was originally considered for the role.)

The film's greatest strength lies in Coppola's sure handling of the sprawling narrative and the brilliance of individual scenes such as the wedding of Talia Shire, and in the superb performances of Pacino, Caan and Duvall, all of whom earned Best Supporting Actor Oscar nominations.

There are no direct mentions of the words 'Mafia' or 'Cosa Nostra' (reportedly the result of discussions at script stage between producer Albert S Ruddy and the Italian American Civil Rights League) and, since it tends to present inherently evil 'heroes' as all-American exemplars battling for a square deal and for honour among thieves, the film appears at times to be a vivid public relations exercise on behalf of organized crime. That said, it remains a seminal gangster film, possessing epic qualities, exciting and compelling, and it deservedly won Academy Awards for Best Picture and Best Screenplay.

'The movie casts a spell far beyond its merits. Warner Brothers would have made it thirty-five years ago as a hundred-minute feature, lively, brilliantly paced, and economical. Now, in the reverent hands of Francis Ford Coppola, it has swelled into an overblown, pretentious, slow, and ultimately tedious three-hour quasi-epic. Gangsters have their *Greatest Story Ever Told*, but minus George Stevens.'
Vogue

'One of the most brutal and moving chronicles of American life ever designed within the limits of popular entertainment ... it's the gangster melodrama come of age, truly

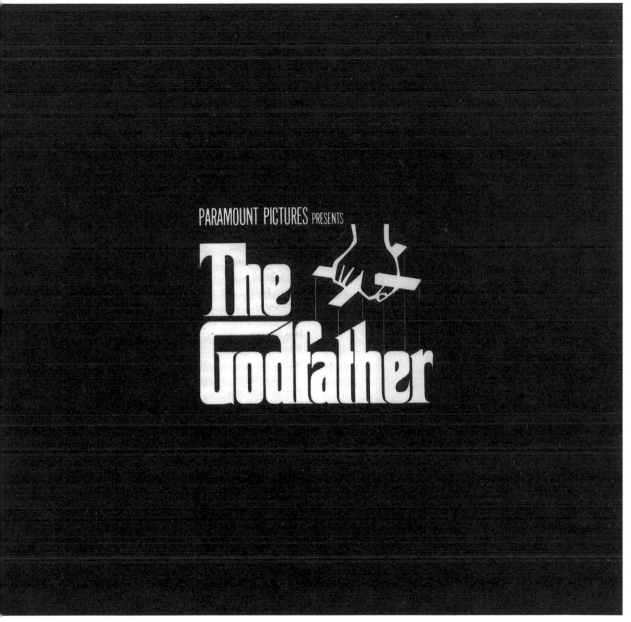

PARAMOUNT PICTURES PRESENTS

The Godfather

THE GODFATHER

sorrowful, exciting, without the false piety of the films that flourished forty years ago.'
The New York Times

'Coppola ... quite deliberately works within the old-fashioned narrative style reminiscent of forties B-pictures and emphasized by the effort at "period" colour photography. It stands as a well-written, well-crafted piece of old-style story-telling.'
Financial Times

'Undoubtedly stunning; it stunned me into the gloom as I ruminated on the number of far better films that have slipped from obscurity to oblivion unheralded and unsung. It is a good film; convincing; directed with a discipline that keeps the complicated plot moving relentlessly; and the competent supporting cast of character actors do all that can be done with

their interchangeable puppet roles ... Brando almost persuaded me that I was watching a great film. But it is not. Like a bauble on a Christmas tree it glitters blood-red but it is equally hollow inside.'
CinemaTV Today

'An incontrovertible demonstration of the continued vitality and artistic power of two things in films whose resources had increasingly been thought to be exhausted: of densely plotted linear narrative, and of natural-ism – social observation and the accu-mulation of authenticating detail – as a method.'
Commentary

THE GODFATHER PART II

(US 1974)
pc Paramount/The Coppola Company. p, d Francis Ford Coppola. co-p Gray Frederickson, Fred Roos. assoc p Mona Skager. w Francis Ford Coppola, Mario Puzo, from the novel *The Godfather* by Mario Puzo. ph Gordon Willis. Colour. ed Peter Zinner, Barry Malkin, Richard Marks. pd Dean Tavoularis. ad Angelo Graham. sfx A D Flowers, Joe Lombardi. cos Theodora Van Runkle. m Nino Rota. add m/md Carmine Coppola. 200 mins

Cast: Al Pacino (Michael Corleone), Robert Duvall (Tom Hagan), Diane Keaton (Kay Corleone), Robert De Niro (Vito Corleone), John Cazale (Fredo Corleone), Talia Shire (Connie), Lee Strasberg (Hyman Roth), Michael V Gazzo (Frankie Pentangeli), G D Spradlin (Senator Geary), Richard Bright (Al Neri), Troy Donahue (Merle Johnson), Roger Corman (Second Senator)

The saga continues with Michael Corleone's post-*Godfather* criminal career and, in flashback, chronicling the early life of Don Vito (Marlon Brando in *The Godfather*, here played by Robert de Niro) growing up in Sicily before going to New York as an orphan in 1901.

Immensely detailed, visually rich and as much a companion piece to *The Godfather* as a sequel since, as well as continuing the saga, it is also a prequel. One of the very few sequels to match the original, it won Oscars for Best Picture, Best Direction, Best Art Direction, Best Score and for Coppola and Puzo's vivid screenplay, which continued to draw a telling parallel between the Mafia and big business in America. Once again Coppola succeeds in making amoral characters sympathetic and engaging audience sympathy for gangsters as well-motivated seekers after the American Dream.

There are times when the film could have benefited from some ruthless pruning (it was alleged Coppola had to reduce an original five-hour version to a more manageable final running time) and there are signs of self-indulgence in leaving redundant scenes in the final cut. Nevertheless, in many ways, *The Godfather Part II*, while inevitably lacking the impact of its predecessor, is a far more impressive and satisfying work. This is due in some measure to the fact that, unencumbered by Brando's emphatic Don Vito Corleone, Coppola has elicited much more balanced performances. Pacino, Shire, Strasberg (the legendary godfather of the Actors Studio, here making his screen debut as Jewish syndicate head Hyman Roth) and Gazzo all received

Academy Award nominations, and De Niro's outstanding portrayal (his career best) won him the Best Supporting Actor Oscar.

It cost some $15,000,000, over twice the budget of the original, but the result more than justifies the expenditure. A dreadful sequel appeared in 1990 (q.v.).

'I'm so excited by this film that if I could sell tickets outside the cinema, I would!'
Daily Mail

'An admirable, responsible production, less emotionally disturbing than its pre-decessor, but a grand historical epic studying the nature of power in the United States' heritage.'
The Hollywood Reporter

'Longueurs there are, but *Godfather II* remains the one sequel that's arguably better than the original.'
The Guardian

'This successor to a blockbuster has better performances, more imaginative use of period decor, sharper photogra-phy, and less lurid violence, but is has nothing to say about the Corleone fami-ly and America that wasn't already evi-dent in Part 1.'
Sight and Sound

'The high points of the first film were moments of violence and suspense; here they are moments of intensely deep and difficult emotions. Taken together, the films are the equivalent of those great, panoramic 19th-century novels that relate the progress of a family and a society.'
Women's Wear Daily

'A third film? Godfather forbid.'
New Statesman

THE GODFATHER PART III
(US 1990)

pc Zoetrope Studios. For Paramount. exec p Fred Fuchs, Nicholas Gage. p, d Francis Ford Coppola. w Francis Ford Coppola, Mario Puzo. ph Gordon Willis. Colour. Panavision. ed Barry Malkin, Lisa Frichtman, Walter Murch. add ed Louise Rubacky, Glen Scantlebury. pd Dean Tavoularis. sup ad Alex Tavoularis. m/md Carmine Coppola. add m Nino Rota. cos Milena Canonero. 162 mins

Cast: Al Pacino (Michael Corleone), Diane Keaton (Kay Adams), Talia Shire (Connie Corleone Rizzi), Andy Garcia (Vincent Mancini), Eli Wallach (Don Altobello), Joe Mantegna (Joey Zasa), George Hamilton (B J Harrison), Bridget Fonda (Grace Hamilton), Sofia Coppola (Mary Corleone), Raf Vallone (Cardinal Lamberto), Franc D'Ambrosio (Anthony Corleone), John Savage (Andrew Hagan)

The saga of Mafia life continues with Michael Corleone attempting to decriminalize his empire and become legitimate. His daughter Mary is romanced by his bastard nephew Vincent, who ultimately triggers off the downfall of his uncle.

A sequel too far. Confused and confusing, over-long, overblown, uninvolving and slower than a stalagmite's growth. The (mostly) perfunctory performances (apart from Pacino, who overacts) match Coppola's (mostly) perfunctory direction. The departure of Winona Ryder, originally slated to play Corleone's daughter, led to the most disastrous error of all – the casting of Coppola's daughter, Sofia. Her painfully inadequate and embarrassing acting is a deadly warning against nepotism. The film itself is simply deadly.

THE GODFATHER PART II

GOLDFINGER

'The picture isn't just unpolished and weakly scored; it lacks coherence. The internal force has vanished from his work, but you still expect some narrative flow, instead he reaches for awesomeness ... *Godfather III* looks like a *Godfather* movie, but it's not about revenge, and it's not about passion and power and survival. It's about a battered movie-maker's king-size depression.'
The New Yorker

'While certain flaws may prevent it from being regarded as the full equal of its predecessors, which are generally ranked among the greatest modern American films, it nonetheless matches them in narrative intensity, epic scope, sociopolitical analysis, physical beauty and deep feeling for its characters and milieu.'
Variety

GOLDFINGER
(GB 1964)

pc Eon. p Harry Saltzman, Albert R Broccoli. d Guy Hamilton. action sequences d Bob Simmons. w Richard Maibaum, Paul Dehn, from the novel by Ian Fleming. ph Ted Moore. Colour. ed Peter Hunt. pd Ken Adam. ad Peter Murton. sfx John Stears, Frank George. m John Barry. title song John Barry, Leslie Bricusse, Anthony Newley, sung by Shirley Bassey. titles Robert Brownjohn. 109 mins

Cast: Sean Connery (James Bond), Honor Blackman (Pussy Galore), Gert Frobe (Goldfinger), Shirley Eaton (Jill Masterson), Tania Mallet (Tilly Masterson), Harold Sakata (Oddob), Bernard Lee ('M'), Lois Maxwell (Miss Moneypenny), Martin Benson (Solo), Cec Linder (Felix Leiter), Austin Willis (Simmons)

Bond foils a supervillain planning to loot Fort Knox.

Connery's third outing as 007, and one of the slickest in the series, a zestful confection of comic-strip thrills and cliffhangers, glamorous girls and gadgets, the latter including a souped-up Aston Martin equipped with an ejector seat, radar and twin machine-guns, and the laser with which Goldfinger plans the bisection of Our Impervious Hero. The villains are up to par: Sakata's lethal bowler hat ranks among the cinema's more outré weapons.

The sets are impressively over-the-top, as is the film, with new director Hamilton getting on with the formula proceedings with infectious relish.

'A bit much? yes, but it's meant to be. Like *Dr No* and *From Russia With Love*, the two previous Bond bombshells, this picture is a thriller, exuberantly travestied.'
Time

'It's all incredible and dreadfully sinister, but you can't help watching.'
Saturday Review

THE GOOD DIE YOUNG
(GB 1954)
pc Remus Films. assoc p Jack Clayton. d Lewis Gilbert. w Vernon Harris, Lewis Gilbert, from the novel by Richard Macauley. ph Jack Asher. B&W. ed Ralph Kemplen. ad Bernard Robinson. m Georges Auric. 98 mins

Cast: Laurence Harvey (Rave), Gloria Grahame (Denise), Richard Basehart (Joe), Joan Collins (Mary), John Ireland (Eddie), Rene Ray (Angela), Stanley Baker (Mike), Margaret Leighton (Eve), Robert Morley (Sir Francis Ravenscourt), Freda Jackson (Mrs Freeman), Lee Patterson (Tod Maslin)

Three men with problems co-opted by a playboy for a mail van robbery in London fall out when the heist goes wrong.

The cast is strong, but the script and direction are over-leisurely and the characters are too clichéd for this made-in-Britain mock-American to work satisfactorily. The mixture of British and American actors set against London locations adds to the general air of unbelievability.

'The trouble with this four-stories-in-one piece is that I couldn't believe in the basic situation – in which three normally honest men, all in low water, are led to crime by one bad 'un. Otherwise, it's a good thriller.'
Picturegoer

THE GRISSOM GANG
(US 1971)
pc Associates and Aldrich/ABS Pictures Corp. p, d Robert Aldrich. assoc p Walter Blake. w Leon Griffith, from the novel *No Orchids for Miss Blandish* by James Hadley Chase. ph Joseph Biroc. Colour. ed Michael Luciano. ad James Dowell Vance. sfx Henry Millar. m Gerald Fried. cos Norma Koch. choreo Alex Romero. 128 mins

Cast: Kim Darby (Barbara Blandish),

Scott Wilson (Slim Grissom), Tony Musante (Eddie Hagan), Robert Lansing (Dave Fenner), Connie Stevens (Anna Borg), Irene Dailey (Ma Grissom), Wesley Addy (John P Blandish), Joey Faye (Woppy), Ralph Waite (Mace), Hal Baylor (Chief McLaine), Matt Clark (Bailey)

In 1931 a young heiress is kidnapped by small-time hoodlums led by a psychopath, with whom she eventually falls in love.

Effective period detail and Aldrich's professional handling fail to disguise the basic silliness of the story. Clichéd characterization and over-large performances don't help either. The violence, relatively tame by today's standards, was regarded as excessive at the time. A remake of 1948's *No Orchids For Miss Blandish*.

'To my shame I was held from the bloody beginning to the even bloodier end. Sickened yes, but inescapably held.'
Daily Mail

'Offensive, immoral and perhaps even lascivious ... carries lurid melodrama and violence to outrageous limits.'
The New York Times

GUMSHOE
(GB 1971)
pc Memorial. p Michael Medwin. assoc p David Barber. d Stephen Frears. w Neville Smith. ph Chris Menges. Colour. sup ed Fergus McDonell. ed Charles Ross. pd Michael Seymour. sfx Bowie Films. m Andrew Lloyd Webber. song *Baby, You're Good For Me* by Andrew Lloyd Webber, Tim Rice. 84 mins

Cast: Albert Finney (Eddie Ginley), Billie Whitelaw (Ellen), Frank Finlay (William), Janice Rule (Mrs Blankerscoon), Carolyn Seymour (Alison Wyatt), Fulton Mackay (John Straker), George Innes (Bookshop Owner), George Silver (Jacob De Fries), Billy Dean (Tommy), Wendy Richard (Anne Scott), Maureen Lipman (Naomi)

A Liverpool bingo caller who fancies himself as a latter-day Humphrey Bogart advertises his services as a private eye and is caught up in mayhem and murder.

Entertaining and affectionate spoof of forties private eye genre films which manages both to pay homage and to function on its own as an exciting and often very funny thriller. There is exemplary playing from all concerned, Finney is superb, making his fantasies seem both logical and inevitable.

Frears's directorial debut is a minor gem, abetted by a terrific script. Only the musical score fails to come up to par.

'A knockout; funny, exciting and far cleverer than it seems at first.'
The Sunday Telegraph

'It is rare enough to find a British film so consistently funny, intelligent and entertaining. That it comes from a debutante director makes a notably cheering end to the year.'
Financial Times

GUNN

(US 1967)
pc Geoffrey Productions. A Blake Edwards Production. p Owen Crump. assoc p Ken Wales, Dick Crockett. d Blake Edwards. w Blake Edwards, William Peter Blatty, based on a story and characters created by Blake Edwards. ph Philip Lathrop. Colour. ed Peter Zinner. ad Fernando Carrere. sfx Paul K Lerpae. m Henry Mancini. 84 mins

Cast: Craig Stevens (Peter Gunn), Laura Devon (Edie), Edward Asner (Jacoby), Sherry Jackson (Samantha), Helen Traubel (Mother), Albert Paulsen (Fusco), Marion Marshall (Daisy Jane), J Pat O'Malley (Tinker), Regis Toomey (The Bishop), Dick Crockett (Leo Gracey), Charles Dierkof (Laszlo Joyce)

A private eye is hired to find out who killed a gang boss and his mistress.

Brisk, fast-moving feature derived from Edwards's television series, which ran for 114 episodes between 1958 and 1960. Another good reason to regret Edwards's move into comedy.

'Unloveable, unpretentious but undeniably enjoyable.'
The Sunday Telegraph

HAMMERHEAD

(GB 1968)

pc Irving Allen Productions. p Irving
Allen. assoc p Andrew Donally. d
David Miller. w William Bast, Herbert
Baker. adap John Briley, from the
novel by James Mayo. ph Kenneth
Talbot, Wilkie Cooper. Colour. ed
Geoffrey Foot. ad John Howell, m
David Whitaker. choreo Ralph Tobert.
99 mins

Cast: Vince Edwards (Charlie Hood),
Judy Geeson (Sue Trenton), Peter
Vaughan (Hammerhead), Diana Dors
(Kit), Michael Bates (Andreas/Sir
Richard), Beverly Adams (Ivory),
Patrick Cargill (Condor), Patrick Holt
(Huntzinger), William Mervyn
(Perrin), Douglas Wilmer (Vendriani),
Tracy Reed (Miss Hull)

British Intelligence recruits an
American agent to hunt down a
master-criminal intent on stealing a
secret nuclear defence system.

    Pallid Bond imitation, complete
with baroque trimmings like the
villain's antique sedan chair. Not inept,
but why bother?

'Quite a lively piece of nonsense, this
should appeal to the many devotees of
special agentry.'
Kine Weekly

HAMMETT

(US 1982)

pc Zoetrope Studios. For Orion. exec p
Francis Coppola. p Fred Roos, Ronald
Colby, Don Guest. assoc p Mona
Skager. d Wim Wenders. w Ross
Thomas, Dennis O'Flaherty. adap
Thomas Pope, from the novel by Joe
Gorea. ph Philip Lathrop, Joseph

Biroc. Colour. ed Barry Malkin, Marc
Laub, Robert Q Lovett, Randy
Roberts. pd Dean Tavoularis, Eugene
Lee. ad Angelo Graham, Leon
Erickson. sfx Howard Jensen, Joseph
Lombardi. sc Terry Leonard. m John
Barry. cos Ruth Morley, Ed Fincher,
Mina Mittleman, Dean Skipworth,
April Ferry. 97 mins

Cast: Frederic Forrest (Samuel Dashiell
Hammett), Peter Boyle (Jimmy Ryan),
Marilu Henner (Kit Conger/Sue
Alabama), Roy Kinnear ('English'
Eddie Hagedorn), Lydia Lei (Crystal
Ling), Elisha Cook (Eli), R G
Armstrong (Lt O'Mara), Richard
Bradford (Det. Bradford), Sylvia
Sidney (Donaldina Cameron)

Writer Dashiell Hammett gets into
trouble when he is approached by a
former Pinkerton Detective Agency
colleague in San Francisco in 1928 and
asked to help locate a missing Chinese
girl.

    Flaccid, ludicrously overrated
hommage which simply demonstrates
imitation is the sincerest form of
tedium. All style and no content.

'*Hammett* has the fussiness of a painting and is similarly static ... the soundtrack is the only thing about *Hammett*
that moves.'
New Musical Express

THE HAND THAT ROCKS THE CRADLE

(US 1992)

pc Buena Vista/InterScope. exec p Ted
Field, Rick Jaffa, Robert W Cort. p
Robert Madden. co-p Ira Halberstadt.
d Curtis Hanson. w Amanda Silver. ph
Robert Elswit. Colour. ed John F Link.

pd Edward Pisoni. ad Mark Zuelske. visual cons Carol Fenelon. sfx co-ord Bob Riggs. sc John A Moio. m Graeme Revell. 110 mins

Cast: Anabella Sciorra (Claire Bartel), Rebecca De Mornay (Peyton Flanders), Matt McCoy (Michael Bartel), Ernie Hudson (Solomon), Julianne Moore (Marlene), Madeline Zima (Emma Bartel), John De Lancie (Dr Mott), Kevin Skousen (Marty), Mitchell Laurance (Lawyer)

A psychotic young widow goes to work as nanny for the two young children of the woman she blames for the suicide of her obstetrician husband in order to destroy her.

Despite predictable plotting (*The Nanny* is given a glossy paint job to bring her up to speed for the nineties) and conventional characterization (De Mornay's nanny from hell makes Mrs Danvers seem like an over-humane social worker), Hanson's slickly suspenseful direction scrapes the nerves efficiently.

'*The Hand That Rocks the Cradle* is meant to scare audiences more or less in the way that the patrons of the early nickelodeons were frightened when they saw the image of a train rushing at them. Audiences aren't asked to think, only to react.'
The New York Times

HARD CONTRACT
(US 1968)
pc 20th Century Fox. p Marvin Schwartz. d, w, st S Lee Pogostin. ph Jack Hildyard. sp ph fx L B Abbott, Art Cruikshank. Colour. Panavision. ed Harry Gerstad. ad Ed Graves. m

Alex North. 106 mins

Cast: James Coburn (John Cuningham), Lee Remick (Sheila Metcalfe), Lilli Palmer (Adrianne), Burgess Meredith (Ramsey Williams), Patrick Magee (Alexei), Sterling Hayden (Michael Carlson), Karen Black (Ellen), Claude Dauphin (Maurice), Helen Cherry (Evelyn Carlson), Sabine Sun (Belgian Woman)

A professional hitman agrees to kill three men in Europe within a month.

Overloaded with pretentious moralizing and equally pretentious dialogue, it succeeds better as a glossy travelogue than as a thriller.

'Oh, Humphrey Bogart. There's still no replacement for you. And a film like *Hard Contract* can barely manage with less.'
The New Yorker

HARPER
(US 1966) (GB: THE MOVING TARGET)
pc Gershwin/Kastner. p Jerry Gershwin, Elliott Kastner. d Jack Smight. w William Goldman, from the novel *The Moving Target* by Ross McDonald. ph Conrad Hall. Colour. Panavision. ed Stefan Arnsten. ad Alfred Sweeney. m Johnny Mandel. song *Livin' Alone* by Dory and André Previn. 121 mins

Cast: Paul Newman (Lew Harper), Lauren Bacall (Mrs Simpson), Julie Harris (Betty Fraley), Arthur Hill (Albert Graves), Janet Leigh (Susan Harper), Pamela Tiffin (Miranda Sampson), Shelley Winters (Fay

Estabrook), Robert Wagner (Alan Taggert), Robert Webber (Dwight Troy), Harry Gould (Sheriff Spanner)

A private eye uncovers intrigue, mystery and murder when a wealthy woman employs him to find her missing husband.

Ross McDonald's Lew Archer (why his name should have been changed is one of the film's biggest mysteries) is a natural literary/celluloid heir to Raymond Chandler's Philip Marlowe, and *Harper* deliberately attempts to recreate the Bogart formula with sixtie gloss and colour, right down to the resonant casting of Bacall.

Newman, while lacking Bogart's charisma, is adequate, and Smight's smooth direction and a clever and witty script make it all very enjoyable. It resembles an expensive, well-made, well above-average made-for-television movie, in that Newman's progress is marked by a series of well-known stars making guest apperances. Newman redundantly reprised the role in *The Drowning Pool* (1975, q.v.).

'A humdinger of a thriller, furiously paced, full of surprise and suspense, with some hard, muscular interludes thrown in.'
The Film Daily

HE WALKED BY NIGHT
(US 1949)
pc Bryan Foy Productions. p Robert Kane. d Alfred Werker. d (uncredited) Anthony Mann. w John C Higgins, Crane Wilbur. add dial Harry Essex. st Crane Wilbur. ph John Alton. ph fx George J Teague. B&W. ed Alfred DeGaetano. ad Edward Ilou. sfx Jack M Rabin. m Leonid Raab. 79 mins

Cast: Richard Basehart (Morgan), Scott Brady (Sgt Marty Brennan), Roy Roberts (Capt. Breen), Whit Bissell Reeves), Jimmy Cardwell (Chuck Jones), Jack Webb (Lee), Bob Bice (Det. Steno), Reed Hadley (Narrator), John Dehner (Assistant Chief), Byron Foulger Avery), Kenneth Tobey (Detective)

Los Angeles policemen track down a cop killer.

Vivid fact-based crime thriller whose semi-documentary style owes much to *Naked City*, but unpretentious and well-handled, with top-flight cinematography.

'One of the best factual crime melodramas produced in the fashionable documentary manner – and the acting is excellent.'
Picturegoer

HEAT

(US 1995)
pc Monarchy Enterprises/Regency Pictures. A Forward Pass production. exec p Arnon Milchan, Pieter Jan Brugge. p Michael Mann, Art Linson. assoc p Kathleen M Shea, Gusmano Cesaretti. d, w Michael Mann. 2nd unit d Ami Canaan Mann. ph Dante Spinotti. Colour. ed Dov Hoenig, Pasquale Buba, William Goldenberg, Tom Rolf. pd Neil Spisak. ad Marjorie Stern. sfx co-ord Terry D Frazee. sc Joel Kramer. m Elliot Goldenthal. tattoos Ken Diaz. 171 mins

Cast: Al Pacino (Vincent Hanna), Robert De Niro (Neil McCauley), Val Kilmer (Chris Shiherlis), Jon Voight (Nate), Tom Sizemore (Michael Cheritto), Diane Venora (Justine Hanna), Ashley Judd (Charlene Shiherlis), Amy Brennan (Eady), Mykelti Williamson (Det. Drucker), Wes Studi (Det. Casals), Ted Levine (Bosko), Dennis Haysbert (Breedan),

HEAT

HELL DRIVERS

William Fichtner (Van Zant), Natalie Portman (Lauren), Tom Noonan (Kelso), Xander Berkeley (Ralp)

A dogged Los Angeles policeman goes on the trail of the psychopathic criminal mastermind behind a $1.6 billion armoured car robbery.

Pacino and De Niro, playing similarly driven characters on opposite sides of the law, meet head-on for the first time (they never appeared in the same scene in *The Godfather Part II*). De Niro, as mannered as ever, pulls every scene-stealing trick in the book (and some yet-to-be-published ones) and at times segués into embarrassing overacting, leaving Pacino to win the dramatic duel hands down. Strong support comes from Voight, Sizemore, Judd and Venora.

Mann never puts a frame wrong as writer and director of a brilliantly-reworked cops-and-robbers crime epic, creating vivid suspense and credible characters and staging some of the most memorable action in recent years – notably the opening armoured car heist, an extraordinary and sustained sequence of an abortive bank robbery that erupts into a massive shooting war in the streets of Los Angeles, and the climactic chase. Taut, violent and exciting, and a genre masterpiece.

'Having revived the historical saga with *The Last of the Mohicans*, he obviously wants to do the same for what has become a much more familiar (and tiresome) genre, the urban action picture. This Mann achieves with truly epic sweep, maniacal conviction and awesome technical proficiency.'
Time

'The Western reinvents itself every decade, but a cop drama is always is always a cop drama. Or so its seemed. With a first-time teaming of its superstar leads, staggering technical virtuosity and a script of rare psychological depth, Michael Mann's *Heat* (* * * * out of four) transcends the genre ... *Heat* is in the cop-movie pantheon with Akira Kurosawa's *High and Low*, and that's as "right" as the genre gets.'
USA Today

'A better crime thriller than anything Scorsese has done.'
VHE

HELL DRIVERS
(GB 1955)
pc Acqua Film Production. exec p Earl St John. p S Benjamin Fisz. d C Raker Endfield. w John Kruse, C Raker Endfield. ph Geoffrey Unsworth. B&W. VistaVision. ed John D

Guthridge. ad Ernest Archer. m Hubert Clifford. 108 mins

Cast: Stanley Baker (Tom), Herbert Lom (Gino), Peggy Cummins (Lucy), Patrick McGoohan (Red), William Hartnell (Cartley), Wilfrid Lawson (Ed), Sidney James (Dusty), Jill Ireland (Jill), Alfie Bass (Tinker), Gordon Jackson (Scottie), David McCallum (Jimmy), Sean Connery (Johnny), Wensley Pithey (Pop), George Murcell (Tub), Marjorie Rhodes (Ma West), Vera Day (Blonde), Beatrice Varley (Mother), Katharine Watson (Newlywed), Marianne Stone (Nurse)

An ex-convict gets a job with a crooked trucking company hauling ballast, whose sadistic 'champion' driver sets out to eliminate him.

Tough (for the time) and hard-boiled in the Hollywood mould, with driving direction that

HELL DRIVERS

eliminates many of the bumps caused by holes in the plot and by clichéd characterization.

Where the film scores is undoubtedly n its action which not only includes numerous scenes of fast lorry-driving, but also some hectic and brutal fist-fight sequences and a tense climax.'
CEA Film Report

HELL ON FRISCO BAY

(US 1955)

pc Jaguar. assoc p George Betholon. d Frank Tuttle. w Sydney Boehm, Martin Rackin, from the novel by William P McGivern. ph John Seitz. Colour. ed Folmar Blangsted. ad John Beckman. m Max Steiner. 98 mins

Cast: Alan Ladd (Steve Rollins), Edward G Robinson (Victor Amato), Joanne Dru (Marcia Rollins), William Demarest (Dan Bianco), Paul Stewart (Joe Lye), Perry Lopez (Mario Amato), Fay Wray (Kay Stanley), Renata Vanni (Anna Amato), Nestor Paiva (Lou Fiaschetti), Stanley Adams (Hammy), Willis Bouchey (Lt Neville)

An embittered ex-policeman framed for manslaughter is released after five years in jail and seeks revenge.

Solid, well-cast, with a cold heart and plenty of action and a lively final duel on board a speeding motor-boat. Robinson plays his familiar role with familiar ease, and Ladd's blandness works well for once.

The film moves quickly and has neat dialogue, well-fought battles and a thrilling climax.'
Picture Show

HENNESSEY

(GB 1975)

pc Hennessey Film Productions. For AIP and Marseilles Enterprises. exec p Samuel Z Arkoff. p Peter Snell. d Don Sharp. w John Gay. st Richard Johnson. ph Ernest Steward. Colour. ed Eric Boyd-Perkins. pd Ray Simm. ad Bert Davey. sfx John Richardson. m John Scott. 104 mins

Cast: Rod Steiger (Niall Hennessey), Lee Remick (Kate), Richard Johnson (Hollis), Trevor Howard (Rice), Eric Porter (Tobin), Peter Egan (Williams), Stanley Lebor (Hawk), Ian Hogg (Gerry), John Hallam (Tipaldi), Hugh Moxey (Burgess), Peter Copley (Home Secretary), Diana Fairfax (Maureen Hennessey), Patsy Kensit (Angie Hennessey)

An Ulsterman whose wife and child are killed in a street battle in Belfast goes to London to blow up the Houses of Parliament during the State Opening by the Queen.

Sloppy and unsuspenseful, decorated with yet another embarrassingly hammy Steiger performance, the film became a minor *cause célèbre* when a major British cinema chain refused to screen it because of its inclusion of newsreel footage of the Royal Family. Without the accompanying media furore it would simply have slipped painlessly into well-deserved obscurity.

'We are asked not only to suspend our disbelief, but to dispense with our intel-ligence altogether as this mirthless, clumsy yarn winds its oh-so-slow way to its inevitable finale ... perhaps the Queen should have cooperated – and

taken a crack at rewriting John Gay's garbled screenplay. She couldn't have done worse.'
Newsweek

HICKEY & BOGGS

(US 1972)

pc Film Guarantors Inc. exec p Richard L O'Connor. p Foaud Said. assoc p Joel Reisner. d Robert Culp. w Walter Hill. ph Wilmer Butler. 2nd unit ph Rexford Metz, Rex Hosea. Colour. ed David Berlatsky. sfx Joe Lombardi. m Ted Ashford. title song by/sung by George Edwards. 111 mins

Cast: Bill Cosby (Al Hickey), Robert Culp (Frank Boggs), Rosalind Cash (Nyone), Sheila Sullavan (Edith Boggs), Isabel Sanford (Nyona's Mother), Louis Moreno (Quemando), Ron Henrique (Florist), Robert Mandan (Mr Brill), Michael Moriarty (Ballard), Lester Fletcher (Rice), Vincent Gardenia (Papadakis)

Two down-and-out Los Angeles detectives hired to trace a missing woman find themselves involved in danger and in the search for $400,000 stolen from a bank.

Culp and Cosby play to excellent effect against the amiable images they created for their popular *I Spy* television series but still retain the characters' easy-going, wise-cracking relationship. Culp directs with originality and assurance but cannot make much sense of Walter Hill's underdeveloped screenplay.

'Starting slow, plottage seldom rises above the confusing stage but later action is sufficiently fast and violent to rate as okay melodrama.'
Variety

HIGH SIERRA

(US 1941)

pc WB-First National. exec p Hall B Wallis. assoc p Mark Hellinger. d Raoul Walsh. w John Huston, W R Burnett, from the novel by W R Burnett. ph Tony Gaudio. B&W. ed Jack Killifer. ad Ted Smith. sfx Byron Haskin, H F Koenekamp. m Adolph Deutsch. 100 mins

Cast: Humphrey Bogart (Roy Earle), Ida Lupino (Marie Garson), Alan Curtis (Babe Kozak), Arthur Kennedy (Red Hattery), Joan Leslie (Velma), Henry Hull (Doc Banton), Henry Travers (Pa Goodhue), Jerome Cowan (Healy) Minna Gombell (Mrs Baughman), Barton MacLane (Ma Kramer), Elisabeth Risdon (Ma Goodhue), Cornel Wilde (Jake Mendoza)

A gangster sprung from jail to carry out a hold-up becomes romantically involved with a crippled girl, and dies in a shoot-out with police in the mountains.

Classic gangster movie that made Bogart at star at 41: he gained the role of Mad Dog Earle after George Raft (who did not want to die at the end of the film), James Cagney, Paul Muni and Edward G Robinson all passed on it.

Bogart cleverly conveyed his inner knowledge of his ultimate fate, and made the character hard-boiled but credibly sympathetic, and able to survive the more maudlin elements of his romance with Lupino and his refusal to abandon a stray dog that brings about his death. The 1955 remake *I Died a Thousand Times* (q.v.) is largely unremarkable.

'Bogart … has had no assignment to match this since *The Petrified Forest*, if then. By painting a character with streaks of white which do not, however, dilute the black, John Huston and W R Burnett, who adapted it from a Burnett novel, drive home their point with power and conviction.'
Motion Picture Herald

'This is what I should call a film worth exposing negative for … like it or not, I'll be damned if you leave before the end or go to sleep.'
The New Republic

HOLLYWOOD STORY

(US 1951)

pc Universal. p Leonard Goldstein. assoc p Bill Grady Jr. d William Castle. w, st Frederick Kohner, Fred Brady. ph Carl Guthrie. B&W. ed Virgil W Vogel. ad Bernard Herzbrun, Richard H Riedel. md Joseph Gershenson. 77 mins

Cast: Richard Conte (Larry O'Brien), Julia Adams (Sally Rousseau), Richard Egan (Lt Lennox), Henry Hull (Vincent St Clair), Fred Clark (Sam Collyer), Jim Backus (Mitch Davis), Housely Stevenson (Mr Miller), Paul Cavanagh (Roland Paul), with Joel McCrea, Richard Neill, 'Baby' Marie Osborne, William Farnum, Betty Blythe, Francis X Bushman, Helen Gibson, Cleo Ridgely, Elmo Lincoln, Dorothy Vernon, Spec O'Donnell, Arline Pretty, Stuart Holmes.

In 1950 a Hollywood producer researching a film about an unsolved 1929 Hollywood murder discovers the identity of the killer.

The poor script makes for a poor movie, but there are compensations in Castle's effective use of Hollywood locations and in the parade of silent-screen stars.

'Dull, pedestrian murder mystery … it is an untidy piece, with a lot of narration.'
Picturegoer

THE HONEYMOON KILLERS

(US 1970)

pc Roxanne. p Warren Steibel. assoc p Paul Asselin. d, w Leonard Kastle. ph Oliver Wood. B&W. ed Stan Warnow, Richard Brophy. m Gustav Mahler. 110 mins

Cast: Shirley Stoler (Martha Beck), Tony Lo Bianco (Ray Fernandez), Mary Jane Rigby (Janet Fay), Doris Roberts (Bunny), Kip McArdle (Delphine Downing), Marilyn Chris (Myrtle Young), Donna Duckworth (Mrs Beck), Ann Morris (Doris), Barbary Cason (Evelyn Long), Mary Breen (Rainelle Downing)

A nurse and a Spanish immigrant pose as sister and brother and murder wealthy women.

A low-key low-budget oddity, based on the real-life 'Lonely Hearts' murderers who were executed in 1951, distinguished by low-key, unsensational direction and *mise-en-scène* and by compelling acting by Stoler and, notably, Lo Bianco.

'The scriptwriter-director has been at such pains to preserve the atmosphere of reality that he has, by slow detail, erased much of the drama.'
Kine Weekly

THE HONEYMOON KILLERS

THE HOODLUM

(US 1951)

pc Jack Schwartz Productions. p Jack Schwartz. d Max Nossek. w Sam Neumann, Nat Tanchuck. ph Clark Ramsey. B&W. ed Jack Killifer. ad Fred Prebble. m Darrell Calker. 61 mins

Cast: Lawrence Tierney (Vincent Lubeck), Liza Golm (Mrs Lubeck), Edward Tierney (Johnny Lubeck), Allene Roberts (Rosa), Eddie Foster (Mickey), Richard Barron (Eddie), Rudy Rama (Harry), Ann Zika (Christie), Stuart Randall (Lt Burdick)

A paroled convict returns to his criminal career.

Typical B-feature crime melodrama: the title tells all.

'This is a heavy and very unrelieved picture ... interest is sustained, but the atmosphere is unhappy throughout.'
CEA Film Report

HOODLUM EMPIRE

(US 1952)

pc Republic. p Herbert J Yates. assoc p, d Joseph Kane. w Bruce Manning, Bob Considine. st Bob Considine. ph Reggie Lanning. B&W. ed Richard L Van Enger. ad Frank Arrigo. m Nathan Scott. 98 mins

Cast: Brian Donlevy (Senator Bill Stephens), Claire Trevor (Connie Williams), Forrest Tucker (Charley Fignatalli), Vera Ralston (Marte Dufour), Luther Adler (Mickey Mancani), John Russell (Joe Gray), Gene Lockhart (Senator Tower), Grant Withers (Rev. Andrews), Taylor Holmes (Benjamin Lawton)

A gangster tries to go straight after World War Two service, but the Syndicate, headed by his uncle, puts pressure on him.

Originally intended as a (fictionalized) biopic of notorious mobster Frank Costello, the emphasis was changed when George Raft turned down the role, which went to Adler: it was reworked as an amalgam of gangland activities and the efforts of Federal investigators out to expose organized crime. Competent but unexceptional.

'Tense, thrilling drama ... made all the more gripping by its authenticity, including the televising of scenes in the court of enquiry ... the well chosen cast does excellent work.'
Picture Show

THE HOT ROCK

(US 1972) (GB: HOW TO STEAL A DIAMOND IN FOUR UNEASY LESSONS)

pc 20th Century Fox. p Hal Landers, Bobby Roberts. d Peter Yates. w William Goldman, from the novel by Donald E Westlake. ph Ed Brown. Colour. Panavision. ed Frank P Keller, Fred W Berger. pd John Robert Lloyd. ad Bob Wrightman. sfx Ira Anderson Jr. m Quincy Jones. 101 mins

Cast: Robert Redford (John Archibald Dortmunder), George Segal (Kelp), Zero Mostel (Abe Greenberg), Ron Liebman (March), Paul Sand (Alan Greenberg), Moses Gunn (Dr Amusa), William Redfield (Lt Hoover), Topo Swope (Sis), Charlotte Rae (Ma Murch), Graham P Jarvis (Warden), Harry Bellaver (Rollo)

Two crooks succeed in stealing a priceless gem from a New York museum, and then proceed to lose their loot more than once.

Lively caper thriller, strong on suspense, thrills and humour, with engaging performances from Segal and Liebman and a witty script and stylish direction.

THE HOT ROCK/HOW TO STEAL A DIAMOND IN FOUR EASY LESSONS

Funny, fast-paced, inventive and infinitely clever crime comedy, so good that it's almost as if *The French Connection* had been remade as a piece of urban humour.'
Glamour

For all its twists and turns, the plot is sublimely logical. The comedy never detracts from the excitement and is often used to excellent effect as a means of moving the story on.'
CinemaTV Today

HOT SUMMER NIGHT
(US 1957)
pc MGM. p Morton S Fine. d David Friedkin. w Morton Fine, David Friedkin, from a story by Edwin P Hicks. ph Harold J Marzorati. B&W. ed Ben Lewis. m André Previn. 86 mins

Cast: Leslie Neilsen (William Joe Partain), Colleen Miller (Irene Partain), Edward Andrews (Lou Follett), Jay C Flippen (Oren Kobble), James Best (Kermit), Paul Richards (Elly Horn), Robert Wilke (Tom Ellis), Claude Akins (Truck Driver), Ruth Childers (Marianna Stewart)

A honeymooning newspaperman trying to get an interview with a holed-up gangster ends up being held for ransom.

Shot in nine days on a low budget by its television-trained director and producer, its plot deficiencies are all too evident, but on its own, admittedly modest, level it is not without interest.

Those who enjoy tough thrillers might find the exciting moments compensate for any improbabilities and for such

audiences it makes fairly good entertainment.'
CEA Film Report.

THE HOUND OF THE BASKERVILLES
(US 1939)
pc 20th Century Fox. exec p Darryl F Zanuck. assoc p Gene Markey. d Sidney Lanfield. w Ernest Pascal, from the novel by Sir Arthur Conan Doyle. ph Peverell Marley. B&W. ed Robert Simpson. ad Richard Day, Hans Peters. m Cyril J Mockridge. 78 mins

Cast: Richard Greene (Sir Henry Baskerville), Basil Rathbone (Sherlock Holmes), Nigel Bruce (Dr Watson), Wendy Barrie (Beryl Stapleton), Lionel Atwill (Dr Mortimer), John Carradine

THE HOUND OF THE BASKERVILLES (1959)

(Barryman), Barlowe Borland (Frankland), Beryl Mercer (Mrs Baskerville), Morton Lowry (John Stapleton), Ralph Forbes (Sir Hugo Baskerville), E E Clive (Cabby), Elly Malyon (Mrs Barryman), Mary Gordon (Mrs Hudson)

Sherlock Holmes solves the mystery of the supernatural hound that terrorizes a baronet on the desolate Dartmoor heathland.

Greene received top billing, but the film (the first of 14 starring Rathbone and Bruce) belongs firmly to Rathbone, who uncannily resembled the Paget drawings of the Great Detective, and whose incisive performance made him the archetypal Holmes and more than compensated for the studio-bound settings and Lanfield's stately direction. Bruce, irritatingly buffoonish as Dr Watson, is a considerable drawback, but the supporting cast, particularly Atwill and Carradine, is fine.

'A startling mystery-chiller developed along logical lines without resorting to implausible situations and over-the-atrics ... Rathbone gives a most effective characterization of Sherlock Holmes which will be relished by mystery lovers.'
Variety

'What we really need in a Holmes picture is far more dialogue and much less action.'
The Spectator

THE HOUND OF THE BASKERVILLES

(GB 1959)
pc Hammer. exec p Michael Carreras. p Anthony Hinds. d Terence Fisher. w

Peter Bryan, from the novel by Sir Arthur Conan Doyle. ph Jack Asher. Colour. ed James Needs. ad Bernard Robinson. m James Bernard. 87 mins

Cast: Peter Cushing (Sherlock Holmes), Andre Morell (Dr Watson), Christopher Lee (Sir Henry Baskerville), Marla Landi (Cecile), Ewen Solon (Stapleton), Francis De Wolff (Dr Mortimer), Miles Malleson (Bishop Frankland), John Le Mesurier (Barrymore), David Oxley (Sir Hugo Baskerville), Helen Goss (Mrs Barrymore)

Sherlock Holmes journeys to Dartmoor to save Sir Henry Baskerville from a legendary ghostly hound that brings death to the Baskervilles.

Handsomely-mounted, well-made Hammer remake with appropriately horrific overtones. Cushing is the definitive colour Holmes, Morell excels as Watson, and Fisher's direction gives the story vivid Gothic overtones.

Cushing played Holmes in a 26-episode BBC television series in 1967, and again in the 1984 made-for-television film *The Masks of Death*. Lee scored a unique double, playing Holmes in Fisher's 1962 *Sherlock Holmes und der Halsband des Todes/Sherlock Holmes and the Deadly Necklace* (filmed in Germany) and playing Holmes's smarter brother, Mycroft, in the 1970 Billy Wilder spoof *The Private Life of Sherlock Holmes*.

'Peter Bryan's script is kept at a good hissing boil by Terence Fisher's brisk direction ... splendid marrow-freezing stuff.'
New Chronicle

'Cushing is a splendid Holmes. The film while being "Very elementary, Watson" has atmosphere and thrills.'
Daily Mirror

THE HOUR BEFORE THE DAWN

(US 1944)
pc Paramount. p William Dozier. d Frank Tuttle. w Michael Hogan. adap Lesser Samuels, from the novel by W Somerset Maugham. ph John Seitz. B&W. ed Stuart Gilmore. ad Hans Dreier, Earl Hedrick. m Miklos Rozsa. 75 mins

Cast: Franchot Tone (Jim Hetherton), Veronica Lake (Dora Bruckmann), John Sutton (Roger Hetherton), Binnie Barnes (May Hetherton), Henry Stephenson (Gen. Hetherton), Philip Merivale (Sir Leslie Buchanan), Nils Asther (Kurt van der Breughel), Edmond Breon (Freddy Merritt), Morton Lowry (Jackson)

An English conscientious objector finds he has married a German spy and kills her.

Stodgy and unconvincing rubbish, with an awesomely inadequate performance by an impassive – not to say frozen – Lake.

'The whole tone of the piece is Hollywood studio.'
Monthly Film Bulletin

HOUSE BY THE RIVER

(US 1950)
pc Republic. A Fidelity Pictures Production. p Howard Welsch. assoc p Robert Peters. d Fritz Lang. w Mel Dinelli, from the novel *Floodtide* by A P Herbert. ph Edward Cronjager.

B&W. ed Arthur Hilton. ad Boris Leven. sfx Howard Lydecker, Theodore Lydecker. m George Antheil. 88 mins

Cast: Louis Hayward (Steven Byrne), Lee Bowman (John Byrne), Jane Wyatt (Marjorie Byrne), Dorothy Patrick (Emily Gaunt), Anne Shoemaker (Mrs Ambrose), Jodie Gilbert (Flora Bantam), Peter Brocco (Coroner), Howland Chamberlin (District Attorney), Margaret Seddon (Mrs Whittaker)

A writer accidentally strangles a man, and implicates his older brother.

Well-photographed but over-theatrical and languidly directed, with more of an eye to tedium than to suspense.

'It seems that when the talents of directors are in decline, their pictures become exceptionally slow: *House by the River* is even slower than the later Hitchcock films.'
Monthly Film Bulletin

THE HOUSE OF THE SEVEN HAWKS

(GB 1959)
pc David E Rose. p David E Rose. d Richard Thorpe. w Jo Eisinger, from the novel *The House of the Seven Flies* by Victor Canning. ph Ted Scaife. B&W. ed Ernest Walter. m Clifford Parker. 92 mins

Cast: Robert Taylor (John Nordley), Nicole Maury (Constanta), Linda Christian (Elsa), Donald Wolfit (Van Der Stoor), David Kossoff (Wilhelm Decker), Eric Pohlmann (Capt. Rohner), Philo Hauser (Charlie Ponz), Gerard Heinz (Insp. Sluiter)

An American small boat owner tangles dangerously with crooks searching for Nazi treasure.

Bland time-passer with a lacklustre star and equally tepid execution.

'Over-complicated to the point of confusion ... the usual thriller about an American adventurer's skirmishes with dishonest Europeans.'
Monthly Film Bulletin

THE HOUSE ON CARROLL STREET

(US 1988)
pc Orion. p Arlene Donovan, Robert Benton. p Robert F Colesberry, Peter Yates. assoc p Nellie Nugiel. d Peter Yates. w Walter Bernstein. ph Michael Ballhaus. Colour. ed Ray Lovejoy. pd Stuart Wurtzel. ad W Steven Graham. m Georges Delerue. 101 mins

Cast: Kelly McGillis (Emily Crane), Jeff Daniels (Cochran), Mandy Patinkin (Ray Salwen), Jessica Tandy (Miss Venable), Jonathan Hogan (Alan), Remak Ramsay (Senator Byington), Kenneth Walsh (Hackett), Christopher Rhodes (Stefan), Charles McCaughan (Salwen Aide No.1), Randle Mell (Salwen Aide No.2), Trey Wilson (Lt Sloan), James Rebhorn (The Official)

In 1951 a woman under surveillance because of her leftish leanings has a tough job persuading an FBI agent that she has stumbled across a scheme to smuggle Nazi war criminals into the United States.

Bernstein's screenplay gives the impression of having been written in 1951, and no amount of smooth direction and detailed period detail can bring it to life.

'Amateur plotting and a guaranteed shelf life – at the video store.'
Variety

THE 'HUMAN' FACTOR

(GB 1975)
pc Eton Film Productions Establishment. exec p Terry Lens. p Frank Avianca. assoc p Peter Inwards. d Edward Dmytryk. w Tom Hunter, Peter Powell. ph Ousama Rawi. Colour. ed Alan Strachen. ad Peter Bates. sfx Les Bowie. m Ennio Morricone. 96 mins

Cast: George Kennedy (John Kinsdale), John Mills (Mike McAllister), Raf Vallone (Dr Lupo), Arthur Franz (Gen. Fuller), Rita Tushingham (Janice), Frank Avianca (Kamal), Haydée Politoff (Pidgeon), Tom Hunter (Taylor), Barry Sullivan (Edmonds), Fiamme Verges (Ann Kinsdale), Shane Rimmer (Carter)

An electronics expert working for NATO uses computer skills to track down the terrorists who murdered his family, and violently eliminates them.

There is a great deal of overacting, presumably to compensate for the hackneyed script and even worse direction by Dmytryk, who had long before gone off the boil.

'This latest entry in the vigilante sweepstakes would be offensive if it weren't so very boring.'
Village Voice

I AM THE LAW

(US 1938)

pc Columbia. p Everett Riskin. d
Alexander Hall. w Jo Swerling, based
on magazine articles by Fred Alhoff.
ph Henry Freulich. B&W. ed Viola
Lawrence. md Morris Stoloff.
83 mins

Cast: Edward G Robinson (John
Lindsay), Barbara O'Neil (Jerry
Lindsay), John Beal (Paul Ferguson),
Wendy Barrie (Frankie Ballou), Otto
Kruger (Eugene Ferguson), Arthur
Loft (Tom Ross), Marc Lawrence
(Eddie Girard), Douglas Wood
(Berry), Ivan Miller (Insp. Gleason),
Charles Halton (Leander)

A law professor is hired as a special
prosecutor to get rid of racketeers.

Zestful melodrama, although at
this stage of his career it is somewhat
hard to accept Robinson on the right
side of the law.

'In spite of the fact that this picture
again dishes up American gangster
life, the film is a combination of
actionful happenings and makes exhilarating entertainment.'
CEA Film Report

I DIED A THOUSAND TIMES

(US 1955)

pc WB. p Willis Goldbeck. d Stuart
Heisler. w W R Burnett, from his
novel. ph Ted McCord. Colour.
CinemaScope. ed Clarence Kolster.
ad Edward Carrere. m David
Buttolph. 109 mins

Cast: Jack Palance (Roy Earle),
Shelley Winters (Marie), Lori Nelson
(Velma), Lee Marvin (Babe),
Gonzalez Gonzalez (Chico), Lon
Chaney Jr (Big Mac), Earl Holliman
(Red), Perry Lopez (Louis Mendoza),
Howard St John (Doc Banton),
Ralph Moody (Pa) Olive Carey (Ma),
Dick Davalos (Lou Dreisser)

A paroled gangster takes part in a
large-scale hotel robbery and is shot
down by the police in a gunfight in
the High Sierras.

Leaden remake of 1941's *High
Sierra* (q.v.): Palance is no Humphrey
Bogart, Stuart Heisler is no Raoul
Walsh, and the film is no great
shakes.

'Proves scarcely more inspired than
its title.'
Monthly Film Bulletin

I, THE JURY

(US 1953)

pc Parklane Productions. p Victor
Saville. d, w Harry Essex, from the
novel by Mickey Spillane. ph John
Alton. B&W. 3-D. ed Frederick Y
Smith. ad Ward Ihnen. m Franz
Waxman. 88 mins

Cast: Biff Elliott (Mike Hammer),
Preston Foster (Capt. Pat Chambers),
Peggie Castle (Charlotte Manning),
Margaret Sheridan (Velda), Alan Reed
(George Kalecki), Frances Osborne
(Myrna), Robert Cunningham (Hal
Kines), Elisha Cook Jr (Bobo), Paul
Dubov (Marty), Mary Anderson
(Eileen Vickers)

Private eye Mike Hammer avenges the
murder of a friend.

Violent and quite sadistic for the
time, although censorship excised the
overt eroticism of Spillane's novel, and
Elliott's colourless Mike Hammer
leaves a dramatic vacuum at the centre.
Remade in 1982 (q.v.).

'Fast-moving but it tends to be rather
too lurid and brutal and well-deserves
its "X" certificate.'
Picture Show

I, THE JURY

(US 1982)

pc Larco/Solo Film/American Cinema Productions. p Robert Solo. assoc p Martin Hornstein. d Richard T Heffron. 2nd unit d Don Pike. w Larry Cohen, from the novel by Mickey Spillane. ph Andrew Laszlo. 2nd unit ph Peter Passas. Colour. ed Garth Graven. pd Robert Gundlach. asst ad Jim Singelis. sfx Conrad Brink, Terry King, Bill Bailes, Bill Nipper, Frank F Liszcak. sc Don Pike, Aaron Norris. m Bill Conti. 111 mins

Cast: Armand Assante (Mike Hammer), Barbara Carrera (Dr Charlotte Stewart), Lauren Landon (Velda), Alan King (Charles Kalecki), Geoffrey Lewis (Joe Butler), Paul Sorvino (Det. Pat Chambers), Judson Scott (Kendricks), Barry Snider (Romero), Julia Barr (Norma Childs), Jessica James (Hilda Kendricks)

Private eye Mike Hammer sets out to avenge the murder of a friend.

Violent, bloody and explicit remake of the 1953 version. While it is certainly no masterpiece, it delivers its quota of well-orchestrated visceral mayhem. The prolific Cohen started as director but, in order to complete it before an actors' strike halted all production, television director Heffron took over. While there are those cultists who believe Cohen would have made a far better film, it is, in fact, perfectly serviceable of its commercial type.

'Richard T Heffron settles for the repellent formula as usual, with the gun and the penis as interchangeable instruments of quick-fire tough-guy virility.'
The Sunday Times

I WAKE UP SCREAMING

(US 1942) (GB: HOT SPOT)
pc 20th Century Fox. exec p Darryl F
Zanuck. p Milton Sperling. d H Bruce
Humberstone. w Dwight Taylor, from
the novel by Steve Fisher. ph Edward
Cronjager. B&W. ed Robert Simpson.
ad Richard Day, Nathan Juran. m
Cyril J Mockridge. 81 mins

Cast: Betty Grable (Jill Lynn), Victor
Mature (Frankie Christopher), Carole
Landis (Vicy Lynn), Laird Cregar (Ed
Cornell), William Gargan
(McDonald), Alan Mowbray (Robin
Ray), Allyn Joslyn (Larry Evans),
Elisha Cook Jr (Harry Williams),
Chick Chandler (Reporter), Morris
Ankrum (District Attorney)

When a young woman is murdered,
the sinister detective assigned to the
case turns out to be the killer.

Unpretentious and, given director
Humberstone's usual output of bland
musicals and equally bland
programmers, surprisingly tense
thriller. Easily his best (and most
atypical) movie, with Grable making
the most of a rare straight role, a good
supporting cast (apart from the ever-
monolithic Mature) and an
extraordinary and chilling
performance by Cregar as the pathetic,
psychopathic detective.

'There are few melodramas a season
that demand to be seen. Here is one
of them.'
Motion Picture Herald

I WAS A COMMUNIST FOR THE FBI

(US 1951)
pc WB. p Bryan Foy. d Gordon
Douglas. w Crane Wilbur, based on
the experiences of Matt Cvetic, as told
to Pete Martin, published in the
Saturday Evening Post. ph Edwin
DuPar. B&W. ed Folmar Blangsted. ad
Leo K Kuter. m Max Steiner. 83 mins

Cast: Frank Lovejoy (Matt Cvetic),
Dorothy Hart (Eve Merrick), Philip
Carey (Mason), James Millican (Jim
Blandon), Richard Webb (Crowley),
Konstantin Shayne (Gerhardt Eisler),
Paul Picerni (Joe Cvetic), Roy Roberts
(Father Novac), Eddie Harris (Harmon),
Ron Haggerthy (Dick Cvetic)

A Pittsburgh steel worker spends nine
years as a member of the Communist
Party as an FBI informer.

Splendid title, shame about the
film, which is an unpleasant example
of Warner Brothers' shameless
sycophancy towards the House
UnAmerican Activities Committee,
rendered all the more unpalatable
because it is well made.

'I conclude there was no more, and no
less, than was implied in the title; but
I would add that the film is a thriller
in its own right, having the snap and
punch of live reportage and the pace
of a first-class newsreel.'
ABC Film Review

IF HE HOLLERS, LET HIM GO

(US 1968)
pc Forward Films. p, d , w Charles
Martin. ph William W Spencer.
Colour. ed Richard Brockway. ad
James W Sullivan. sfx Justus Gibbs. m
Harry Sukman. 106 mins

Cast: Raymond St Jacques (James
Lake), Dana Wynter (Ellen Whitlock),
Kevin McCarthy (Leslie Whitlock),
Barbara McNair (Lily), John Russell
(Sheriff), Ann Prentiss (Thelma
Wilson), Arthur O'Connell
(Prosecutor), Royal Dano (Carl
Blaire), Steve Sandor (Harry), James
Craig (Police Chief), James McEachin
(Defence Counsel)

A wrongly-imprisoned man escapes
from jail to clear himself and gets
caught up in a man's scheme to
murder his wife.

Melodramatic rubbish whose cast
is left stranded by the inadequate
script and direction.

'Belying the title of its production
company this film must be vying for
the honours as the most old-fashioned
movie both in style and content of this
or any other year.'
Films and Filming

ILLEGAL

(US 1955)
pc WB. p Frank J Rosenberg. d Lewis
Allen. w W R Burnett, James R Webb,
from the play *The Mouthpiece* by
Frank J Collins. ph Peverell Marley.
B&W. ed Thomas Reilly. ad Stanley
Fleischer. m Max Steiner. 88 mins

Cast: Edward G Robinson (Victor
Scott), Nina Foch (Ellen Miles), Hugh
Marlowe (Ray Borden), Jayne
Mansfield (Angel O'Hara), Albert
Dekker (Frank Garland), Howard St
John (E A Smith), Ellen Corby (Miss
Hinkle), Robert Ellenstein (Joe
Knight), De Forrest Kelley (Edward
Clary), Jay Adler (Joseph Carter)

A District Attorney resigns and starts
to drink after sending an innocent

man to the chair, but makes a comeback as a defence lawyer working for a racketeer.

Lively remake of 1932's *The Mouthpiece* (q.v.) with Robinson clearly relishing being back at his old studio. The direction is brisk and to the point, and the screenplay is vigourously idiomatic.

Illegal lacks depth and subtlety, but its hard-driving vitality makes it unusu-ally enjoyable on its own level.'
Monthly Film Bulletin

IN A LONELY PLACE
(US 1950)

pc Columbia/Santana. p Robert Lord. assoc p Henry S Kesler. d Nicholas Ray. w Andrew Solt. adapt Edmund H North, from the novel by Dorothy B Hughes. ph Burnett Guffey. B&W. ed Viola Lawrence. ad Robert Peterson. m George Antheil. 94 mins

Cast: Humphrey Bogart (Dixon Steele), Gloria Grahame (Laurel Gray), Frank Lovejoy (Brun Nicolai), Carl Benton Reid (Capt. Lochner), Art Smith (Mel Lippman), Jeff Donnell (Sylvia Nicolai), Martha Stewart (Mildred Atkinson), Robert Warwick (Charlie Waterman), Morris Ankrum (Lloyd Barnes), William Ching (Ted Barton)

When a neurotic Hollywood scriptwriter is suspected of murder, his

IN A LONELY PLACE

neighbour gives him an alibi and they fall in love – until she starts to suspect he may actually be the killer.

Bogart's jaundiced, perfectly-judged performance and vivid support from Grahame raise it well above average of its type, although whether Ray's competent but unremarkable direction really adds to his cult *auteur* status is a matter for debate.

'Will excite any moviegoer with that orthodox play upon nerves and feelings which is the charm of the thriller.'
New Statesman

IN THE HEAT OF THE NIGHT

(US 1968)
pc Mirisch. p Walter Mirisch. d Norman Jewison. w Stirling Silliphant, from the novel by John Ball. ph Haskell Wexler. Colour. ed Hal Ashby. ad Paul Groesse. m Quincy Jones. title song Marilyn and Alan Bergman, sung by Ray Charles. 109 mins

Cast: Sidney Poitier (Virgil Tibbs), Rod Steiger (Sheriff Bill Gillespie), Warren Oates (Sam Wood), Quentin Dean (Delores Purdy), William Schallert (Webb Schubert), Lee Grant (Mrs Leslie Colbert), Scott Wilson (Harvey Oberst), Matt Clark (Packy Harrison), Anthony James (Ralph Henshaw)

A bigoted Southern small-town sheriff unwillingly co-operates with a black Philadelphia police homicide expert to find a killer.

Ingenious and riveting blend of involving whodunnit and powerful plea for racial tolerance, tautly directed and very well acted by

Poitier and, surprisingly, by Steiger, who abandoned his usual irritating mannerisms and as a result won the Best Actor Academy Award. The film won the Best Picture Oscar, deservedly pipping *Bonnie and Clyde*, *The Graduate*, *Doctor Dolittle* and *Guess Who's Coming to Dinner* (which also had a racial theme) at the post, and also picking up the Oscars for Screenplay, Editing and Sound.

'A tense, fascinating film, benefitting from a tight, well-written script by Stirling Silliphant, and from the sure direction of Mr Jewison, who gets better and better with each picture.'
Saturday Review

'Chalk up a new milestone in movie detective stories. This is a modern classic of its genre, one that combines all of the traditional elements of good detective suspense with intriguing characters, and tops it off with a modern setting that makes the film as topical as the 1960's headlines.'
Cue

'A sound, serious and altogether excellent film that is quite possible the best we have had from the US this year.'
Life

INNOCENT BYSTANDERS

(GB 1972)
pc Sagittarius. p George H Brown. d Peter Collinson. w James Mitchell, from the novel by James Munro. ph Brian Probyn. Colour. ed Alan Pattillo. ad Maurice Carter. sfx Pat Moore. m John Keating. song *What Makes The Man?* by/sung by Hurricane Smith. 111 mins

Cast: Stanley Baker (John Craig), Geraldine Chaplin (Miriam Loman), Dana Andrews (Blake), Donald Pleasence (Loomis), Sue Lloyd (Joanna Benson), Vladek Sheybal (Aaron Kaplan), Derren Nesbitt (Toyce), Warren Mitchell (Omar), Ferdy Mayne (Marcus Kaplan), John Collin (Asimov), Frank Maher (Daniel)

A middle-aged agent joins the hunt for a Russian scientist who escapes from prison in Siberia.

Typically jaundiced seventies spy thriller, whose formula writing and unremarkable direction are partly redeemed by above-average performances.

'When a project is conceived in cinematic terms, and graced with a first rate team of actors, as in *Innocent Bystanders*, the effect makes for taut and gripping entertainment.'
Films and Filming

INNOCENT LIES

(GB/FRANCE 1995)
pc Red Umbrella Films/Septieme/Cinea/Polygram. p Simon Perry, Phillipe Guez. assoc p Philippe Carcassone. d Patrick Dewolf. w Kerry Crabbe, Patrick Dewolf. ph Patrick Blossier. Colour. ed Chris Wimble, Joelle Hache. pd Bernd Lepel. ad Nicolas Prier, Charlie Smith. m Alexandre Desplat. 88 mins

Cast: Adrian Dunbar (Alan Cross), Joanna Lumley (Lady Helena Graves), Gabrielle Anwar (Celia Graves), Stephen Dorff (Jeremy Graves), Florence Hoath (Angela Cross), Sophie Aubry (Solange Montfort), Alexis Benisof (Christopher Wood),

Marianne Denicourt (Maud Graves), Melvil Poupaud (Louis Bernard)

A British policeman investigates murder on the French coast in September 1938.

Inept, sub-Agatha Christie whodunnit with a dire screenplay and even worse direction, which are impressively matched by performances that embarrass both actors and audience.

'Competence is certainly not much in evidence in *Innocent Lies*, the worst film of the week and possibly of the year.'
The Independent

INSIDE THE WALLS OF FOLSOM PRISON

(US 1951)
pc WB. p Bryan Foy. d, w Crane Wilbur. ph Edwin DuPar. B&W. ed Owen Marks. ad Douglas Bacon. m William Lava. 84 mins

Cast: Steve Cochran (Chuck Daniels), David Brian (Mark Benson), Philip Carey (Red Pardue), Ted de Corsia (Warden), Scott Forbes (Frazier), Lawrence Toland (Leo Daley), Dick Wesson (Tinker), Paul Picerni (Jeff Riordan), William Campbell (Ferretti), James Griffith (Gebhardt), Matt Willis (Dunnevan)

A humane prison guard attempts to instigate reforms in a California jail.

Warner Bros competently reprise a thirties-style Big House thriller replete with thirties-style clichés but with little particular impact.

'Photographed in the prison itself, its

authentic backgrounds lend even greater reality to this realistic story, which is based on fact. It is strongly directed and acted.'
Picture Show

INTERPOL

(GB 1957) (US: PICK-UP ALLEY)
pc Warwick. p Irving Allen, Albert R Broccoli. d John Gilling. location d Max Varnel. w John Paxton, from the book by A J Forrest. ph Ted Moore, Stan Pavey. B&W. Scope. ed Richard Best. ad Paul Sheriff. m Richard Rodney Bennett. song *Anyone For Love* by Lester Lee, Ned Washington, sung by Yana. 92 mins

Cast: Victor Mature (Charles Sturgis), Anita Ekberg (Gina Broger), Trevor Howard (Frank McNally), Bonar Colleano (Amalio), Marne Maitland (Guido), Eric Pohlmann (Fayala), Alec Mango (Salko), Peter Illing (Capt. Baria), Sydney Tafler (Curtis), Martin Benson (Varolli), Andre Morell (Breckner)

An American investigator is sent to Europe to wreck an organization headed by the madman who murdered his sister.

Despite its A-film pretensions, this is a ripe example of the traditional British B-picture, with an ageing American star being filmed on picturesque European locations with remarkably little to indicate his journeys were really necessary.

'Despite the scrappy and confused nature of the plot, the film should please less critical enthusiasts of crime stories on account of its action-filled and fast-moving qualities.'
CEA Film Report

THE IPCRESS FILE

(GB 1965)
pc Steven/Lowndes. exec p Charles Kasher. p Harry Saltzman. assoc p Ronald Kinnoch. d Sidney J Furie. w Bill Canaway, James Doran, from the novel by Len Deighton. ph Otto Heller. Colour. Techniscope. ed Peter Hunt. pd Ken Adam. ad Peter Murton. m John Barry. 109 mins

Cast: Michael Caine (Harry Palmer), Nigel Green (Dalby), Guy Doleman (Ross), Sue Lloyd (Jean), Gordon Jackson (Carswell), Aubrey Richards (Radcliffe), Frank Gatliff (Bluejay), Thomas Baptiste (Barney), Oliver Macgreevy (Housemartin), Freda Bamford (Alice), Anthony Blackshaw (Edwards)

A British Intelligence officer is assigned to find a kidnapped scientist, and unmasks his superior as an enemy agent.

Caine's laconic performance as Deighton's smart-alec secret agent (named in the film, unlike Deighton's original), light years removed from the comic-strip tradition of the Bond films, holds the over-complex proceedings together, but he finally falls victim to Furie's 'look-at-me!' direction, with its deliberate and increasingly irritating plethora of tortured camera angles and vertiginous zooms which make the film resemble a frenetic kaleidoscope.

Caine survived for two more sixties sequels, *Funeral in Berlin* (1967, q.v.) and *Billion Dollar Brain* (1967, q.v.). Only a complete sadist would mention his dismal return to the role in the nineties.

'It is in fact a slow, dull and very long counter espionage story, totally

unromantic and weighed down with what sounds like a load of pseudo-scientific jargon.'
Sunday Express

THE ITALIAN JOB
(GB 1969)
pc Oakhurst/Paramount. p Michael Deeley. assoc p Bob Porter. d Peter Collinson. 2nd unit d Philip Wrestler. w Troy Kennedy Martin. ph Douglas Slocombe. 2nd unit ph Norman Warwick. Colour, Panavision. ed John Trumper. pd Disley Jones. ad Michael Knight. sfx Pat Moore. stunt driving L'Équipe Rémy Julienne. m Quincy Jones. songs Quincy Jones, Don Black. 100 mins

Cast: Michael Caine (Charlie Croker), Noel Coward (Mr Bridger), Benny Hill (Prof. Peach), Raf Vallone (Altabani), Tony Beckley (Camp Freddie), Rosanno Brazzi (Beckerman), Maggie Blye (Lorna), Irene Handl (Miss Peach), John Le Mesurier (Prison Governor), Fred Emney (Birkenshaw), John Clive (Garage Manager), Graham Payne (Keats)

A gang pulls off a $4,500,000 gold bullion robbery in Turin and make an extraordinary escape driving through the vehicle-clogged streets after sabotaging the computerized Traffic Control Centre.

Blithe, crowd-pleasing crime caper with a sharp sense of humour, a memorably amusing performance by Noel Coward as a suave criminal mastermind and, best of all, amazing stunt driving in three Mini Coopers.

'No attempt is made to present the plot as credible and no audience will care about that, for the fun is an excellent mixture of witty burlesque of crime and criminals and of comedy excitement.'
Kine Weekly

JACK THE RIPPER

(GB 1958)
pc Mid-Century. p, d, ph Robert S
Baker, Monty Berman. w Jimmy
Sangster. st Peter Hammond, Colin
Craig. B&W. ed Peter M Bezencenet.
m Stanley Black. 84 mins

Cast: Lee Patterson (Sam Lowry),
Eddie Byrne (Insp. O'Neill), Betty
McDowall (Anne Ford), Ewen Solon
(Sir David Rogers), John Le Mesurier
(Dr Tranter), George Rose (Clarke),
Philip Leaver (Music Hall Manager),
Barbara Burke (Kitty), Denis Shaw
(Simes), George Woodbridge (Blake),
Esma Cannon (Nelly)

An American detective on vacation in
London helps Scotland Yard hunt for
Jack the Ripper.

    Atmospheric with leanings towards
the horrific, not surprising since the
screenplay is by Jimmy Sangster, who
wrote *The Curse of Frankenstein* and
other shockers for Hammer. It betrays
its basic B-feature origins with its
American hero.

'Well-made, with turn-of-the-century
atmosphere and settings convincing.
There is suspense and excitement with
the killings bloodthirsty in effect without being too horrific in presentation,
and the identity of the murderer is
well concealed until the climax.'
CEA Film Report

JACK'S BACK

(US 1988)
pc Palisades Entertainment. exec p
Elliott Kastner. p Tim Moore, Cassian
Elwes. d, w Rowdy Herrington. ph
Shelly Johnson. Colour. ed Harry B
Miller III. pd Piers Plowden. sfx m-u

John Naulin. m Danny Di Paolo.
97 mins

Cast: James Spader (John/Rick
Westford), Cynthia Gibb (Chris
Moscari), Jim Haynie (Sgt Gabriel),
Robert Picardo (Dr Carolos Battera),
Rod Loomis (Dr Sidney Tannerson),
Rex Ryon (Jack Pendler), Chris
Mulkey (Scott Morofsky), Wendell
Wright (Capt. Walter Prentis), John
Wesley (Sam Hillard), Bobby Hosea
(Tom Dellerton)

A man who psychically witnesses the
murder of his doctor brother sets out
to track down the perpetrator of a
series of Jack the Ripper-style slayings
of Los Angeles prostitutes.

    Production values are nothing to
shout about, but Spader scores in a
dual role and writer-director
Herrington makes rather more than
might be expected of his material.

'A movie like this is nothing without
contrivance, and one of its pleasures
is to watch the plot gimmicks as
they twist inward upon themselves,
revealing one level of surprise
after another.'
Chicago Sun-Times

JADE

(US 1995)
pc Paramount. exec p William J
Macdonald. p Robert Evans, Craig
Baumgarten, Gary Adelson. co-p George
Goodman. d William Friedkin. w Joe
Eszterhas. ph Andrzej Bartkowiak.
Colour. ed Augie Hess. pd Alex
Tavoularis. ad Charles Breen. sc Buddy
Joe Hooker. m James Horner. 95 mins

Cast: David Caruso (David Corelli),

Linda Fiorentino (Trina Gavin), Chazz Palminteri (Matt Gavin), Richard Crenna (Governor Lou Edwards), Michael Biehn (Lt Hargrove), Donna Murphy (Karen Heller), Ken King (Oetey Vesko), Holt McCallany (Bill Barrett), David Hunt (Pat Callendar), Kevin Tighe (DA Arnold Clifford), Jay Jacobus (Justin Henderson), Angie Everhart (Patrice Jacinto)

An ambitious San Francisco District Attorney uncovers high-level sleaze and corruption that threatens his career when he investigates the murder of a kinky multi-millionaire.

Eszterhas's cynically-calculated follow-up to *Basic Instinct* offers the same basic high-sex content, low-intelligence exploitation tosh as before, whose high-gloss treatment by Friedkin simply underlines its basic exploitation-movie spuriousness. If, as reported, Eszterhas received $2,500,000 for his screenplay (which works out at a whopping $26,315 a minute), he was overpaid, and viewers certainly did not receive value for money.

'*Jade* tries to hard to be a serious, lush *noir* but, like the cheap sex it revels in, it is ultimately a hollow, anti-climactic experience.'
Empire

'A long haul through a shoal of shoddy red herrings, with contrived shocks and suspense, coupled with understandably lacklustre performances.'
Daily Star

THE JANUARY MAN
(US 1989)
pc MGM. p Norman Jewison, Ezra

Swerdlow. assoc p Christopher Cook. d Pat O'Connor. w John Patrick Shanley. ph Jerzy Zielinski. Colour. ed Lou Lombardo. pd Philip Rosenberg. ad Dan Davies. sc Greg Walker. m Marvin Hamlisch. add m Moe Koffman. 97 mins

Cast: Kevin Kline (Nick Starkey), Susan Sarandon (Christine Starkey), Mary Elizabeth Mastrantonio (Bernadette Flynn), Harvey Keitel (Frank Starkey), Danny Aiello (Vincent Alcoa), Rod Steiger (Eamon Flynn), Alan Rickman (Ed), Faye Grant (Alison Hawkins), Kenneth Walsh (Roger Culver), Jayne Haynes (Alma), Tandy Cronyn (Lana)

An unorthodox New York policeman goes on the trail of a serial strangler.

Quirky comedy-thriller which just about gets by on sheer effrontery, with an unintentionally hilarious – and very bad – turn from Steiger.

'Baffling attempt to blend mystery, comedy and romance.'
Empire

JET STORM
(GB 1959)
pc Pendennis. A Steven Pallos-Cy Endfield Production. p Steven Pallos. d C Raker Endfield. w C Raker Endfield, Sigmund Miller. st Sigmund Miller. ph Jack Hildyard. B&W. ed Oswald Hafenrichter. ad Scott MacGregor. m Thomas Rajan. song Marty Wilde. 99 mins

Cast: Richard Attenborough (Ernest Tilley), Stanley Baker (Capt. Barrow), Diane Cilento (Angelica Como), Mai Zetterling (Carol Tilley), Hermione

Baddeley (Mrs Satterley), Virginia Maskell (Pam Leighton), Harry Secombe (Binky Meadows), Elizabeth Sellars (Inez Barrington), Sybil Thorndike (Emma Morgan), George Rose (James Brock), Megs Jenkins (Rose Brock), Patrick Allen (Mulliner), Marty Wilde (Billy Forrester), Bernard Braden (Otis Randolf), Barbara Kelly (Edwina Randolf), Paul Carpenter (George Towers)

A madman plants a bomb on board an airliner and threatens to detonate it over the Atlantic.

All-star suspenser pre-dating the *Airport* movies by at least a decade. The characters are one-dimensional, the dialogue is clichéd, but it is nevertheless very watchable.

'The result may not be great drama, but it certainly makes for a tense thriller with unusual interest-value.'
Picturegoer

JOE VALACHI: I SEGRETI DI COSA NOSTRA
(ITALY/FRANCE 1972) (US, GB: THE VALACHI PAPERS)
pc Euro France Films/Productions De Laurentiis Intermarco. exec p Nino E Krisman. p Dino De Laurentiis. d Terence Young. w Stephen Geller, from the book *The Valachi Papers* by Peter Maas. ph Aldo Tonti. Colour. ed John Dwyre. ad Mario Carbuglia. m Riz Ortolani. 127 mins

Cast: Charles Bronson (Joseph 'Joey Cago' Valachi), Mario Pilar (Salerno), Fred Valleca (Johnny Beck), Giacomino De Michelis (Little Augie), Arny Freeman (Warden, Atlanta Penitentiary), Gerald S O'Loughlin

(FBI Agent Ryan), Lino Ventura (Vito Genovese), Walter Chiari (Dominick 'The Gap' Petrilli), Joseph Wiseman (Salvatore Maranzano), Jill Ireland (Maria Valachi)

Convict Joe Valachi talks to an FBI agent about his life in the Mafia after gangster boss Vito Genovese puts out a $20,000 contact on him.

Flatulent, sloppy and over-long, with a flashback structure that adds further confusion to to the poor script and direction. Bloody and violent (for the time), with performances that range from the barely adequate (Bronson) to unbelievably awful (Wiseman). It was launched in the wake of *The Godfather*, and sank without trace.

'It takes considerable ineptitude to produce a gangster movie this energating. Every shrewd, image-conscious mobster should rush to endorse it, since organized crime emerges not as the traditional threat to society or vivid source of film melodrama and social criticism but simply as a crashing bore.'
The Washington Post

JOHNNY COOL

(US 1963)
pc Chrislaw. exec p Peter Lawford. p, d William Asher. assoc p Milton Ebbins. w Joseph Landon, from the novel *The Kingdom of Johnny Cool* by John McPartland. ph Sam Leavitt. B&W. ed Otto Ludwig. ad Frank T Smith. m Billy May. title song Sammy Cahn, Jimmy Van Heusen. 102 mins
Cast: Henry Silva (Johnny Cool/Giordano), Elizabeth Montgomery (Dare Guiness), Jim

Backus (Louis Murphy), Brad Dexter (Lennart Crandall), Marc Lawrence (Colini), John McGiver (Oby Hinds), Sammy Davis Jr (Educated), Gregory Morton (March), Mort Sahl (Ben Morro), Telly Savalas (Santangeolo), Wanda Hendrix (Miss Connolly), John Dierkes, Elisha Cook Jr, Robert Armstrong, Douglas Dumbrille (Gang Members), Joseph Calleia (Tourist)

An expatriate American gangster trains a young Sicilian bandit and sends him to the US to kill the men responsible for his deportation.

More cold than cool, with an unpleasantly impassive performance by Silva in a rare leading role. Interestingly cast, though, and efficient, heartless direction by Asher, who shows a considerable change in pace and style from his usual brainless AIP beach movies.

'Technically *Johnny Cool* is an interesting picture but the point of it is never clear. There is no moral attitude visible except that it is poor policy to buck the syndicate.'
The Hollywood Reporter

JOHNNY STOOL PIGEON

(US 1949)
pc Universal. p Aaron Rosenberg. d William Castle. w Robert L Richards. st Henry Jordan. ph Maury Gertsman. B&W. ed Ted J Kent. ad Bernard Herzbrun, Emrich Nicholson. sfx David S Horsley. m Milton Schwartzwald. 76 mins

Cast: Howard Duff (George Morton), Shelley Winters (Terry), Dan Duryea (Johnny Evans), Tony Curtis (Joey

Hayatt), John McIntire (Avery), Gar Moore (Sam Harrison), Leif Erickson (Pringle), Barry Kelley (McCandles), Hugh Reilly (Charlie), Wally Maher (Benson), Charles Drake (Hotel Clerk)

A jailed gangster helps a federal agent to infiltrate and break up a narcotics ring.

Competent, directed at a cracking pace by Castle in his pre-horror movie days, and rather better than its material.

'Brisk meller that will satisfy the action situations ... novel story treatment.'
Variety

JOURNEY INTO FEAR

(US 1942)
pc Mercury Productions. exec p George J Schaeffer. p Orson Welles. d Norman Foster, Orson Welles (uncredited). w Joseph Cotten, Orson Welles, from the novel by Eric Ambler. ph Karl Struss. B&W. ed Mark Robson. ad Albert D'Agostino, Mark-Lee Kirk. sfx Vernon L Walker. m Constantin Bakaleinikoff. 71 mins

Cast: Joseph Cotten (Howard Graham), Dolores Del Rio (Josette Martel), Orson Welles (Col. Maki), Ruth Warrick (Stephanie Graham), Agnes Moorehead (Mrs Mathews), Everett Sloane (Kopelkin), Jack Moss (Banat), Jack Durant (Gogo), Eustace Wyatt (Dr Haller), Frank Readick (Mathews)

A Turkish military official helps an American gunnery officer to escape from Turkey during World War Two.

A disappointment considering its

pedigree. Confused, with some thrills and moderate suspense, but the ending, reshot by Welles months after completion of principal photography, does little to ameliorate the prevailing incoherence. Poorly remade in 1975 with Sam Waterston in the Cotten role.

'This Mercury Players production does not reach the high standard of novelty or interest achieved by its predecessors; indeed, we find it rather difficult to believe that Orson Welles contributed much towards it.'
The Cinema

'It is good to see so likeable an entertainer as Welles making an unpretentious pleasure-picture; but to make a good one you need to be something of an artist, and Welles has little if any artistry.'
The Nation

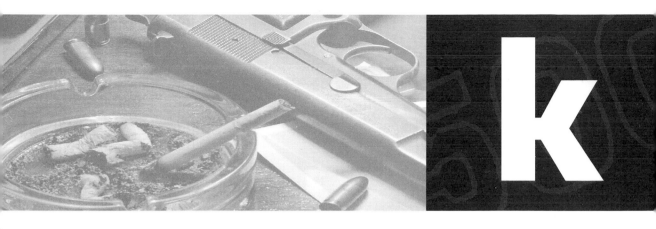

THE KIDNAPPING OF THE PRESIDENT

(CANADA 1979)

pc Sefel Pictures International. For Presidential Productions. exec p Joseph Seafel. p John Ryan, George Mendeluk. d George Mendeluk. 2nd unit d Larry Paul, Barry Pearson. w Richard Murphy, from the novel by Charles Templeton. st cons Barry Pearson. ph Michael Malloy. Colour. ed Michael McLaverty. ad Douglas Higgins. sfx Peter Hutchinson, Richard Albain. sfx m-u Greg Cannom. m Paul M Zaza. 113 mins

Cast: William Shatner (Jerry O'Connor), Hal Holbrook (President Scott), Van Johnson (Vice President Richards), Ava Gardner (Beth Richards), Miguel Fernandez (Roberto Assanti), Cindy Girling (Linda Steiner), Michael J Reynolds (MacKenzie), Elizabeth Shepherd (Joan Scott), Maury Chaykin (Harvey Cannon)

The American President is kidnapped by terrorists while on a state visit to Toronto and held to ransom in a booby-trapped security truck.

After the gory, exploitative opening sequence of terrorist carnage in the jungles of Argentina it settles down to a tense – if implausible – thriller with a naive view of politics that delivers what the title promises.

'Pure baloney, but with an element of uncomfortable realism around the edges ... you get the feeling that it could all just happen.'
Cosmopolitan+

KILL HER GENTLY

(GB 1958)

pc Fortress. p Guido Coen. d Charles Saunders. w Paul Erickson. ph Walter J Harvey. B&W. ed Margery Saunders. ad Harry White. m Edwin Astley. 75 mins

Cast: Griffith Jones (Jeff Martin), Maureen Connell (Kay Martin), Marc Lawrence (William Connors), George Mikell (Lars Svenson), Shay Gorman (Dr Landers), Marianne Brauns (Raina), Frank Hawkins (Inspector)

A madman hires two escaped convicts to kills his wife.

Typical fifties British B-picture with a derivative plot and a token American (Lawrence). Adequate of its type. (Later cut to 63 minutes.)

'On the whole the average material produces a moderately effective second-feature thriller for the masses.'
CEA Film Report

THE KILLER ELITE

(US 1975)

pc Exeter Associates/Persky-Bright. An Arthur Lewis-Baum/Dantine production. exec p Helmut Dantine. p Martin Baum, Arthur Lewis. assoc p, p sup Joel Freeman. d Sam Peckinpah. 2nd unit d Frank Kowalski. w Marc Norman, Stirling Silliphant, from the novel *Monkey in the Middle* by Robert Rostand. ph Phil Lathrop. 2nd unit ph Duke Callaghan. Colour. Panavision. sup ed Garth Craven. ed Tony De Zarraga, Monte Hellman. pd Ted Haworth. sfx Sass Bedig. sc Whitey Hughes. m Jerry Fielding. 120 mins

Cast: James Caan (Mike Locken), Robert Duvall (George Hansen), Arthur Hill (Cap Collis), Gig Young (Lawrence Weyburn), Mako (Yuen Chung), Bo Hopkins (Jerome Miller), Burt Young (Mac), Tom Clancy (O'Leary), Tiana (Tommy Chung), Kate Heflin (Amy), Sondra Blake (Josephine), Helmut Dantine (Vorodny), Matthew Peckinpah (Mat)

Mercenaries fall out and end up on opposite sides of a bloodbath involving the CIA and Japanese assassins in America.

A waste of Peckinpah, who makes the action vivid and exciting but can do nothing (who could?) with the daft, over-convoluted plot, which throws the CIA, sword-wielding Japanese killers and martial arts mayhem and double-crossing galore into the indigestible stew, and whose sole *coup de cinéma* was killing its executive producer (and former actor), Helmut Dantine, early on.

'Craftily marrying the martial arts fad to the anti-CIA craze to produce a sort of *Enter the Dragon meets Three Days of the Condor*, the script is of course a mixture of opportunism and joke ... compared to Peckinpah's last two shamefully mistreated masterpieces, *Pat Garrett and Billy the Kid* and *Bring Me the Head of Alfredo Garcia*, *The Killer Elite* is merely a commercial chore, but one that is infinitely less faceless than *The Getaway*.'
Monthly Film Bulletin

THE KILLERS

(US 1946)
pc Universal. p Mark Hellinger. d Robert Siodmak. w Anthony Veiller, (uncredited) John Huston, from the short story by Ernest Hemingway. ph Woody Bredell. sfx ph David s Horsley. B&W. ed Arthur Hilton. ad Jack Otterson, Martin Obzina. m Miklos Rosza. 105 mins

Cast: Edmond O'Brien (Riordan), Ava Gardner (Kitty Collins), Albert Dekker (Colfax), Burt Lancaster (Swede), Sam Levene (Luninsky), John Miljan (Jake), Virginia Christine (Lilly), Vince Barnett (Charleston), Charles D Brown (Packy), Donald MacBride (Kenyon), Phil Brown (Nick), Charles McGraw (Al), William Conrad (Max), Charles Middleton (Farmer Brown)

A boxer offers no resistance when two gangsters track him down to a small town and shoot him, and an insurance investigator unravels the motive for the murder.

Lancaster made a powerful and charismatic screen debut as the fatalistic murder victim, and O'Brien (the investigator) and Gardner (as a corrupt and corrupted *femme fatale*) make strong impressions. Flashbacks give it a sometimes spurious depth. Subsequent viewings suffer from the law of diminishing returns and tend to show there is less than meets the eye, and the Hemingway story simply serves as a prologue to the core of the drama. Remade in 1964 (q.v.).

'Seldom does a melodrama maintain the high tension that distinguishes this one.'
Variety

'It piles one tense situation upon another until *Dillinger* is a bedtime story in comparison.'
Kine Weekly

THE KILLERS

(US 1964)
pc Revue/Universal International. p, d Donald Siegel. w Gene L Coon, from the short story by Ernest Hemingway. ph Richard L Rawlings. Colour. ed Richard Belding. ad Frank Arrigo, George Chan. tech adv Hall Brock. m Johnny Williams. song *Too Little Time* by Henry Mancini, Don Raye. 95 mins

Cast: Lee Marvin (Charlie), Angie Dickinson (Sheila Farr), John Cassavetes (Johnny North), Ronald Reagan (Browning), Clu Gulager (Lee), Claude Akins (Earl Sylvester), Norman Fell (Mickey), Virginia Christine (Miss Watson), Don Haggerty (Mail Truck Driver), Robert Philips (George), Seymour Cassell (Desk Clerk)

Two hired hitmen shoot a man, who makes no attempt to escape in spite of having been warned. The killers investigate to find the reason for his fatalism.

Tough, unsubtle and overrated remake of the 1946 film (q.v.), and even further removed from the Hemingway original. The Universal Studios backlot streets are less than convincing, and Siegel's direction, while firm, is not particularly inspired. There are compensations in the vivid acting of Marvin and Gulager as the killers, and a fascinating performance by Reagan as a criminal mastermind: it was his final film before entering full-time politics and achieving greater international stardom in his greatest role.

Filmed as a made-for-television movie, it was deemed to be too violent for the small screen and was given a theatrical release. Virginia Christine, incidentally, appeared in both versions.

'A sizzling, tense, electrically charged adventure in melodrama.'
The Film Daily

93 minutes of sock-em-in-the-mouth rough stuff that beats the original story to a bloody pulp.'
Newsweek

KILLER'S KISS

(US 1955)

pc Stanley Kubrick. p Stanley Kubrick, Morris Bousel. d, w, ph, ed Stanley Kubrick. B&W. m Gerald Fried. choreo David Vaughan. 67 mins

Cast: Frank Silvera (Vincent Rapallo), Jamie Smith (Davy Gordon), Irene Kane (Gloria Price), Jerry Jarret (Albert, Fight Manager). Mike Dana, Felice Orlandi, Ralph Roberts, Phil Stevenson (Hoodlums), Julius Adelman (Mannequin Factory Owner), David Vaughan, Alec Rubin (Conventioneers)

An unsuccessful boxer falls for a dance hall hostess who is the mistress of her boss, and murder and kidnapping result.

Kubrick's second feature, filmed largely on location in New York for $75,000 (raised from his family and friends), shows an excellent understanding of character and involves some interesting location work. Unfortunately, his overuse of flashbacks and an ill-judged nightmare sequence shown in negative dilute the impact. More interesting in terms of his overall canon than for its minor inherent virtues. Kubrick's then wife, Ruth Sobotka, appears in a ballet sequence.

Killer's Kiss served as the (largely fictional) background for 1984's *Stranger's Kiss*.

'Producer-director-writer-editor Stanley Kubrick appears here to have tried to substitute freshness of approach *à la* Orson Welles for stars and costly production values. The result is certainly different than the average commercial film that is, but it fails to be fresh or incidentally entertaining.'
The Film Daily

THE KILLING

(US 1956)

pc Harris-Kubrick Productions. p James B Harris. d, w Stanley Kubrick, from the novel *Clean Break* by Lionel White. add dial Jim Thompson. ph Lucien Ballard. B&W. ed Betty Steinberg. ad Ruth Sobotka Kubrick. m Gerald Fried. 84 mins

Cast: Sterling Hayden (Johnny Clay), Jay C Flippen (Marvin Unger), Marie Windsor (Sherry Peatty), Elisha Cook Jr (George Peatty), Colleen Gray (Fay), Vince Edwards (Val Cannon), Ted de Corsia (Randy Kennan), Joe Sawyer (Mike O'Reilly), Tim Carey (Nikki Arane), Jay Adler (Leo), Joseph Turkell (Tiny)

A former convict plans the ingenious robbery of $2 million from a heavily-guarded racetrack, but he and his accomplices are ultimately betrayed.

Minor low-budget classic, and arguably (with *Paths of Glory* and *Spartacus*) Kubrick's least self-consciously pretentious film, vividly handled, with exemplary use of flashbacks and excellent performances, notably those of Cook Jr, Windsor and de Corsia. *The Asphalt Jungle* revisited in fine second-feature style.

'Harris and Kubrick are two very talented young men who know how to create a motion picture and, even more important, how to assemble the kind of talent that will help them achieve their objectives. It will be interesting to see what they can do with a bigger picture because they are inevitably going to be doing them.'
The Hollywood Reporter

'Though *The Killing* is composed of familiar ingredients and it calls for further explanations, it evolves as a fairly diverting melodrama.'
The New York Times

KILLING ZOE

(US 1994)

pc A Davis Film Production. exec p Becka Boss, Quentin Tarantino, Lawrence Bender. p Samuel Hadida. d, w Roger Avary. ph Tom Richmond. Colour. ed Kathryn Himoff. pd David Wasco. ad Charles Collum. m-u sfx Tom Savini. m Tomandandy. 96 mins

Cast: Eric Stoltz (Zed), Julie Delpy (Zoe), Jean-Hugues Anglade (Eric), Gary Kemp (Oliver), Bruce Ramsay (Ricardo), Kario Salem (Jean), Tai Thai (François), Salvator Xuereb (Claude), Gian Carlo Scandiuzzi (Bank Manager), Cecilia Peck (Martina), Eric Pascal Chaltei (Bellboy)

An American ex-convict goes to Paris to take part in a big bank robbery which goes badly wrong.

Executive producer Quentin Tarantino's one-time video store colleague turned screenplay collaborator (*Pulp Fiction*) Avary takes a stab at direction which strikes oceans of blood on screen but fatally misses on every other count, apart from vestigial, ill-remembered memories of other and better genre films. In other words, a true Tarantino acolyte. Avary's

THE KILLING

embarrassingly portentous dialogue has the profundity of a fortune cookie without its concomitant depth, the acting is even less convincing, and, unless over-abundance of gratuitous nastiness rather than accomplishment is counted a cinematic virtue, his debut is well worth missing.

'Has the bloodshed and pretensions down pat, but in other respects it is noticeably slack ... it wears its excess- es as a sign of daring, and it revels in a near-sexual enjoyment of events inside the bank, turning one slow-motion shooting into an ecstatic moment that would have given Sam Peckinpah pause.'
The New York Times

KISS ME DEADLY

(US 1955)
pc Parklane Productions. exec p Victor Saville. p, d Robert Aldrich. w A I Bezzerides, from the novel by Mickey Spillane. ph Ernest Laszlo. B&W. ed Michael Luciano. ad William Glasgow. m Frank DeVol. song *Rather Have The Blues* by Frank DeVol, sung by Nat 'King' Cole. 105 mins

Cast: Ralph Meeker (Mike Hammer), Albert Dekker (Dr Soberin), Paul Stewart (Carl Evello), Maxine Cooper (Velda), Gaby Rogers (Gabrielle/Lily Carver), Wesley Addy (Pat), Juano

Hernandez (Eddie Yeager), Nick Dennis (Nick), Cloris Leachman (Christina), Marian Carr (Friday), Jack Lambert (Sugar), Jack Elam (Charlie Max), Percy Helton (Mortuary Doctor)

A private eye picks up a woman escapee from a mental home and is pitchforked into a bizarre slew of hoods, homicide and a sinister nuclear device dubbed 'the great whatsit'.

Aldrich certainly deserved congratulations for turning a trashy Spillane novel into a hard-boiled, atmospherically-photographed *film noir* that was hailed as great art in some critical quarters and a prime case of the Emperor's New Clothes in others. It is luridly over-directed, strains far too hard for significance and, while never boring, the narrative is often confusing. The violence was surprisingly sadistic for the fifties.

'A series of amorous dames, murder-minded plug-uglies and dangerous adventures that offer excitement but have little clarity to let the viewer know what's going on.'
Variety

'If this production had not been made so relentlessly "arty", it might have been thoroughly artistic.'
The Hollywood Reporter

KISS OF DEATH
(US 1947)
pc 20th Century Fox. p Fred Kohlmar. d Henry Hathaway. w Ben Hecht, Charles Lederer. st Eleazar Lipsky. ph Norbert Brodine. B&W. ed J Watson Webb Jr. ad Lyle Wheeler, Leland Fuller. sfx Fred Sersen. m David Buttolph. 99 mins

Cast: Victor Mature (Nick Bianco), Brian Donlevy (D'Angelo), Colleen Gray (Nettie), Richard Widmark (Tom Udo), Taylor Holmes (Earl Howser), Howard Smith (Warden), Karl Malden (Sgt William Cullen), Anthony Ross (Williams), Mildred Dunnock (Mrs Rizzo), Millard Mitchell (Max Schultz), Temple Texas (Blondie)

An ex-convict persuaded by a District Attorney to turn informer is hunted by a psychopathic killer.

Well-made and punchily directed by Hathaway, mostly on location in New York, and atmospherically photographed by Norbert Brodine. Widmark made his memorable screen debut as a giggling and sadistic psychopath. Remade as the 1958 Western *The Fiend Who Walked the West* and, as *Kiss of Death*, in 1995.

'Tensely-made underworld thriller; but Hollywood's mischievously false values once more destroy its moral tone ... best thing in the picture is a new personality, Richard Widmark, who, as a grinning, ruthless killer, delivers the most chilling study of vileness seen for a long time.'
Daily Herald

KISS TOMORROW GOODBYE
(US 1950)
pc WB. p William Cagney. d Gordon Douglas. w Harry Brown, from the novel by Horace McCoy. ph Peverell Marley. B&W. ed Truman K Wood, Walter Hannemann. ad Wiard Ihnen. m Carmen Dragon. 102 mins

Cast: James Cagney (Ralph Cotter), Barbara Payton (Holiday Carleton), Helena Carter (Margaret Dobson),

Ward Bond (Insp. Webber), Luther Adler (Cherokee Mandon), Barton MacLane (Reece), Steve Brodie (Jinx Raynor), Rhys Williams (Vic Mason), Herbert Heyes (Ezra Dobson), Neville Brand (Carleton)

A brutal killer breaks out of jail and returns to a life of crime until the law finally catches up with him.

Violent thriller made to cash in on the success of *White Heat* (1949, q.v.), which emerges are rather more of a parody than one imagines was intended, despite a feisty turn by Cagney.

'On the whole, an unpleasant and rather complicated narrative, which certainly does not do James Cagney, nor any of the artists concerned, justice, in spite of its high production values.'
Picturegoer

KLUTE
(US 1971)
pc WB. p, d Alan J Pakula. assoc p C Kenneth Deland. w Andy K Lewis, Dave Lewis. ph Gordon Willis. Colour. Panavision. ed Carl Lerner. ad George Jenkins. m Michael Small. 114 mins

Cast: Jane Fonda (Bree Daniel), Donald Sutherland (John Klute), Charles Cioffi (Cable), Roy Scheider (Frank Ligourin), Dorothy Tristan (Arlyn Page), Rita Gam (Trina), Vivian Nathan (Psychiatrist), Nathan George (Lt Trask), Morris Strassberg (Mr Goldberg), Barry Snider (Berger)

A private eye searching for a missing scientist is led to a high-class New York

call girl who once had the man as
a client.

Pakula takes a fairly predictable
plot and turns it into engrossing
drama, thanks to a clever screenplay
and an Oscar-winning performance by
Fonda as the actress and model turned
prostitute. The sex scenes do it no
harm either. Sutherland's lugubrious
shamus is little more than a cipher and
a lot more than a bore, and the film
itself has dated badly.

'The film's wandering through the
sordid side of urban life come across
more as titillation than logical dramatic exposition. The only rewarding
element is Miss Fonda's performance.'
Variety

'Tepid, rather tasteless mush.'
The New York Times

LA DAME DANS L'AUTO AVEC LES LUNETTES ET UN FUSIL

(FRANCE 1970) (US, GB: THE LADY IN THE CAR WITH GLASSES AND A GUN)

pc Lira Film/Columbia. p Raymond Danon, Anatole Litvak. d Anatole Litvak. w Richard Harris, Eleanor Perry, from the novel by Sébastien Japrisot. ph Claude Renoir. Colour. Panavision. ad Willy Holt. m Michel Legrand. song *On The Road* by Michel Legrand, Hal Shaper, sung by Petula Clark. 105 mins

Cast: Samantha Eggar (Dany Lang), Oliver Reed (Michael Caldwell), John McEnery (Philip), Stéphane Audran (Anita Caldwell), Billie Dixon (Secetary), Bernard Fresson (Jean), Philippe Nicaud (Highway Policeman), Marcel Bozzuffi (Manuel), Jacques Fabbri (Doctor), Yves Pignot (Baptisin)

An English secretary working in Paris ends up involved in murder when she agrees to drive her employer's car back from the airport.

Convoluted, totally unbelievable suspenser which puts everything on Eggar's shoulders. Unfortunately, she proves inadequate to the task, although the direction and screenplay give her little help.

'An inflated, foggy, complicated thriller with some suspense and colour, but a let-down ending. For undemanding audiences.'
Kine Weekly

LA MARIÉE ÉTAIT EN NOIR

(FRANCE/ITALY 1967) (US, GB: THE BRIDE WORE BLACK)

pc Les Films du Carosse/Artistes Associés/Dino De Laurentiis Cinematografica. p Marcel Herbert. d François Truffaut. w François Truffaut, Jean-Louis Richard, from the novel *The Bride Wore Black* by William Irish (rn Cornell Woolrich). ph Raoul Coutard. Colour. ed Claudine Bouché. ad Pierre Guffroy. m Bernard Herrmann. 107 mins

Cast: Jeanne Moreau (Julie Kohler), Jean-Claude Brialy (Corey), Michel Bouquet (Robert Coral), Charles Denner (Fergus), Claude Rich (Bliss), Daniel Boulanger (Holmes), Michel Lonsdale (René Morane), Serge Rousseau (David), Jacques Robiolles (Charlie), Luce Fabiole (Julie's mother), Van Doude (Insp. Fabri), Sylvie Delannoy (Mrs Morane), Alexandra Stewart (Miss Becker)

A woman seeks revenge against the man who shot her husband on their wedding day.

Impressive and informed *hommage* to Hitchcock, complete with a Bernard Herrmann score, sharply directed with an equal eye to humour and suspense, and boasting fine leading performances.

'It is not a great, great picture but it is touching and fun at a level so much higher than other films that it is just a great relief to have it to see.'
The New York Times

LADY IN CEMENT

(US 1968)

pc Arcola/Millfield. p Aaron Rosenberg. d Gordon Douglas. underwater sequence d Ricou Browning. w Marvin H Albert. Jack Guss, from the novel by Marvin H

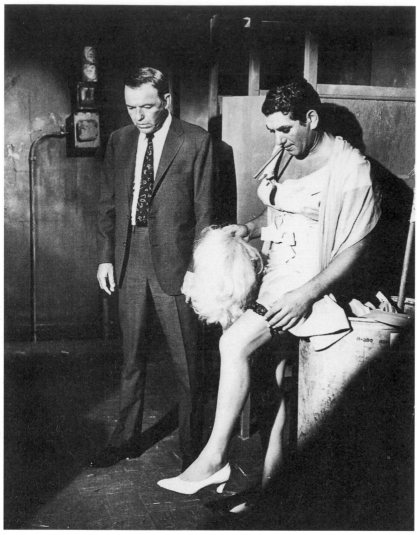

LADY IN CEMENT

Albert. ph Joseph Biroc. sfx ph L B Abbott, Art Cruikshank. Colour. Panavision. ed Leroy Deane. m Hugo Montenegro. 93 mins

Cast: Frank Sinatra (Tony Rome), Raquel Welch (Kit Forrest), Richard Conte (Lt Santini), Dan Blocker (Earl Gronsky), Martin Gabel (Al Mungar), Lainie Kazan (Maria Baretto), Pat Henry (Hal Rubin), Steve Peck (Paul Mungar), Virginia Wood (Audrey), Richard Deacon (Arnie Sherwin),

Alex Stevens (Shev)

An ex-convict hires private eye Tony Rome to find out if a girl found naked with her feet encased in a block of concrete at the bottom of Biscayne Bay is his missing girlfriend.

'The sum total of this mess of pseudo-reality wil be titillation for some, repulsion for those looking for the slightest relationship to the human condition.'
Film and Television Daily

THE LADY VANISHES
(GB 1938)

pc Gainsborough. p Edward Black. d Alfred Hitchcock. w Sidney Gilliat, Frank Launder, from the novel *The Wheel Spins* by Ethel Lina White. add dial. Alma Reville. ph Jack Cox. B&W. ed Alfred Roome, R E Dearing. ad Alec Vetchninsky, Maurice Carter, Albert Juillon. m Louis Levy. 97 mins

Cast: Margaret Lockwood (Iris Henderson), Michael Redgrave (Gilbert), Paul Lukas (Dr Hartz), Dame May Whitty (Miss Froy), Googie Withers (Blanche), Cecil Parker (Mr Todhunter), Linden Travers (Mrs Todhunter), Mary Clare (The Baroness), Naunton Wayne (Caldicott) Basil Radford (Charters)

A young woman and an amateur musicologist returning to England from Switzerland are involved in international espionage when a fellow passenger is kidnapped by foreign spies.

Ingenious, fast-paced and wittily-scripted, and the best of Hitchcock's pre-war thrillers. The original director was American Roy William Neill: when he quit, Hitchcock took over and shot the entire film on a 90 foot-long sound stage at Islington Studios in north London, using a single railway carriage and a mixture of miniatures and back projection to create 'locations'. Redgrave, who was appearing on stage in London while filming took place, made his initially reluctant screen debut, and the acting throughout is excellent, with Wayne and Radford standing out as the cricket-mad Charters and Caldicott, who, concerned to get back to England for the last day of the Test Match, blithely

nore the skulduggery all around
hem. The suspense rarely lets up.
Iitchcock made his traditional cameo
appearance hurrying along the
platform at Victoria Station. The
dismal 1979 remake (q.v.)
demonstrates Hitchcock's superiority
in every department.

A brilliantly handled and briskly played
slice of mystery drama, consistently
gripping, not only well textured with
suspense and punctuated with dramatic action but subtly and refreshingly flavoured with a most delectable

quality.'
Motion Picture Herald

'Well, Hitchcock has done it again …
possibly the best, certainly the most
successful of all his pictures …
Hitchcock plays up to the full the chill
and panic of the situation.'
The Observer

'If it were not so brilliant a melodrama, we should class it as a brilliant
comedy. Seeing it imposes a double, a
blessedly double, strain: when your
sides are not aching from laughter

your brain is throbbing in its attempts
to outguess the director.'
The New York Times

THE LADY VANISHES

(GB 1979)
pc Hammer Films. For Rank Film
Productions. exec p Michael Carreras,
Arlene Sellers, Alex Winitsky. p Tom
Sachs. d Anthony Page. w George
Axelrod, from the novel *The Wheel
Spins* by Ethel Lina White & the
screenplay by Frank Launder & Sidney
Gilliat. ph Douglas Slocombe. 2nd unit
ph John Harris. Colour. Panavision. ed

THE LADY VANISHES

LAS VEGAS, 500 MILLIONES

Russell Lloyd, pd Wilfred Shingleton. ad Bill Alexander, George von Kieseritzky. sfx Martin Gutteridge. m Richard Hartley. 97 mins

Cast: Elliott Gould (Robert Condon), Cybill Shepherd (Amanda Kelly), Angela Lansbury (Miss Froy), Herbert Lom (Dr Hartz), Arthur Lowe (Charters), Ian Carmichael (Caldicott), Gerald Harper (Mr Todhunter), Jean Anderson (Baroness Kisling), Jenny Runacre (Mrs Todhunter), Vladek Sheybal (Trainmaster)

A *Life* magazine reporter and a three-times-married American heiress deal with Nazi spies when a fellow passenger is kidnapped on board a train travelling from Germany to England in 1939.

More ham than Hammer. Unwise and unwelcome: the miscast leads are leaden, the script is diffuse, and Page is no Hitchcock. Only Lowe and Carmichael as the cricket-obsessed Englishmen emerge with any credit.

'A mid-Atlantic mish-mash with some moderately amusing moments but no cohesive style. Slapstick hokum, bland suspense and mystery elements that will fool almost no one add up to a heavy-handed affair.'
Variety.

LAS VEGAS, 500 MIL-LIONES/LES HOMMES DE LAS VEGAS/AN EINEM FRE-ITAG IN LAS VEGAS/RADI-OGRAFIA D'UN COLPO D'ORO (SPAIN/ FRANCE/WEST GER-MANY/ITALY 1968) (US, GB: THEY CAME TO ROB LAS VEGAS)

pc Isasi/Capitole/Eichberg Film/Franca Film. exec p Nat Waschberger. d Antonio Isasi. w Antonio Isasi, Jo Eisinger, L Comeron, J Illa. dial Jo Eisinger. ph Juan Gelpi. Colour. Techniscope. ed Elena Jaumandreu, Emilio Rodriguez. ad Tony Cortes, Juan Alberto. sfx Antonio Baquero. m Georges Garaventz. 129 mins

Cast: Gary Lockwood (Tony), Elke Sommer (Anne), Lee J Cobb (Skorsky), Jack Palance (Douglas), Georges Géret (Leroy), Gustavo Re (Salvatore), Daniel Martin (Merino), Jean Servais (Gino), Roger Hanin (The Boss), Maurizio Arena (Clark), Armand Mestral (Mass), Fabrizio Capucci (Cooper)

A gang robs a security truck carrying money from Las Vegas casinos and becomes involved with the Mafia and US Treasury agents.

Over-long European mock-American crime caper, lethargically executed.

'All pretty predictable, updating the basic B-Western plot, and some fast cutting during the various gunplays only tends to confuse the action.'
Films and Filming

THE LAST GANGSTER
(US 1937)
pc MGM. p J J Cohn. d Edward Ludwig. w John Lee Mahin. st William A Wellman, Robert Carson. ph William Daniels. B&W. ed Ben Lewis. ad Cedric Gibbons, Danieth Cathcart. montages Slavko Vorkapich. 81 mins

Cast: Edward G Robinson (Joe Krozac), James Stewart (Paul North Sr), Rose Stradner (Talya Krozac), Lionel Stander (Curly), Douglas Scott (Paul North Jr), John Carradine (Casper), Sidney Blackmer (San Francisco Editor), Edward Brophy (Fats Garvey), Alan Baxter (Frankie 'Acey' Kile), Grant Mitchell (Warden)

A gangster gets out of jail after ten years and seeks revenge on his wife for deserting him.

Languid direction makes less of the drama than the script and cast warrant but Robinson's performance has its compensations.

'It is eminently fitting that Edward G Robinson should be the hero of what we fervently hope is the last Hollywood gangster film.'
The New York Times

LAST MAN STANDING
(US 1996)
pc New Line Productions/Lone Wolf. exec p Sara Risher, Michael de Luca. p Walter Hill, Arthur Sarkissian. co-p Ralph Singleton. assoc p Paula Heller. d, w Walter Hill, from a story by Akira Kurosawa & Ryuzo Kikushima. ph Lloyd Ahern. Panavision. Colour. ed Freeman Davies. pd Gary Wisner. ad Barry Chusid. sc Allan Graf. m Ry Cooder. 100 mins

Cast: Bruce Willis (John Smith), Christopher Walken (Hickey), Bruce Dern (Sheriff Ed Galt), Alexandra Powers (Lucy), David Patrick Kelly (Doyle), William Sanderson (Joe Monday), Karina Lombard (Felina), Ned Eisenberg (Strozzi), Leslie Mann (Wanda), Michael Imperioli (Giorgio), R D Call (McCool), Ken Jenkins (Capt. Pickett)

stranger sets rival gangs of bootleggers running a small Texas border town during Prohibition at each other's throats.

Hill made a welcome return to form, smartly reworking Kurosawa's 1961 classic *Yojimbo* (remade in 1964 as Leone's seminal spaghetti Western *A Fistful of Dollars*) as a bloody gangster opus with an awesome expenditure of ammunition and huge body count that would not disgrace a minor civil war, and brilliantly-staged action and gunfights. Characterization is by-the-book but satisfactory

'Confrontations, shoot-outs, tension and violence create an adrenaline high that lasts all the way to the climactic confrontation.'
Daily Star

'As predictable as it is perfunctory.'
Variety

THE LAST MILE
(US 1932)
pc KBS Film Co./World Wide Pictures. p E W Hammons. d Sam Bischoff. w Seton I Miller, from the play by John Wexley. ph Arthur Edeson. B&W. ed Martin G Cohn, Rose Loewinger. ad Ralph DeLacy. md Val Burton. 84 mins

Cast: Howard Philips (Richard Walters), Preston S Foster (Killer Mears), George E Stone (Berg), Noel Madison (D'Amoro), Alan Roscoe (Kirby), Paul Fix (Werner), Al Hill (Mayer), Daniel L Haynes (Jackson), Frank Sheridan (Warden Lewis), Alec B Francis (Father O'Connor), Edward Van Sloan (Rabbi)

Killers awaiting execution on Death Row stage a doomed revolt.

Vigorous, although lacking the dramatic punch of the stage original.

'Picture is depressing, prison and death being two things the mass of normal people put away from their thoughts.'
Variety

THE LAST MILE
(US 1959)
pc Vanguard. p Max J Rosenberg, Milton Subotsky. assoc p Robert Hodes, Herman Klappert. d Howard W Koch. w Milton Subotsky, Seton I Miller, from the play by John Wexley. ph Joseph Biroc. B&W. ed Robert Brockman, Patricia Jaffe. ad Paul Barnes. sfx Milton Olson, Vincent Brady. m Van Alexander. 81 mins

Cast: Mickey Rooney ('Killer' John Mears), Clifford David (Richard Walters), Frank Conroy (O'Flaherty), Frank Overton (Father O'Connors), Leon Janney (Callagan), Donald Barry (Drake), Alan Bunce (Warden), Harry Millard (Fred Mayor), Michael Constantine (Ed Warner), Ford Rainey (Red Kirby), Milton Seltzer (Peddie)

Men awaiting execution on Death Row plan a revolt.

Grim (for the period) and powerful, if somewhat under-cast, film of the play that brought stage stardom to Spencer Tracy and Clark Gable. Preston Foster starred in the 1932 film (q.v.). Koch directs in an appropriately downbeat style, and Rooney is surprisingly effective.

'It is difficult to discern the entertain-ment value of such bestiality, except that the later scenes might appeal to masculine devotees of tough fare.' *CEA Film Report*

'Packs quite a wallop.'
Variety

THE LAST OF SHEILA
(US 1973)
pc WB. exec p Stanley O'Toole. p, d Herbert Ross. w Stephen Sondheim, Anthony Perkins. ph Gerry Turpin. Colour. ed Edward Warschilka. pd Ken Adam. ad Tony Roman. m Billy Goldenberg. song *Friends* sung by Bette Midler. 123 mins

Cast: Richard Benjamin (Tom), Dyan Cannon (Christine), James Coburn (Clinton Greene), Joan Hackett (Lee), James Mason (Philip), Ian McShane (Anthony), Raquel Welch (Alice), Yvonne Romain (Sheila Greene), Pierro Rosso (Vittorio)

A Hollywood producer invites six friends on a Mediterranean yacht cruise in order to discover who killed his wife a year previously.

Relentlessly camp and cuter than a chorus girl on the make, this film's convoluted and self-satisfied screenplay filled with twists and red herrings must have been a shriek to write but is largely uninvolving. It is like being at a party where you know nobody, and everyone else is determined to enjoy themselves without allowing you to join in the fun.

'Films like this make one wonder how movies ever caught on. Or if they will continue to do so.'
The Guardian

THE LAST SHOT YOU HEAR
(GB 1968)
pc Lippert Films. exec p Robert Lippert, p Jack Parsons. d Gordon Hessler. w Tim Shields, from the play *The Sound of Murder* by William Fairchild. ph David Holmes. B&W. ed Robert Winter. ad Ken Ryan. m Bert Shefter. song Bert Shefter, Stella Stevens, sung by Stella Stevens.
90 mins

Cast: Hugh Marlowe (Charles Nordeck), Zena Walker (Eileen), Patricia Haines (Anne Nordeck), William Dysart (Peter Marriott), Thorley Walters (Gen. Jowett), Lionel Murton (Ruben), Helen Horton (Dodie Rubens), John Nettleton (Nash), John Wentworth (Chambers), Alistair Williamson (CID Officer)

A woman and her lover plan the murder of her marriage guidance counsellor husband.

Banal B-feature throwback to the second features of the fifties, complete with a fading Hollywood star, and betraying its stage origins at every turn.

'Shoddily written, laboriously directed, and no suprises in the surprise twist ending.'
Sight and Sound

THE LATE SHOW
US 1977)
pc WB. p Robert Altman. assoc p Robert Eggenweiler, Scott Bushnell. d, w Robert Benton. ph Chuck Rosher. Colour. ed Lou Lombardo, Peter Appleton. set design Bob Gould. sc Paul Baxley. m Kenn Wannberg.
93 mins

Cast: Art Carney (Ira Wells), Lily Tomlin (Margo), Bill Macy (Charlie Hatter), Ruth Nelson (Mrs Schmidt), Howard Duff (Harry Regan), Joanna Cassidy (Laura Birdwell), Eugene Roche (Ron Birdwell), John Considine (Lamar), John Davey (Sgt Dayton)

An ageing, unwell private detective comes out of retirement to find out who killed his former partner.

Benton's directorial debut is a self-conscious and tedious homage to Chandler et al., burdened with a snail-paced screenplay and a typically irritating and mannered performance by Tomlin. The Los Angeles locations underline the essential redundancy of the proceedings.

'If the film, as a whole, never quite comes off it is because of the failure to establish the credibility of Lily Tomlin's character or of the relation-ship which develops between her and Caney, which is obviously intended to move beyond the realm of caricature.'
Films and Filming

THE LAUGHING POLICEMAN
(US 1973) (GB: AN INVESTIGATION OF MURDER)
pc 20th Century Fox. p, d Stuart Rosenberg. w Thomas Rickman, from the novel *Den Skrattande Polisen* by Maj Sjöwall, Per Wahlöö. ph David Walsh. Colour. ed Robert Wyman. ad Doug Von Koss. m Charles Fox. 112 mins

Cast: Walter Matthau (Jake Martin), Bruce Dern (Leo Larsen), Lou Gossett (James Larrimore), Albert Paulsen (Camerero), Anthony Zerbe (Lt Steiner), Val Avery (Pappas), Cathy Lee Crosby (Kay Butler), Mario Gallo (Bobby Mow), Joanna Cassidy (Monica), Shirley Ballard (Collins), Paul Koslo (Haygood)
San Francisco policemen hunt a mass murderer.

Sjöwall and Wahlöö's prize-winning novel is translated and transposed from Stockholm to San Francisco and loses in the transition, not helped by a confused screenplay and lacklustre direction. The locations help, though, and Dern is good.

'Incomprehensible thrillers are not always bad, but when they start out by insisting in a complexity that ends up simple, one is entitled to feel a bit peeved.'
The Observer

LAURA
(US 1944)
pc 20th Century Fox. p, d Otto Preminger. w Jay Dratler, Samuel Hoffenstein, Betty Reinhardt, from the novel by Vera Caspary. ph Joseph La Shelle. B&W. ed Louis Loeffler. ad Lyle Wheeler, Leland Fuller. sfx Fred Serson. m David Raksin. title song *Laura* by David Raksin, Johnny Mercer. 88 mins

Cast: Gene Tierney (Laura Hunt), Dana Andrews (Mark McPherson), Clifton Webb (Waldo Lydecker), Vincent Price (Shelby Carpenter), Judith Anderson (Ann Treadwell), Dorothy Adams (Bessie Clary), James Flavin (McAvity), Clyde Fillmore (Bullitt), Ralph Dunn (Fred Callahan), Grant Mitchell (Corey), Kathleen Howard (Louise)

A detective falls in love with the dead

woman whose murder he is investigating – fortunately, he turns out not to be a necrophile.

Smooth, stylish with a haunting theme and a satisfying denouement. The movie established Preminger (replacing Rouben Mamoulian, who had shot only a few scenes as director), and Webb's waspish portrait of a columnist brought him stardom. Hollywood Golden Age film-making at its best, burnished by Joseph La Shelle's atmospheric Oscar-winning monochrome cinematography.

'Well above the average in its own class. A murder story told with an intelligent deliberation and an effort to interest the audience in the personalities of the protagonists.'
The Times

'One of the best thrillers ever made, as good as *Double Indemnity*, better than *Casablanca* or *The Maltese Falcon* ... the plot is brilliantly contrived, the characters live, the dialogue is witty without being forced, laconic without a lot of hammy biting on the bullet.'
The Daily Telegraph

LE CERCLE ROUGE
(FRANCE/ITALY 1970) (US, GB: THE RED CIRCLE)
pc Corona/Selenia. p Robert Dorfman. d, w, p manager Jean-Pierre Melville. ph Henri Decae. Colour. ad Théo Meurisse. m Eric de Marsan. 150 mins

Cast: Alain Delon (Corey), André Bourvil (Mattei), Yves Montand Jensen), François Périer (Santi), Gian Maria Volonté (Vogel), André Eykan

(Rico), Pierre Collet (Prison Warder), Paul Crauchet (The Fence), Paul Amiot (Chief of Police), Jean Pierre Posier (Mattei's Assistant)
A criminal intends to go straight after five years in jail but soon reverts to wrongdoing.

Pallid European attempt to ape American crime thrillers, with an exciting robbery sequence. Otherwise simply a series of attractively-photographed picture-postcard views with uninteresting action in the foreground.

'Undoubtedly superior to the majority of thrillers that come our way.'
Films and Filming

LE SALAIRE DE LA PEUR
(FRANCE/ITALY 1953) (US, GB: THE WAGES OF FEAR)
pc Filmsonor/CICC/Vera Film/Fono Roma. p, d Henri-Georges Clouzot. w Henri-Georges Clouzot, Jérome Géronimo, from the novel by Georges Arnaud. ph Armand Thiraud. B&W. ed Madeleine Gug, Henri Rust, E Muse. ad Rene Renoux. m Georges Auric. 140 mins

Cast: Yves Montand (Mario), Charles Vanel (Jo), Vera Clouzot (Linda), Folco Lulli (Luigi), Peter Van Eyck (Bimba), William Tubbs (O'Brien), Antonio Centa (Chief, 'Boss' Camp), Mario Moreno (Hernandez), Jo Dest (Smerloff)

Four men stranded in a squalid South American oil town are hired to drive two trucks loaded with unstable nitroglycerine 300 miles over treacherous roads to a burning oil well.

Pessimistic, brilliantly-directed and riveting suspenser, with the drive – which takes up some two-thirds of the picture – reaching relentless, near-unbearable peaks of tension. It won the Grand Prix at the 1953 Cannes Film Festival. The 1977 remake *Sorcerer* (q.v.) was dismal.

'One of the greatest shockers of all time. The suspense it generates is close to prostrating. Clouzot is not interested in tingling the customer's spine, but rather in giving him the symptoms of a paralytic stroke.'
Time

'It is fine suspense stuff, the kind of film that should make Alfred Hitchcock, an expert in this thing, very jealous indeed.'
Daily Herald

THE LEAGUE OF GENTLEMEN
(GB 1959)
pc Allied Film Makers. p Michael Relph. d Basil Dearden. w Bryan Forbes, from the novel by John Boland. ph Arthur Ibbetson. B&W. ed John D Guthridge. ad Peter Proud. m Philip Green. 116 mins

Cast: Jack Hawkins (Mr Hyde), Nigel Patrick (Peter Race), Roger Livesey (Mycroft), Richard Attenborough (Lexy), Bryan Forbes (Porthill), Kieron Moore (Stevens), Robert Coote (Bunny Warren), Terence Alexander (Rupert), Melissa Stribling (Peggy), Norman Bird (Weaver), Patrick Wymark (Wylie), Nanette Newman (Elizabeth), David Lodge (CSM), Doris Hare (Molly Weaver), Gerald Harper (Capt. Saunders)

LEPKE

A redundant officer recruits seven ex-servicemen with shady pasts to execute a big bank robbery as a by-the-book military operation.

Ideally cast, witty, smartly directed and thoroughly entertaining crime caper. Sadly, prevailing censorship insisted that crime had to be seen to not to pay, thus ruining an otherwise excellent enterprise.

'A first class crook-thriller which has an ingenious story, well-maintained suspense, agreeable comedy relief, a vivid action sequence in the detail of the actual robbery, and extremely likeable characterization and occasionally pungent dialogue.'
CEA Film Report

LEPKE

(US 1974)
pc AmeriEuro Pictures Corporation. exec p Yoram Globus. p, d Menahem Golan. w Wesley Lau, Tamar Hoffs. st Wesley Lau. ph Andrew Davis. Colour. Panavision. ed Dov Hoenig, Aaron Stell. pd Jack Degovia. sfx Cliff Wenger. m Ken Wannberg. cos Jodie Tillen. 110 mins

Cast: Tony Curtis (Louis 'Lepke' Buchalter), Anjanette Comer (Bernice Meyer), Michael Callan (Robert Kane) Warren Berlinger (Gurrah Shapiro), Gianni Rosso (Albert Anastasia), Vic Tayback (Lucky Luciano), Mary Wilcox (Marion), Milton Berle (Mr Meyer), John Durren (Dutch Schultz), Erwin Fuller (J Edgar Hoover), Jack Ackerman (Little Augie), Louis Guss (Max Rubin)

ES DIABOLIQUES

he rise and fall of Jewish gangster
ouis 'Lepke' Buchalter.

A crude, cut-price, kosher version
f *The Godfather*, equally strewn with
orpses and clichés, and directed with a
udding absence of style, sympathy or
ophistication. Curtis's performance
ves hoodlums a bad name.

epke seems quite devoid of the kind
f zest and enthusiasm that any num-
er of B-grade variations on the theme
ave effortlessly attained.'
Monthly Film Bulletin

LES DIABOLIQUES
(FRANCE 1954) (US:
DIABOLIQUE, GB: THE FIENDS)
pc Filmsonor. p, d Henri-Georges
Clouzot. w Henri-Georges Clouzot, G
Geronomi, from the novel *The Woman
Who Was* by Pierre Boileau & Thomas
Narcejac. ph Armand Thiraud. B&W.
ed Madeleine Gug. ad Leon Barsacq.
m Georges Van Parys. 114 mins

Cast: Simone Signoret (Nicole
Horner), Vera Clouzot (Christina
Delasalle), Paul Meurisse (Michel

Delasalle), Charles Vanel (Insp.
Fichet), Pierre Larquey (Drain), Michel
Serrault (Raymond), Jean Brochard
(Plantiveau), Therese Dorney
(Madame Herboux), Noel Roquevert
(Herboux), Georges Poujouly
(Soudieu)

The wife of a schoolmaster and his
mistress plan his perfect murder, but
things go awry when his corpse
vanishes and the police start to
close in.

Classic, unbearably suspenseful

thriller with one of the most ingenious (and most recycled, notably by *Fatal Attraction*, q.v.) plot twists in the genre. The made-for-television remake, *Reflections of Murder* (1976), only served to underline the fact that the pre-eminence of *Les Diaboliques* is not simply a reflection of its clever plot, but owes considerably more to Clouzot's consummate direction and to the acting. One of Signoret's finest performances. The less said about the crass 1996 Sharon Stone-Isabelle Adjani remake, the better.

'One of the dandiest mystery dramas that has shown here in goodness knows when. To tell anybody the surprises that explode like shotgun blasts in the last reel is a crime that should be punishable by consigning the culprit to an endless diet of grade-B films.'
The New York Times

'I confess that I could sit through the film again, for more than curiosity's sake: for the quality of the narrative development. Clouzot fixes you, not with a glittering eye but with the eye of a mackerel two days dead; you cannot escape the dreadful hypnosis.'
The Sunday Times

LETHAL WEAPON
(US 1987)
pc WB/Silver Pictures. p Richard Donner, Joel Silver. assoc p Jennie Lew. d Richard Donner. w Shane Black. ph Stephen Goldblatt. underwater ph Frank Holgate, Ron Vidor. aerial ph Frank Holgate. Colour. Panavision. ed Stuart Baird. pd J Michael Riva. ad Eva Bohn, Virginia L Randolph. sfx co-ord Chuck Gaspar. sc Bobby Bass. m Michael

Kamen, Eric Clapton. 109 mins

Cast: Mel Gibson (Martin Riggs), Danny Glover (Roger Murtaugh), Gary Busey (Mr Joshua), Mitchell Ryan (Gen. McAllister), Tom Atkins (Michael Hunsaker), Darlene Love (Trish Murtaugh), Traci Wolfe (Rianne Murtaugh), Jackie Swanson (Amanda Hunsaker), Damon Hines (Nick Murtaugh), Ebonie Smith (Carrie Murtaugh)

A semi-suicidal Los Angeles cop and his straight-arrow partner break up a major drug-smuggling operation headed by a psychotic Vietnam veteran.

Attractive chemistry between the leads gives a welcome human dimension to a deftly-calculated, briskly-directed (if essentially unbelievable) melange of mayhem, thrills and violence in which the protagonists are as interesting as what happens to them. Sequels were inevitable.

'*Lethal Weapon* adroitly blends a whole range of current genres, stitching together bits and pieces of everything from buddy movies and cop thrillers to vigilante and Vietnam war films.'
Monthly Film Bulletin

'*Lethal Weapon* is one part "Rambo Comes Home" and one part *48 Hrs.* It's a film teetering on the brink of absurdity when it gets serious, but thanks to its unrelenting energy and insistent drive, it never quite falls.'
Variety

L'HOMME DE RIO/L'UOMO DI RIO
(France/Italy 1964)

pc Films Ariane/Productions Les Artistes Associés/Dear Film/Vides. p Alexandre Mnouchkine, Georges Dancigers. d Philippe de Broca. w J P Rappaneau, Ariane Mnouchkine, Daniel Boulanger, Philippe de Broca. dial Daniel Boulanger. ph Edmond Séchan. Colour ed Françoise Javet. m Georges Delerue. 114 mins

Cast: Jean-Paul Belmondo (Adrien Dufourquet), Françoise Dorleac (Agnés), Jean Servais (Prof. Catalan), Simone Renant (Lola), Milton Ribiero (Tupac), Ubiracy De Oliveira (Sir Winston), Adolfo Celi (Senor De Castro)

A Frenchman goes to Brazil to rescue his fiancée who has been kidnapped by crooks hunting for statuettes that hold the key to a fortune in gems.

Engaging and fast-moving, amusingly sending up genre conventions while creating vivid thrills of its own. Belmondo's swashbuckling exploits outdo Douglas Fairbanks and James Bond; the screenplay is inventive and De Broca rarely allows the breakneck pace to flag.

'Virtually every complication, every crisis involving imminent peril, that have ever been pulled in the movies, especially the old silent ones, is pulled in this. And they are pulled in such rapid continuity and so expansively played, with such elan and against such brilliant backgrounds, that they take your breath away.'
The New York Times

LICENCE TO KILL
(US 1988)
pc UA/Danjaq. p Albert R Broccoli,

Michael G Wilson. assoc p Tom Pevsner, Barbara Broccoli. d John Glen. 2nd unit d, ph Arthur Wooster. underwater d Ramon Bravo. w Michael G Wilson, Richard Maibaum. ph Alec Mills. aerial ph Phil Pastuhov. Colour. Panavision. ed John Grover, Carlos Puente, Matthew Glen. pd Peter Lamont. ad Michael Lamont, Dennis Bosher, Ken Court. fx sup John Richardson. stunt sup Paul Weston. m Michael Kamen. song *Licence to Kill* by Narada Michael Walden, Jeffrey Cohen, Walter Afanasieff, sung by Gladys Knight. titles Maurice Binder. 133 mins

Cast: Timothy Dalton (James Bond), Carey Lowell (Pam Bouvier), Robert Davi (Franz Sanchez), Talisa Soto (Lupe Lamora), Anthony Zerbe (Milton Krest), Frank McRae (Sharkey), Everett McGill (Killifer), Wayne Newton (Prof. Joe Butcher), Benicio Del Toro (Dario), Anthony Starke (Truman-Lodge), Pedro Armendariz Jr (President Hector Lopez), Desmond Llewellyn ('Q'), David Hedison (Felix Leiter), Robert Brown ('M'), Caroline Bliss (Miss Moneypenny), Don Stroud (Heller)

James Bond has his licence to kill revoked when he turns vigilante to avenge the near-murder of a friend.

Dalton, second time out as 007, consolidates his status as the best Bond since Connery: he gets on with the business in hand with physical vigour and without worrying, Moore-fashion, about how he looks.

The splendid pre-credits stunt is followed by plentiful action and an exciting climactic chase. The continued switch of emphasis from comedy and gimmicks to a strong storyline works well. David Hedison first played the role of Felix Leiter in *Live and Let Die* (1973, q.v.).

LICENCE TO KILL

'The people at the Bond factory have wisely gone easy on the indulgent in-jokery that threatened to smother the Bonds of the early 80s ... a simple biff-bang yarn which avoids getting bogged down in weapons fetishism and lifestyle shopping ... the action is well-handled.'
Empire

'A cocktail of high-octane action, spectacle and drama ... exotic settings now serve the narrative rather than provide a glossy travelogue.'
Variety

'The major difference between Dalton and the earlier Bonds is that he seems to prefer action to sex. But then so do movie audiences, these days. *Licence to Kill* is one of the best of the recent Bonds.'
Chicago Sun-Times

LIGHTNING STRIKES TWICE
(US 1951)
pc WB. p Henry Blanke. d King Vidor. w Lenore Coffe, from a novel by Margaret Echard. ph Sid Hickox. B&W. ed Thomas Reilly. ad Douglas Bacon. m Max Steiner. 91 mins

Cast: Richard Todd (Richard Trevelyan), Ruth Roman (Shelley Carnes), Mercedes McCambridge (Liza McStringer), Zachary Scott (Harvey Turner), Nacho Gallado (Pedro), Darryl Hickman (String), Frank Conroy (Nolan), Kathryn Givney (Myra Nolan), Rhys Williams (Father Paul)

A man is acquitted of murder, remarries, and his new wife starts to wonder if he is really a killer.

Low on suspense and thrills in spite of its creditable credits, with only an over-talky screenplay to punctuate the tedium.

'A veritable mouse of a picture ... Hollywood, as our Mr Todd might well reflect after this one, is not always, alas, the land of opportunity.'
Picturegoer

LITTLE CAESAR
(US 1931)
pc First National/WB. p Hal Wallis. d Mervyn LeRoy. w Francis Farogoh, from the novel by W R Burnett. ph Tony Gaudio. B&W. ed Ray Curtiss. ad Anton Grot. md Emo Rapee. 77 mins

Cast: Edward G Robinson (Cesare Enrico Bandello/Rico), Douglas Fairbanks Jr (Joe Massara), Glenda Farrell (Olga Strassoff), William Collier Jr (Tony Passa), Ralph Ince (Diamond Pete Montana), George E Stone (Otero), Thomas Jackson (Lt Tom Flaherty), Stanley Fields (Sam Vettori), Armand Kaliz (DeVoss), Sidney Blackmer (Big Boy), Landers Stevens (Commissioner McClure)

The rise and fall of an Italian-American gangster from New York's East Side.

Seminal genre piece whose success triggered off the spate of thirties gangster movies and made Robinson a star: his power-crazed, trigger-happy hoodlum is still highly impressive. He dominates the proceedings, and established the archetype of villain-as-hero with a characterization clearly – and admiringly – based on Al Capone.

The film itself now seems sluggish, although the highlights – notably William Collier Jr shooting down Robinson on the steps of a church and his famous last words, 'Mother of Mercy – is this the end of Rico?', still have impact.

'The strong story is vividly illustrated and allows for plenty of tensely dramatic situations.'
CEA Film Report

'Robinson's brilliant character study as the bombastic gang leader overshadows all the hackneyed gunning and racketeering business generally. The character enlists no sympathy but it lives vividly. At times there is a satirical touch which helps soften the grimness of the story.'
Picturegoer

'One of the best gangster pictures yet turned out.'
Variety

LIVE AND LET DIE
(GB 1973)
pc Eon. p Harry Saltzman, Albert R Broccoli. d Guy Hamilton. shark scenes d William Grefé. w Tom Mankiewicz, from the novel by Ian Fleming. ph Ted Moore. 2nd unit ph John Harris. sp ph fx Charles Staffell. Colour. ed Bert Bates, Raymond Poulton, John Shirley. sup ad Syd Cain. ad Stephen Hendrickson, Bob Laing, Peter Lamont. sfx Derek Meddings. sc Bob Simmons, Jery Comeaux, Ross Kananga, Bill Bennett, Eddie Smith, Joie Chitwood. m George Martin. title song Paul McCartney, Linda McCartney, sung by Paul McCartney and Wings. choreo Geoffrey Holder. titles Maurice Binder. 121 mins

Cast: Roger Moore (James Bond), Yaphet Kotto (Dr Kananga), Jane

Seymour (Solitaire), Clifton James (Sheriff Pepper), Julius W Harris (Tee Hee), Geoffrey Holdfer (Baron Samedi), David Hedison (Felix Leiter), Gloria Hendry (Rosie), Bernard Lee ('M'), Lois Maxwell (Miss Moneypenny), Tommy Lane (Adam), Earl Jolly Brown (Whisper), Roy Stewart (Quarrel)

Bond faces mayhem, murder and voodoo on the trail of a black master-criminal in the Caribbean.

Slickly-processed serial-style action and thrills with some splendid set pieces, best of all being a powerboat chase across Louisiana bayous. By now the Bond films had become a formulaic institution requiring only a new plot, new gimmicks and better-than-before cliffhangers.

The introduction of a new 007 was painlessly achieved, with Moore simply making minor variations on his bland-as-cottage-cheese characterization from his television series *The Saint*. Connery's laconic toughness and underlying menace were sorely missed. For those still counting, this was the eighth in the series.

'His adventures here are splendidly, outrageously entertaining and highly imaginative. Relax, take it easy and feel confident. The new James Bond will do very nicely thank you.'
Daily Express

'Setting aside an all-right speedboat spectacular over land and water, the film is both perfunctory and pre-dictable – leaving the mind free to wander into the question of its overall taste. Or lack of it?'
Time

THE LIVING DAYLIGHTS

(GB 1987)
pc Eon. p Albert R Broccoli, Michael G Wilson, assoc p Tom Pevsner, Barbara Broccoli. d John Glen. 2nd unit d, ph Arthur Wooster. w Richard Maibaum, Michael G Wilson. ph Alec Mills. add ph Phil Pastuhov, Tom Sanders. Colour. Panavision. ed John Grover, Peter Davies. pd Peter Lamont. sup ad Terry Ackland-Snow. add ad Michael Lamont, Ken Court, Fred Hole, Bert Davey, Thomas Riccabona, Peter Manhard. sfx sup John Richardson. stunt arr Paul Weston. driving stunt arr Rémy Julienne. m John Barry. song *The Living Daylights* by John Barry, Pal Waaktaar, sung by a-ha. titles Maurice Binder. 131 mins

Cast: Timothy Dalton (James Bond), Maryam D'Abo (Kara Milovy), Jeroen Krabbé (Gen. Gerogi Koskov), Joe Don Baker (Brad Whitaker), John Rhys-Davies (Gen. Leonid Pushkin), Art Malik (Kamran Shah), Andreas Wisniewski (Necros), Thomas Wheatley (Saunders), Desmond Llewellyn ('Q'), Robert Brown ('M'), Geoffrey Keen (Minister of Defence), Walter Gotell (Gen. Anatol Gogol), Caroline Bliss (Miss Moneypenny), John Terry (Felix Leiter), Julie T Wallace (Rosika Miklos)

James Bond seeks out a renegade American mercenary turned arms dealer in cahoots with a fake Soviet defector.

The series gains a new lease of life with the replacement of smirking Roger Moore by Dalton, who, as the fourth Bond, is refreshingly streets ahead as an actor, relies more on intelligence than on gadgets and wisecracks, takes the role seriously and

possesses genuine authority.

Stunts and action are plentiful and exciting and, in keeping with the age of AIDS and herpes, Bond no longer leaps into bed with every female he meets.

'The new, Timothy Dalton version of Bond is relatively sleek, tough and thoughtful; his occasional flash of a fey pixie-ish expression oddly evokes another multimorphous British hero, Dr Who ... the film is essentially an "action circus", Douglas Fairbanks swashbuckle updated by secret-agent costume (cloak-and-gadget), and sex-with-everything.'
Monthly Film Bulletin

'Dalton's a class act, be it in Shakespeare on the London stage or as the new 007 ... he's an actor, not just a pretty face with a dimpled chin, and in *Daylights* he's abetted by mate-rial that's a healthy cut above the series norm of super hero fantasy ... pic isn't just a high-tech action replay with the usual ravishing vistas and ditto dames. Everyone seems to have tried a little harder this time.'
Variety

'Belongs somewhere on the lower rungs of the Bond ladder. But there are some nice stunts.'
Chicago Sun-Times

THE LONG GOOD FRIDAY

(GB 1979)
pc Calendar Productions. For Black Lion Films. p Barry Hanson. assoc p Chris Griffin. d John MacKenzie. w Barrie Keefe. ph Phil Meheux. Colour. ed Mike Taylor. ad Vic Symonds. sfx Ian Wingrove. sc Roy Alon. m Francis Monkman. 114 mins

Cast: Bob Hoskins (Harold Shand), Helen Mirren (Victoria), Dave King (Parky), Bryan Marshall (Harris), Derek Thompson (Jeff Hughes), Eddie Constantine (Charlie), Brian Hall (Alan), Stephen Davis (Tony), P H Moriarty (Razors), Paul Freeman (Colin), Charles Cork (Eric), Patti Love (Carol), Pierce Borsnan (First Irishman), Roy Alon (Captain Death)

A London gangland boss fights to pull off a multi-million-pound dockland deal with the Mafia while his criminal empire comes under attack.

Originally intended for television but found to be far too violent for small-screen sensibilities and given a theatrical release. An excellently updated *Little Caesar* cleverly transposed to the London underworld, with a muscular script and visceral direction and a towering central performance (his best) by Hoskins. Certainly vicious, bloody and sadistic, but also a minor milestone in British genre films.

'The first British thriller to even approach the crackling vitality of the classic Hollywood gangster movies.'
Daily Mail

THE LONG GOODBYE
(US 1973)
pc Lion's Gate Films. exec p Elliott Kastner. p Jerry Blick. assoc p Robert Eggenweiler. d Robert Altman. w Leigh Brackett, from the novel by Raymond Chandler. ph Vilmos Zsigmond. Colour. Panavision. ed Lou Lombardo. m John Williams. song *The Long Goodbye* by John Williams, Johnny Mercer.
111 mins

Cast: Elliott Gould (Philip Marlowe), Nina Van Pallandt (Eileen Wade), Sterling Hayden (Roger Wade), Mark Rydell (Marty Augustine), Henry Gibson (Dr Verringer), David Arkin (Harry), Jim Bouton (Terry Lennox), Warren Berlinger (Morgan), Jo Ann Brody (Jo Ann Eggenweiler), Steve Coit (Det. Farmer)

When private eye Philip Marlowe helps a friend who is having marital problems, murder ensues and he investigates.

Altman's perverse and pointless reworking of Chandler's novel is as near as makes no different a cruel act of necrophilia towards the author (screenwriter Brackett also contributed to the 1946 version of *The Big Sleep*, although you would never guess it from this flatulent farrago).

Nothing remains of the atmosphere of the original, and Marlowe comes across as simply another hollow vehicle for the director's egocentricity. Confused and tedious and barely watchable, even for devout *auteur* buffs.

'Altman's lazy, haphazard put-down is without affection or understanding, a nose thumb not only at the idea of Philip Marlowe but at the genre that his tough-guy soft-heart epitomized. It is a curious spectacle to see Altman mocking a level of achievement to which at best he could only aspire.'
Time

'*The Long Goodbye* looks like a very late American imitation of a French imitation of earlier American films.'
New Society

A LOVELY WAY TO DIE
(US 1968) (GB: A LOVELY WAY TO GO)
pc Universal. p Richard Lewis. d David Lowell Rich. a A J Russell. ph Morris Hartzband. Colour. Scope. ed Sidney Katz. ad William Levitas. m Kenyon Hopkins. title song Kenyon Hopkins, Judy Spencer. 104 mins

Cast: Kirk Douglas (Jim Schuyler), Sylva Koscina (Rena Westerbrook), Eli Wallach (Tennessee Fredericks), Kenneth Haigh (Jonathan Fleming), Sharon Farrell (Carol), Gordon Peters (Eric), Martyn Green (Finchley), Doris Roberts (Feeney), Carey Nairnes (Harris), Ralph Waite (Magruder), Philip Bosco (Fuller), Ali McGraw (Melody)

A former cop hired to protect a woman accused of murder saves her from death and proves her innocence.

Glossy, made-for-television movie-style blend of mystery and humour that probably looked better in the page than on the screen. Standard sixties hokum.

'Racy comedy thriller containing some excellent visual humour and some good moments of black comedy ... but marred by an overflow of plot, inadequately linked.'
The Daily Cinema

LUCKY LUCIANO
(ITALY/FRANCE 1973)
pc Vides/Films de La Boetie. p Franco Cristaldi. assoc p Andre Genovese. d, st Francesco Rosi. w Francesco Rosi, Lino Jannuzzi, Tonino Guerra. w (English version) Jerome Chodorov. ph Pasqualino De Santis. Colour. ed Ruggero Mastroianni. ad Andrea

Crisanti. m Piero Piccioni. 115 mins

Cast: Gian Maria Volonte (Lucky Luciano), Rod Steiger (Gene Giannini), Edmond O'Brien (Harry J Anslinger), Charles Stragusa (Himself), Vincent Gardenia (American Colonel), Charles Cioffi (Vito Genovese), Silverio Blasi (Italian Captain of Police), Jacques Monod (French Commissioner), Karin Petersen (Igea), Larry Gates (Herlands), Magda Konopka (Countess)

Biopic of the Mafia narcotics boss from his deportation from the United States to his death in Italy.

Over-long and over-romanticized but with a good performance by Volonte, although he plays Luciano more as a saint than a hoodlum. The other performances are best ignored.

'To see a fragmented film such as this, which leaps about in time like a jumping bean, without being made aware beforehand that it is a dramatized documentary, is like trying to sight read *Hamlet* in its original Elizabethan English.'
Cinema TV Today

M

(GERMANY 1930)

pc Nero Film/Vereinighte Star-Film. p Seymour Nebenzal. d Fritz Lang. w Fritz Lang, Thea von Harbou, Paul Falkenberg, Adolf Jansen, Karl Vash, from an article by Egon Jacobson. ph Fritz Arno Wagner, Gustav Rathje. B&W. ed Karl Vollbrecht, Emil Hasler. m from *Peer Gynt* by Edvard Grieg. 118 mins

Cast: Peter Lorre (Franz Becker), Otto Wernicke (Karl Lohmann), Gustav Gründgens (Schraenker), Theo Lindgren (Bauernfaenger), Theodor Loos (Police Commissioner Groeber), Georg John (Blind Pedlar), Ellen Widman (Frau Beckman), Inge Landgut (Elsie), Ernst Stahl-Nachbaur (Police Chief), Paul Kemp (Pickpocket), Franz Stein (Minister), Rudolf Blümmer (Defence Lawyer)

A psychopathic child murderer is hunted by both the Düsseldorf police and the criminal underworld.

Classic Lang thriller, his first sound film, and using the new medium to considerable creative effect, notably when Lorre whistles the theme from Grieg's *Peer Gynt* as an accompaniment to his killings. It was based on the real-life mass murderer Peter Kürten, who was arrested in Düsseldorf in May 1930.

Lang and von Harbou used their clever screenplay to try to explore the psychopathic mind and to make strong, often satirical, social comment within the context of mounting unease and tension. Lorre gave his finest performance, and the impact of the film was further enhanced by atmospheric cinematography. Remade by Joseph Losey in 1951 (q.v.).

'Lorre depicts the murderer as a terribly childish monster, now abject, now formidable, so that our horror is tempered with pity, and our pity qualified by disgust. Herr Fritz Lang's direction of the whole film is a most subtle and effective essay in the Grand Guignol manner. The curdling of blood is as delicate a business as the tickling of trout, and Herr Lang achieves the macabre unobtrusively, without distracting crudities.'
The Spectator

'A brilliant and delicate study of a pathological type ... not only is the film brilliantly directed, with a vast amount of that inspired type-casting at which the Germans are so good, but Peter Lorre acts the part of the insane murderer with great insight and inspired skill.'
The New Republic

M

(US 1951)

pc Superior Films. p Seymour Nebenzal. d Joseph Losey. w Norman Reilly Raine, Leo Katcher, from the 1931 screenplay by Fritz Lang, Thea Van Harbou, Peter Falkenberg, Adolf Jansen & Karl Vash. add dial Waldo Salt. ph Ernest Laszlo. B&W. ed Edward Mann. ad Martin Obzina. m Michel Michelet. 87 mins

Cast: David Wayne (M), Howard Da Silva (Carney), Martin Gabel (Marshall), Luther Adler (Langley), Steve Brodie (Lt Becker), Glenn Anders (Riggert), Norman Lloyd (Sutro), Walter Burke (McMahan), Raymond Burr (Pottsy)

A child murderer is hunted down by both the police and the criminal underworld in Los Angeles.

An effective and surprisingly faithfu reworking of Fritz Lang's 1931 classic (q.v.), but while Wayne works hard, he cannot reach the chill factor achieved by Peter Lorre in the original. One of Losey's best, least self-conscious movies.

'Produced with an eye to pictorial values and a flair for moments of suspense, but on the whole it is slow-moving and ponderous. Those who like pleasant entertainment will not find it in this film.'
CEA Film Report

THE MACKINTOSH MAN

(GB 1973)
pc Newman-Foreman/John Huston Productions. p John Foreman. assoc p William Hill. d John Huston. 2nd unit d James Arnett. w Walter Hill, from the novel *The Freedom Trap* by Desmond Bagley. ph Oswald Morris. Colour. ed Russell LLoyd. pd Terry Marsh. ad Alan Tomkins. sfx Cliff Richardson, Ron Balinger. m Maurice Jarre. 99 mins

Cast: Paul Newman (Joseph Rearden), Dominique Sanda (Mrs Smith), James Mason (Sir George Wheeler), Harry Andrews (Angus Mackintosh), Ian Bannen (Slade), Michael Hordern (Brown), Nigel Patrick (Soames-Trevelyan), Peter Vaughan (Brunskill), Roland Culver (Judge), Percy Herbert (Taafe), John Bindon (Buster), Hugh Manning (Prosecutor), Leo Genn (Rollins), Robert Lang (Jack Summers), Jenny Runacre (Gerda)

A British Intelligence agent is given a false identity and sent to prison to infiltrate a gang organizing escapes for wealthy jailbirds.

Over-complex and hardly worth following, with a dull performance by Newman and little evidence of Huston taking much interest in the proceedings.

'For all the high speed car chases and suave dirty work, the highly improbable story is badly stitched together and starts coming apart at the seams well before the end.'
Daily Mirror

MADIGAN

(US 1968)
pc Universal. p Frank P Rosenberg. d Don Siegel. w Henri Simoun, Abraham Polonsky, from the novel *The Commissioner* by Richard Dougherty. ph Russell Metty. Colour. Scopc. ed MIlton Shifman. ad Alexandxer Golitzen, George C Webb. m sup Joseph Gershenson. m Don Costa. 101 mins

MAGNUM FORCE

Cast: Richard Widmark (Det. Daniel Madigan), Henry Fonda (Commissioner Russell), Inger Stevens (Julia Madigan), Harry Guardino (Det. Rocco Bonaro), James Whitmore (Chief Insp. Charles Kane), Susan Clark (Tricia Bentley), Michael Dunn (Midget Castiglione), Steve Inhat (Barney Benesch), Don Stroud (Hughie), Sheree North (Jonesy), Warren Stevens (Ben Williams), Bert Freed (Chief of Detectives Hap Lynch), Raymond St Jacques (Dr Taylor)

A New York police detective and his partner are given three days to recapture an escaped murder suspect.

Slick and efficient action thriller with a fashionably jaundiced view of big-city police, and a taut script that provides the protagonists with believable backgrounds and problems. Madigan, well played by Widmark, died in the final shootout but was revived for Widmark's 1972 TV Movie *Brock's Last Case*, which served as the pilot for the subsequent *Madigan* television series (September 1972–August 1973).

'Some excellent acting and intelligent dialogue make this first class entertainment.'
Sunday Express

MAGNUM FORCE
(US 1973)
pc Malpaso. p Robert Daley. d Ted Post. 2nd unit d Buddy Van Horn. w John Milius, Michael Cimino. st John Milius, based on the character created by Harry Julian Fink, Rita N Fink. ph Frank Stanley. Colour. Panavision. ed Ferris Webster. ad Jack Collis. m

Lalo Schifrin. 122 mins

Cast: Clint Eastwood (Insp. Harry Callahan), Hal Holbrook (Lt Neil Briggs), Mitchell Ryan (Charlie McCoy), David Soul (Ben Davis), Felton Perry (Early Smith), Robert Urich (John Grimes), Kip Niven (Red Astrachan), Tim Matheson (Phil Sweet), Christine White (Carol McCoy), Richard Devon (Carmine Ricca)

San Francisco policeman Harry Callan takes on a squad of renegade cops who are executing criminals outside the reach of the law.

Eastwood refines the character he created in 1971's *Dirty Harry* (q.v.) and makes him even more amoral and ignores any trace of emotion, turning him into a vigilante in the true Western tradition.

While the film lacks the style of its predecessor and the script abandons nuances of characterization in favour of straight action and violence, underscored by Post's hell-for-leather direction, it is nevertheless powerful and exciting, and dominated by its star's undoubted charisma.

'Year's best crime picture ... bolder, bloodier and better than before ... a wild, wooly, all-the-way out movie that's action crammed with excitement ... the suspense of a Hitchcock thriller.'
The Spectator

MAKE HASTE TO LIVE
(US 1954)
pc Republic. assoc p, d William A Seiter. w Warren Duff, from the novel by The Gordons. ph John L Russell Jr. B&W. ed Fred Allen. ad Frank

Hotaling. m Elmer Bernstein. 90 mins

Cast: Dorothy McGuire (Crystal Benson), Stephen McNally (Steve), Mary Murphy (Randy Benson), John Howard (Josh), Edgar Buchanan (Sheriff Lafe), Ron Hagerthy (Hack), Pepe Hern (Rudolfo Gonzales), Argentina Brunetti (Mrs Gonzales), Eddy Waller (Bud Kelly), Carolyn Jones (Mary Rose)

A man leaves prison and embarks on a reign of terror against his wife prior to killing her.

Economical suspenser with vivid central performances more than compensating for some of the screenplay contrivances.

'When it comes to a war of nerves, there should be no half measures. There are none here, in this suspense thriller that really builds up the tension.'
Picturegoer

MALONE
(US 1987)
pc Orion. p Leo L Fuchs. d Harley Cokliss. w Christopher Frank, from the novel *Shotgun* by William Wingate. ph Gerald Hirschfeld. Colour. ed Todd C Ramsay. pd Graeme Murray. sc Bud Davis. m David Newman. 93 mins

Cast: Burt Reynolds (Malone), Cliff Robertson (Delaney), Kenneth McMillan (Hawkins), Cynthia Gibb (Jo Barlow), Scott Wilson (Paul Barlow), Lauren Hutton (Jamie), Philip Anglim (Harvey), Tracey Walter (Dan Bollard), Alex Diakun (Madrid), Mike Kirton (Frank), Duncan Fraser (Malone's Target), Janne Mortil (Helen)

THE MALTESE FALCON

A disillusioned CIA hitman tangles with a millionaire trying to take over a small town in Oregon as a base for a planned paramilitary empire.

Pale Rider rides again, but the pony finally stumbles in spite of a better-than-average straight performance by Reynolds.

'Cokliss has a knack for good angles and builds well to some nice action scenes.'
Variety

THE MALTESE FALCON
(US 1941)
pc WB-First National. exec p Hal B Wallis. assoc p Henry Blanke. d, w John Huston, from the novel by Dashiell Hammett. ph Arthur Edeson. B&W. ed Thomas Richards. ad Robert Haas. m Adolph Deutsch. 100 mins

Cast: Humphrey Bogart (Sam Spade), Mary Astor (Brigid O'Shaughnessy), Gladys George (Iva Archer), Peter Lorre (Joel Cairo), Bardon MacLane

(Lt Dundy), Lee Patrick (Effie Perrine), Sydney Greenstreet (Casper Gutman), Ward Bond (Det. Tom Polhaus), Jerome Cowan (Miles Archer), Elisha Cook Jr (Wilmer Cook), James Burke (Luke), Murray Alper (Frank), John Hamilton (DA Bryan), Emory Parnall (Mate of *La Paloma*), Walter Huston (Capt. Jacobi)

A private detective becomes dangerously involved with a *femme fatale* and a gang of crooks searching for a fabled jewel-encrusted statuette.

A genre classic and one of the most purely enjoyable private eye thrillers ever, to be savoured through repeated viewings. It marked Huston's memorable directorial debut and gave Bogart one of his best roles, which he received only after George Raft, who was unwilling to work with a tyro director, turned it down.

Huston's inspired direction, his script, which wisely retained the spirit and much of the dialogue of the Hammett original, Arthur Edeson's fine cinematography and ideal casting and performances make it an archetype – tense, laconic and cleverly characterized – and Bogart was an equally archetypal shamus. Greenstreet, too, made a memorable film debut and was nominated for the Academy Award for Best Supporting Actor. Lorre, Astor and Elish Cook Jr were equally good, and the director's father, Walter Huston, made an unbilled appearance as Captain Jacobi, who turns up in Spade's office with the Falcon and then dies.

The film, made for $324,000 in 34 days, was a critical success, Huston was nominated for an Oscar for his screenplay and the film received a Best Picture nomination. *The Maltese Falcon* had been filmed twice before – under that title in 1931, with Ricardo Cortez and Bebe Daniels, and in 1936 as *Satan Met a Lady* (q.v.) with Warren William and Bette Davis.

'The trick which Mr Huston has pulled is a combination of American ruggedness with the suavity of the English crime school – a blend of mind and muscle – plus a slight touch of pathos.'
The New York Times

'*The Maltese Falcon* has nearly everything a mystery film should have. Enough mystery to keep us guessing … a wonderfully convincing set of characters … admirable photography … rich in sardonic revelation, it belongs to the vintage period of American gangsterism.'
New Statesman

'There is character in the picture and this, as well as the swift succession of its contrived excitements and very shrewd dialogue, is what gives the temporary but sufficient meaning required by its violent fantasy.'
The New Republic

'The most interesting and imaginative detective film to come out of America, or anywhere else, since the first *Thin Man*, another Hammett story. Bogart is as good as he can be.'
The Sunday Times

MAN AFRAID
(US 1957)
pc Universal-International. p Gordon Kay. d Harry Keller. w Herb Meadow. st Dan Ullman. ph Russell Metty. B&W. Scope. ed Ted J Kent. ad Alexander Golitzen, Philip Barber. m Henry Mancini. 84 mins

Cast: George Nader (Rev. David Collins), Phyllis Thaxter (Lisa Collins), Tim Hovey (Michael Collins), Eduard Franz (Carl Simmons), Harold J Stone (Lt Marlin), Judson Pratt (Wilbur Fletcher), Reta Shaw (Nurse Willis), Butch Bernard (Ronnie Fletcher), Mabel Albertson (Maggie)

A preacher and his family are terrorized by the mentally unbalanced father of a young man accidentally killed by the reverend.

First-rate revenge thriller, tensely directed and scripted, with a genuinely unnerving performance by Franz as the persecutor.

'Vivid characterization and dramatic scenes help to make it absorbing if emotional entertainment.'
CEA Film Report

MAN HUNT
(US 1941)
pc 20th Century Fox. assoc p Kenneth Macgowan. d Fritz Lang. w Dudley Nichols, from the novel *Rogue Male* by Geoffrey Household. ph Arthur Miller. B&W. ed Allen McNeil. ad Richard Day, Wiard B Ihnen. m Alfred Newman. 102 mins

Cast: Walter Pidgeon (Capt. Thorndike), Joan Bennett (Jerry), George Sanders (Quive-Smith), John Carradine (Mr Jones), Roddy McDowall (Vaner), Ludwig Stössel (Doctor), Heather Thatcher (Lady Risborough), Roger Imhof (Capot Jensen), Egon Brecher ('Whiskers'), Lester Matthews (Major), Holmes Herbert (Farnsworthy), Eily Malyon (Postmistress), Herbert Evans (Reeves)

An English big-game hunter sets out to shoot Hitler. Caught with the Führer in his sights, he is beaten and left for dead but escapes to London, where he is hunted by Gestapo agents.

Supremely suspenseful chase thriller with impeccable direction – particularly effective in the long stretches without dialogue that recall Lang's background in silent films – and fine cinematography, although the Hollywood version of London is risible.

'A masterly job of motion picture make-believe ... Lang, whose place in film-making was already established by *M*, has directed the work with consummate imagination and skill. And the players never fail to make it both a vastly compelling entertainment and an arresting evaluation of a lot of ideas which most of us are considering at the moment.'
New York Herald Tribune

THE MAN IN THE ATTIC

(US 1953)
pc Panoramic Productions. p Robert L Jacks. d Hugo Fregonese. w Robert Pressnell Jr, Barre Lyndon, from *The Lodger* by Marie Belloc-Lowndes. ph Leo Tover. B&W. sup ed Paul Weatherwax. ed Marjorie Fowler. ad Lyle Wheeler, Leland Fuller. md Lionel Newman. 82 mins

Cast: Jack Palance (Slade), Constance Smith (Lily Bonner), Byron Palmer (Paul Warwick), Frances Bavier (Helen Harley), Rhys Williams (William Harley), Sean McClory (First Constable), Leslie Bradley (Second Constable), Tita Phillips (Daisy), Lester Matthews (Insp. Melville), Harry Cording (Sgt Bates), Lilian Bond (Annie Rowley), Lisa Daniels (Mary Lenham)

An eccentric lodger in a Victorian boarding house turns out to be Jack the Ripper.

Unremarkable remake of *The Lodger*, with Palance going entertainingly over the top.

'A really good thriller. Full marks to all concerned.'
Picturegoer

THE MAN INSIDE

(GB 1958)
pc Warwick. p Harold Huth. d John Gilling. w John Gilling, David Shaw, from the novel by M E Chaber. ph Ted Moore. 2nd unit ph Cyril Knowles. B&W. CinemaScope. ed Bert Rule. ad Ray Simms. m Richard Rodney Bennett. songs *The Man Inside* by Len Braverman, *Trudie* by Joe Henderson. 97 mins

Cast: Jack Palance (Milo March), Anita Ekberg (Trudie Hall), Nigel Patrick (Sam Carter), Anthony Newley (Ernsto), Bonar Colleano (Martin Lomer), Sean Kelly (Rizzio), Sidney James (Frank King), Donald Pleasence (Organgrinder), Eric Pohlmann (Tristano), Josephine Brown (Mrs Frazur), Gerard Heinz (Stone), Naomi Chance (Jane Leyton), Alec Mango (Lopez)

A book-keeper who steals a priceless diamond from his employer in New York is pursued to Lisbon, Madrid and Paris by a private detective.

Confused plotting and an unintentionally hilarious performance from Ekberg make for a competently-made but less than interesting piece which offers some attractive locations but little else.

'All the well-tried tricks of the trade have gone to the making of this eventful crime thriller – expert direction, slick characterization, fast-moving action, holding suspense and tingling thrill – resulting in good solid entertainment for Δpopular tastes.'
CEA Film Report

THE MAN OUTSIDE

(GB 1967)
pc Trio Films/Group W. p William Gell. d, w Samuel Gallu, from the novel *Double Agent* by Gene Stackleborg. add dial Julian Bond, Roger Marshall. ph Gilbert Taylor. Colour. Scope. ed Tom Noble. ad Peter Mullins. m Richard Arnell. 98 mins

Cast: Van Heflin (Bill Maclean), Heidilinde Weis (Kay Sebastian), Pinkas Braun (Rafe Machek), Peter Vaughan (Nikolai Volkov), Charles Gray (Charles Griddon), Paul Maxwell (Judson Murphy), Ronnie Barker (George Venaxas), Linda Marlowe (Dorothy), Gary Cockrell (Bruno Parry), Bill Nagy (Morehouse), Archie Duncan (Det. Supt Barnes), Larry Cross (Austen)

A dismissed CIA agent is used as a decoy to test the loyalty of another agent in London.

Downbeat, jaundiced spy thriller, well performed by Heflin, with confused and confusing use of London locations.

'The taut direction of Samuel Galli ensures that suspense is kept to a maximum.'
The Daily Cinema

THE MAN WHO KNEW TOO MUCH

THE MAN WHO KNEW TOO MUCH

(US 1955)
pc Filwite Productions. p, d Alfred
Hitchcock. w John Michael Hayes,
Angus McPhail, from a story by
Charles Bennett & D B Wyndham-
Lewis. ph Robert Burks. Colour.
VistaVision. ed George Tomasini. ad
Hal Pereira, Henry Bumstead, Sam
Comer, Arthur Krams. sfx John P
Fulton. m Bernard Herrmann. *Storm
Cloud Cantata* by Arthur Benjamin, D
B Wyndham-Lewis. songs *Que Sera,
Sera, We'll Love Again* by Jay Livington,
Ray Evans. 119 mins

Cast: James Stewart (Dr Ben
McKenna), Doris Day (Jo McKenna),
Bernard Miles (Mr Drayton), Brenda
de Banzie (Mrs Drayton), Chris Olson
(Hank McKenna), Ralph Truman
(Buchanan), Daniel Gelin (Louis
Bernard), Reggie Nalder (Rien, the
Assassin), Mogens Wieth
(Ambassador), Alan Mowbray (Val
Parnell), Betty Bascomb (Edna), Hilary
Brooke (Jan Peterson)

A dying secret agent tells an American
couple holidaying in Morocco of a
plan to assassinate a statesman in
London, where their young son is
kidnapped to ensure their silence.

Hitchcock's over-long remake of
his 1934 thriller is sadly
disappointing, with the director
apparently seduced into flatulent
film-making by exotic locations and
VistaVision, delivering scenes which
look lovely but do little to advance
the narrative or increase the
suspense. Nevertheless, he succeeds
in finding an occasion for Day
(surprisingly effective in a dramatic
role) to sing *Che Sera, Sera*, which
received an Oscar nomination and
became a hit.

The actual business of the
attempted assassination in the
Albert Hall still grips, however, and
Reggie Nalder looks the part of a
would-be killer.

'His facile directorial paint-brush, plus
the intriguing backgrounds and interesting characters combine to hold
audience interest keyed up at all
times. It's like a long novel that could
be tightened yet many would prefer it
as it is.'
The Hollywood Reporter

'Stewart himself is poorly directed (he
was petulant when he should have
been Stewart-ish). Bernard Miles and
Brenda de Banzie are also poorly
directed. And there are one or two
other signs that Alfred Hitchcock may
need a vacation.'
Films in Review

THE MAN WITH THE GOLDEN GUN

(GB 1974)
pc Eon Productions. p Harry
Saltzman, Albert R Broccoli. assoc p
Charles Orme. d Guy Hamilton. w
Richard Maibaum, Tom Mankiewicz,
from the novel by Ian Fleming. ph
Ted Moore, Oswald Morris. 2nd unit
ph John Harris. Colour. ed Ray
Poulton. pd Peter Murton. ad Peter
Graysmark, Peter Lamont. sfx John
Stears. miniatures Derek Meddings.
sc W J Milligan Jr. m John Barry.
title song John Barry, Don Black,

sung by Lulu. titles Maurice Binder. 125 mins

Cast: Roger Moore (James Bond), Christopher Lee (Scaramanga), Britt Ekland (Mary Goodnight), Maud Adams (Andrea), Herve Villechaize (Nick Nack), Clifton James (J W Pepper), Soon Taik Oh (Hip), Richard Loo (Hai Fat), Marc Lawrence (Rodney), Bernard Lee ('M'), Lois Maxwell (Miss Moneypenny), Marne Maitland (Lazar), Desmond Llewellyn ('Q'), James Cossins (Colthorpe)

Bond goes east to terminate a professional assassin.

The mixture as before – exotic locations, exotic women, exotic villains and exotic sets – hampered by pedestrian script and direction and a leading man who is less interesting than his stunt doubles. As a result it loses steam and becomes tedious. Still, the commanding presence of Lee (the only actor to have played a man with three nipples) as Scaramanga and the diminutive Herve Villechaize playing Laurel to Lee's Hardy (or vice versa) give it a much-needed shot in the arm.

'He should be packed off to a sanitarium, where he can give his liver a rest and wait in leisure for his moment to come again. Bond has been around too long to be fresh, but not long enough to qualify as a genuine antique.'
Time

THE MAN WITH THE GOLDEN GUN

MC-42(71-31)

THE MANCHURIAN CANDIDATE

'There are no essential changes in a sure-fire formula that director Guy Hamilton perfected as far back as *Goldfinger*.'
Playboy

THE MANCHURIAN CANDIDATE
(US 1962)

pc MC Productions/Essex Productions. exec p Howard W Koch. p George Axelrod, John Frankenheimer. d John Frankenheimer. w George Axelrod, from the novel by Richard Condon. ph Lionel Lindon. optical sfx Howard Anderson Company. B&W. ed Ferris Webster. pd Richard Sylbert. sfx Paul Pollard. m David Amram. 126 mins

Cast: Frank Sinatra (Bennett Marco), Laurence Harvey (Raymond Shaw), Janet Leigh (Rosie), Angela Lansbury (Raymond's Mother), Henry Silva (Chunjin), James Gregory (Senator John Iselin), Leslie Parrish (Jocie Jordan), John McGiver (Senator Thomas Jordan), Khigh Dhiegh (Yen Lo), James Edwards (Corporal Melvin), Douglas Henderson (Colonel), Albert Paulsen (Zilkov), Madame Spivi (Berezovo's Female Counterpart), Barry Kelley (Secretary of Defense), Whit Bissell (Medical Officer), Reggie Nalder (Gomel)

An American prisoner is brainwashed by Chinese Communists during the Korean War and sent back to the United States to assassinate a presidential candidate.

A witty, satirical screenplay and stylish direction transform a basically improbable premise into a sharp and exciting thriller. Casting Harvey as a brainwashed zombie was inspired, the acting throughout is first-rate and Frankenheimer, making his best movie, stages a nerve-shredding climax.

'The thriller has done what it was meant to do – it has held us in increasing suspense for over two hours.'
The Guardian

'Many loud hurrahs for *The Manchurian Candidate*, a thriller guaranteed to raise all but the limpest hair. It comes to us from a little, half-abandoned western village called Hollywood and shines with all the characteristics – energy, pell-mell pace, a smooth, hard, bright surface – for which that village grew world-

famous and which we keep hearing, and fearing, it has lost forever.'
The New Yorker

MANNEN PÁ TAKET

SWEDEN 1976) (US, GB: THE MAN ON THE ROOF)
c Svenska Filminstitutet/Svensk Filmindusti. p Per Berglund. d, w Bo Widerberg, from the novel *Den Vedervärdige Mannen Fran Säffle* by Maj Sjöwall & Per Wahlöö. ph Odd Geir Saether, Per Källberg, Hans Welin, Ake Astrand, Roland Sterner, John Olsson, Lars-Ake Pahlén, Tina Svensson, Hanno Fuchs, Dan Myrman. Colour. ed Silvia Ingemarsson, Bo Widerberg. ad Alf Axén. m Björn J Lindh. 109 mins

Cast: Carl Gustaf Lindstedt (Chief Insp. Martin Beck), Gunnel Wadner (Mrs Beck), Hakan Serner (Insp. Einer Rönn), Sven Volter (Lennart Kohlberg), Eva Remaeus (Mrs Kohlberg), Thomas Hellberg (Gunvald Larsson), Carl Axel-Heiknert (Palmon Hult), Torgny Anderberg (Supt Malm), Birgitta Valberg (Mrs Nyman), Harald Hamrell (Stefan Nyman)

Stockholm police hunt down a cop killer who turns out to be a former policeman.

Excellent police procedural with stylish direction, unfamiliar locations,

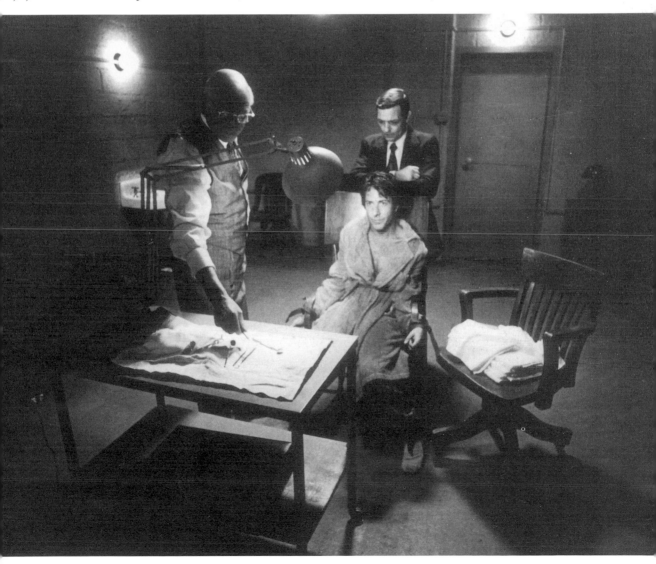

MARATHON MAN

and a good eye for detail and characterization.

'Here is a thriller richly wrought: one that augments its initial mystery and its ultimate blaze of action with penetrating analyses of several of the persons involved, and also with a shrewd perception of the degrees of good and evil promoted by the social environemt in which officers of law and order are functioning.'
Films and Filming

MARATHON MAN
(US 1976)
pc Paramount. p Robert Evans, Sidney Beckerman. assoc p George Justin. d John Schlesinger. 2nd unit d, sc Everett Creach. w William Goldman, from his novel. ph Conrad Hall. special ph Garrett Brown. Colour. ed Jim Clark. pd Richard MacDonald. ad Jack De Shields. sfx Richard Johnson, Charles Spurgeon. m Michael Small. 126 mins

Cast: Dustin Hoffman (Babe Levy), Laurence Olivier (Szell), Roy Scheider (Doc Levy), William Devane (Janeway), Marthe Keller (Elsa), Fritz Weaver (Prof. Blumenthal), Richard Bright (Karl), Marc Lawrence (Erhard), Allen Joseph (Babe's Father), Tito Goya (Melendez), Jacques Marin (LeClerc)

When his brother is murdered, a student becomes dangerously involved with a Nazi war criminal who has come to New York from his hideaway in Uruguay to collect a fortune in diamonds.

Although there are times when it is over-plotted to the point of incoherence, Schlesinger turns the screenplay into a glossy and riveting suspenser with a strong, if mannered, performance by Hoffman and a vivid portrait of unalloyed evil from Olivier, who tries out the ripe 'mittel-European' accent that was to serve him so well – and so frequently – in subsequent movies.

The violence can be gruelling at times, and anyone with a fear of dentists should be ready to close their eyes and ears when Olivier tortures Hoffman with a dental drill.

'Totally absorbing, first-rate jigsaw-like thriller … one of the most gripping and fascinating suspense stories since *The Day of the Jackal*.'
Photoplay

'A staggering but Pyrrhic victory of slick filmmaking know-how and high-powered acting over sleazy, piddling material … Schlesinger … knows how to grab an audience, and he'll hit you with anything to keep your attention – illogical emotional histrionics, baffling plot gimmicks, disorienting editing and, most of all, extravagant violence.'
New York Post

MARLOWE
(US 1979)
pc Katzka-Berne Productions/Cherokee Productions. In association with Beckerman Productions. p Gabriel Katzka, Sidney Beckerman. d Paul Bogart. w Stirling Silliphant, from the novel *The Little Sister* by Raymond Chandler. ph William H Daniels. Colour. ed Gene Ruggiero. ad George W Davis, Addison Heher. sfx Virgil Beck. m Peter Matz. 95 mins

Cast: James Garner (Philip Marlowe), Gayle Hunnicutt (Mavis Wald), Carroll O'Connor (Lt Christy French), Rita Moreno (Dolores Gonzales), Sharon Farrell (Orfamy Quest), H M Wynant (Sonny Steelgrave), Jackie Coogan (Grant W Hicks), Kenneth Tobey (Sgt Fred Beifus), Nate Esformes (Paleface), Bruce Lee (Winslow Wong), Christopher Cary (Chuck), Paul Stevens (Dr Lagardie)

Private eye Philip Marlowe lands deep in trouble with gangsters, blackmail and murder when he is hired by a young woman to find her missing brother.

Engaging, with a good sense of humour and a suitably Chandleresque atmosphere, and an enjoyably laconic portrait of Marlowe that is rather more Garner than Chandler. It is packed with modish violence and red herrings, and Bogart (no relation!) moves fast enough to skid over the lacunae in the plot. The highlight is Bruce Lee, in an early screen appearance, trashing Marlowe's office in an orgy of martial arts mayhem.

'The action moves too fast to need explaining and the dialogue … has the irony and the throwaway wit which one remembers from the best Chandler.'
The Sunday Times

MARNIE
(US 1964)
pc Geoffrey Stanley Inc/Universal-International. p, d Alfred Hitchcock. w Jay Presson Allen, from the novel by Winston Graham. ph Robert Burks. Colour. ed George Tomasini. pd Robert Boyle. pictorial design Albert Whitlock. m Bernard Herrmann. 130 mins

Cast: Sean Connery (Mark Rutland), Tippi Hedren (Marnie), Diane Baker

(Lil Mainwaring), Martin Gabel (Sidney Strutt), Louise Latham (Bernice Edgar), Bob Sweeney (Cousin Bob), Alan Napier (Mr Rutland), S John Launer (Sam Ward), Mariette Hartley (Susan Claborn), Bruce Dern (Sailor), Henry Beckman (First Detective), Edith Evanson (Rita), Meg Wylie (Mrs Turpin)

A wealthy publisher marries a compulsive kleptomaniac and discovers her neuroses and sexual frigidity stem from her murder of one of her prostitute mother's clients when she was a child.

Hitchcock takes on Freud and loses. A rotten script, indifferent acting and insulting special effects and back projection promote rigor mortis-inducing tedium. For uncritical idolators only.

'When an unknown director turns out suspense melodrama as dreary and unconvincing as this, moviegoers revel in the thought of what it might have been if Hitchcock had done it. It is disconcerting to come away from *Marnie* feeling precisely the same way.'
Time

'It might conceivably satisfy an audience that has nothing more stimulating than a commercial to look forward to, but certainly not to anyone who remembers Hitchcock in his prime.'
Saturday Review

THE MARSEILLES CONTRACT
(GB/FRANCE 1974) (US: THE DESTRUCTORS)
pc Kettledrum Films/PECF. For WB and AIP. p, w Judd Bernard. assoc p Patricia Casey. d Robert Parrish. ph

Douglas Slocombe. Colour. ed Willy Kemplen. ad Willy Holt. sfx Paul Trielli. m Roy Budd. 90 mins

Cast: Michael Caine (John Deray), Anthony Quinn (Steve Ventura), James Mason (Jacques Brizzard), Alexandra Stewart (Mrs Matthews), Maureen Kerwin (Lucienne Brizzard), Marcel Bozzufi (Calmet), Catherine Rouvel (Brizzard's Mistress), Maurice Ronet (Briac), Vernon Dobtcheff (Lazar)

An American Narcotics Bureau agent hires a hitman in Paris to kill a smuggler he is unable to bring to justice.

Under-written, hazily-plotted co-production, with most of the cast – honourably excepting Caine's barely skin-deep but cheerfully characterized assassin – looking as though they would rather be somewhere else.

'A thriller that throws most of the current clichés ... into one uneasy story and comes up with not very much.'
The Sunday Telegraph

THE MASK OF DIMITRIOS
(US 1944)
pc WB. p Henry Blanke. d Jean Negulesco. w Frank Gruber, from the novel *A Coffin for Dimitrios* by Eric Ambler. ph Arthur Edeson. B&W. ed Frederick Richards. ad Ted Smith. m Adolph Deutsch. 95 mins

Cast: Sydney Greenstreet (Mr Peters), Zachary Scott (Dimitrios), Faye Emerson (Irana Preveza), Peter Lorre (Cornelius Latimer Leyden), George Tobias (Fedor Muishkin), Victor Francen (Wladislaw Grodek), Steve Geray (Bulic), Florence Bates

(Madame Chavez), Eduardo Cianelli (Marukakis), Kurt Katch (Col. Haki), George Metaxa (Hans Werner), John Abbott (Mr Pappas)

A Dutch thriller writer is drawn into a web of mystery, intrigue and espionage when he investigates the murder of a notorious master-criminal.

Scott made his screen debut in a well-cast thriller which suffers from an over-complicated screenplay and overuse of flashbacks. The performances, though, are a delight, notably those of Greenstreet and Lorre.

'Strong melodrama ... the film is heavy entertainment and demands concentration, and is, therefore, addressed to more intelligent patrons.'
CEA Film Report

'The main trouble about this international spy melodrama is that its plot is, at times, very obscure and the dialogue tends to become overbearing.'
Picturegoer

MASQUERADE
(US 1988)
pc MGM. A Michael Levy Enterprises production. exec p, w Dick Wolf. p Michael I Levy. assoc p Kelliann Ladd. d Bob Swaim. ph David Watkin. Colour. ed Scott Conrad. pd John Kasarda. ad Dan Davis. sfx Connie Brink. sc Peter Hock. m John Barry. 91 mins

Cast: Rob Lowe (Tim Whalen), Meg Tilly (Olivia Lawrence), Kim Cattrall (Brooke Morrison), Doug Savant (Micke McGill), John Glover (Tony Gateworth), Dana Delany (Anne

MCQ

MCQ

Briscoe), Erik Holland (Chief of Police), Brian Davies (Granger Morrison), Bernie McInerney (Harland Fitzgerald), Bill Lopatto (Weyburn)

A cocky young yachtsman makes a play for a wealthy woman with marriage and murder in mind.

Glossy, complex and intriguing in spite of shallow characterization and rather too many echoes of other and better films.

'How any director responsible for the meticulously precise orchestration of mood, locale and character in *La Balance* could produce anything so flaccid and flavourless and *Masquerade* is the real mystery.'
Monthly Film Bulletin

McQ
(US 1974)
pc Batjac/Levy Gardner. exec p Michael A Wayne. p Jules Levy, Arthur Gardner, Lawrence Roman. d John Sturges. 2nd unit d Ron R Rondell. w Lawrence Roman. ph Harry Stradling Jr. Colour. Panavision. ed William Ziegler. pd Walter Simonds. sfx Howard Jensen. m Elmer Bernstein. 111 mins

Cast: John Wayne (Lon McQ), Eddie Albert (Capt. Ed Kosterman), Diana Muldaur (Lois Boyle), Colleen Dewhurst (Myra), Clu Gulager (Franklin Toms), David Huddleston (Pinky Farrow), Jim Watkins (JC), Al Lettieri (Manny Santiago), Julie Adam (Elaine Forrester), Roger E Mosley (Rosey), William Bryant (Sgt Stan Boyle), Joe Tornatore (LaSalle), Kim Sanford (Ginger)

When his partner is gunned down, a Seattle policeman resigns from the force to go after the killer.

Dreary *Dirty Harry* clone, with Wayne looking tired and uncomfortable, and a clichéd script and limp direction adding to the general air of ennui. The score is dreary, too.

'A good contemporary crime actioner.'
Variety

THE MECHANIC/KILLER OF KILLERS

(US 1972)

pc United Artists. A Robert Chartoff-Irwin Winkler-Lewis J Carlino Production. p Irwin Winkler, Robert Chartoff. d Michael Winner. 2nd unit d Antonio Tarruella. w Lewis John Carlino. ph Richard Kline, Robert Paynter. Colour. sup ed Freddie Wilson. ad Roger Maus, Herbert Westbrook. sfx Richard F Albain. m Jerry Fielding. 100 mins

Cast: Charles Bronson (Arthur Bishop), Jan-Michael Vincent (Steve McKenna), Keenan Wynn (Harry McKenna), Jill Ireland (Prostitute), Linda Ridgeway (Louise), Frank de Kova (The Man), Linday H Crosby (Policeman), Takayuki Kubote (Karate Master), Martin Gordon (American Tourist), James Davidson (Intern)

A professional assassin specializing in making hits look like accidents teaches the tricks of the trade to a young newcomer who has a hidden agenda of his own.

Typically brisk, typically meretricious Winner opus. Busy direction fails to elicit from the monolithic Bronson

anything approaching a lively performance. The twist in the tail is barely worth waiting for.

'Like its protagonist, Michael Winner's latest excursion into the improbable is cold, calculating, efficient, flashy, and – despite its cultural and philosophical pretensions – vacuous.'
Monthly Film Bulletin

MIDNIGHT CROSSING

(US 1987)

pc The Midnight Crossing Film Partners. A Team Effort Production. In association with Limelite Studios. exec p Dan Ireland, Gary Barber, Gregory Cascante, Wanda S Rayle. p Mathew Hayden. d Roger Holzberg. 2nd unit d Don Edmunds. w Roger Holzberg, Doug Weiser. st Roger Holzberg. ph Henry Vargas. 2nd unit ph Orson Ochoa. underwater ph Gary Shlifer. ed Earl Watson. pd José Duarte. ad Carter Lee Cullen. sc Artie Melesci. m Paul Buckmaster, Al Gorgoni, Adam Gorgoni. 104 mins

Cast: Faye Dunaway (Helen Barton), Daniel J Travanti (Morely Barton), Kim Cattrall (Alexa Schubb), John Laughlin (Jeff Shubb), Ned Beatty (Ellis), Pedro de Pool (Capt. Mendoza), Doug Weiser (Miller), Michael Thompson (Shore Patrol Officer), Chick Bernhardt (Young Morely)

The man who charters a young couple's yacht to take him and his blind wife on a 20th anniversary yacht cruise in the Caribbean has a sinister hidden motive.

In spite of enough plot twists to give a pretzel an inferiority complex, this leaden thriller sinks with all hands.

'Tedious, grossly over-acted ... filled with gratuitous sex and violence ... awful dialogue, unbelievable characters, and disjointed scenes which make no sense.'
Variety

MIDNIGHT LACE

(US 1960)

pc Ross Hunter/Arwin/Universal-International. p Ross Hunter, Martin Melcher. d David Miller. w Ivan Goff, Ben Roberts, from the play *Mathilda Shouted Fire* by Janet Green. ph Russell Metty. Colour. ed Russell F Schoengarth, Leon Barsha. ad Alexander Golitzen, Robert Clatworthy. m Frank Skinner. gowns Irene. 105 mins

Cast: Doris Day (Kit Preston), Rex Harrison (Tony Preston), Myrna Loy (Aunt Bea), Natasha Parry (Peggy Thompson), John Williams (Insp. Byrnes), John Gavin (Brian Younger), Herbert Marshall (Charles Manning), Anthony Dawson (Ash), Roddy McDowall (Malcolm), Doris Lloyd (Nora), Hermione Baddeley (Dora), Richard Ney (Daniel), Rhys Williams (Victor Elliott)

The rich American wife of a London businessman subjected to a reign of terror is marked for murder.

Glossy suspenser requiring considerable suspension of disbelief, but entertaining in its undemanding way, although its Hollywood-London settings take almost as much swallowing as the plot. Indifferently remade for television in 1980 with the locale changed to San Francisco.

'Under the direction of David Miller suspense builds up with teasing impact until the last final surprise and unexpected conclusion.'
The Film Daily

THE MIDNIGHT MAN

(US 1974)

pc Norlan/Universal. p, d, w Roland Kibbee, Burt Lancaster, from the novel *The Midnight Lady and the Morning Man* by David Anthony. ph Jack Priestley. Colour. ed Frank Morris. ad James D Vance. sc Alan Gibbs. m Dave Grusin. song *Come On Back Where You Belong* by Dave Grusin, Morgan Ames, sung by Yvonne Elliman. 119 mins

Cast: Burt Lancaster (Jim Slade), Susan Clark (Linda), Cameron Mitchell (Quartz Willinger), Morgan Woodward (Clayborne), Harris Yulin (Sheriff Casey), Robert Quarry (Dr Pritchett), Joan Lorring (Judy Willinger), Ed Lauter (Leroy), Lawrence Dobkin (Waldo Mason), Mills Watson (Cash), William T Hicks (Charlie), Catherine Bach (Natalie Clayborne), Nick Cravat (Gardener)

A former policeman, paroled after killing his wife's lover, goes to work as a security guard at a South Carolina college, where he solves the murder of a young woman.

Confusing, over-long and slow, with enough red herrings to feed a host, but offering little to feed the imagination.

'Glossy whodunit with more twists than thrills ... efficient enough but lifeless, and burdened with portentous sentiments about solitude, violence and the nature of the beast.'
Sight and Sound

THE MIGHTY QUINN

(US 1989)

pc MGM in association with Star Partners II. And A & M Films procution. exec p Dale Pollock, Gil Friesen. p Sandy Lieberson, Marion Hunt, Ed Elbert. assoc p Jack Cummins. d Carl Schenkel. w Hampton Fancher, from the novel *Finding Maubee* by A H Z Carr. ph Jacques Steyn. 2nd unit ph Karl Kases. Colour. ed John Jympson. pd Roger Murray-Leach. ad Gregory Keen. sc Dean Ferrandini, Dan Bradley. m Anne Dudley. 98 mins

Cast: Denzel Washington (Xavier Quinn), Robert Townsend (Maubee), James Fox (Elgin), Mimi Rogers (Hadley Elgin), M Emmett Walsh (Miller), Sheryl Lee Ralph (Lola Quinn), Art Evans (Jump). Esther Rolle (Ubu Pearl), Norman Beaton (Governor Chalk), Alex Colon (Patina), Keye Luke (Dr Raj), Tyra Ferrell (Isola)

The black police chief of a Carribean island tracks down the killer of a decapitated white businessman.

Interesting, interestingly-cast and underrated whodunnit with attractive location work.

'*The Mighty Quinn* is a spy thriller, a buddy movie, a musical, a comedy and a picture that is wise about human nature. And yet will all these qualities, it never seems to strain: this is a graceful, almost charmed, entertainment.'
Chicago Sun-Times

MINISTRY OF FEAR

(US 1945)

pc Paramount. p, w Seton I Miller, from the novel by Graham Greene. d Fritz Lang. ph Henry Sharp. B&W. ed Archie Marshek. ad Hal Pereira, Hans Dreier. m Victor Young. 85 mins

Cast: Ray Milland (Stephen Neale), Marjorie Reynolds (Carla Hilfe), Carl Jaffe (Willi Hilfe), Hillary Brooke (Second Mrs Bellaire), Percy Waram (Insp. Prentice), Dan Duryea (Cost/Travers), Alan Napier (Dr Forrester), Erskine Sanford (Mr Rennit), Thomas Loudon (Mr Newland), Byron Foulger (Mr Newby), Aminta Dyne (First Mrs Bellaire), Lester Matthews (Dr Norton)

A man released from an insane asylum after serving time for the mercy killing of his wife becomes involved in a World War Two Nazi spy ring.

Atmospheric, nerve-stretching, with Lang on good form and even managing to distract the viewer from the patently phoney studio-built London settings. Duryea is memorably unpleasant.

'The movie version of *Ministry of Fear* has stripped away the mystic and psychic trappings of Graham Greene's novel and left an ingenious, tense spy story, from this morning on, the Paramount screen becomes one of the exciting, baffling places around town.'
New York World-Telegram

THE MIRROR CRACK'D

(GB 1980)

pc G W Films. p John Brabourne, Richard Goodwin. d Guy Hamilton. w Jonathan Hales, Barry Sandler, from the novel *The Mirror Crack'd From Side to Side* by Agatha Christie. ph Christopher Challis. Colour. ed Richard Marden. pd Michael Stringer.

...d John Roberts. m John Cameron. cos Phyllis Dalton. 105 mins

Cast: Angela Lansbury (Miss Marple), Elizabeth Taylor (Marina Gregg), Rock Hudson (Jason Rudd), Tony Curtis (Marty N Fenn), Edward Fox (Insp. Craddock), Kim Novak (Lola Brewster), Geraldine Chaplin (Ella Zielinsky), Charles Gray (Bates, the Butler), Maureen Bennett (Heather Babcock), Margaret Courtenay (Mrs Bantry), Charles Lloyd Pack (Vicar), Richard Pearson (Dr Haydock), *Murder at Midnight* cast: Anthony Steel (Sir Patrick Ridgeley), Dinah Sheridan (Lady Amanda Ridgeley), Kenneth Fortescue (Charles Foxwell), Hildegarde Neil (Lady Foxcroft), Alan Cuthbertson (Peter Montrose), Nigel Stock (Insp. Gates), John Bennett (Barnaby)

A killer strikes among Americans making a movie at a British studio in 1953.

Overstuffed with names and featuring a badly undernourished screenplay, a miscast Lansbury and star performances that range from barely adequate to downright embarrassing, with direction to match. The brief opening pastiche of a British B-feature mystery movie is infinitely more entertaining than the tosh that follows.

'A film in which the acting is so wooden a trail of sawdust is left in the characters' wake.'
Now! Magazine

THE MOB
(US 1951) (GB: REMEMBER THAT FACE)
pc Columbia. p Jerry Bresler. d Robert Parrish. w William Bowers, from the novel *Waterfront* by Ferguson Findley. ph Joseph Walker. B&W. ed Charles Nelson. ad Cary Odell. m George Duning. 87 mins

Cast: Broderick Crawford (Johnny Damico), Betty Buehler (Mary Kiernan), Richard Kiley (Thomas Clancy), Otto Hulett (Lt Banks), Matt Crowley (Smoothie), Neville Brand (Gunner), Ernest Borgnine (Joe Castro), Walter Clavun (Sgt Bennion), Lynne Baggett (Peggy), Charles Bronson (Jack), John Marley (Tony), Ralph Dumke (Police Commissioner)

A detective goes undercover to smash a waterfront racket.

Effectively-executed thick-ear programmer with little new in plot or characterization.

'It makes no attempt to be pretty, and its violence is as exciting and fast-paced as you could ask for ... what it offers, precisely, is an hour and a half of physical mayhem, served up hot with pistols and blackjacks.'
The New York Times

MOONRAKER
(GB/FRANCE 1979)
pc Eon/Les Productions Artistes Associes. p Albert R Broccoli. exec p Michael G Wilson. assoc p William P Cartlidge. d Lewis Gilbert. 2nd unit d Ernest Day, John Glen. w Christopher Wood, from the novel by Ian Fleming. ph Jean Tournier. 2nd unit ph Jacques Renoir. visual fx ph Paul Wilson. optical fx ph Robin Browne. Colour. Panavision. ed John Glen. pd Ken Adam. ad Max Douy, Charles Bishop, Peter Lamont, Harry Lange. sfx John Richardson, Rene Albouze, Serge Ponvianne. visual fx sup Derek Meddings. visual fx Jean Berard. stunt arr Bob Simmons, Claude Carliez. m John Barry. title song John Barry, Hal David, sung by Shirley Bassey. titles Maurice Binder. 126 mins

Cast: Roger Moore (James Bond), Lois Chiles (Holly Goodhead), Michael (Michel) Lonsdale (Hugo Drax), Richard Kiel ('Jaws'), Corinne Clery (Corinne Dufour), Emily Bolton (Manuela), Bernard Lee ('M'), Lois Maxwell (Miss Moneypenny), Toshiro Suga (Chang), Desmond Llewellyn ('Q'), Walter Gotell (Gen. Gogol), Geoffrey Keen (Frederick Gray), Brian Keith (US Shuttle captain)

James Bond saves mankind again, this time from a megalomaniac intent on taking over the world after wiping life off the planet with poison bombs fired from space.

The mixture much as before, with Moore delivering the wisecracks and significant glances, and stuntmen delivering the action. The sequence in space could well carry the subtitle *007 versus Star Wars*. Bond is now as indestructible (and about as credible) as Bugs Bunny, and his exploits have much the same overall improbability. No-expense-spared gadgetry, special effects and locations help compensate for dull patches, but it was a mistake to bring back steel-toothed villain Richard Kiel ('Jaws') from *The Spy Who Loved Me* (1977, q.v.) only to reform him in a saccharine sub-plot.

French co-production meant the replacement of originally-cast heavy Stewart Granger with French actor Lonsdale, whose Christian name was Anglicized to 'Michael' for the occasion.

'Perhaps we've been spoiled by too many galactic spectaculars but I'm afraid the sight of men floating in space and blasting each other with laser guns now seems as routine as any Western shoot out and the film races wearily through its two hours length.'
The Spectator

'This £15 million romp has much more to offer too. The funniest dialogue, the most lavish locations, astonishing gadgetry and thrilling non-stop action. Certainly the most sensational Bond film yet.'
News of the World

THE MOUTHPIECE

(US 1932)
pc WB. p Lucien Hubbard. d James Flood, Elliott Nugent. w Earl Baldwin, Joseph Jackson. st Frank Collins. ph Barney McGill. B&W. ed George Amy. 90 mins

Cast: Warren William (Vincent Day), Sidney Fox (Celia), Aline MacMahon (Miss Hickey), William Janney (John), John Wray (Barton), Polly Walters (Gladys), Ralph Ince (J B), Mae Madison (Elaine), Noel Francis (Miss DeVere), Morgan Wallace (Smith), Paulette Goddard (Girl at Party), J Carrol Naish (Tony), Guy Kibbee (Bartender), Jack LaRue (Garland)

An Assistant District Attorney ends up defending gangsters after sending an innocent man to the chair.

No-nonsense exposure of corrupt justice, allegedly based on real-life New York attorney William J Fallon, and voted one of the ten best films of the year by *The New York Times*.

Remade in 1940 as *The Man Who Talks Too Much* with George Brent, and in 1955 as *Illegal* (q.v.) with Edward G Robinson.

'A thrilling and exciting melodrama.'
New York World-Telegram

MURDER

(GB 1930)
pc British International. p John Maxwell. d Alfred Hitchcock. w Alma Reville, from the play *Enter Sir John* by Clemence Dane, Helen Simpson. ph Jack Cox. B&W. sup ed Emile de Ruelle. ed Rene Harrison. ad John Mead, Peter Proud. 92 mins

Cast: Herbert Marshall (Sir John), Norah Baring (Diana Baring), Phyllis Konstam (Dulcie Markham), Edward Chapman (Ted Markham), Miles Mander (Gordon Druce), Esme Percy (Handel Fane), Donald Calthrop (Ion Stewart), Esme Chaplin (Prosecuting Counsel), A Brandon Thomas (Defending Cousel), Joynson Powell (Judge), Marie Wright (Miss Mitcham), R E Jeffrey (Jury Foreman)

A juror, convinced of the innocence of a young actress accused of murder, turns sleuth and unmasks the real killer.

Hitchcock made a good job of one of his infrequent whodunnits, considerably helped by Marshall's strong performance in his first talking picture. Hitchcock also made a German version at the same time, with Alfred Abel in the Marshall role.

'One acquires considerable admiration for this Hitchcock as a director of drama on the screen.'
Variety

'Originality and artistry of production, with fine acting, make this engrossing mystery story a film of unique interest. Recording is excellent. Clever and thrilling enough to please anywhere.'
Bioscope.

MURDER BY CONTRACT

(US 1958)
pc Orbit. p Leon Chooluck. d Irving Lerner. w Ben Simcoe. ph Lucien Ballard. B&W. ed Carlo Lodato. ad Jack Poplin. m Perry Botkin. 81 mins

Cast: Vince Edwards (Claude), Philip Pine (Marc), Herschel Bernardi (George), Caprice Toriel (Billie Williams), Cathy Browne (The Blonde), Michael Granger (Mr Moon), Frances Osborne (The Maid)

A professional killer is hired to dispose of a federal witness, but his plans go awry.

Interesting, well-directed, well-acted, low-budget second feature whose pretentions to significance are not entirely realized, and with rather too much naive moralizing.

'I thought it self-conscious but not pretentious: a constant pleasure to watch and a lesson in timing, economy and control; and explosively exciting.'
The Spectator

MURDER BY DEATH

(US 1976)
pc Rastar. For Columbia. p Ray Stark. assoc p Roger M Rothstein. d Robert Moore. w Neil Simon. ph David M Walsh. Colour. ed Margaret Booth, John F Burnett, Michael A Stevenson. pd Stephen Grimes. ad Harry Kemm. sfx Augie Lohman. m Dave Grusin.

MURDER BY DEATH

cos Ann Roth. titles Charles Addams, Wayne Fitzgerald. 95 mins

Cast: Eileen Brennan (Tess Skeffington), Truman Capote (Lionel Twain), James Coco (Milo Perrier), Peter Falk (Sam Diamond), Alec Guinness (Bensonum), Elsa Lanchester (Jessica Marbles), David Niven (Dick Charleston), Peter Sellers (Sidney Wang), Maggie Smith (Dora Charleston), Nancy Walker (Yetta), Estelle Winwood (Nurse Withers), Richard Narita (Willie Wang)

An eccentric invites the world's greatest detectives for the weekend and involves them in a bizarre murder mystery.

Entertainingly silly parody that almost comes off, apart from the denouement, which is both ludicrous and largely incomprehensible. It helps, too, to have at least a nodding acquaintance with the fictional creations being satirized by Simon.

The sleuths are sharply satirized, apart from Sellers, who appears to have believed he was appearing in a provincial pantomime, while Guinness's imperturbable blind butler wins the acting honours by a whisker. As an actor, Capote puts up an unanswerable case for writers sticking to writing.

'Neil Simon's parody murder mystery contains a great many one liners delivered by a half-dozen of our favourite stars with fine expertise. The stars obviously relish their roles satirizing some of detective fiction's best-loved sleuths as they appeared both in print and on screen ... it is the flair with which this unsubstantial material is presented that counts.'
Film Information

'One murder is certain: the kings and queens of detective fiction have been memorably done in. Mass murder with style.'
Evening Standard

MURDER BY DECREE

(CANADA/GB 1978)
pc Saucy Jack Inc/Decree Productions. In association with the Canadian Film Development Corporation/Famous Players Film Company/Wow!!! Entertainment Incorporation. A Robert A Goldstone presentation. exec p Len Herberman. p René Dupont, Bob Clark. d Bob Clark. w John Hopkins, from *The Ripper File* by John

Lloyd, Elwyn Jones. ph Reginald H Morris. Colour. ed Stan Cole. pd Harry Pottle. ad Peter Childs. sfx Michael Albrechtson. m Carl Zittrer, Paul Zaza. 112 mins

Cast: Christopher Plummer (Sherlock Holmes), James Mason (Dr Watson), David Hemmings (Insp. Foxborough), Susan Clark (Mary Kelly), Anthony Quayle (Sir Charles Warren), John Gielgud (The Prime Minister), Frank Finlay (Insp. Lestrade), Donald Sutherland (Robert Lees), Genevieve Bujold (Annie Crook)

Sherlock Holmes investigates the Jack the Ripper killings and uncovers a high-level Establishment cover-up.

Lurid, bloody and ingenious, if hardly convincing. Plummer and Mason make an excellent, if idiosyncratic, Holmes and Watson, other roles are interestingly cast, the nineteenth-century atmosphere is laid on with a steam shovel, it maintains a lively dramatic momentum and is rarely boring.

The whirring noise you may hear is Conan Doyle spinning in his grave.

'Uncomplimentary, my dear Watson.'
Daily Express

'There is a sense of atmosphere and period struggling to get out, too, but it is mostly Hammered into the ground.'
The Guardian

MURDER BY PROXY
(GB 1955) (US: BLACKMAIL)
pc Hammer. p Michael Carreras. d Terence Fisher. w Richard Landau, from the novel by Helen Nielsen. ph

Jimmy Harvey. B&W. ed Maurice Rootes. ad Jim Elder Wills. m Ivor Slaney. 87 mins

Cast: Dane Clark (Casey Morrow), Belinda Lee (Phyllis Brunner), Betty Ann Davies (Alicia Brunner), Eleanor Summerfield (Maggie Doone), Andrew Osborn (Lance Gordon), Harold Lang (Travis), Michael Golden (Insp. Johnson), Delphi Lawrence (Linda), Alfie Bass (Ernie), Cleo Laine (Singer), Gillian Frank (Miss Darling), Jill Melford (Miss Nardis)

An American drunk who accepts £500 to marry a woman he does not know ends up having to clear himself of suspicion of murder.

Above-average British B-feature with a glum, imported, second-league Hollywood star and brisk, better-than-it-deserves direction.

'The treatment is sufficiently persuasive to bring a fair amount of excitement to well-tried material ... competently made and the dialogue is agreeably convincing.'
Monthly Film Bulletin

MURDER, INC
(US 1960) (GB: MURDER, INCORPORATED)
pc 20th Century Fox. p Burt Balaban. assoc p Larry Joachim. d Burt Balaban, Stuart Rosenberg. w Irv Tunick, Mel Barr, from the book by Burton Turkus & Sid Feder. ph Gaine Rescher. B&W. CinemaScope. ed Ralph Rosenblum. ad Dick Sylbert. m Frank De Vol. 103 mins

Cast: Stuart Whitman (Joey Collins), May Britt (Eadie Collins), Henry

Morgan (Burton Turkus), David J Stewart (Louis 'Lepke' Buchalter), Simon Oakland (Det. Tobin), Peter Falk (Abe Reles), Warren Fennerty (The Bug), Joseph Bernard (Mendy Weiss), Vincent Gardenia (Laslo), Morey Amsterdam (Walter Sage)

A tough Brooklyn District Attorney smashes a thirties crime syndicate.

Fact-based B-feature directed in effective, fast-moving, semi-documentary style but rather lacking in convincing period detail. Falk's fascinating if mannered performance adds impact.

'The gangster action is brutal and vivid ... the appeal is essentially masculine, but devotees of tough gangster fare will certainly like this one.'
CEA Film Report

MURDER, MY SWEET
(US 1944) (GB: FAREWELL, MY LOVELY)
pc RKO. exec p Sid Rogell. p Adrian Scott. d Edward Dmytryk. w John Paxton, from the novel *Farewell, My Lovely* by Raymond Chandler. ph Harry J Wild. B&W. ed Joseph Noriega. ad Albert D'Agostino, Carroll Clark. sfx Vernon Walker. montage Douglas Travers. md Constantin Bakaleinikoff. m Roy Webb. 95 mins

Cast: Dick Powell (Philip Marlowe), Claire Trevor (Velma/Mrs Grayle), Anne Shirley (Ann), Otto Kruger (Amthor), Mike Mazurki (Moose Malloy), Miles Mander (Mr Grayle), Douglas Walton (Marriott), Don Douglas (Lt Randall), Ralf Harolde (Dr Sonderborg), Esther Howard (Mrs Florian), John Indrisano (Chauffeur), Ernie Adams (Bartender)

private eye Philip Marlowe lands up in mounting trouble when an ex-convict hires him to find his missing girlfriend.

Complex, suspenseful and fast-moving, with razor-sharp dialogue and atmospheric *film noir* direction that combines pace and economy with visual flair. The playing is uniformly good, and the off-beat casting of Powell, then best known for playing allow romantic leads in musicals, comes off very well indeed: he comes cross as both tough and convincing.

A seminal private eye thriller,

remade with surprising success in 1975 as *Farewell, My Lovely* (q.v.) with Robert Mitchum as Marlowe.

'It is slick, sensational, shallow, sordid and scintillating.'
Manchester Guardian

'In short, *Murder, My Sweet* is pulse quickening entertainment.'
The New York Times

'As smart as it is gripping. Ace direction and fine camera-work

combine with a neat story and top performances.'
Variety

MURDER ON THE ORIENT EXPRESS

(GB 1974)
pc G W Films. For EMI. p John Brabourne, Richard Goodwin. d Sidney Lumet. w Paul Dehn, from the novel by Agatha Christie. ph Geoffrey Unsworth. process ph Charles Staffell. Colour. ed Anne V Coates. pd, cos Tony Walton. ad Jack

MURDER SHE SAID

MURDER ON THE ORIENT EXPRESS

Stephens. m Richard Rodney
Bennett. 131 mins

Cast: Albert Finney (Hercule Poirot),
Lauren Bacall (Mrs Hubbard),
Martin Balsam (Bianchi), Ingrid
Bergman (Greta Ohlsson), Jacqueline
Bissett (Countess Adrenyi), Jean-
Pierre Cassel (Pierre Paul Michel),
Sean Connery (Col. Arbuthnot),
John Gielgud (Beddoes), Wendy
Hiller (Princess Dragomiroff),
Anthony Perkins (Hector McQueen),
Vanessa Redgrave (Mary Debenham),
Rachel Roberts (Hildegarde
Schmidt), Richard Widmark
(Rachett), Michael York (Count
Andrenyi), George Coulouris (Dr
Constantine)

In 1934 Hercule Poirot investigates
homicide on board the snowbound
Istanbul–Paris express.

Over-long and basically faithful
adaptation, impeccably mounted and
carefully directed to allow an all-star
cast to do their party pieces in
enjoyably varying styles. Finney is
somewhat over the top as Poirot, but
compared to the role's subsequent
screen incumbent, Peter Ustinov, he
seems remarkably restrained.

Finney, Ingrid Bergman, the
screenplay, music and cinematography
were all nominated for Academy
Awards. In the event, only Bergman
won, for Best Supporting Actress.

**'A joy-ride that traverses a stagger-
ing complexity of points and doesn't
come off the rails once.'**
Evening Standard

**'No more or less than the book
itself, it is a perfectly pleasant**
entertainment, a couple of hours
of nostalgic escape.'
The Times

MURDER SHE SAID
(GB 1961)
pc MGM. p George H Brown. d
George Pollock. w David Pursall, Jack
Seddon, from the novel *4.50 from
Paddington* by Agatha Christie. ph
Geoffrey Faithfull. B&W. ed Ernest
Walter. ad Harry White. m Ron
Goodwin. 86 mins

Cast: Margaret Rutherford (Miss Jane
Marple), Arthur Kennedy (Quimper),
Muriel Pavlow (Emma), James
Robertson Justice (Ackenthorpe),
Charles Tingwell (Craddock), Thorley
Walters (Cedric), Conrad Phillips
(Harold), Ronnie Raymond
(Alexander), Joan Hickson (Mrs
Kidder), Ronald Howard (Eastley),
Gerald Cross (Albert), Michael Golden
(Hillman)

An elederly spinster turns detective after
witnessing a murder in a passing train.

Engaging minor romp, with
Rutherford resolutely Rutherford and
nothing like Christie's Jane Marple, and
a reasonably surprising denouement.

Joan Hickson, who appears in a
minor role, went on to play Miss
Marple in a popular eighties and
nineties British television series.
Rutherford made three more (and
disappointing) Miss Marple
whodunnits, *Murder at the Gallop*
(1963), *Murder Most Foul* (1964) and
Murder Ahoy (1964).

'Gentle fun and mild thrills.'
Evening News

ADINE

(US 1987)

TriStar-ML Delphi Premier
roductions. exec p, unit p manager
olfgang Glattes. p Arlene Donovan.
d Robert Benton. ph Nestor
mendros. Colour. ed Sam O'Stccn.
Paul Sylbert. ad Peter Lansdown
nith, Cary White. sc Diamond
rnsworth. m Howard Shore. 83 mins

ast: Jeff Bridges (Vernon Hightower),
im Basinger (Nadine Hightower),
p Torn (Buford Pope), Gwen Verdon
era), Glenne Headly (Renee), Jerry
iller (Raymond Escobar), Jay
tterson (Dwight Estes), William
umans (Boyd), Gary Grubbs (Cecil),
ue Deckert (Mountain), Harlan
rdan (Sheriff Rusk)

hairdresser and her estranged
sband become involved in murder in
ties small-town Texas.

   Lighthearted comedy-thriller with
ss depth than hair lacqueur.

n innocuous soufflé.'
ariety

HE NAKED EDGE

(US/GB 1961)

Pennebaker (Glass-Seltzer)-
aroda/Jason/Monica/Monmouth/Ben
ey. exec p Marlon Brando. p Walter
lzter, George Glass. d Michael
nderson. w Joseph Stefano, from the
ovel *First Train to Babylon* by Max
lich. ph Erwin Hillier. B&W. ed
ordon Pilkington. ad Carmen Dillon.
William Alwyn. 99 mins

ast: Gary Cooper (George Radcliffe)
eborah Kerr (Martha), Eric Portman
eremy Clay), Michael Wilding

(Morris Brooke), Diane Cilento (Mrs
Heath), Hemione Gingold (Lilly
Harris), Ray McAnally (Donald
Heath), Peter Cushing (Wrack),
Ronald Howard (Claridge), Sandor
Eles (Manfridi), Wilfrid Lawson
(Pom), Helen Cherry (Miss Osborne),
Joyce Carey (Victoria Hicks)

A woman suspects her businessman
husband may be a murderer.

   Competent but implausible, with a
cast that is more interesting than the
plot and a lacklustre performance from
Cooper in his final film. Anderson
appears to think he is Hitchcock;
he isn't.

'While the "spine-chiller" unfolds, it
not only holds, but steadily tightens its
grip and, what's more, has a terrifying
denouement.'
Kine Weekly

'The sort of dishonest, trick-filled
thriller which has become something
of a staple commodity recently.'
Monthly Film Bulletin

THE NAKED RUNNER

(GB 1967)

pc Artanis. A Sinatra Enterprises
Production. p Brad Dexter. d Sidney J
Furie. w Stanley Mann, from the
novel by Francis Clifford. ph Otto
Heller. Colour. Techniscope. ed Barry
Vince. ad Peter Proud. m Harry
Sukman. 103 mins

Cast: Frank Sinatra (Sam Laker), Peter
Vaughan (Martin Slattery), Derren
Nesbitt (Col Harman), Nadia Gray
(Karen Gisevius), Toby Robins (Ruth),
Inger Stratton (Anna), Cyril Luckham
(Cabinet Minister), Edward Fox (Ritchie

Jackson), J Dubin-Behrmann (Joseph), Michael Newport (Patrick Laker)

The 14-year-old son of an American businessman who agrees to take a message from London to Leipzig for British Intelligence is kidnapped to force his father to kill a man in Copenhagen.

Implausible, slackly-written, frenetically and flashily over-directed by Furie and boringly acted by Sinatra, who seems to have as much trouble staying awake as audiences did.

'The story is full of opportunities for drama, but the audience has only the script's word that *The Naked Runner* is a suspense film ... as in many another amateurish spy film, Sinatra and company have forgotten to look for the enemy within – a soggy scenario that gummed up the caper from the start.'
Time

THE NAME OF THE GAME IS KILL

(US 1968) (US TV: THE FEMALE TRAP)
pc Poore and Todd Productions/Fanfare. exec p Joe Solomon. assoc exec p Richard J Todd. p Robert Poore. assoc p Robert L Rosen. d Gunnar Hellstrom. w Gary Crutcher. ph William Szigmond. Colour. ed Lou Lombardo. ad Ray Markham. m Stu Phillips. song *Shadows* by Stu Phillips, Mike Gordon, sung by The Electric Prunes. 88 mins

Cast: Jack Lord (Symcha Lipa), Susan Strasberg (Mickey Terry), Collin Wilcox (Diz Terry), Tisha Sterling (Nan Terry), T C Jones (Mrs

Terry/Mr Terry), Mort Mills (Sheriff Kendall), Marc Desmond (The Doctor)

A hitchhiker taken by a woman to the lonely Arizona desert home where she lives with her mother and her two sisters finds himself targeted for death.

Offbeat, macabre to the point of parody but consistently intriguing, although the denouement is hardly credible.

'Quite frankly, a piece of melodramatic invention designed to chill the marrow (which it does not do very well) and to entertain (which it does quite well in an unsophisticated way).'
Kine Weekly

THE NEW CENTURIONS

(US 1972) (GB: PRECINCT 45 – LOS ANGELES POLICE)
pc Chartoff-Winkler Productions. p Irwin Winkler, Robert Chartoff. assoc p Henry Gellis. d Richard Fleischer. w Stirling Silliphant, from the novel *The New Centurions* by Joseph Wambaugh. ph Ralph Woolsey. Colour. Panavision. ed Robert C Jones. pd Boris Leven. m Quincy Jones. 103 mins

Cast: George C Scott (Sgt Kilvinsky), Stacy Keach (Roy Fehler), Jane Alexander (Dorothy Felder), Scott Wilson (Gus), Rosalind Cash (Lorrie), Erik Estrada (Sergio), Clifton James (Whitey), Richard Kalk (Milton), James B Sikking (Sgt Anders), Beverly Hope Atkinson (Alice), William Atherton (Johnson), Ed Lauter (Galloway), Dolph Sweet (Sgt Runyon), Burke Byrnes (Phillips)

A rookie joins a seasoned veteran

policeman to patrol Los Angeles.

The 'older mentor/keen youngster' formula long ago worked to death on television works well enough on the big screen. The routine of big-city police work is convincingly depicted with a fashionably jaundiced eye, and it compels attention in spite of its episodic, largely plotless structure.

'There is no "story" in the accepted sense, no very significant development of character. But the succession of highly-charged incidents, and the men's varied reactions to them add up to a film that never loses its steel-fisted grip.'
Evening News

NEW YORK CONFIDENTIAL

(US 1955)
pc A Greene-Rouse Production, presented by Edward Small. p Clarence Green. d Russell Rouse. w Clarence Greene, Russell Rouse, suggested by the book by Jack Lait & Lee Mortimer. ph Edward Fitzgerald. B&W. ed Grant Whytock. pd Fernando Carrere. ad Joseph W Holland. sfx Willis Cook. m Joseph Mullendore. 87 mins

Cast: Broderick Crawford (Charles Lupo), Richard Conte (Nick Magellan), Marilyn Maxwell (Iris Palmer), Anne Bancroft (Katherine Lupo), J Carrol Naish (Ben Dagajanian), Onslow Stevens (Johnny Achilles), Barry Kelley (Frawley), Mike Mazurki (Andie Wendler), Celia Lovsky (Mama Lupo), Steven Geray (Morris Franklin), Nestor Paiva (Martinelli), Joe Vitale (Batista)

A New York Syndicate boss makes a hitman his minder, but eventually his protégé is ordered to kill him.

Slick, allegedly authentic, and fairly unusual for the period in its presentation of criminals as big businessmen. Excellent cinematography and editing.

'Exciting and thrilling, it nevertheless well deserves its "X" certificate.'
Picture Show

NIAGARA
(US 1953)
pc 20th Century Fox. p Charles Brackett. d Henry Hathaway. w Charles Brackett, Walter Reisch, Richard Breen. ph Joe MacDonald. sfx ph Ray Kellogg. Colour. ed Barbara McLean. ad Lyle Wheeler, Maurice Ransford. m Sol Kaplan. song *Kiss* by Lionel Newman, Haven Gillespie, sung by Marilyn Monroe. 92 mins

Cast: Marilyn Monroe (Rose Loomis), Joseph Cotten (George Loomis), Jean Peters (Polly Cutler), Casey Adams (Ray Cutler), Dennis O'Dea (Insp. Sharkey), Richard Allan (Patrick), Don Wilson (Mr Kettering), Lurene Tuttle (Mrs Kettering), Russell Collins (Mr Qua), Will Wright (Boatman), Lester Matthews (Doctor), Carleton Young (Policeman), Sean McClory (Sam)

An unfaithful woman and her lover plot the murder of her husband.
Ordinary but handsomely-

NIAGARA

appointed thriller that manages the not inconsiderable feat of taking itself seriously. It was designed to showcase two great North American icons – Monroe and the Niagara Falls. Both were photographed to advantage by Joe MacDonald.

'I approached this richly idiotic film with caution but, as time went on, abandoned myself to an enjoyment which I hope was shared by the rest of the audience.'
The Sunday Times

NICK CARTER, MASTER DETECTIVE
(US 1939)
pc MGM. p Lucien Hubbard. d Jacques Tourneur. w Bertram Millhauser, Harold Buckley, based on the character created by John R Coryell. ph Charles Lawton. B&W. ed Elmo Veron. 57 mins

Cast: Walter Pidgeon (Nick Carter/Robert Chalmers), Rita Johnson (Lou Farnsby), Henry Hull (John A Keller), Stanley C Ridges (Dr Frankton), Donald Meek (Bartholomew), Addison Richards (Hiram Streeter), Henry Victor (J Lester Hammil), Milburn Stone (David Krebs), Martin Kosleck (Otto King)

The Master Detective is assigned to break up a spy ring stealing plans from an aircraft factory.

Compact second feature (the first of three starring Pidgeon as the sleuth created by John R Coryell in *New York Weekly* in 1884) which passes the time painlessly but leaves little impression.

'Subsequent releases of the series will have to have stronger and more thrilling content, if Carter's screen life is to carry along for any length of time.'
Variety

NIGHT AND THE CITY
(GB 1950)
pc 20th Century Fox. p Samuel G Engel. d Jules Dassin. w Jo Eisinger, from the novel by Gerald Kersh. ph Max Greene. B&W. ed Sidney Stone. ad C P Norman. m Benjamin Frankel. 101 mins

Cast: Richard Widmark (Harry Fabian), Gene Tierney (Mary Bristol), Googie Withers (Helen Nosseros), Hugh Marlowe (Adam Dunn), Francis L Sullivan (Phil Nosseros), Herbert Lom (Kristo), Mike Mazurki (The Strangler), Stanislaus Zbyszko (Gregorius), James Hayter (Figler), Edward Chapman (Hoskins), Charles Farrell (Beer), Ada Reeve (Molly), Eliot Makeham (Pinkney)

A small-time crook sets out to be a wrestling promoter in London and runs into opposition from the Greek gangster who controls the sport.

A dismal attempt to do for London what *Naked City* did for New York. Dassin's direction is self-conscious and dull, and he uses locations like an undiscriminating tourist determined to prove he has been to London, while the Anglo-American cast seem ill at ease with the story and with each other. Remade, very badly, by Irwin Winkler in 1992, with Robert De Niro in the Widmark role.

'*Night and the City* should be a great help in sending American tourists to Paris.'
Evening Standard

NIGHT MOVES
(US 1975)
pc Hiller Productions/Layton. P Robert M Sherman. assoc p Gene Lasko. d Arthur Penn. w Alan Sharp. ph Bruce Surtees. underwater ph Jordan Klein. Colour. ed Dede Allen, Stephen A Rotter. pd George Jenkins. sfx Marcel Vercoutere, Joe Day. m Michael Small, 99 mins

Cast: Gene Hackman (Harry Moseby), Jennifer Warren (Paula), Edward Binns (Joey Ziegler), Harris Yulin (Marty Hiller), Kenneth Mars (Nick), Janet Ward (Arlene Iverson), James Woods (Quentin), Anthony Costello (Marv Ellman), John Crawford (Tom Iverson), Melanie Griffith (Delly Gastner), Susan Clark (Ellen Moseby), Ben Archibel (Charles)

A Hollywood private eye hired to find a runaway teenage girl is enmeshed in a slew of murder and the smuggling of archaeological treasures out of Mexico.

Densely-plotted, well-observed, with a tense climax and an overdose of violence, but ultimately unfocused. Over-indulgence of the hero's marital problems ultimately becomes counterproductive. Not as good as its Penn-prone idolators would have you believe.

'The latest entry in the private-detective genre, *Night Moves*, is basically a light-weight, but there's something about it that keeps you glued – even though it's burdened with stereotypes and a script that almost too glib for its own good, has a plot and subplot as convoluted as

bent corkscrew, and is about as memorable as last week's newspaper.'
Women's Wear Daily

A stunning, stylish detective mystery in the classic Raymond Chandler-Ross Macdonald Mould ... also a fast, often funny movie with lots of compassionate-observed real, living breathing people.'
Los Angeles Times

THE NIGHT OF THE FOLLOWING DAY

(US 1968)

Gina/Universal. exec p Jerry Jershwin, Elliott Kastner. p, d Hubert Cornfield. w Hubert Cornfield, Robert Phippeny, from the novel *The Snatchers* by Lionel White. ph Willy Kurant. Colour. ed Ann Vogler. ad Jean Boulet. m Stanley Myers. song *One Early Morning* by Stanley Myers, Jon Hendricks. 93 mins

Cast: Marlon Brando (Bud), Richard Boone (Leer), Rita Moreno (Vi), Pamela Franklin (The Girl), Jess Hahn (Wally), Gerard Buhr (Gendarme), Jacques Marin (Bartender), Hughes Wanner (The Father), Al Lettieri (Pilot)

Four men abduct a young girl and hold her for ransom in an isolated French seaside villa, but the scheme finally collapses.

Brando sinks to the occasion and sleepwalks through the film. Boone, who also took over direction near the end of shooting, gives the only involving performance in a pretentious, poorly-written and badly-directed thriller which is flabby where it should be tense and whose cop-out ending effectively destroys what minor interest there is.

NIGHT AND THE CITY

'Strikingly bad, an under-charged and over-heated thriller.'
Financial Times

NIGHT WATCH
(GB 1973)
pc Brut Productions. p Martin Poll, George W George, Bernard Straus. assoc p David White. d Brian G Hutton. w Tony Williamson, from the play by Lucille Fletcher. add dial Evan Jones. ph Billy Williams. Colour. ed John Jympson. ad Peter Murton. m John Cameron. 98 mins

Cast: Elizabeth Taylor (Ellen Wheeler), Laurence Harvey (John Wheeler), Billie Whitelaw (Sarah Cooke), Robert Lang (Appleby), Tony Britton (Tony), Bill Dean (Insp. Walker), Michael Danvers-Walker (Sgt Norris), Rosario Serrano (Dolores), Pauline Jameson (Secretary), Linda Hayden (Girl in Car)

A neurotic woman witnesses a murder, but no one will believe her.

A hackneyed story receieves lacklustre treatment on both sides of the camera, and the final twist is forgettable.

'What's amazing about the film is that it's so *bad*. In fact it almost defies description.'
Films and Filming

NIGHTHAWKS
(US 1981)
pc Universal. In association with Herb Nanas. exec p Michael Wise, Franklin R Levy. p Martin Poll. assoc p Kathryn Stellmack. d Bruce Malmuth. 2nd unit d Bill Casidy. w David Shaber. st David Shaber, Paul Sylbert. ph James A Contner. Colour. ed Christopher

Holmes, Stanford C Allen. pd Peter Larkin. sfx Walter Tatro, Nick Allder. special m-u Dick Smith. m Keith Emerson. 99 mins

Cast: Sylvester Stallone (Deke DaSilva), Billy Dee Williams (Matthew Fox), Lindsay Wagner (Irene), Persis Khambatta (Shakka), Nigel Davenport (Insp. Peter Hartman), Rutger Hauer (Wulfgar), Hilarie Thompson (Pam), Joe Spinell (Lt Munafo), Walter Matthews (Commissioner), Charles Duval (Dr Ghiselin)

Interpol recruit two New York policemen to help hunt down a ruthless international terrorist.

Fast-moving, brainless, by-numbers action and suspense with a memorable performance by Hauer as a terrorist and one from Wagner that fades while you watch.

'The film looks much like a television pilot for a new series, no better or worse. It suffices, but only just!'
Cosmopolitan

NIGHTMARE
(US 1956)
pc A Pine-Thomas-Shane Production. p William Thomas, Howard Pine. d, w Maxwell Shane, from the short story by Cornell Woolrich. ph Joseph Biroc. B&W. ed George Gittens. ad Frank Sylos. m Herschel Burke Gilbert. 89 mins

Cast: Edward G Robinson (Rene Bressard), Kevin McCarthy (Stan Grayson), Connie Russell (Gina), Virginia Christine (Sue), Rhys Williams (Torrence), Gage Clark (Belnap), Barry Atwater (Warner),

Marian Carr (Madge), Billy May (Louis Simes)

When a New Orleans jazz musician dreams he has committed a murder, his detective brother-in-law proves he was hypnotized into becoming a killer.

Shane's preposterous remake of his own *Fear in the Night* (1947) still fails to carry much conviction. McCarthy makes a good impression as the tortured musician, Robinson makes none.

'Surely the most ingenious thriller of the year. Sometimes it oversteps the bounds of logic. But, then, what nightmare was ever logical?'
Picturegoer

NIGHTMARE IN THE SUN
(US 1963)
pc Afilmco. p Marc Lawrence, John Derek. assoc p Douglas Stewart. d Marc Lawrence. w Ted Thomas, Fanya Lawrence. st Marc Lawrence, George Fass. ph Stanley Cortez. Colour. ed Douglas Stewart, William Shenberg. a Paul Sylos. m Paul Glass. 81 mins

Cast: Ursula Andress (Marsha), John Derek (Steve), Aldo Ray (Sheriff Max Ilrod), Arthur O'Connell (Sam Wilson), John Marley (Hogan), Rober Duvall (Motorcyclist), Richard Jaeckel (Motorcyclist), Sammy Davis Jr (Trucker), George Tobias (Gideon), Lurene Tuttle (Gideon's Wife), Keenan Wynn (Junkyard Proprietor), Allyn Joslyn (Mr Dawson)

A corrupt small-town sheriff attempts to frame a hitchhiker for the murder o a wealthy citizen's wife.

Perennial screen heavy Marc

Lawrence displays an interesting visual style in his directorial debut, and off-beat casting of the minor roles helps, but the over-contrived story loses momentum.

'The fact that it has an attitude and this clearly comes through makes it preferable any day to a smoothly-tailored absence of purpose.'
Films and Filming

99 AND 44/100% DEAD/CALL HARRY CROWN
(US 1974)

pc Joe Wizan/Vashon. p Joe Wizan. assoc p Mickey Borofsky. d John Frankenheimer. underwater d Paul Stader. w Robert Dillon. ph Ralph Woolsey. underwater ph Lamar Boren. Colour. Panavision. ed Harold F Kress. ad Herman Blumenthal. sfx Ira Anderson Jr, Paul Pollard Sr. m Henry Mancini. song *Easy, Baby* by Henry Mancini, Alan Bergman, Marilyn Bergman. 98 mins

Cast: Richard Harris (Harry Crown), Edmond O'Brien (Uncle Frank), Bradford Dillman (Big Eddie), Ann Turkel (Buffy), Chuck Connors (Marvin 'Claw' Zuckerman), Constance Ford (Dolly), David Hall (Tony), Kathrine Baumann (Baby), Janice Heiden (Clara), Roy Jenson (Jake), Max Kleven (North)

A mobster hires a professional killer to take out a rival.

The title and the opening titles rouse interest, but the messy melange of comic-strip action, cardboard characters and bad acting that follows does not. Another Frankenheimer dud.

'Apart from the grand folly of the title – literally unspeakable – Frankenheimer's new movie is the bruised victim of its own worst excesses.'
Films Illustrated

NO WAY OUT
(US 1986)

pc Orion. exec p Mace Neufeld. p Laura Ziskin, Robert Garland. d Roger Donaldson. w Roger Garland, from the novel *The Bog Clock* by Kenneth Fearing. ph John Alcott, Alun Bollinger. Colour. ed Neil Travis. pd Dennis Washington, Kai Hawkins. ad Anthony Brokliss. sc Richard Diamond Farnsworth, Peter Bell. m Maurice Jarre. 115 mins

Cast: Kevin Costner (Tom Farrell), Gene Hackman (David Bryce), Sean Young (Susan Atwell), Will Patton (Scott Pritchard), Howard Duff (Sen Duvall), George Dzundza (Sam Hesselman), Iman (Nina Beka), Fred Dalton Thompson ((Marshall), Leon Russom (Kevin O'Brien), Dennis Burkley (Mate), Marshall Bell (Contra No.1), Chris D (Contra No.2), Michael Shillo (Schiller)

A navy officer working in the Pentagon for the Secretary of Defense is assigned to find a vital witness to the murder of the woman he shared as a mistress with the Secretary, and ends up as prime suspect.

Ingenious remake of 1948's *The Big Clock* (q.v.) with a new, hard-to-swallow climactic twist and solid central performances.

'A superior example of the genre, a film in which a simply situation grows more and more complex until it turns into a nightmare not only for the hero but also for everyone associated with him.'
Chicago Sun-Times

NO WAY TO TREAT A LADY
(US 1967)

pc Sol C Siegel Productions. p Sol C Siegel. d Jack Smight. w John Gay, from the novel by William Goldman. ph Jack Priestley. Colour. ed Archie Marshak. ad Hal Pereira, George Jenkins. m Stanley Myers. song *A Quiet Place* by Stanley Myers, Andrew Belling, sung by The American Breed. 108 mins

Cast: Rod Steiger (Christopher Gill), George Segal (Morris Brummel), Lee Remick (Kate Palmer), Eileen Heckart (Mrs Brummel), Murray Hamilton (Insp. Haines), Michael Dunn (Mr Kupperman), Martine Bartlett (Alma Mulloy), Barbara Baxley (Belle Poppie), Irene Dailey (Mrs Fitts), Ruth White (Mrs Himmel), Doris Roberts (Sylvie Poppie), Val Bisoglio (Det. Monaghan), David Doyle (Lt Dawson)

A New York detective tracking down a deranged, mother-dominated killer of women trades insults with the murderer and finally puts his girlfriend in danger.

Witty, immensely enjoyable and blackly comic thriller whose humour is well integrated with the thrills and suspense. Steiger assumes a series of disguises, and while he is no Alec Guinness in *Kind Hearts and Coronets*, he is well suited to the role, and Smight's slick direction succeeds in using his usual tendency to overact to advantage. A small gem.

NORTH BY NORTHWEST

NORTH BY NORTHWEST
(US 1959)
pc Alfred Hitchcock/MGM. p, d Alfred Hitchcock. assoc p Robert Coleman. w Ernest Lehman. ph Robert Burks. Colour. ed George Tomasini. ed William A Horning, Merrill Pye. sfx A Arnold Gillespie, Lee LeBlanc. m Bernard Herrmann. titles Saul Bass. 136 mins

Cast: Cary Grant (Roger Thornhill), Eva Marie Saint (Eve Kendall), James Mason (Phillip Vandamm), Jessi Royce Landis (Clara Thornhill), Leo G Carroll (The Professor), Philip Ober (Lester Townsend), Martin Landau (Leonard), Adam Williams (Valerian), Edward C Platt (Victor Larrabee), Josephine Hutchinson ('Mrs Townsend'/Housekeeper), Robert Ellenstein (Licht), Les Tremayne (Auctioneer)

NORTH BY NORTHWEST

A Madison Avenue executive is mistaken for a secret agent, kidnapped and framed for murder, and ends up on the run from the law and from foreign spies.

Hitchcock at his tongue-in-cheek best, taking a tall story that barely holds water and leading it from one unforgettable set-piece to the next at such a pell-mell pace that disbelief is willingly suspended. Grant's drunken downhill drive, his strafing by a crop-dusting aircraft and the final perilous climb up a president's face on Mount Rushmore are deserved genre classics.

Hitchcock misses few tricks, and panders to cineastes by quoting from other of his films, including *The 39 Steps*, *Saboteur* and *Notorious*, and climaxes *North By Northwest* with (by his own assessment) one of the cinema's greatest phallic symbols as the train carrying Grant and Saint enters a tunnel.

Grant is at his suave best, but the acting honours go to Mason's silky villain, whose homosexual relationship with his henchman, Martin Landau, is surprisingly overt for the period.

May not be his best-ever piece of suspense but it is certainly his most mischievously outrageous attack on public credulity.'
Sunday Express

Too long or not, *North by Northwest* is a film to see. You get a lot of entertainment for your money. You get a couple of clever, sophisticated screen actors and an elegant actress with a fine-drawn, exciting face. You get one scene that will be talked about as long as people talk about films at all. And everything for little more than the price of a glossy, colour-plated magazine, which in many ways this much resembles.'
The Observer

NOTORIOUS
(US 1946)
pc RKO. p, d Alfred Hitchcock. assoc p Barbara Keon. w Ben Hecht, from an idea by Alfred Hitchcock. ph Ted Tetzlaff. B&W. ed Theron Warth. ad Albert D'Agostino, Carroll Clark, Darrell Silvera, Claude Carpenter. sfx Vernon L Walker, Paul Eagler. m Roy Webb. 102 mins

Cast: Ingrid Bergman (Alicia Huberman), Cary Grant (Devlin), Claude Rains (Alexander Sebastian), Louis Calhern (Paul Prescott), Reinhold Schünzel (Dr Anderson), Leopoldine Konstantin (Mrs Sebastian), Ivan Triesault (Eric Mathis), Moroni Olsen (Walter Beardsley), Alex Minotis (Joseph), Wally Brown (Mr Hopkins), Sir Charles Mendl (Commodore)

The daughter of a convicted German spy is persuaded by American agent to marry a neo-Nazi spy in postwar Rio de Janeiro in order to bring him and his organization to book.

Sophisticated and ironic suspenser with some splendid set-pieces, notably a swooping crane shot ending up in a

close-up of a significant key. But Hitchcock's concentration on the torrid (for the time) romance of Bergman and Grant, particularly their 'longest kiss in history', tends to undercut the tension. Grant and Bergman are excellent, Rains as the Nazi leader is outstanding.

'One of the most absorbing pictures of the year … a romantic melodrama which is just about as thrilling as they come – velvet smooth in dramatic action, sharp and sure in its characters and heavily charged with the intensity of warm emotional appeal.'
The New York Times

'*Notorious* lacks many of the qualities which made the best of Alfred Hitchcock's movies so good, but it has more than enough good qualities of its own.'
The Nation

'Hitchcock has used all his box of tricks to jolt, to unnerve: the distortions, the shadows, the watchful faces of melodrama … the movement of the camera is over-ruling; and possible distastes of the elements of Ben Hecht's script is most of the time lost in the interest of watching the rhythm of motion, the sidling or the sudden approaches, the swoops and swerves and horizontal swings.'
The Sunday Times

NUMBER SEVENTEEN
(GB 1932)
pc British International Pictures. p John Maxwell. d Alfred Hitchcock. w Alfred Hitchcock, Alma Reville,

Rodney Ackland, from the play & novel by J Jefferson Farjeon. ph Jack Cox, Bryan Langley. B&W. ed A C Hammond. ad Wilfred Shingleton. m A Hallis. 64 mins

Cast: Leon M Lion (Ben), Anne Gray (The Young Girl), John Stuart (The Detective), with Donald Calthrop, Barry Jones, Garry Marsh, Ann Casson, Henry Caine

A detective rounds up crooks with the help of a tramp and a girl from the gang who falls for him.
    The cliché-ridden original was turned into a cliché-ridden melodrama by Hitchcock, who showed his dislike of the project to which he had been assigned in a film that is short, confusing and below par, with a disappointing climactic chase between a train and a bus that employs all-too-obvious miniatures.

'The producer [sic] has concentrated more on camera angles than the telling of the story, which is constantly held up, whilst its development is full of obscurities.'
CEA Film Report

'A disaster!'
Alfred Hitchcock

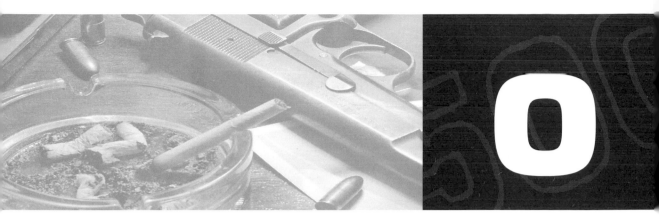

OBSESSION
(US 1976)

pc Yellow Bird Films. exec p Robert S Bremson. p George Litto, Harry N Blum. d Brian De Palma. w Paul Schrader. st Paul Schrader, Brian De Palma. ph Vilmos Zsigmond. Colour. Panavision. ed Paul Hirsch. ad Jack Senter. sfx Joe Lombardi, Special Effects Unlimited. m Bernard Herrmann. 98 mins

Cast: Cliff Robertson (Michael Courtland), Genevieve Bujold (Elizabeth Courtland/Sandra Portinari), John Lithgow (Robert LaSalle), Sylvia 'Kuumba' Williams (Judy), Wanda Blackman (Amy Courtland), Patrick McNamara (Third kidnapper), Stanley Reyes (Insp. Brie), Nick Krieger (Farber), Don Hood (Ferguson), Stockard Fontelieu (Dr Ellman), Regis Cordic (Newscaster)

Sixteen years after his wife is killed in a kidnapping, a businessman falls in love with her 'double' in Italy and is drawn into sinister intrigue.

Inept and self-regarding rehash of *Vertigo* (1958, q.v.), and yet another disastrous attempt by De Palma to pass himself off as the new Hitchcock. Even the climax is muffed.

'An unholy mess. Intended as an *hommage* to Hitchcock – especially to his murky and pretentious *Vertigo* (itself a kind of unwitting tribute to Clouzot's *Diabolique*) – *Obsession* attitudinizes in three directions: towards the Hitchcockian thriller, towards the old-fashioned tearjerker, and towards the sophisticated European film, with cultural references strewn like bread crumbs along the way of Hansel and Gretel.'
New York Magazine

'The only really obsessive thing about it is director Brian De Palma's desire to make a slavish imitation of a Hitchcock film. Echoes abound, most notably of *Rebecca*, *Vertigo* and *Marnie*; but whereas personal involvement (his own and the audience's) is the trademark of even the most mechanical Hitchcock movie, here the whole thing seems to have been assembled by numbers.'
The Observer

ODDS AGAINST TOMORROW
(US 1959)

pc Harbel. p, d Robert Wise. assoc p Phil Stein. w John O Killens, Nelson Gidding, from the novel by William P McGivern. ph Joseph Brun. B&W. ed Dede Allen. ad Leo Kerz. m John Lewis. 96 mins

Cast: Harry Belafonte (Johnny Ingram), Robert Ryan (Earl Slater), Gloria Grahame (Helen), Shelley Winters (Lorry), Ed Begley (Dave Burke), Will Kuluva (Bacco), Mae Barnes (Annie), Kim Hamilton (Ruth), Richard Bright (Coco), Carmen DeLavallade (Kitty), Lou Gallo (Moriarty), Wayne Rogers (Soldier)

A former policeman recruits two men, one black, to rob a small bank in New York State, but racial tension wrecks the enterprise.

A taut, expertly-directed thriller that suffers from some overwrought plotting, sincere but unconvincingly-integrated racial tension, and weak acting by Belafonte. The score and cinematography are distinct assets.

'There is a splurge of melodramatics in the climax and these, together with suspense and sustained incident, help to make it exciting fare of modern appeal.'
CEA Film Report

ON DANGEROUS GROUND

(US 1951)

pc RKO. p John Houseman. d
Nicholas Ray. w A I Bezzerides, from
the novel by Gerald Butler. ph George
E Diskant. B&W. ed Roland Gross. ad
Albert D'Agostino, Ralph Berger. m
Bernard Herrmann. 82 mins

Cast: Robert Ryan (Jim Wilson), Ida
Lupino (Mary Malden), Ward Bond
(Walter Brent), Charles Kemper (Bill
Daly), Anthony Ross (Pete Santos), Ed
Begley (Capt. Brawley), Ian Wolfe
(Carrey), Sumner Williams (Danny
Malden), Gus Schilling (Lucky), Frank
Ferguson (Willows), Cleo Moore
(Myrna), Olive Carey (Mrs Brent)

A tough killer sent to track down an out-
of-town killer falls for his blind sister.

Interesting *film noir*, although not
quite the seminal work its reputation
would have you believe. Good
performances and a relatively short
running time redeem its self-
consciousness.

'The combination of unlikely incident
and pretentious dialogue makes for a
distinctly odd film.'
Monthly Film Bulletin

ON HER MAJESTY'S
SECRET SERVICE

(GB 1969)

pc Eon/Danjaq. p Harry Saltzman,
Albert R Broccoli. assoc p Stanley
Sopel. d Peter Hunt. 2nd unit d John
Glen. stock car sequences d Anthony
Squire. w Richard Maibaum, from
the novel by Ian Fleming. add dial
Simon Raven. ph Michael Reed.
2nd unit ph Egil Woxholt, Emil
Ford. aerial ph John Jordan. skiing

ON HER MAJESTY'S SECRET SERVICE

ph Willy Bogner Jr, Alex Barbey.
Colour. ed John Glen. pd Syd Cain.
ad Bob Laing. sfx John Stears. stunt
arr George Leech. m John Barry,
song *We Have All The Time In The
World* by John Barry, Hal David,
sung by Louis Armstrong. titles
Maurice Binder. 140 mins

Cast: George Lazenby (James Bond),
Diana Rigg (Tracy), Telly Savalas (Ernst
Blofeld), Ilse Steppat (Irma Blunt),
Gabriele Ferzetti (Marc Ange Draco),
Yuri Borienko (Grunther), Bernard
Horsfall (Campbell), George Baker (Sir
Hilary Bray), Bernard Lee ('M'), Lois
Maxwell (Miss Moneypenny),
Desmond Llewellyn ('Q'), Angela

Scoular (Ruby), Catherina von Schell
(Nancy), Joanna Lumley (English Girl),
Dani Sheridan (American Girl), Julie
Ege (Scandinavian Girl), Anoushka
Hempel (Australian Girl), Jenny Hanley
(Italian Girl), Bessie Love (American
Guest), Geoffrey Cheshire (Tousaint)

James Bond tangles with arch-villain
Blofeld in Switzerland and marries
the wilful daughter of an
international racketeer.

No amount of thrills, inventively-
staged action and attractive locations
can disguise the fact that one-time-only
007 George Lazenby is as wooden as
Pinocchio, so one is left with peripheral
pleasures and an embarrassing dramatic

vacuum at the centre.

Former Bond editor Peter Hunt turned to direction to excellent effect, and future Bond director John Glen did a capable job as second unit director and editor.

'Producers Albert R Broccoli and Harry Salztman and director Peter Hunt have packed so much break-neck physical excitement and stunning visual attractions into *On Her Majesty's Secret Service* that the initial disappointment of George Lazenby replacing Sean Connery as James Bond is almost forgotten by the film's climax.'
Variety

'An attempt, repeated and strenuous, is made to substitute quantities of violence for quality.'
New York Post

'As the new Bond, George Lazenby sums it all up: large, solidly put together, but beyond the predictable motions with little sense of what should be happening or how it should be done.'
Monthly Film Bulletin

ONLY WHEN I LARF
(GB 1968)
pc Beecord Productions. p Len Deighton, Brian Duffy. assoc p Hugh Atwooll. d Basil Dearden. w John Salmon, from the novel by Len Deighton. ph Anthony Richmond. Colour. ed Fergus McDonnell. ad John Blezard. m Ron Grainer. 103 mins

Cast: Richard Attenborough (Silas), David Hemmings (Bob), Alexandra Stewart (Liz), Nicholas Pennell (Spencer), Melissa Stribling (Diana), Terence Alexander (Gee Gee Gray), Edric Connor (Awana), Clifton Jones (Gen. Sakut), Calvin Lockhart (Ali Lin), Brian Grellis (Spider), David Healy (Jones), Alan Gifford (Poster)

Three confidence tricksters fall out in a welter of double-, triple- and quadruple-crosses.

The caper is underdeveloped to the point of anorexia, with only Attenborough in a series of disguises working hard enough to overcome some of the lacklustre material. The sole surprise is Len Deighton's involvement.

'Wavers between moods until it is neither funny enough for a comedy nor exciting enough for a thriller.'
Daily Mail

THE PARALLAX VIEW

(US 1974)

pc Gus Productions. In association with Harbor Productions and Doubleday Productions. For Paramount. exec p Gabriel Katzka. p, d Alan J Pakula. assoc p Charles H Maguire, Robert E Jiras. w David Giler, Lorenzo Semple Jr, from the novel by Loren Singer. ph Gordon Willis. Colour. Panavision. ed John W Wheeler. ad George Jenkins. sfx Tim Smyth. m Michael Small. 102 mins

Cast: Warren Beatty (Joe Frady), Paula Prentiss (Lee Carter), William Daniels (Austin Tucker), Walter McGinn (Jack), Hume Cronyn (Rintels), Kelly Thorsden (LD), Chuck Waters (Assassin), Earl Hindmar (Red), Bill Joyce (Senator Carroll), Bettie Johnson (Mrs Carroll), Bill McKinney (Art), Ted Gehring (Schecter), Jim Davis (Senator Hammond), Anthony Zerbe (Schwartzkopf), Kenneth Mars (Turner)

A reporter investigates the assassination of a US senator and discovers key witnesses are dying one after the other.

Sharply directed, but with an excess of style that too frequently obscures the multilayered, deliberately opaque narrative, and infused with a mounting atmosphere of political paranoia that even Oliver Stone might envy.

Parallels with the John F Kennedy assassination are effectively drawn, and the editing and production design add strongly to the overall impact. The denouement owes a debt to *The Manchurian Candidate* (q.v.).

'Complex in structure, demanding and deserving the closest concentration, this sociological thriller ... is a very stylish affair ... a thinking thriller has made its mark.'
Films and Filming

'Pakula's film suffers from the modern screen tendency to tell an exciting and intricate story so obliquely that it is impossible to follow at a single viewing.'
Evening News

PAYROLL

(GB 1961)

pc Lynx. A Julian Wintle-Leslie Parkyn Production. p Norman Priggen. d Sidney Hayers. w George Baxt, from the novel by Derek Bickerton. ph Ernest Steward. B&W. ed Tristan Cones. ad Jack Shampan. m Reg Owen. song *It Happens Every Day* by Tony Osborne, sung by Eddie Ellis. 105 mins

Cast: Michael Craig (Johnny Mellors), Billie Whitelaw (Jackie Parker), Françoise Prevost (Katie Pearson), William Lucas (Dennis Pearson), Tom Bell (Blackie), Kenneth Griffith (Monty), Barry Keegan (Langridge), William Peacock (Harry Parker), Joan Rice (Madge Moore), Glyn Houston (Frank Moore), Andrew Faulds (Det. Insp. Carberry), Stanley Meadows (Bowen)

A woman whose driver husband dies during the hijacking of an armoured van in Newcastle seeks revenge against the small-time crooks who killed him.

Tense, American-influenced second feature with (largely realized) A-film aspirations, with well-used locations and driving direction, notably the hijacking sequence, but with a endency towards cliché and melodrama.

'Moves at a cracking, high-powered pace from one exciting incident to another, peopled with intriguingly contrasted characters.'
ABC Film Review

PENNY GOLD
(GB 1973)
pc Fanfare Films. p George H Brown. d Jack Cardiff. w David Osborne, Liz Charles-Williams. ph Ken Hodges. Colour. ed John Trumper. ad Bert Davey. m John Scott. 90 mins,

Cast: Francesca Annis (Delphi Emerson), James Booth (Matthews), Nicky Henson (Roger), Una Stubbs (Anna), Joseph O'Connor (Charles Blachford), Richard Heffer (Claude Grancourt), Joss Ackland (Jones), Sue Lloyd (Model), George Murcell (Dr Merrick), Marianne Stone (Mrs Parsons)

Murders are committed over a priceless postage stamp.

A dreadful throwback to fifties British B-features, minus the merit of an imported Hollywood star and with no discernible redeeming features.

'The kind of stolid murder mystery spoonfed to addicts on television several times a week and it is surprising that it came to be considered as feature material in the first place.'
Films and Filming

PHANTOM LADY
(US 1944)
pc Universal. exec p Milton Feld. assoc p Joan Harrison. d Robert Siodmak. w Bernard C Schoenfeld, from the novel by William Irish (rn Cornell Woolrich). ph Woody Bredell. B&W. ed Arthur Hilton. ad John B Goodman, Robert Clatworthy. 'phantom hat' created by Kenneth Hopkins. md Hans J Salter. 87 mins

Cast: Franchot Tone (Jack Marlow), Ella Raines (Carol 'Kansas' Richman), Alan Curtis (Scott Henderson), Aurora (Estela Monteiro), Thomas Gomez (Insp. Burgess), Fay Helm (Ann Terry), Elisha Cook Jr (Cliff March), Andrew Tombes Jr (Barman), Regis Toomey, Joseph Crehan (Detectives), Virginia Brissac (Dr Chase), Milburn Stone (District Attorney)

When a man is convicted of strangling his wife, his secretary and a detective find the real killer.

Taut direction by Siodmak, who also raises the sexual temperature to a surprising (for the time) level, and the involvement of long-time Hitchcock associate Joan Harrison is evident in the overall *mise-en-scène*.

'An expertly contrived, suspenseful mystery meller developing along unusual cinematic lines.'
Variety

THE PHENIX CITY STORY
(US 1955)
pc Allied Artists. p Samuel Bischoff, David Diamond. d Phil Karlson. w Crane Wilbur, Daniel Mainwaring. ph Harry Neumann. B&W. ed George White. ad Stanley Fleischer. m Harry Sukman. song *Phenix City Blues* by Harold Spina. 100 mins

Cast: John McIntire (Albert Patterson), Richard Kiley (John Patterson), Kathryn Grant (Ellie Rhodes), Edward Andrews (Rhett Tanner), Biff Mcguire (Fred Gage), Lenka Peterson (Mary Jo Patterson), Truman Smith (Ed Gage), Jean Carson (Cassie), Meg Myles (Judy), John Larch (Clem Wilson), James Edwards (Zeke)

A young lawyer helps clean up Phenix City at the time it was known as 'the wickedest city in the United States'.

Hard-edged and punchy B-feature, thanks to a fact-based story, location filming and a cast of unknowns. Not as daring, however, as it would have liked to be. If they wanted, Exhibitors could feature a 13-minute prologue in which Phenix City residents involved in the 1954 murder of Albert Patterson were interviewed.

'My choice of best film of the week goes to *Phenix City Story*, every minute of which justifies its X certificate. It has no star names but I found the story so gripping – and at times so shocking – that it doesn't need them.'
Daily Herald

PICKUP ON SOUTH STREET
(US 1953)
pc 20th Century Fox. p Jules Schermer. d, w Samuel Fuller, from the story *Blaze of Glory* by Dwight Taylor. ph Joe Macdonald. sfx ph Ray Kellogg. B&W. ed Nick de Maggio. ad Lyle Wheeler, George Patrick. m Leigh Harline. 83 mins

Cast: Richard Widmark (Skip McCoy), Jean Peters (Candy), Thelma Ritter (Moe), Murvyn Vye (Capt. Dan Tiger), Richard Kiley (Joey),

Willis B Bouchey (Zaza), Milburn Stone (Wineki), Henry Slate (MacGregor), Jerry O'Sullivan (Enyart), George E Stone (Police Clerk), Parley Baer (Stranger)

A pickpocket who steals a woman's purse in the New York subway finds himself involved with a Communist spy ring and under pressure from the police and the FBI.

Lurid anti-Red melodrama which benefits from the veneer of gritty realism Fuller gives it and from Ritter's Academy Award-nominated performance. Slick and efficient, but not nearly as good as the director's later cult *auteur* status might have you believe. Indifferently remade as *Capetown Affair* in 1968.

'I found it entertaining hokum.'
Picturegoer

'The film monotonously turns to violence for its excitement and the mixture of crime and anti-Communist propaganda jars.'
Monthly Film Bulletin.

P.J.
(US 1967) (GB: NEW FACE IN HELL)
pc Universal. p Edward J Montaigne. d John Guillermin. w Philip Reisman Jr. st Philip Reisman Jr, Edward J Montaigne. ph Loyal Griggs. Colour. Techniscope. ed Sam Waxman. ad Alexander Golitzen, Philip Harrison. m Neal Hefti. 109 mins

Cast: George Peppard (P J Detweiler), Raymond Burr (William Orbison), Gayle Hunnicutt (Maureen Prebble), Coleen Gray

(Betty Orbison), Susan Saint James (Linette), Jason Evers (Jason Grenoble), Wilfrid Hyde White (Billings-Browne), Severn Darden (Shelton Quell), H Jane Van Duser (Elinor Silene), George Furth (Sonny Silene), Brock Peters (Waterpark), Ken Lynch (Thorson)

A down-and-out private eye comes up against blackmail and murder when he is hired as bodyguard for a rich tycoon's mistress.

Glossy but empty-headed thick-ear thriller with a depressingly glum hero.

'*P.J.* is a sassy series of blood-drenched beatings, stompings and shootings, strung on a plot as implausible as a bad dream.'
Time

PLAY MISTY FOR ME
(US 1971)
pc Universal/Malpaso. A Jennings Lang Presentation. p Robert Daley. assoc p/p manager/asst d Bob Larson. d Clint Eastwood. w Joe Heims, Dean Riesner. st Joe Heims. ph Bruce Surtees. Colour. ed Carl Pingitore. ad Alexander Golitzen. m Dee Barton. 102 mins

Cast: Clint Eastwood (Dave Garland), Jessica Walter (Evelyn Draper), Donna MIlls (Tobie Williams), John Larch (Sgt McCallum), Jack Ging (Frank Dewan), Irene Hervey (Madge Brenner), James McEachin (Al Monte), Clarice Taylor (Birdie), Donald Siegel (Murphy), Duke Everts (JJ), George Fargo (Man), Mervin W Frates (Locksmith), Tim Frawley (Deputy Sheriff)

A California disc jockey becomes involved with a woman fan who turns out to be a homicidal psychopath.

Eastwood made a powerful and assured directorial debut, handling his chores on both sides of the camera with impressive skill, and drew from Walter her best performance by far as his dangerously deranged one-night stand. There is exemplary pacing, sustained suspense and some vivid set-pieces. Eastwood's frequent collaborator, Don Siegel, has a cameo as a barman.

'On an informal Richter scale of movie terror, *Play Misty for Me* registers a few gasps, some *frissons* and at least one spleen-shaking shudder. A good little scare show, in other words, despite various gaps in logic and probability.'
Time

'A surprisingly auspicious directorial debut.'
Village Voice

POINT BLANK
(US 1967)
pc MGM. A Judd Bernard-Irwin Winkler Production. p Judd Bernard, Robert Chartoff. d John Boorman. w Alexander Jacobs, David Newhouse, Rafe Newman, from the novel *The Hunter* by Richard Stark. ph Philip H Lathrop. sfx ph J McMillan Johnson. Colour. Panavision. ed Henry Berman. ad George W Davis, Albert Brenner. m Johnny Mandel. song *Mighty Good Times* by Stu Gardner. 92 mins

Cast: Lee Marvin (Walker), Angie Dickinson (Chris), Keenan Wynn (Yost), Carroll O'Connor (Brewster),

Lloyd Bochner (Frederick Carter), Michael Strong (Stegman), John Vernon (Mal Reese), Sharon Acker (Lynne), James B Sikking (Hired Gun), Kathleen Freeman (Citizen), Felix Silla (Bellhop)

A gangster is double-crossed after a big robbery and left for dead in the deserted Alacatraz prison. Two years later he seeks vengeance.

Violent, with a basically thin story that is all too often wilfully obscured by arty direction and gratuitous camera angles, Boorman's first American film is – depending on your point of view – either irritatingly idiosyncratic and overrated or a crime film classic. The editing is impeccable, however. Naturally, it has become a cult movie.

'One leaves a blank, pointless movie like *Point Blank* feeling cheapened by it and, yes, by the adolescent fantasies it awakens and caters to as one sits alone in the darkness with it. Surely it will win this year's sweaty palm award – hands down.'
Life Magazine

'Riveting; the screenplay is intelligent; and the performances are just right ... an absolute must.'
The Guardian

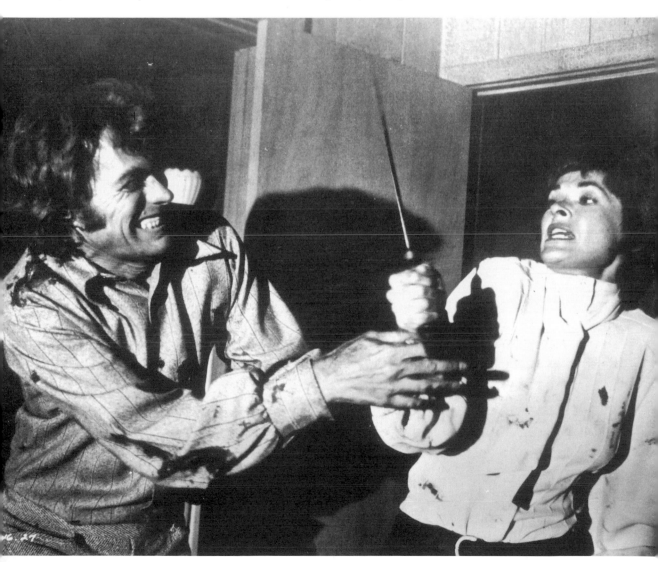

PLAY MISTY FOR ME

POINT OF NO RETURN

(US 1993) (GB: ASSASSIN)
pc WB. p Art Linson. co-p James
Herbert. assoc p D J Caruso, David
Sosna. d John Badham. 2nd unit d D
J Caruso. w Robert Getchell,
Alexandra Seros, from the film *Nikita*
by Luc Besson. ph Michael Watkins.
2nd unit ph Michael Ferris. Colour.
Panavision. ed Frank Morris. pd Philip
Harrison. ad Sydney Z Litwack. sc
Mic Rodgers. m Hans Zimmer, Nick
Glennie-Smith. 108 mins

Cast: Bridget Fonda (Maggie), Gabriel
Byrne (Bob), Dermot Mulroney (JP),
Miguel Ferrer (Kaufman), Anne
Bancroft (Amanda), Olivia D'Abo
(Angela), Richard Romanus (Fahd
Bahktiar), Harvey Keitel (Victor the
Cleaner), Lorraine Toussaint (Beth),
Geoffrey Lewis (Drugstore Owner),
Mic Rodgers (Cop)

A young female junkie sentenced to
be executed for killing a policeman is
given the choice of death or working
as a government assassin. She chooses
the latter.

   Slavish, redundant remake of Luc
Besson's *Nikita* (1990) with an
inadequate leading lady. The direction,
however, is less self-consciously clever.

'Lacking its Gallic sheen, and weighed
down by a bombastic Hans Zimmer
score, the remake reveals the true
nature of the original – a puerile day-
dream.'
The Daily Telegraph

THE POPPY IS ALSO A
FLOWER

(UNITED NATIONS 1966) (GB:
DANGER GROWS WILD)
pc TelsUN. p Euan Lloyd. delegate p
Simon Schiffrin. d Terence Young.
2nd unit d Georges Lampin. w Joe
Eisinger, from a story idea by Ian
Fleming. ph Henri Alékan. 2nd unit
ph Tony Brown. Colour. ed Monique
Bonnot, Peter Thornton, Henry
Richardson. ad Maurice Colasson,
Tony Roman. sfx Paul Pollard. m
Georges Auric. 105 mins

Cast: E G Marshall (Jones), Trevor
Howard (Lincoln), Gilbert Roland
(Marco), Rita Hayworth (Monique),
Anthony Quayle (Captain), Angie
Dickinson (Linda), Yul Brynner
(Col. Salem), Eli Wallach (Locarno),
Harold Sakata (Martin), Senta Berger
(Nightclub Entertainer), Hugh
Griffith (Tribal Chief), Marcello
Mastroianni (Insp. Mosca), Georges
Géret (Supt Roche), Howard Vernon
(Police Analyst), Stephen Boyd
(Benson), Omar Sharif (Dr Rad),
Jack Hawkins (Gen. Bahar), Trini
Lopez (Himself), Amadeo Nazzari
(Capt. Dinonno)

Two UN agents are assigned to smash
a narcotics syndicate.

   An unwatchable oddity made for
charitable motives by the United
Nations, who would have been a lot
more charitable if they had kept to
peace-keeping and kept out of movie-
making.

   A starry cast flounder through
banal dialogue, tedious plotting and
lethargic direction. First shown on
television in the US and then released
in cinemas.

'Slow, silly and optimistically star-
studded thriller.'
Sight and Sound

THE POSTMAN ALWAYS
RINGS TWICE

(US 1946)
pc MGM. p Carey Wilson. d Tay
Garnett. w Harry Ruskin, Niven
Busch, from the novel by James M
Cain. ph Sidney Wagner. B&W. ed
George White. ad Cedric Gibbons,
Randall Duell. m George Bassman.
113 mins

Cast: Lana Turner (Cora Smith),
John Garfield (Frank Chambers),
Cecil Kellaway (Nick Smith), Hume
Cronyn (Arthur Keats), Leon Ames
(Kyle Sackett), Audrey Totter (Madge
Gorland), Alan Reed (Ezra Kennedy),
Jeff York (Blair), Charles Williams
(Jimmie White), Cameron Grant
(Willie), Wally Cassell (Ben), William
Halligan, Morris Ankrum (Judges)

A woman and a drifter become lovers
and conspire to murder her elderly
husband.

   Double Indemnity revisited to fine
dramatic effect, with Garnett cleverly
evoking vivid, overt sexual tension
that was quite remarkable for the
time and the studio, even after
contemporary censorship insisted on
sanitizing Cain's novel. He even
succeeded in convincing audiences
that Turner could act as well as
simply look sultry. She and Garfield
were first-rate, although Kellaway
gave the most potent performance as
the husband.

   The novel had been filmed
before, in France as *Le Dernier
Tournant* in 1939 and in Italy in
1942 where Visconti made an
unauthorized version, *Ossessione*. A
dire remake followed in 1981 (q.v.).

POINT OF NO RETURN

'The producer has attempted to gain sympathy for the seducer-murderer and his completely immoral accomplice. Because of this the film leaves a nasty taste in the mouth, and defeats its own dramatic ends ... it's strong meat, spoilt by weak concessions to film traditions.'

Picturegoer

'The approach to lust and murder is as adult and matter-of-fact as that used by James M Cain in his book ... pic seems almost certain to be marked with controversy over such a frank display of adultery and the murder to which it leads.'

Variety

THE POSTMAN ALWAYS RINGS TWICE

(US 1981)
pc Lorimar. A Northstar International Picture. In association with CIP-Europäische Treuhand AG. exec p Andrew Braunsberg. p Charles Mulvehill, Bob Rafelson. assoc p Michael Barlow. d Bob Rafelson. w David Mamet, from the novel by James M Cain. ph Sven Nykvist. Colour. ed Graeme Clifford. pd George Jenkins. sfx Jerry Williams. m Michael Small. 121 mins

Cast: Jack Nicholson (Frank Chambers), Jessica Lange (Cora Papadakis), John Colicos (Nick Papadakis), Michael Lerner (Katz), John P Ryan (Kennedy), Angelica Huston (Madge), William Traylor (Sackett), Tom Hill (Barlow), Jo Van Ness (Motorcycle Cop), Don Calfa (Goebel)

A drifter and his mistress plan the perfect murder of her middle-aged husband.

Overwrought, operatic and unnecessary remake (set, like the novel, during the Depression) which, in spite of its would-be tumescent eighties explicitness, carries far less of an erotic charge than the 1946 John Garfield-Lana Turner version.

The much-publicized sex scenes look more cheerless and uncomfortable than enticing, for both actors and audience. Nicholson's laughable encounter with naked lion-tamer Huston is a bizarre highlight in a movie composed almost entirely of lowlights.

'They haven't pulled it off. Just when Mamet's script should be tightening the screws, it grows diffuse.'

Newsweek

'Above all, the film lacks the one vital quality that distinguished the flawed, 1940s version with Lana Turner and John Garfield: the electric charge between the two lovers that lights up their grim and shocking affair.'

Daily Mail

THE PRESIDIO

(US 1988)
pc Paramount. exec p Jonathan A Zimbert. p D Constantine Conte. co-p Fred Caruso. d, ph Peter Hyams. Colour. Panavision. w Larry Ferguson. ed James Mitchell, Diane Adler. Beau Barthel-Blair. pd Albert Brenner. ad Kandy Stern. sfx co-ord Philip C Cory. sc Glenn Wilder. m Bruce Broughton. 98 mins

Cast: Sean Connery (Lt Col. Alan Caldwell), Mark Harmon (Jay Austin),

Meg Ryan (Donna Caldwell), Jack Warden (Sgt Major Ross Maclure), Mark Blum (Arthue Peale), Dana Gladstone (Col. Paul Lawrence), Jenette Goldstein (Patti Jean Lynch), Marvin J McIntyre (MP Zeke), Don Calfa (Howard Buckley), James Hooks Reynolds (George Spota), Curtis W Sims (Sgt Moeller)

An army provost marshal and a civilian policeman clash over their enforced joint investigation of murders committed on a large military base – The Presidio – in San Francisco.

Standard crime story with the (almost inevitable) *Bullitt*-style car chase and a well-staged chase on foot through San Francisco's Chinatown.

'*The Presidio* begins with an assembly line screenplay and never rises above it ... the whole movie has the feeling of a clone, of a film assembled out of spare parts from other movies, out of the cinematic junkyard, from the opening chase sequence ... there's hardly an element we haven't seen before.'

Chicago Sun-Times

PRETTY BOY FLOYD

(US 1959)
pc Le-Sac/Pretty Boy Productions. p Monroe Sachson. d, w Herbert J Leder. ph Chuck Austin. B&W. ed Ralph Rosenblum. m Del Sirino, William Sanford. 96 mins

Cast: John Ericson (Pretty Boy Floyd), Barry Newman (Al Riccardo), Joan Harvey (Lil Courtney), Herb Evers (Blackie Faulkner), Carl York (Curly), Roy Fant (Jed Watkins), Shirley Smith (Ann Courtney), Phil Kenneally (Baker), Effie Afton (Ma Parks), Peter

Falk (Shorty Walters), Norman Burton (Bill Courtney)

Heavily fictionalized biopic of the thirties Public Enemy.

The budget is low, its aspirations and execution even lower.

'With John Ericson in the title role and enough violence in the script to pass for excitement, film should do okay in the exploitation market.'
Variety

PRETTY MAIDS ALL IN A ROW
(US 1971)
pc MGM. p, w Gene Roddenberry, from the novel by Francis Pollini. d Roger Vadim. ph Charles Rosher. Colour. ed Bill Brame. ad George W Davis, Preston Ames. m Lalo Schifrin. song *Chilly Winds* by Lalo Schifrin, Mike Curb, sung by The Osmonds. 92 mins

Cast: Rock Hudson (Tiger), Angie Dickinson (Miss Smith), Telly Savalas (Surcher), John David Carson (Ponce), Roddy McDowall (Proffer), Keenan Wynn (Poldaski), James Doohan (Follo), William Campbell (Grady), Susan Tolsky (Miss Cramire), Barbara Leigh (Jean), Gretchen Burrell (Marjorie), Joy Bang (Rita)

A high-school guidance counsellor seduces and then murders his female pupils.

Bizarre blend of homicide, sex and black comedy with much emphasis on nudity, as one might expect from director Roger Vadim, who was making his Hollywood bow. Rather more entertaining than it deserves to

be. Given the producer-writer, a must for *Star Trek* completists?

'The result, though sporadically funny … is peculiarly pointless.'
Monthly Film Bulletin

PRETTY POISON
(US 1968)
pc 20th Century Fox/Lawrence Turman/Mollino Production. exec p Lawrence Turman. p Marshal Blacklar, Noel Black. d Noel Black. w Lorenzo Semple Jr, from the novel *She Let Him Continue* by Stephen Geller. ph David Quaid. Colour. ed William Ziegler. ad Jack Martin Smith, Harold Michelson. sfx Ralph Winigar, Billy King. m Johnny Mandel. 89 mins

Cast: Anthony Perkins (Dennis Pitt), Tuesday Weld (Sue Ann Stepanek), Beverly Garland (Mrs Stepanek), John Randolph (Azenauer), Dick O'Neill (Bud Munsch), Clarice Blackburn (Mrs Bronson), Joseph Bova (Pete), Ken Kercheval (Harry)

A psychotic arsonist, released from an institution after 15 years, fascinates a high-school student with his fantasies of being a secret agent. She, being a homicidal paranoid, involves him in her murderous schemes.

A minor gem, twisted, taut, cleverly-scripted and directed (Black was making his feature directorial debut) with a compellingly creepy performance by Weld. Perkins is good, too, in yet another variation on *Psycho*'s Norman Bates.

'A truly marvellous thriller.'
Newsweek

PRIME CUT
(US 1972)
pc Cinema Center Films. exec p Kenneth Evans. p Joe Wizan. assoc p Mickey Borofsky. d Michael Ritchie. w Robert Dillon. ph Gene Polito. Colour. Panavision. cd Carl Pingitore. ad Bill Malley. sfx Logan Frazee. m Lalo Schifrin. 86 mins

Cast: Lee Marvin (Nick Devlin), Gene Hackman (Mary Ann), Angel Tomkins (Clarabelle), Gregory Walcott (Weenie), Sissy Spacek (Poppy), Janit Baldwin (Violet), William Morey (Shay), Clint Ellison (Delaney), Howard Platt (Shaugnessy), Les Lannom (O'Brien), Eddie Egan (Jake)

A ruthless Chicago enforcer is sent to eliminate a Kansas gangster.

Violent, silly and trashy, with a few memorable set-pieces, notably the opening sequence in which a man is killed and fed into a meat-processing plant to emerge as a string of sausages, and an attack by an agricultural reaping machine in a wheat field. Sissy Spacek made her screen debut.

'Another contemporary underworld "western" bloodletting, which is drawn, quartered and ground according to an overused recipe for hash.'
Variety

THE PRIZE
(US 1963)
pc Roxbury. p Pandro S Berman. assoc p Kathryn Hereford. d Mark Robson. w Ernest Lehmann, from the novel by Irving Stone. ph William H Daniels. Colour. Panavision. ed Adrienne Fazan. ad George W Davis, Urie McCleary. sfx J McMillan Johnson,

PRIME CUT

A Arnold Gillespie, Robert H Hoag. m Jerry Goldsmith. 136 mins

Cast: Paul Newman (Andrew Craig), Edward G Robinson (Dr Max Stratman), Elke Sommer (Inger Andersen), Diane Baker (Emily Stratman), Micheline Presle (Dr Denise Marceau), Gerard Oury (Dr Marceau), Sergio Fantoni (Dr Farelli), Kevin McCarthy (Dr Garratt), Leo G Carroll (Count Bertil Jacobssen), Sascha Pitoeff (Daranyi), Jacqueline Beer (Monique Souvir), John Wengraf (Hans Eckart), Don Dubbins (Ivar Cramer), Anna Lee (Reporter)

An American in Stockholm to receive the Nobel Prize for Literature foils a Communist plan to kidnap the winner of the Physics Prize and substitute his twin brother to deliver an anti-American acceptance speech.

Ernest Lehmann's blithe screenplay unashamedly plays homage to his *North by Northwest* script and makes more of Irving Stone's best-selling novel than Stone did. Comedy and suspense are smoothly blended and, although over-long, it adds up to pleasing mock-Hitchcock. The Swedes and the Nobel Prize Committee were not amused.

'Robson couldn't go far wrong with *The Prize*. And although the film has its longueurs, Robson manages for the most part to keep it moving along joyously on its well-laid tracks.'
Monthly Film Bulletin

'Stands barefaced amid the pomp of Panavision, Metrocolor and Elke Sommer's physique as a pretentious and silly spy story guaranted to test – or rather try – Swedish-American relations, let alone the idiocy-threshold of the moviegoer.'
New York Herald Tribune

THE PROWLER

(US 1951)
pc Horizon Pictures. p S P Eagle (rn Sam Spiegel). d Joseph Losey. w Hugo Butler. st Robert Thoeren, Hans Wilhelm. ph Arthur Miller. B&W. ed Paul Weatherwax. ad Boris Leven. m Lyn Murray. 92 mins

Cast: Van Heflin (Webb Garwood), Evelyn Keyes (Susan Gilvray), John Maxwell (Bud Crocker), Katherine Warren (Mrs Crocker), Emerson Treacy (William Gilvray), Madge Blake (Martha Gilvray), Wheaton Chambers (Dr James), Robert Osterloh (Coroner), Sherry Hall (John Gilvray)

A corrupt Los Angeles policeman has an affair with the wife of a late-night radio disc jockey and murders him so that he can marry the widow and collect the insurance.

Atmospheric *film noir*, all the more effective if you recall *Double Indemnity*, and tautly directed by Losey, although he fails to prevent it tipping over into melodrama in the later scenes.

'Its sordidness detracts from its human appeal. It is, however, holding and has a strong element of suspense. It is intelligently acted ... good entertainment of a novel but not too pleasant kind.'
CEA Film Report

PUBLIC ENEMY

(US 1931) (GB: ENEMIES OF THE PUBLIC)
pc WB-Vitaphone. p Darryl F Zanuck. d William A Wellman. w Kubec Glasmon, John Bright. adapt, dial Harvey Thew, from the story *Beer and Blood* by John Bright. ph Dev Jennings. B&W. cd Ed McCormick. ad Max Parker. md David Mendoza. 83 mins

Cast: James Cagney (Tom Powers), Jean Harlow (Gwen Allen), Edward Woods (Matt Doyle), Joan Blondell (Mamie), Beryl Mercer (Ma Powers), Donald Cook (Mike Powers), Mae Clarke (Kitty), Mia Marvin (Jane), Leslie Fenton (Nails Nathan), Robert Emmett O'Connor (Paddy Ryan), Rita Flynn (Molly Doyle), Ben Hendrick Jr (Bugs Moran), Frank Coghlan Jr (Tom as a Boy), Frankie Darrow (Matt as a Boy), Adele Watson (Mrs Doyle), Murray Kinnell (Putty Nose)

A policeman's son and his pal who grow up together in a Chicago slum graduate from petty crime to big-time racketeering.

Gangster classic that still compels attention, thanks to a sharply-characterized screenplay that credibly delineates the genesis of gangsterdom, Wellman's well-paced, documentary-style direction and, particularly, to Cagney's swaggering, vividly-conceived

performance. The celebrated scene in which he grinds half a grapefruit into the face of his mistress, Mae Clarke, still has considerable force, as does the climax in which Cagney's bullet-ridden body is delivered to his mother's door.

'Well-told and its intensity is relieved by scenes of the central characters slugging bartenders and slapping their women across the face. US audiences, long trained by the press to glorify thugs, last week laughed loudly at such comedy and sat spell-bound through the serious parts ... it carries to its ultimate absurdity the fashion for romanticizing gangsters, for even in defeat the public enemy is endowed with grandeur.'
Time

'A grim and terrible document, with no attempt to soften or humanize the character. Of all racketeer films it is the most brutal and least like movie fiction. For this reason it is the most arresting.'
Picture Play

PULP

(GB 1972)
pc A Klinger-Caine-Hodges Production. p Michael Klinger. d, w Mike Hodges. ph Ousama Rawi. Colour. ed John Glen. pd Patrick Downing. ad Darrell Lass. m George Martin. 95 mins

Cast: Michael Caine (Mickey King), Mickey Rooney (Preston Gilbert), Lionel Stander (Ben Dinuccio), Lizabeth Scott (Princess Cippola), Nadia Cassini (Liz Adams), Al Lettieri (Miller), Dennis Price (Mysterious Englishman), Amerigo Toy (Sotgio),

PULP FICTION

Leopoldo Trieste (Marcovic), Robert Sacchi (Jim Norman), Victor Mercieca (Prince Cippola), Mary Caruana (Mae West), Jeanne Lass (Marlene Dietrich), Kate Sullivan (Joan Crawford), Anna Pace Donnela (Jean Harlow), Jennifer Gauci (Shirley Temple), Tondi Barr (Gloria Swanson)

A pulp fiction writer living in the Mediterranean is caught up in real-life mob machinations when he is hired to ghost the biography of a retired gangster,

Occasionally amusing parody of gangster movies, with a rather too knowing attitude towards the genre, improved no end by brightly-photographed Malta locations and a lively performance from Rooney.

'The whole movie has the look of a magazine spread, with actors not so much living as posing before a camera which invariably regards them from derisively satiric angles.'
Village Voice

PULP FICTION
(US 1994)
pc Miramax-A Band Apart/Jersey Films production. exec p Danny DeVito, Michael Schamberg, Stacey Sher. co-exec p Bob Weinstein, Harvey Weinstein, Richard N Gladstein. p Lawrence Bender. d Quentin Tarantino. w, st Quentin Tarantino, Roger Avary. ph Andrzej Sekula. 2nd unit ph Alan Sherrod. Colour. ed Sally Menke. pd David Wasco. ad Charles Collum. sfx co-ord Larry Fioritto. sc Ken Lesco. m sup Laryn Rachtman, Kathy Nelson. 154 mins

Cast: Tim Roth (Pumpkin), Amanda Plummer (Honey Bunny), John Travolta (Vincent Vega), Samuel L Jackson (Jules Winnfield), Uma Thurman (Mia Wallace), Harvey Keitel (The Wolf), Bruce Willis (Butch Coolidge), Rosanna Arquette (Jody), Ving Rhames (Marcellus Wallace), Eric Stoltz (Lance), Christopher Walken (Capt. Koons), Maria de Medeiros (Fabienne)

A pair of small-time crooks prepare to hold up a diner. Two hitmen set out to kill punks who double-cross a crimelord. One of the hitmen takes the crimelord's mistress out on a date which ends in near disaster when she overdoses on heroin. A boxer, paid to take a drive, wins the fight and goes on the run.

Tarantino makes expert use of his (mostly) good cast, large budget and over-long running time to deliver a slick, cynically-constructed crowd-pleaser that won the Palme D'Or at the Cannes Film Festival, confirmed his cult status and brought him and Roger Avary the Best Screenplay Academy Award. Critics and movie buffs hungry for a new *auteur* to idolize were overwhelmed by ecstasy. Others found it nasty, meretricious and coasting along on the director's by now familiar fetish for full-frontal violence.

For all its surface gloss and smart dialogue (which sounds increasingly less clever on subsequent viewings), *Pulp Fiction* too often simply resembles a more expensive remix of the pulpy, everything-goes mess of blood, brutality, sadism, bad language, crass comedy and over-the-top characters that made *Reservoir Dogs* so popular.

'The consensus among reviewers of Quentin Tarantino's *Pulp Fiction* seems to be that the new film is even more violent than his *Reservoir Dogs*, "but at least it's funny". Pardon me while I clutch at comprehension. You mean it is all right to watch people being shot, stabbed, tortured, sodomised or drug-injected if we laugh at it, but not if we take it seriously?.'
Financial Times

'The film's very gusto keeps total nihilism at bay; and while the over-indulgence may be regrettable, you have to admire the spectacle of a filmmaker grabbing his talent and running hard.'
The Times

'The most acclaimed film-maker of his decade. You can argue all you want about Tarantino's cinematic talent; but as the foremost practitioner of the cinematic Heimlich manoeuvre, he is without peer.'
The Sunday Times

'A spectacularly entertaining piece of pop culture ... on any number of important levels, *Pulp Fiction* is a startling, massive success.'
Variety

'One cannot help wondering whether the appropriate response to this sort of souped-up trailer-park trash might be to acquire a gun and blow the director's head off. I mean, strictly for laughs, OK? In Tarantinos world, no doubt, it would be a scream.'
The Daily Telegraph

'*Reservoir Dogs* is like an action

painting; by comparison, *Pulp Fiction* is a mosaic.'
Quentin Tarantino

PUPPET ON A CHAIN

(GB 1970)
pc Big City Productions. p Kurt Unger. d Geoffrey Reeve. boat chase, add sequences d Don Sharp. w Alistair MacLean. add material Paul Wheeler, Don Sharp. ph Jack Hildyard. 2nd unit ph Skeets Kelly. Colour. ed Bill Lenny. pd Peter Mullins. ad Geoffrey Tiozer. stunt arr Joe Dunne. boat stunts Wim Wagenaar, John Terhaak. m Piero Piccioni. 98 mins

Cast: Sven-Bertil Taube (Paul Sherman), Barbara Parkins (Maggie), Alexander Knox (Col. De Graaf), Patrick Allen (Insp. Van Gelder), Vladek Sheybal (Meegeren), Ania Marson (Astrid Lemay), Penny Castaldi (Trudi), Peter Hutchins (Assassin), Henni Orri (Herta), Drewe Henley (Jimmy Duclos)

An American agent goes to Amsterdam after a gang of heroin smugglers.

Run-of-the-mill programmer with pallid performers displaying the dramatic range of marionettes. The speedily-staged climactic speedboat chase is hugely exciting and makes one wish Don Sharp had directed the whole film.

'This picture has its exciting moments but somehow fails to catch fire until the last reel when spectacular action and suspense redeem the rest.'
Kine Weekly

q

QUE LA BÊTE MEURE/UCCIDERO UN UOMO

(FRANCE/ITALY 1969) (US: THIS MAN MUST DIE, GB: KILLER!)
pc Les Films la Boetie/Rizzoli Films. p André Genovese. d Claude Chabrol. w Paul Gegauff, from the novel *The Beast Must Die* by Nicholas Blake (rn C Day Lewis). ph Jean Rabier. Colour. ed Jacques Galliard. ad Guy Littaye. m André Girard. 110 mins

Cast: Michel Duchaussoy (Charles Thenier), Caroline Cellier (Helene Lanson), Jean Yanne (Paul Decourt), Anouk Ferjac (Jeanne), Marc Di Napoli (Philippe), Maurice Pialat (Police Inspector), Guy Marly (Jacques Ferrand), Lorraine Rainer (Anna Ferrand)

A man tracks down and kills the hit-and-run driver who killed his son.

Tense, superbly-realized film of the Nicholas Blake novel, effectively transposed to beautifully-photographed French settings and directed in his most telling Hitchcockian style by Chabrol, with excellent performances by Duchaussoy as the hunter and Yanne as his quarry.

'Chabrol again interweaves threads of classic tragedy, Hitchcock thriller and social satire to achieve another perfect film.'
Sight and Sound

THE QUILLER MEMORANDUM

(GB/US 1966)
pc Rank/Ivan Foxwell Productions/Carthay. p Ivan Foxwell. d Michael Anderson. w Harold Pinter, from the novel *The Berlin Memorandum* by Adam Hall (rn Elleston Trevor). ph Erwin Hillier. 2nd unit ph H A R Thompson. Colour. ed Frederick Wilson. ad Maurice Carter. sfx Les Bowie, Arthur Beavis. m John Barry. song *Wednesday's Child* by John Barry, David Mack. 103 mins

Cast: George Segal (Quiller), Alex Guinness (Pol), Max Von Sydow (Oktober), Senta Berger (Inge), George Sanders (Gibbs), Robert Helpmann (Weng), Robert Flemyng (Rushington), Peter Carsten (Hengel), Edith Schneider (Headmistress), Günther Meisner (Hassler), Ernst Walder (Grauber)

A British secret agent investigates a sinister neo-Nazi organization in Berlin.

The stodgy script and even stodgier direction slows an already snail-like pace to near-standstill and defeats a good cast who deserve better. The suspense largely derives from trying to figure out when it will all end.

'A B movie, never mind the big budget and the famous names, is what MEMORANDUM is. The plot is generally aimless, the lines are merely cute. Incredible that it was written by one of Britain's most brilliant playwrights.'
Time

RANSOM!

(US 1955)

pc MGM. p Nicholas Nayfack. d Alex Segal. w Cyril Hume, Richard Maibaum, from their television play *Fearful Decision*. ph Arthur E Arling. B&W. ed Ferris Webster. ad Cedric Gibbons, Arthur Lonergan. m Jeff Alexander. 109 mins

Cast: Glenn Ford (David Stannard), Donna Reed (Edith Stannard), Leslie Nielsen (Charlie Telfer), Juano Hernandez (Jesse Chapman), Robert Keith (Chief Jim Beckett), Jim Gaines (Langly), Mabel Albertson (Mrs Partridge), Alexander Scourby (Dr Paul Gorman), Bobby Clark (Andy Stannard), Ainslie Pryor (Al Stannard)

The family of a kidnapped boy come under strain when the father refuses to pay the ransom.

Grim and tense, but betraying its television origins by taking place almost entirely in the home of the kidnap victim, and marred by an overwrought performance by Ford.

'Almost entirely a dialogue play, there is little action and the pace is leisure-ly, but the story is so holding that it grips the attention throughout.'
CEA Film Report

REAR WINDOW

(US 1954)

pc Patron Inc. An Alfred Hitchcock Production. p, d Alfred Hitchcock. w John Michael Hayes, from the story *It Had to be Murder* by Cornell Woolrich. ph Robert Burks. Colour. ed George Tomasini. ad Hal Pereira, Joseph McMillan Johnson, Sam Comer, Ray Moyer. sfx John P

Fulton. m Franz Waxman. 112 mins

Cast: James Stewart (L B Jeffries), Grace Kelly (Lisa Fremont), Wendell Corey (Det. Thomas J Doyle), Raymond Burr (Lars Thorwald), Thelma Ritter (Stella), Judith Evelyn (Miss Lonely Hearts), Georgine Darcy (Miss Torso), Sara Berner (Woman on Fire Escape), Frank Cady (Man on Fire Escape), Ross Bagdasarian (Composer), Jesslyn Fax (Miss Hearing Aid), Rand Harper (Honeymooner), Irene Winston (Mrs Thorwald)

A magazine photographer confined to his apartment with a broken leg passes the time watching his neighbours across the courtyard. When he sees a man murder his wife, he is unable to convince a detective friend and almost loses his life to the killer.

Hitchcock's gimmick – confining the action to the Stewart's apartment and limiting the audience's view of the crime to what he sees – comes off very effectively. You can't help wondering, though, why a man who makes his living taking photographs and who is snooping through a telephoto lens doesn't take even one snap to confirm his story. The reason, presumably, is that such obvious logic would simply terminate the film prematurely.

Hayes's screenplay is one of his best, Hitchcock makes his artificial universe credible, and Stewart's choice performance more than compensates for Kelly's acting deficiencies.

'It is a nearly perfect cinematic reflection of life in the Hitchcock world, perilous, macabre and

REAR WINDOW

sophisticated and is recommended on all counts without qualification.'
Motion Picture Herald

'Tension is almost non-existent in the first hour and a half of *Rear Window*, but the last twenty minutes are as exciting as anything Hitchcock has ever done.'
Films in Review

'Mr Hitchcock is no greenhorn. When he takes on a stunt like this kind he may be counted on to pull it off with a maximum of build-up to the punch, a maximum of carefully tricked deception and incidents to divert and amuse.'
The New York Times

REMAINS TO BE SEEN
(US 1953)
pc MGM. p Arthur Hornblow Jr. d Don Weis. w Sidney Sheldon, from the play by Howard Lindsay, Russel Crouse. ph Robert Planck. B&W. ed Cotton Warburton. ad Cedric Gibbons, Hans Peters. md Jeff Alexander. 89 mins

Cast: June Allyson (Jody Revere), Van Johnson (Waldo Williams), Louis Calhern (Benjamin Goodman), Angela Lansbury (Valeska Chauvel), John Beal (Dr Glenson), Dorothy Dandridge (Herself), Barrey Kelley (Lt O'Falir), Sammy White (Ben), Kathryn Card (Mrs West)

The police are called in after a millionaire dies of an apparent heart attack and a carving knife mysteriously appears in his chest.

A witless comedy-thriller that is deficient on both counts.

That one-time favourite, the thriller-comedy, makes a feeble come-back.'
Picturegoer

REPORT TO THE COMMISSIONER

(US 1974) (GB: OPERATION UNDERCOVER)

pc Frankovich Productions. For UA p M J Frankovich. d Milton Katselas. w Abby Mann, Ernest Tidyman, from the novel *Report to the Commissioner* by James Mills. ph Mario Tosi. Colour. ed David Blewitt. pd Robert Clatworthy. sfx Robert MacDonald. m Elmer Bernstein. 112 mins

Cast: Michael Moriarty (Beauregard Bo' Lockley), Yaphet Kotto (Richard 'Crunch' Blackstone), Susan Blakely (Patty Butler), Hector Elizondo (Capt. D'Angelo), Tony King (Thomas 'The Stick' Henderson), Michael McGuire (Lt Hanson), Edward Grover (Capt. Strichter), Dana Elcar (Chief Perna), Robert Balaban (Joey Egan), William Devane (Assistant DA Jackson), Stephen Elliott (Police Commissioner), Richard Gere (Billy), Vic Tayback (Lt Seidensticker)

An idealistic rookie cop accidentally kills an undercover policewoman and becomes involved in a cover-up by his superior officers.

Rather too keen to make its (valid) sociological points at the expense of the narrative drive and tending to become over-melodramatic at moments of emphasis, it is nevertheless quite exciting. Richard Gere's screen debut.

The pace of the direction by Milton Katselas is so keen and the characters are so absorbingly realized

that one goes along with it all, and one knows at last that something devastating has been said, within the thriller context, about eternal ironies of crime and punsihment.'
Films and Filming

RESERVOIR DOGS

(US 1992)

pc Live America Inc. A Dog Eat Dog production. exec p Richard N Gladstein, Ronna B Wallace, Monte Hellman. p Lawrence Bender. co-p Harvey Keitel. d, w Quentin Tarantino. background radio dial Quentin Tarantino, Roger Avary. ph Andrezj Sekula. 2nd unit ph Alan Sherrod. ed Sally Menks. pd David Wasco. sfx co-ord Larry Fioritto. sc Ken Lesco. 99 mins

Cast: Harvey Keitel (Mr White [Larry]), Tim Roth (Mr Orange [Freddy]), Michael Madsen (Mr Blonde [Vic]), Chris Penn (Nice Guy Eddie), Steve Buscemi (Mr Pink), Lawrence Tierney (Joe Cabot), Randy Brooks (Holdaway), Kirk Baltz (Marvin Nash), Eddie Bunker (Mr Blue), Quentin Tarantino (Mr Brown), Michael Sottile (Teddy), Lawrence Bender (Young Cop)

Thieves fall out after a jewel heist goes badly wrong.

One of the most lauded debuts since Welles and *Citizen Kane*, but infinitely less deserving of the excessive praise shovelled onto it. If it had actually been even half as good as Tarantino and his idolators claim, by now Welles would have been relegated to a mere footnote in cinema history.

Tarantino is a skilled dialogue writer, notably in the opening scene

with its strong echoes of *Tin Men*, but his characters are clichés, and gain what resonance they possess as the result of casting, not writing. His direction is flashy but uninteresting, and he allows any actor who wants to to go over the top. Most of the cast, with the honourable exception of Lawrence Tierney, do just that.

The robbery itself is only glimpsed in flashbacks. The bulk of the action takes place in an abandoned warehouse and gives a strong impression that *Reservoir Dogs* might have been conceived as a one-set play and subsequently opened out.

Tarantino must have spent much of the time when he worked in a video store watching the stock and, as a result, his film is a treasure-trove for eager film buffs. The most obvious influence is *The Killing*, but one of the key reasons for its extraordinary success among cineastes is that almost any better film and/or film-maker can convincingly be dragged in to give cultural depth to the shallow proceedings. All the now well-established trademark Tarantino tics are already firmly in place – fast, facile direction, excessive violence seasoned with sadism, four-letter-word-splattered dialogue and ciphers instead of characters.

Few films in recent years have been so amazingly overrated, especially by those critics who require regular new cultural bandwagons on which to leap in order to keep their street cred in peak condition and who seized on Tarantino as a fresh icon to cultivate. Trendy moviegoers, in particular, reacted well to its unsubtle but undoubtedly visceral appeal, turning what was basically a second feature with intellectual pretensions into a cult, and turning Tarantino into a star-*auteur*. However, a few misguided souls insisted he was simply an unclothed emperor, but their voices were barely heard above the sycophantic critical and media hubbub. (Tarantino was originally going to make the film in black and white with friends instead of actors, but when Keitel came on board as star and co-producer, enough money was raised to make it in colour with a professional cast.)

'The free-wheeling mix of generic elements and left-field characterization in *Reservoir Dogs* is reminiscent of the crime movie sub-plot of Larry Cohen's *Q: The Winged Serpent* ... an astute mix of wit and cynicism which washes down its melodramatic excesses with sly satire on the blood-and-guts elements of the crime movie, this is a film of considerable acuity and power.'
Sight and Sound

'Few films in recent memory can boast such an unrelenting power over its audience. Intelligent, brutal and original, *Reservoir Dogs* will shock, disturb and provoke for years to come.'
Film Review

'Here is the ideal date movie, assuming you're dating a psychopathic sadist with a high tolerance for dillydalling.'
People

'A show-off piece of filmmaking that will put debut writer-director Quentin Tarantino on the map, *Reservoir Dogs* is an intense, bloody, in-your-face crime drama about a botched robbery and its gruesome aftermath.'

RESERVOIR DOGS

Colourfully written in vulgar gangster vernacular and well played.'
Variety

The plot is about as fresh as a Christmas cracker motto and the casual violence and sadism grow increasingly wearisome and leave a bad taste in the mouth ... few films could live up to all the fatuous, fawning flattery that's been heaped on it. *Reservoir Dogs* certainly doesn't.'
Daily Star

If it's flamboyance you want, head straight for *Reservoir Dogs*, a lurid mélange of crime caper and homoerotic bloodbath.'
Gay Times

RING OF FEAR
(US 1954)
pc Wayne-Fellows. p Robert M Fellows. d James Edward Grant. w Paul Fix, Philip MacDonald, James Edward Grant. ph Edwin DuPar. Colour. Scope. ed Fred MacDowell. circus wardrobe/production numbers Jane Beatty. m Emil Newman, Arthur Lange. Mickey Spillane's *Velda* and *The Mike Hammer Theme* by Stan Purdy. 93 mins

Cast: Clyde Beatty (Himself), Mickey Spillane (Himself), Pat O'Brien (Frank Wallace), Sean McClory (Dublin O'Malley), Marian Carr (Valerie St Denis), John Bromfield (Armand St Denis), Pedro Gonzales-Gonzales (Gonzales), Emmett Lynn (Twitchy), Jack Strang (Paul Martin), Kenneth Tobey (Shreveport)

A homicidal maniac escapes from an asylum, returns to the circus where he

once worked, and blackmails an alcoholic clown into committing acts of sabotage.

Tosh under the big top, notable only for writer Mickey Spillane making a bizarre appearance as himself and playing detective so unconvincingly he would be rapidly disowned by his private eye, Mike Hammer.

'Violent melodrama and over-coloured acting.'
Monthly Film Bulletin

ROADBLOCK
(US 1951)
pc RKO. p Lewis J Rachmil. d Harold Daniels. w Steve Fisher, George Bricker. st Richard Landau, Geoffrey Holmes. ph Nicholas Musuraca. B&W. ed Robert Golden. ad Albert D'Agostino, Walter E Keller. m Paul Sawtell. 73 mins

Cast: Charles McGraw (Joe Peters), Joan Dixon (Diane), Lowell Gilmore (Kendall Webb), Louis Jean Heydt (Harry Miller), Milburn Stone (Egan), Joseph Crehan (Thompson), Harry Lauter (Saunders), John Butler (Hotel Clerk), Dave Willock (Airport Clerk), Peter Brocco (Bank Heist Man)

An insurance investigator in love with a woman who refuses to marry a poor man gives a gangster inside information in exchange for a share of the loot from a train robbery.

Compact, above-average second feature with solid direction and a strong finish.

'A little too overblown in plot, perhaps, for a routine thriller, but the detection stuff, particularly a clever

bit of business at the beginning, is plausibly managed.'
Picturegoer

THE ROARING TWENTIES
(US 1938)
pc WB/First National. exec p Hal B Wallis. assoc p Samuel Bischoff. d Raoul Walsh. w Jerry Wald, Richard Macaulay, Robert Rossen. st Mark Hellinger. ph Ernest Haller. B&W. ed Jack Kilifer. ad Max Parker. sfx Byron Haskin, Edwin DuPar. m Heinz Roemheld, Ray Heindorf. 106 mins

Cast: James Cagney (Eddie Barlett), Priscilla Lane (Jean Sherman), Huphrey Bogart (George Hally), Gladys George (Panama Smith), Jeffrey Lynn (Lloyd Hart), Frank McHugh (Danny Green), Paul Kelly (Nick Brown), Elizabeth Risdon (Mrs Sherman), Edward Keane (Pater Henderson), Joseph Sawyer (Sgt Pete Jones), Joseph Crehan (Mr Fletcher), Abner Biberman (Lefty)

Three GIs return to the US after World War One, where one of them becomes a bootlegger during Prohibition and draws his friends into life as gangsters.

Walsh's muscular, documentary-influenced direction – complemented by strong performances from Cagney and Bogart, and evocative Warner Bros art direction which stylishly recreated the Prohibition era – makes this one of the studio's best genre efforts, in spite of its soft, sentimental centre. Walsh replaced originally-slated director Anatole Litvak.

'A brilliantly-made thriller.'
The Spectator

THE ROARING TWENTIES

ROBIN AND THE 7 HOODS

(1964)

pc A P-C Productions Picture, exec p
Howard W Koch. p Frank Sinatra.
assoc p William H Daniels. d Gordon
Douglas. ph William H Daniels.
Colour. Panavision. w David R
Schwartz. ed Sam O'Steen. ad LeRoy
Deane. m Nelson Riddle. songs Sammy
Cahn, James Van Heusen. 123 mins

Cast: Frank Sinatra (Robbo), Dean
Martin (John), Sammy Davis Jr
(Will), Bing Crosby (Alan A Dale),

Edward G Robinson (Big Jim), Peter
Falk (Guy Gisborne), Barbara Rush
(Marian), Victor Buono (Sheriff
Potts), Hank Henry (Six Seconds),
Allen Jenkins (Vermin), Jack LaRue
(Tomatoes), Robert Foulk (Sheriff
Glick), Robert Carricart (Blue Jaw),
Phil Crosby (Hood), Richard
Bakalyan (Hood), Richard Sinatra
(Hood), Sig Rumann (Hammacher),
Hans Conreid (Mrs Ricks)

The legend of Robin Hood reworked as
a gangster saga set in Chicago in 1928.

Flatulent, over-long and
unsophisticated excuse for Sinatra and
'The Clan' to enjoy themselves, which
is more than most audiences would.
Robinson had the good sense to
remain unbilled.

'Almost as strained and archaic in the
fable it has to tell of Prohibition era
gangsters in Chicago as the fable of
Robin Hood it travesties ... for all
those magnificent talents, it is an
artless and obvious film.'
The New York Times

ROBIN AND THE 7 HOODS

ROGUE COP
(US 1954)

pc MGM. p Nicholas Nayfack. d Roy Rowland. w Sidney Boehm, from the novel by William P McGivern. ph John Seitz. B&W. ed James E Newcom. ad Cedric Gibbons, Hans Peters. sfx A Arnold Gillespie. m Jeff Alexander. 88 mins

Cast: Robert Taylor (Christopher Kelvaney), Janet Leigh (Karen Stephanson), George Raft (Dan Beaumonte), Steve Forrest (Eddie Kelvaney), Anne Francis (Nancy Corlane), Robert Ellenstein (Sidney Myers), Robert F Simon (Ackerman), Anthony Rose (Father Ahearn), Alan Hale Jr (Johnny Stark), Peter Broco (Wrinkles Fallon), Vince Edwards (Langley), Olive Carey (Selma)

A corrupt cop turns on his gangland paymasters when they have his brother killed.

Brisk, efficient and downbeat, with a surprisingly good performance by Taylor and a stand-out portrait of an underworld kingpin by Raft.

'A simple, streamlined movie about crookedness.'
New York Herald-Tribune

ROPE
(US 1948)

pc Transatlantic Pictures. p Sidney Bernstein, Alfred Hiichcock. d Alfred Hitchcock. w Arthur Laurents. adap Hume Cronyn, from the play by Patrick Hamilton. ph Joseph Valentine,

William V Skall. Colour. ed William H Ziegler. ad Perry Ferguson. m Leo F Forbstein, based on a theme by Poulenc.

Cast: James Stewart (Rupert Cadell), Farley Granger (Philip), John Dall (Shaw Brandon), Joan Chandler (Janet Walker), Cedric Hardwicke (Mr Kentley), Constance Collier (Mrs Atwater), Edith Evanson (Mrs Wilson), Douglas Dick (Kenneth Lawrence), Dick Hogan (David Kentley)

Two homosexual students murder a college friend to prove their superiority, then throw a party for the dead boy's family, fiancee and their former teacher, and hide the body in an unlocked chest as an extra 'guest'.

Slow, ultimately pointless fictionalization of the twenties Leopold and Loeb murder (which also served as the basis for 1959's *Compulsion*, q.v.), rendered flat, slow and tedious by Hitchcock's use of the 'ten-minute take'. This involved filming continuously for the (approximately) ten minutes it took to use up a single magazine of film, with the camera prowling around the single set and following the actors. No conventional cuts or dissolves were used.

The breaking up of the action into eight takes was ultimately self-defeating, except as a demonstration of technical virtuosity, since it simply served to underline already dangerously stagey material and turn the film into little more than a photographed stage play. Fortunately, the failure of *Rope* purged the technique from Hitchcock's system and he never used it again.

Interestingly, however, producer Sidney Bernstein went on to co-found the British commercial television company Granada: the medium, with its lower technical and dramatic aspirations became the natural home for the time-saving 'ten-minute take' technique.

Rope is mainly significant as Hitchcock's first colour film and as a cinematic curiosity, in spite of valiant acting by Dall and Granger.

'The story moves at an even and monotonous speed and the eye, instead of being rested by the smoothness of the camera movement, is tired by it. Hitchcock, who used to terrify us by his handling of sudden detail, has condemned himself to meaningless deliberation. Instead of tension, we have exhaustion.'
The Sunday Times

'One must bluntly observe that the method is neither effective nor does it appear that it could be. For, apart from the tedium of waiting for someone to open that chest and discover the hidden body which the hosts have tucked away for the sake of a thrill, the unpunctuated flow of image becomes quite monotonous.'
The New York Times

'The film has been brilliantly conceived and presented with great polish and artistry, and the direction is masterly.'
CEA Film Report

RUSSIAN ROULETTE
(US 1975)
pc Bulldog Productions. exec p Elliott Kastner. p Jerry Blick. assoc p Marion Segal, Denis Holt. d Lou Lombardo. w

Tom Ardies, Stanley Mann, Arnold Margolin, from the novel *Kosygin is Coming* by Tom Ardies. ph Brian West. Colour. ed Richard Marden. ad Roy Walker. sfx Robert Macdonald, Joe Day, Thomas Clark. sc Bill Couch. m Michael J Lewis. 90 mins

Cast: George Segal (Timothy Shaver), Cristina Raines (Bogna Kirchoff), Denholm Elliott (Petapiece), Gordon Jackson (Hardison), Richard Romanus (Raymond 'Rags' Ragulia), Bo Brundi (Sergei Vostick), Val Avery (Rudolph Henke), Louise Fletcher (Midge), Nigel Stock (Ferguson), Peter Donat (McDermott)

A suspended Royal Canadian Mounted Police corporal prevents the assassination of USSR premier Alexei Kosygin in Vancouver.

Lombardo, Robert Altman's former editor, makes a spirited directorial debut and maintains a speedy enough pace to distract from illogicalities in the storyline.

'An entertaining and exciting film that will not tax your intellect or viscera.'
Film Information

SABOTAGE

(GB 1936) (US: THE WOMAN ALONE)

pc Gaumont British. p Michael Balcon. assoc p Ivor Montagu. d Alfred Hitchcock. w Charles Bennett. dial Ian Hay, Helen Simpson, E V H Emmett, Alma Reville, from the novel *The Secret Agent* by Joseph Conrad. ph Bernard Knowles. B&W. ed Charles Frend. ad Otto Werndorff, Albert Jullion. m Louis Levy. 77 mins

Cast: Sylvia Sidney (Sylvia Verloc), Oscar Homolka (Carl Verloc), John Loder (Ted Spencer), Desmond Tester (Steve), Joyce Barbour (Renee), Matthew Boulton (Supt Talbot), S J Warmington (Hollingshead), William Dewhurst (A S Chatman), Austin Trevor (Vladimir), Torin Thatcher (Yunct), Aubrey Mather (Greengrocer), Peter Bull (Michaelis), Charles Hawtrey (Youth)

An anarchist manages a London cinema while plotting to blow up the city.

Patchy thriller with an insipid hero (Alexander Korda refused to release Hitchcock's original choice, Robert Donat). There are, however, two classic sequences: Sidney's murder of Homolka with a knife, played without dialogue, is a dramatic *tour de force*, and the boy's journey across London unknowingly carrying a primed bomb in a packed bus generates nerve-scraping tension. Hitchcock later admitted he had made a major mistake in having the bomb detonate prematurely on the bus and kill the boy, since moviegoers, now sympathetic to his predicament, resented his death.

'*Sabotage* hangs together. In that respect it is his best picture. The picture is full of shrewd observation and cockney humour and the cutting throughout is fine.'
The Daily Telegraph

'It has been designed as a thriller and it thrills.'
Daily Mail

SABOTEUR

(US 1942)
pc Universal. p Frank Lloyd. assoc p Jack H Skirball. d, st Alfred Hitchcock. w Peter Viertel, Joan Harrison, Dorothy Parker. ph Joseph Valentine.

SABOTEUR

B&W. ed Otto Ludwig. ad Jack Otterson. m Charles Previn, Frank Skinner. 108 mins

Cast: Robert Cummings (Barry Kane), Priscilla Lane (Pat Martin), Otto Kruger (Charles Tobin), Alma Kruger (Henrietta Sutton), Alan Baxter (Freeman), Pedro de Cordoba (Bones, the Human Skeleton), Vaughan Glaser (Philip Martin), Ian Wolfe (Butler), Norman Lloyd (Frank Fry), Dorothy Peterson (Mrs Mason), Bill Curtis (Mayer, the Midget), Clem Bevans (Neilsen), Gus Glassmire (Mr Pearl), Samuel S Hinds (Foundation Leader)

A World War Two aircraft factory worker suspected of sabotage is chased across country by the police as he tries to track down the real perpetrators.

Minor and uneven, redeemed by a stand-out suspense climax set on the torch of the Statue of Liberty and a bizarre, if unmotivated, sequence in a circus freak show. A miracle would have been needed to elicit a good performance from Cummings: there is none.

'Not all the turns in *Saboteur* are new, but the pace is kept up. The phoney thrill leads to the real thrill. And when the Hitchcock situation comes it is irreproachable.
New Statesman

THE SAINT IN NEW YORK
(US 1938)
pc RKO. p William Sistrom. d Ben Holmes. w Charles Kauffman, Mortimer Offner, from the novel by Leslie Charteris. ph Joseph August, Frank Redman. B&W. ed Harry Marker. ad Van Nest Polglase. 72 mins

Cast: Louis Hayward (Simon Templar, 'The Saint'), Kay Sutton (Fay Edwards), Sig Rumann (Hutch Rellin), Jonathan Hale (Insp. Fernack), Jack Carson (Red Jenks), Paul Guilfoyle (Hymie Fanro), Frederick Burton (William Valcross), Ben Welden (Papinoff), Charles Halton (Vincent Nather), Cliff Bragdon (Sebastian)

The Saint is hired to dispose of six gangsters in New York.

The first film featuring the suave, not-entirely-honest crimefighter created by Leslie Charteris in *Meet the Tiger* (1928) is a well-crafted B-feature that gets on with the business in hand at lively pace.

George Sanders took over the role in RKO's next film, *The Saint Strikes Back* (1939) and played it in four subsequent movies. Hugh Sinclair was Templar in two 1941 British films (*The Saint's Vacation*, *The Saint Meets the Tiger* and Hayward returned in 1953 for *The Saint's Vacation*). Templar's last cinema appearance was in *Le Saint mène la Danse* in 1959, after which the character seguéd to television, where it was processed and pasteurized into little more than a well-tailored grin by Roger Moore. Val Kilmer played Templar in the character's expensively mounted 1997 big screen comeback.

'Highly fantastic in plot, but intriguing ... making no pretensions in being more than a B picture, this happens to be one of the top B's of the current crop of film fare.'
Variety

THE SAINT'S RETURN
(GB 1953) (US: THE SAINT'S GIRL FRIDAY)
pc Hammer. p Anthony Hinds. d Seymour Friedman. w Allan McKinnon, based on characters created by Leslie Charteris. ph Walter Harvey. B&W. ed James Needs. ad J Elder Wills. m Ivor Slaney. 73 mins

Cast: Louis Hayward (Simon Templar, 'The Saint'), Naomi Chance (Lady Carol Denbigh), Sydney Tafler (Lennar), Charles Victor (Chief Insp. Teal), Harold Lang (Jarvis), Thomas Gallagher (Hoppy Uniatz), Jane Carr (Katie), Fred Johnson (Irish Cassidy), Russell Enoch (Keith Merton), Ian Fleming (Lord Merton), Diana Dors (Margie), Russell Napier (Col. Stafford)

The Saint investigates a murder in London and unmasks the leader of a gambling ring.

Routine, predictable British B-picture with imported American star and director.

'Although it is little more than hokum, however, it moves at a good pace and provides murder and detective drama of a popular type.'
CEA Film Report

SAPPHIRE
(GB 1959)
pc Artna. p Michael Relph. d Basil Dearden. w Janet Green. add dial Lukas Heller. ph Harry Waxman. Colour. ed John Guthridge. ad Carmen Dillon. m Philip Green. title song Philip Green, Sonny Miller, sung by Jimmy Lloyd. 92 mins

Cast: Nigel Patrick (Det. Supt Hazard), Yvonne Mitchell (Mildred arr), Michael Craig (Det. Insp. Learoyd), Paul Massie (David Harris), Bernard Miles (Mr Harris), Olga Lindo (Mrs Harris), Earl Cameron (Dr Robbins), Gordon Heath (Paul Slade), Jocelyn Britton (Patsy), Harry Baird (Johnnie Fiddle), Rupert Davies (Ferris), Freda Bamford (Sgt Cook), Yvonne Buckingham (Sapphire)

London police investigating the murder of a young woman are caught up in racial tension when they discover she was of mixed race.

A compelling combination of whodunnit and racial drama, with a sharp screenplay and advanced (for the time) views on racism in Britain.

'It is first and foremost a very fine, tantalizing edge-of-your-seat thriller.'
The Star

SATAN MET A LADY
(US 1936)
pc WB p Henry Blanke. d William Dieterle. w Brown Holmes, from the novel The Maltese Falcon by Dashiell Hammett. ph Arthur Edeson. B&W. md Max Parker, Warren Low. md Leo F Forbstein. 75 mins

Cast: Bette Davis (Valerie Purvis), Warren William (Ted Shayne), Alison Skipworth (Madame Barabbas), Arthur Treacher (Anthony Travers), Winifred Shaw (Astrid Ames), Marie Wilson (Murgatroyd), Porter Hall (Mr Ames), Maynard Holmes (Kenneth), Charles Wilson (Pollock), Olin Howland (Dunhill)

A private eye hunts for a gem-incrusted ram's horn and tangles with crooks.

Pointless remake of 1931's The Maltese Falcon, churned out on the Warner Bros assembly line and heartily – and rightly – disliked by Davis. Sam Spade becomes Ted Shayne, Caspar Gutman becomes Madame Barrabas, the Falcon becomes a ram's horn and the film becomes another less than fine mess.

'There is no story, merely a farrago of nonsense representing a series of practical studio compromised with an unworkable script.'
The New York Times

SCARFACE/SCARFACE, SHAME OF A NATION
(US 1932)
pc Howard Hughes. p, sup Howard Hughes. d Howard Hawks. w Ben Hecht, Seton I Miller, John Lee Mahin, W R Burnett, Fred Palsey, from the novel by Armitage Trail. ph Lee Garmes, L William O'Connell. B&W. ed Edward D Curtiss. m Adolph Tandler, Gus Arnheim. 99 mins

Cast: Paul Muni (Tony Camonte), Ann Dvorak (Cesca Camonte), Karen Morley (Poppy), Osgood Perkins (Johnny Lovo), Boris Karloff (Gaffney), George Raft (Guido Rinaldo), C Henry Gordon (Guarino), Purnell Pratt (Publisher), Vince Barnett (Angelo), Inez Palange (Mrs Camonte), Henry J Vejar (Costillo), Edwin Maxwell (Chief of Detectives), Tully Marshall (Managing Editor), Henry Armetta (Pietro), Dennis O'Keefe (Dance Extra), Howard Hawks (Man on Bed)
The rise and fall of a big-time gangster in twenties Chicago.

Seminal gangster movie, loosely based on the career of Al Capone. There are recreations of the St Valentine's Day Massacre and the slaying of 'Big Jim' Colosimo and Dion O'Banion. However, Muni's motivation (incestuous feelings towards his sister) was, needless to say, entirely fictional, as was his character's end. His vivid performance is a genre archetype and confirmed his stardom, and Scarface also made a star of George Raft, playing Muni's coin-flipping henchman. Boris Karloff, soon to be typecast in horror roles, is memorable as Muni's main rival.

Hawks's muscular direction is outstanding, and the innovatory use of colloquial dialogue rather than the usually more stylized speech prevalent in films of the time adds considerable force.

It took six weeks to shoot, was completed in November and then ran into problems with both censors and public, and Hawks was forced to make cuts in order to show the 'hero' less sympathetically. Several endings were shot (including one with Muni hanging from the gallows) but the most frequently-used ending has him begging for mercy.

Tough, violent and amoral, Scarface is a major influence, with most of its innovations later being assimilated into other genre movies.

'Had Scarface been released a year or so ago it would have been hailed as a masterpiece of dramatic realism by those who had never seen anything like it in the cinema before. But we've already seen Little Caesar and Public Enemy ... as a result ... the edge has been somewhat taken off

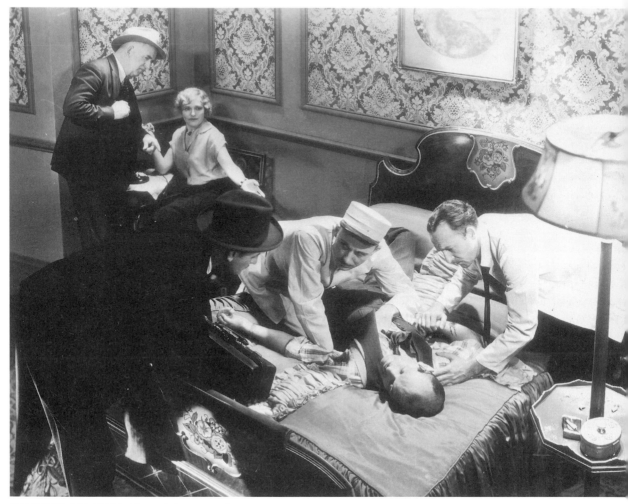

SCARFACE/SCARFACE, SHAME OF A NATION

gangster shockers.'
New York Evening Journal

'The slaughter in *Scarface* ... is like that of a Shakespearian tragedy ... a stirring picture, efficiently directed and capably acted.'
The New York Times

'The most vicious and demoralizing gangster pic produced.'
Harrison's Reports

SEA OF LOVE
(US 1989)

pc Universal. p Martin Bregman, Louis A Stroller. assoc p Michael Scott Bregman. d Harold Becker. w Richard Price. ph Ronnie Taylor. add ph Adam Holender. Colour. ed David Bertherton, John Wright. pd John Jaye Moore. sc Dick Ziker. m Trevor Jones. 113 mins

Cast: Al Pacino (Frank Keller), Ellen Barkin (Helen), John Goodman (Sherman Towley), Michael Rooker (Terry), William Hickey (Frank Sr), Richard Jenkins (Gruber), Paul Calderon (Serafino), Gene Canfield

(Struk), Larry Joshua (Dargan), John Spencer (Lieutenant), Christine Estabrook (Gina Gallagher), Barbara Baxley (Miss Allen), Jacqueline Brooks (Helen's Mother)

A jaded veteran New York policeman investigating serial murders in which the killer finds victims through 'lonely hearts' advertisements falls for his prime suspect.

Evident sexual chemistry between Pacino (ending a major career slump) and Barkin goes a long way towards disguising the fact that the plot is riddled with holes and has a pretty predictable resolution, while tasteful nudity (using a body double for Barkin) helped it towards success, as did the tense, no-nonsense direction.

'Taut, racy, sublimely witty ... crackles with verve and erotic overtones.'
Today

'Suspenseful film noir boasting a superlative performance by Al Pacino.'
Variety

SEBASTIAN
(GB 1967)
pc Maccius. p Herbert Brodkin, Michael Powell. assoc p John Pellatt. d David Greene. w Gerald Vaughan-Hughes. st Leo Marks. ph Gerald Fisher. Colour. ed Brian Smedley-Aston. pd Wilfred Shingleton. ad Fred Carter. m Jerry Goldsmith. song Here Comes the Night by Jerry Goldsmith, Hal Shafer. titles Richard Williams Films. 100 mins

Cast: Dirk Bogarde (Sebastian), Susannah York (Becky Howard), Lilli Palmer (Elsa Shahn), John Gielgud (Head of Intelligence), Janet Munro (Carol), Margaret Johnston (Miss Elliott), Nigel Davenport (Gen. Phillips), Ronald Fraser (Tony), John Ronane (Jameson), Ann Beach (Pamela), Donald Sutherland (American)

An Oxford don is recruited as a codebreaker by British Intelligence.

Amiable, glossy and diverting, but unsure whether it is meant as a send-up or intended to be taken seriously.

'It's just classy pulp, but the whole thing goes by before one has time to hate it.'
The New Yorker

SECRET AGENT
(GB 1936)
pc Gaumont British. p Michael Balcon, Ivor Montagu. d Alfred Hitchcock. w Charles Bennett. adap Alma Reville, from the play by Campbell Dixon, based on the short stories The Traitor & The Hairless Mexican by W Somerset Maugham. dial Ian Hay, Jesse Lasky Jr. ph Bernard Knowles. B&W. ed Charles Frend. ad Otto Werndorff, Albert Jullion. m Louis Levy. 83 mins

Cast: Madeleine Carroll (Elsa Carrington), John Gielgud (Richard Ashenden), Peter Lorre (The Mexican), Robert Young (Robert Marvin), Percy Marmont (Caypor), Florence Kahn (Mrs Caypor), Lilli Palmer (Lilli), Charles Carson ('R'), Michel Saint-Denis (Coachman), Andrea Malandrinos (Manager), Tom Helmore (Capt. Anderson), Howard Marion Crawford (Carl), Dino Galvanni (Receptionist), Rene Ray (Maid), Michael Redgrave (Man)

A novelist is recruited by British Intelligence and, with another agent posing as his wife, is sent to Switzerland to eliminate a German spy.

The hero is miscast, but some splendid suspenseful sequences – notably the chase through the chocolate factory where the spies have their headquarters and a memorable portrait of villainy from Lorre – salvage an otherwise minor and unmemorable Hitchcock thriller. Michael Redgrave's screen debut.

'Secret Agent dallies much on the way and does lots of looping to get over a dramatic point, but withal rates as good spy entertainment.'
Variety'

'His [Hitchcock's] films consist of a series of small "amusing" melodramatic situations ... very perfunctorily he builds up to these tricky situations (paying no attention on the way to inconsistencies, loose ends, psychological absurdities) and then drops them: they mean nothing: they lead to nothing.'
The Spectator

THE SECRET BEYOND THE DOOR
(US 1948)
pc Diana Productions-Universal. exec p Walter Wanger. p, d Fritz Lang. w Sylvia Richards, from the story Museum Piece No 13 by Rufus King. ph Stanley Cortez. B&W. ed Arthur Hilton. ad Max Parker. m Miklos Rosza. 99 mins

Cast: Joan Bennett (Celia Lamphere), Michael Redgrave (Mark Lamphere), Anne Revere (Caroline Lamphere), Barbara O'Neil (Miss Robey), Natalie Schaefer (Edith Potter), Paul Cavanagh (Rick Barrett), Anabel Shaw (Society Girl), Rosa Rey (Paquita), James Seay (Bob Dwight), Mark Dennis (David), Donna Di Mario (Gypsy), Virginia Brissac (Sarah), Houseley Stevenson (Andy)

A woman married to a man with an obsession for murder cases starts to believe he intends to kill her.

High-style direction, but low-credibility content. Atmospherically photographed, though.

SEVEN

Lang gets a few wood-silky highlights out of this sow's ear, but it is a hopeless job and a worthless movie.'
The Nation

SIEGE OF PINCHGUT

(GB 1959) (US: FOUR DESPERATE MEN)

pc Ealing Films. A Michael Balcon Production. assoc p Eric Williams. d Harry Watt. w Harry Watt, John Cleary. add w Alexander Baron. ph Gordon Dines. B&W. ed Gordon Stone. ad Alan Withy. m Kenneth V Jones. 104 mins

Cast: Aldo Ray (Matt Kirk), Heather Sears (Ann Fulton), Neil McCallum (Johnny Kirk), Victor Maddern (Bert), Carlo Justini (Luke), Alan Tilvern (Supt Hanna), Barbara Mullen (Mrs Fulton), Gerry Duggan (Pat Fulton), Kenneth Warren (Police Commissioner), Grant Taylor (Constable Macey), Derek Barnes (Sgt Drak), Richard Verson (Under Secretary)

A man claiming innocence escapes on the way to prison and, with his brother and two others, holes up on an island in Sydney Harbour with three hostages.

Unexceptional, with uninteresting characters. Compensations include the Australian locations and taut, documentary-style set-pieces.

The film raises many issues, but explores none of them satisfactorily. In the end, it rates as just a thunderingly exciting thriller.'
Picturegoer

SEVEN

(US 1995)

pc New Line. exec p Gianni Nunnari, Dan Kolsrud, Anne Kopelson. co-exec p Lynn Harris, Richard Saperstein. p Arnold Kopelson, Phyllis Carlisle. co-p Stephen Brown, Nana Greenwald, Sanford Panitch. line p William C Gerrity. assoc p Michele Platt. d David Fincher. w Andrew Kevin Walker. ph Darius Khondji. add ph Vincent Reynaud. Colour. ed Richard Francis-Bruce. pd Arthur Max. ad Gary Wissner. sfx sup Danny Cangemi. sfx m-u Rob Bottin. m Howard Shore. 127 mins

Cast: Brad Pitt (Mills), Morgan Freeman (Somerset), Gwyneth Paltrow (Tracy), Kevin Spacey (John Doe), Richard Roundtree (Talbot), R Lee Ermey (Police Captain), John C McGinley (California), Julie Araskog (Mrs Gould), Mark Boone Jr (Greasy FBI Man), John Cassini (Officer Davis), Reginald E Cathey (Dr Santiago), Peter Crombie (Dr O'Neill), Hawthorne James (Library Night Guard), Steve Watson (Hacker), Richard Portnow (Dr Beardsley), Pamela Tyson (Vagrant)

A veteran big-city policeman on the verge of retirement is joined by a rookie to track down the deranged serial killer who uses the Seven Deadly Sins as blueprints for his homicides.

Fincher makes impressive amends for his dreary directorial debut (*Alien 3*) with a riveting suspenser that is the stuff of which nightmares are made. An inspired screenplay is matched by taut, stylish direction and complemented by bleak cinematography that drains the colour from the grim, rain-drenched city in vivid *noir* fashion.

The visceral impact of its memorably grisly shock sequences and set-pieces is potentiated by clever staging, which appears to reveal more than is actually seen on screen and forces the viewer to become a voyeur-accomplice. The atmosphere of mounting terror and unease is sustained and chilling, the acting, especially by Spacey, is exemplary.

'A film you won't be able to shake from your memory.'
The Independent

'This is a nerve-shredder that will keep you on the edge of your seat from the first reel.'
The People

'Gruesome, though more by suggestion than what's shown; also poetic and powerful.'
The Daily Telegraph

'*Seven* has the scariest ending since George Sluizer's original *The Vanishing* (*Spoorloos*, 1988) ... and stands as the most complex and disturbing entry in the serial killer genre since *Manhunter*.'
Sight and Sound

SEVEN DAYS IN MAY

(US 1964)

pc Seven Arts/Joel Produtions/John Frankenheimer. p Edward Lewis. d John Frankenheimer. w Rod Serling, from the novel by Fletcher Knebel & Charles W Bailey II. ph Ellsworth Fredericks. B&W. ed Ferris Webster. ad Cary Odell. m Jerry Goldsmith. 118 mins

Cast: Burt Lancaster (Gen. James M Scott), Kirk Douglas (Col Martin 'Jiggs' Casey), Frederic March (President

SEVEN DAYS TO NOON

Lyman), Ava Gardner (Eleanor
Holbrook), Edmond O'Brien (Senator
Raymond Clark), Martin Balsam (Paul
Girard), George Macready (Christopher
Todd), Whit Bissell (Senator Prentice),
Hugh Marlowe (Harold McPherson),
Bart Burns (Corwin), Richard Anderson
(Col. Murdock), Jack Mullaney (Lt
Hough), Andrew Duggan (Col.
Henderson), John Houseman (Admiral
Barnswell)

An American Army colonel discovers a
plot by high-ranking military men to
overthrow the US President.

Riveting political thriller, with
Frankenheimer in top form, excellent
casting, and a taut, intelligent
screenplay. Lancaster, playing against his
usual heroic type, is particularly good.

'An entertainment, in Graham
Greene's sense of the word, and an
intelligent one.'
Monthly Film Bulletin

'Suspense mounts increasingly as the
deadline approaches, and credit for
this must be shared between a brilliant cast and director.'
ABC Film Review

SEVEN DAYS TO NOON
(GB 1950)
pc A Boulting Brothers Production for
London Films. p, ed Roy Boulting.
d John Boulting. w Frank Harvey,
Roy Boulting. st Paul Dehn, James
Bernard. ph Gilbert Taylor. B&W.
ad John Elphick. m John Addison.
94 mins

Cast: Barry Jones (Prof. Willingdon)
Olive Sloane (Goldie), Andre Morell
(Supt Folland), Sheila Manahan
(Ann Willingdon), Hugh Cross
(Stephen Lane), Joan Hickson (Mrs

SEVEN DAYS TO NOON

Peckett), Ronald Adam (Prime Minister), Marie Ney (Mrs Willingdon), Merrill Mueller (American Commentator)

A deranged nuclear scientist steals an atom bomb and threatens to destroy London in a week unless all nuclear research is halted.

The low-key, semi-documentary direction and an uncomfortably credible storyline, reinforced by unfamiliar faces in key roles, adds to the mounting suspense. The scenes of the evacuation of London are notably impressive, and the clever location work potentiates the persuasive air of reality. The original story, by film critic Dehn and composer Bernard, won an Academy Award.

'A film of great tension and excitement with a climax that is reached after breathless suspense.'
The Star

SEVEN THIEVES
(US 1960)
pc 20th Century Fox. p, w Sidney Boehm, from the novel *Lions at the Kill* by Max Catto. d Henry Hathaway. ph Sam Leavitt. B&W. CinemaScope. ed Dorothy Spencer. ad Lyle R Wheeler, John De Cuir. m Dominic Frontiere. 102 mins

Cast: Edward G Robinson (Theo Wilkins), Rod Steiger (Paul Mason), Joan Collins (Melanie), Eli Wallach (Pancho), Alexander Scourby (Raymond Le May), Berry Kroeger (Hugo Baumer), Michael Dante (Louis), Sebastian Cabot (Monte Carlo Director), Marcel Hillaire (Duc Di Salins), Jonathan Kidd (Seymour)

An elderly criminal devises an ingenious scheme to steal $4 million from a Monte Carlo casino.

Smart, thoroughly professional, perfect crime caper with forceful (if anonymous) direction that maintains pace and tension until the inevitable moment in the last reel when current censorship dictated that crime should not pay.

'The plot isn't new and it doesn't make you think. Yet it's the kind of first-rate precision job that signifies entertainment with a capital E. This fool-proof thriller, capably directed, expertly cast, reminds us that before Hollywood became the factor for wide-screen spectacle it was the home of professional story-telling.'
Picturegoer

THE SEVEN-UPS
(US 1973)
pc 20th Century Fox/Philip D'Antoni Productions. exec p Kenneth Utt, Barry J Weitz. p, d Philip D'Antoni. assoc p Jerry Greenberg. w Albert Ruben, Alexander Jacobs. st Sonny Grosso. ph Uhrs Furrer. Colour. ed Stephen A Rotter, John C Horger, Jerry Greenberg. pd Ed Wittstein. sfx Albert Griswold. m Don Ellis. 103 mins

Cast: Roy Scheider (Buddy), Victor Arnold (Barilli), Jerry Leon (Mingo), Ken Kercheval (Ansel), Tony Lo Bianco (Vito Lucia), Larry Haines (Max Kalish), Richard Lynch (Moon), Bill Hickman (Bo), Lou Polan (Carmine Coltello), Matt Russo (Festa), Joe Spinell (Toredano), Robert Burr (Lt Hines), Rex Everhart (Insp. Gilson), David Wilson (Bobby)

A New York detective leads a secret unit against a group of leading gangsters.

The storyline is routine, and director D'Antoni (who produced *The French Connection*, q.v.) is often unsure in his handling of actors. The action, especially an exciting and sustained car chase, gets it by.

'The film keeps tidily clear of the moral endorsements of *Magnum Force* and *Walking Tall*; it is as an action thriller that *The Seven-Ups* asks to be judged, and as such it largely succeeds.'
Monthly Film Bulletin

SHADOW OF A DOUBT
(US 1943)
pc Universal. p Jack H Skirball. d Alfred Hitchcock. w Thornton Wilder, Sally Benson, Alma Reville. st Gordon McDonnell. ph Joseph Valentine. B&W. ed Milton Carruth. ad Robert Boyle, R A Gausman, L R Robinson. m Dimitri Tiomkin. 108 mins

Cast: Joseph Cotten (Charlie Oakley), Teresa Wright (Charlie Newton), Macdonald Carey (Jack Graham), Patricia Collinge (Emma Newton), Henry Travers (Joseph Newton), Hume Cronyn (Herbie Hawkins), Wallace Ford (Fred Saunders), Edna May Wonicott (Ann Newton), Charles Bates (Roger Newton), Irving Bacon (Stationmaster), Clarence Muse (Pullman Porter), Janet Shaw (Louise)

A young girl is delighted when her favourite uncle comes to visit, but slowly comes to suspect him of being a psychotic serial killer.

An engrossing blend of sharply-observed, beautifully-detailed American small-town life, suspense and cleverly-conceived character study, and reportedly Hitchcock's favourite among his own movies.

Thornton Wilder's original screenplay – inspired by the real-life twenties 'Merry Widow Killer', Earl Leonard Nelson, and polished by Sally Benson, author of *Meet Me In St Louis*, and Mrs Hitchcock (Alma Reville) – works very well as both social comment and suspenser, and location shooting in Santa Rosa in northern California (interiors were filmed at Universal Studios) adds telling atmosphere.

Once curiously underrated, *Shadow of a Doubt* is, without doubt, one of the best films in the Hitchcock Hollywood canon.

'Hitchcock again proves himself a master director … suspense is gripping and dramatic and thrilling situations are piled up to a terrific climax.'
CEA Film Report

'The essence of such a tale is the solidity and ordinariness of the background against which the strangeness of murder is disclosed. Hitchcock, from long ago a master of this kind of solid plausbility, has, I fancy, learned from Orson Welles the value of the interrupted broken conversation, the dialogue drowned in chatter. I do not think I was mistaken in seeing the Welles influence elsewhere in this admirably made film; in the use of close-ups, the pictorial handling of the solitary figure, and the suggestion of the voice overheard.'
The Sunday Times

'There are points in *Shadow of a Doubt* which suggest that Hitchcock has been taking an intensive course of Orson Welles, unless one assumes that Orson Welles made an intensive study of Hitchcock in the first place.'
The Observer

SHAFT
(US 1971)
pc MGM/Shaft Productions. A Stirling Silliphant/Roger Lewis Production. p Joel Freeman. assoc p David Golden. d Gordon Parks. w Ernest Tidyman, John D F Black, from the novel by Ernest Tidyman. ph Urs Furrer. Colour. ed Hugh A Robertson. ad Emmanuel Gerard. m Isaac Hayes. 100 mins

Cast: Richard Roundtree (John Shaft), Moses Gunn (Bumpy Jonas), Charles Cioffi (Vic Androzzi), Christopher St John (Ben Buford), Gwen Mitchell (Ellie Moore), Lawrence Pressman (Ton Hannon), Victor Arnold (Charlie), Sherri Brewer (Marcy), Rex Robbins (Rollie), Margaret Warnecke (Linda), Joseph Leon (Byron Leibowitz), Camille Yarbrough (Dina Greene)

Black private eye John Shaft is told his licence will be suspended unless he helps the New York police investigate a Harlem gangster.

Brisk, competent blaxploitation thriller that spawned two sequels and a television series which also starred Roundtree.

'In the main a highly workmanlike and enjoyable thriller.'
Monthly Film Bulletin

SHAMUS
(US 1972)
pc Robert M Weitman Productions. For Columbia. p Robert M Weitman. assoc p Jim Di Gangi. d Buzz Kulik. w Barry Beckerman. ph Victor J Kemper. Colour. ed Walter Thompson. ad Philip Rosenberg. m Jerry Goldsmith. 98 mins

Cast: Burt Reynolds (Shamus McCoy), Dyan Cannon (Alexis), John Ryan (Col. Hardcore), Joe Santos (Lt Promuto), Giorgio Tozzi (Il Dottore), Ron Weyland (E J Hume), Larry Block (Springy), Beeson Carroll (Bolton), Kevin Conway (The Kid), John Glover (Johnnie)

A private eye is pitchforked into danger when a wealthy industrialist hires him to recover stolen jewels.

Confused and fast-moving, the film recalls a lot of better genre films, including *The Big Sleep*, but in spite of a plot that takes more effort than it is worth to follow, it provides moderate, thick-ear entertainment.

'The characters may be largely colourless but in their unendearing, unedifying way they pack in enough action for half a dozen such pictures.'
Daily Mail

SHARKY'S MACHINE
(US 1981)
pc Deliverance Productions. For Orion. p Hank Moonjean. assoc p Edward Teets. d Burt Reynolds. w Gerald Di Pego, from the novel by William Diehl. ph William A Fraker. Colour. ed William Gordean. Dennis Virkler. pd Walter Scott Herndon. sfx Phil Cory. sc, Bobby Bass. m sup Snuff Garrett. 120 mins

Cast: Burt Reynolds (Tom Sharky), Vittorio Gassman (Victor D'Anton), Brian Keith (Papa), Charles Durning (Frisco), Earl Holliman (Hotchkins), Bernie Casey (Arch), Henry Silva (Billy Score), Richard Libertini (Nosh), Darryl Hickman (Smiley), Rachel Ward (Dominoe), Joseph Mascolo (Joe Tipps), Hari Rhodes (Highball Mary), Carol Locatell (Mabel), John Fiedler (Barrett)

Demoted after an undercover narcotics operation goes wrong, an Atlanta cop forms his own unofficial police squad and investigates political corruption and a high-class call girl racket.

Reynolds gives a typically tough-funny performance in a tailor-made role and, as director, demonstrates a slick ability to stage exciting action in a power-paced movie that takes him successfully into *Dirty Harry* territory.

'A solidly made cop movie with an added dimension. Seen sympathetically it's a provocative and even subversive movie.'
The Guardian

SHORT CUT TO HELL
(US 1957)

pc Paramount. p A C Lyles. d James Cagney. w Ted Berkman, Raphael Batt, W R Burnett, from the novel *This Gun For Sale* by Graham Greene. ph Haskell Boggs. B&W. VistaVision. ed Ken

SHARKY'S MACHINE

McAdo. ad Hal Pereira, Roland Anderson. m Irving Colbert. 89 mins

Cast: Robert Ivers (Kyle), Georgann Johnson (Glory), William Bishop (Stan), Jacques Aubuchon (Bahwell), Peter Baldwin (Adams), Yvette Vickers (Daisy), Murvyn Vye (Nichols), Milton Frome (Los Angeles Police Captain), Richard Hale ('AT')

A man hired by a gangster to commit a double murder tries to double-cross him.

Interesting if ultimately flawed remake of 1942's *This Gun for Hire* (q.v.), with efficient if not particularly inspired direction by James Cagney in his only film as director. He also appears on screen to introduce the movie.

'The picture has its moments, and the plot is still fresh and Greene enough. Director James Cagney ... manages to beauty-spot a few of the bare places with some characteristic Cagney touches.'
Time

SIGNPOST TO MURDER
(US 1964)
pc MGM. p Lawrence Weingarten. d George Englund. w Sally Benson, from the play by Monte Doyle. ph Paul C Vogel. B&W. Panavision. ed John McSweeney Jr. ad George W Davis, Edward Carfagno. sfx J McMillan Johnson. m Lynn Murray. 74 mins

Cast: Joanne Woodward (Molly Thomas), Stuart Whitman (Alex Forrester), Edward Mulhare (Dr Mark Fleming), Alan Napier (The Vicar), Joyce Worsley (Mrs Barnes), Leslie

Denison (Supt Bickley), Murray Matheson (Dr Graham), Hedley Mattingly (Rogers), Carol Vezie (Auntie)

A killer escapes from an asylum, takes refuge in a lonely house, holds a woman at gunpoint, and a bizarre murder takes place.

Ludicrous, with an unbelievable plot and denouement that the audience – although, amazingly, not the players – can see coming a mile off, set in a make-believe England that only exists in Hollywood.

'Quite the sorriest film I've seen in many months.'
Films and Filming

THE SILENT PARTNER
(US/CANADA 1978)
pc Carolco Inc. ex p Garth H Drabinsky. p Joel B Michaels, Stephen Young. d Darryl Duke. w Curtis Hanson, from the novel *Think of a Number* by Anders Bodelson. ph Billy Williams. 2nd unit ph Stephen Katz. Colour. ed George Appleby. pd Trevor Williams. sfx Bill Woods. m Oscar Peterson. song *C'mon Downtown* by Nancy Simmonds. 105 mins

Cast: Elliott Gould (Miles Cullen), Christopher Plummer (Harry Reikle), Susannah York (Julie), Celine Lomez (Elaine), Michael Kirby (Charles Packard), Sean Sullivan (Bank Guard), Ken Pogue (Det. Willard), John Candy (Simonsen), Gail Dahms (Louise), Charlotte Blunt (Mrs Packard)

A Toronto bank clerk who foils a hold-up and appropriates most of the loot is terrorized by the robber, who escapes from jail and demands a

share of the stolen money.

Neatly-plotted but crassly-directed, with Plummer going well over the top. His appearance in drag is unintentionally risible.

'Unacceptable levels of sadism and gratuitous violence mar this ingenious Canadian caper movie.'
Sight and Sound

SINGLE WHITE FEMALE
(US 1992)
pc Columbia. exec p Jack Baran. p, d Barbet Schroeder. co-p Roger Joseph Pugliese. assoc p Susan Hoffmann. w Don Roos, from the novel *SWF Seeks Same* by John Lutz. ph Luciano Tovoli. Colour. ed Lee Percy. pd Milena Canonero. ad P Michael Johnston. sfx Eddie Etan Surkin. sc Edward J Ulrich. m Howard Shore. 108 mins

Cast: Bridget Fonda (Allison Jones), Jennifer Jason Leigh (Hedra Carlson), Steven Weber (Sam Rawson), Peter Friedman (Graham Knox), Steven Tobolosky (Mitchell Myerson), Frances Bay (Elderly Neighbour), Michele Farr (Myerson's Assistant), Tara Karsian (Mannish Applicant), Christiana Capetillo (Exotic Applicant), Jessica Landy (Talkative Applicant), Rene Estevez (Perfect Applicant), Ken Tobey (Desk Clerk)
A successful young woman throws out her unfaithful boyfriend and takes in a shy room-mate who becomes her friend, but turns out to be a murderous psychotic out to take over her life and her identity.

Slickly-dressed, well-acted and rather unpleasant, with strong suspense and more than enough directorial style to paper over most of the inconsistencies of plot and characterization and the uneasy segué from pyschological thriller to slasher.

With its astonishing sets, acute observation and chilling conclusion, *Single White Female* is a modern thriller of note, even if its slickness sometimes works against it.'
Movies

SITTING TARGET

(GB 1972)

pc MGM. p Barry Kulik. assoc p Basil Keys. d Douglas Hickox. w Alexander Jacobs, from the novel by Laurence Henderson. ph Edward Scaife. 2nd unit ph Alan McCabe. Colour. ed John Glen. pd Jonathan Barry. sfx John Stears. chase sequence arr Romo Gorrara. m Stanley Myers. 93 mins

Cast: Oliver Reed (Harry Lomart), Jill St John (Pat Lomart), Ian McShane (Birdy Williams), Edward Woodward (Insp. Milton), Frank Finlay (Marty Gold), Freddie Jones (MacNeil), Jill Townsend (Maureen), Robert Beatty (Gun Dealer), Tony Beckley (Soapy Trucker), Mike Pratt (Prison Warder Accomplice)

A violent criminal breaks out of jail, seeking vengeance against his unfaithful wife.

Lumpy, pastiche-Hollywood thick-ear thriller, tranposed to Britain with, in the best B-feature tradition, an imported American star. Slickly done, but pointless.

'Another glib and glossy thriller along the lines of *Get Carter* and *Villain*, considerably shallower and more stereotyped than either ... it has absolutely nothing to offer except its gleeful, plentiful and largely unmotivated violence.'
Monthly Film Bulletin

SKYJACKED

(US 1972)

pc MGM/Walter Seltzer Productions. p Walter Seltzer. assoc p James Pratt. d John Guillermin. 2nd unit d James W Gavin. w Stanley R Greenberg, from the novel *Hijacked* by David Harper. ph Harry Stradling Jr. 2nd unit ph Don Morgan. Colour. Panavision. ed Robert Swink. ad Edward R Carfagno. sfx Ralph Schwartz. tech adv Ed Connelly. m Perry Botkin Jr. 101 mins

Cast: Charlton Heston (Capt. Hank O'Hara), Yvette Mimieux (Angela Thatcher), James Brolin (Sgt Jerome W Weber/Weller), Claude Akins (Sgt Puzo), Jeanne Crain (Clara Shaw), Roosevelt 'Rosey' Grier (Gary Brown), Walter Pidgeon (Senator Lindner), Leslie Uggams (Lovejoy Wells), Mariette Hartley (Harries Stevens), Mike Henry (Co-pilot), Ken Swofford (Navigator) Susan Dey (Elly Brewster), Nicholas Hammond (Peter Lindner), Maureen Connell (Mrs O'Hara)

A deranged hijacker forces an internal American flight to divert to Alaska and then fly on to Moscow.

Guillermin deserves praise for wringing as much suspense as he does from a familiar planeload of clichéd characters, ranging from the woman who gives birth on board to the air stewardess in love with the captain. It loses momentum during the second half and, with Heston at the controls, no one could *really* believe the bad guy would win.

'Over the years there have been several rather good thrillers about aeroplanes. This one is no exception, the tension is acute throughout.'
CinemaTV Today

SLAUGHTER ON TENTH AVENUE

(US 1957)

pc Universal. p Albert Zugsmith. d Arnold Laven. w Lawrence Roman, from the book *The Man Who Rocked the Boat* by William J Keating, Richard Carter. ph Fred Jackman. B&W. ed Russell F Schoengarth. ad Alexander Golitzen, Robert E Smith. md Joseph Gershenson. m Richard Rodgers. 103 mins

Cast: Richard Egan (William Keating), Jan Sterling (Madge Pitts), Dan Duryea (John Jacob Masters), Julie Adams (Dee), Walter Matthau (Al Dahlke), Charles McGraw (Lt Vosnick), Sam Levene (Howard Drysdale), Mickey Shaughnessy (Solly Pitts), Harry Bellaver (Benjy Karp), Nick Dennis (Midget), Ned Weaver (Eddie 'Cockey' Cook), Mickey Hargitay (Big John)

A Deputy District Attorney investigates corruption and homicide on the New York waterfront.

Something of a comic-strip-style riff on *On the Waterfront*, happily less self-satisfied, with competent performances and a good score.

'The sort of stevedore special Hollywood has been serving up ever since On the Waterfront, when the moviemakers discovered that the public likes a pier with a yegg on it.'
Time

SLAUGHTER ON TENTH AVENUE

SLEUTH

(GB 1972)

pc Palomar Pictures. exec p Edgar J Scherick. p Morton Gottlieb. assoc p David Middlemass. d Joseph L Mankiewicz. w Anthony Shaffer, from his play. ph Oswald Morris. Colour. ed Richard Marden. pd Ken Adams. ad Peter Lamont. m John Addison. 139 mins

Cast: Laurence Olivier (Andrew Wyke), Michael Caine (Milo Tindle/Insp. Doppler), Margo Channing (Marguerite), John Matthews (Det. Sgt Tarrant), Teddy Martin (Constable Higgs)

A cuckolded thriller writer seeks revenge by involving his wife's lower-class hairdresser lover in bizarre game-playing with a sinister hidden agenda.

Nothing is what it seems, including the cast, but what worked well in the artificial environment of the stage simply comes over as camp and unconvincing on film. Olivier overdoes it while Caine tries, and fails, to keep up – so, naturally, they were both nominated for Oscars. The Academy Award nominations for Mankiewicz and composer John Addison were rather more deserved.

'It's an honourable and often intriguing attempt to prove that a good play can be as good a film without too much reshaping. But at this length you see the sleight of hand that the theatre masked, even in the performances.'
The Guardian

SLITHER

(US 1973)

pc MGM. A Jack Sher and Talent Associates Production. p Jack Sher. assoc p, w W D Richter. d Howard Zieff. ph Laszlo Kovacs. Colour. ed David Bretherton. ad Dale Henessey. sfx John Coles. m Tom McIntosh. 96 mins

Cast: James Caan (Dick Kanipsia), Peter Boyle (Barry Fenaka), Sally Kellerman (Kitty Kopetzky), Louise Lasser (Mary Fenaka), Allen Garfield (Hallenbeck/Palmer), Richard B Shull (Harry Moss), Alex Rocco (First Brother), Alex Hentelhoff (Second Brother), Gerry Goodrow (Third Brother)

Crooks engage in a wild hunt for the loot from a robbery.

Engaging and easy-to-watch, with off-beat characters. A promising directorial debut for Zieff, who smoothly meshes humour and straight-faced mayhem.

'A very well cast comedy-enhanced thriller which can only be described as very entertaining.'
Films and Filming

SOME GIRLS DO
(GB 1969)
pc Ashdown Film Productions. p Betty E Box. assoc p James Ware. d Ralph Thomas. w David Osborn, Liz Charles-Williams, based on the character created by Sapper. ph Ernest Steward. Colour. ed Ernest Hosler. ad Edward Marshall. sfx Kit West. m Charles Blackwell. title song lyric Don Black, sung by Lee Vanderbilt. 93 mins

Cast: Richard Johnson (Hugh Drummond), Daliah Lavi (Baroness Helga Hagen), Bebe Loncar (Pandora), James Villiers (Carl Petersen), Sydne Rome (Flicky), Ronnie Stevens

(Peregrine Carruthers), Robert Morley (Miss Mary), Maurice Denham (Mr Mortimer), Vanessa Howard (Robot No.7), Florence Desmond (Lady Manderly)

Bulldog Drummond investigates the sabotage of a new supersonic airliner.

Dismally unfunny spy spoof, inadequate in all departments.

'Bulldog Drummond would turn in his grave if he could see what has happened to him.'
Monthly Film Bulletin

SOMEBODY KILLED HER HUSBAND
(US 1978)
pc Simon Productions. For Columbia. p Martin Poll. assoc p William Craver. d Lamont Johnson. w Reginald Rose. ph Andrew Laszlo, Ralf D Bode. Colour. ed Barry Malkin. pd Ted Haworth. ad David Chapman. m Alex North. song *Love Keeps Getting Stronger Every Day* by Neil Sedaka, Howard Greenfield. 97 mins

Cast: Farrah Fawcett-Majors (Jenny Moore), Jeff Bridges (Jerry Green), John Wood (Ernest Van Santen), Tammy Grimes (Audrey Van Santen), John Glover (Hulbert Little), Patricia Elliott (Helene), Mary McCarty (Flora), Laurence Guittard (Preston Moore), Beeson Carroll (Frank Danziger)

A woman and her lover turn sleuth to find her husband's killer.

A thin comedy-thriller, low on laughs and thrills, with Fawcett-Majors leaving a vacuum where her performance should be.

'It is indeed a pretty dim affair.'
The Guardian

SORCERER
(US 1977) (GB: WAGES OF FEAR)
pc Film Properties International. p, d William Friedkin. assoc p Bud Smith. w Walon Green, from the novel *Le Salaire de la Peur* by Georges Arnaud. ph John M Stephens, Dick Bush. Colour. ed Bud Smith, Robert K Lambert. pd John Box. ad Roy Walker. optical fx Marv Ystron. sound fx Charles L Campbell. m fx Ron Nagle, Scott Mathews. m Tangerine Dream, *Spheres (Movement 3)* by Keith Jarrett. 121 mins

Cast: Roy Scheider (Jackie Scanlon, 'Juan Dominguez'), Bruno Cremer (Victor Mazon, 'Serrano'), Francisco Rabal (Nilo), Amidou (Kassem, 'Martinez'), Ramon Bieri (Corlette), Peter Capell (Lartigue), Karl John (Angerman, 'Marquez'), Frederick Ledebur (Carlos), Joe Spinell (Spider), Chico Martinez (Bobby Del Rios), Rosario Almontes (Agrippa)

Four men wanted by the law risk their lives by driving trucks carrying nitroglycerine over dangerous terrain to put out an oil well fire.

Overblown, hugely expensive, largely pointless, handsome-looking remake of the classic 1953 suspenser *Le Salaire de la Peur/ The Wages of Fear* (q.v.) with a few impressive scenes. The title probably compounded its commercial failure, since the natural assumption was that Friedkin had made another horror movie in the wake of *The Exorcist*

SORRY, WRONG NUMBER

'A visual and aural textbook on every-thing that is wrong with current movies; no narrative flow, no psycho-logical development of character, no interaction of performers, no true unity of locale ... no build ups, no structure ... not a single scene with dramatic tension.'
Village Voice

SORRY, WRONG NUMBER
(US 1948)

pc Paramount/Hall B Wallis Productions. p Hal B Wallis, Anatole Litvak. d Anatole Litvak. w Lucille Fletcher, from her radio play. p Sol Polito. B&W. ed Warren Low. ad Hans Dreier, Earl Hedrick. sfx Farciot Edouart, Gordon Jennings. m Gene Merritt, Walter Oberst. 89 mins

Cast: Barbara Stanwyck (Leona Stevenson), Burt Lancaster (Henry Stevenson), Ann Richards (Sally Lord Dodge), Wendell Corey (Dr Alexander), Harold Vermilyea (Waldo Evans), Ed Begley (James Cotterill), Leif Erickson (Fred Lord), William Conrad (Morano), John Broomfield (Joe), Jimmy Hunt (Peter Lord), Dorothy Neumann (Miss Jennings)

A bedridden heiress tries desperately to save herself after overhearing a telephone conversation between men planning to kill her.

Very well acted and tense, although there are narrative problems arising from the extension of the story from the radio play's original 22 minutes' running time. It grips throughout, and it is only after it is over that its inherent artificiality become evident.

'Tension taut as a bow string makes

Sorry, Wrong Number about as exciting a thriller as your nerves will stand.'
The Star

SPEED
(US 1994)

pc 20th Century Fox. exec p Ian Bryce. p Mark Gordon. co-p Allison Lyon. d Jan De Bont. 2nd unit d Alexander Witt. w Graham Yost. ph Andrzej Bartkowiak. add ph David Drziecki, Garry Waller. visual fx sup Boyd Shermis. Colour. ed John Wright. pd Jackson De Govia. ad John R Jensen. sfx co-ord John Frazier. sc Gary M Hymes. m Mark Mancina. add m John Van Tongeren. 116 mins

Cast: Keanu Reeves (Jack Traven), Dennis Hopper (Howard Payne), Sandra Bullock (Annie), Joe Morton (Capt. McMahon), Jeff Daniels (Harry), Alan Ruck (Stephens), Glenn Plummer (Jaguar Owner), Richard Lineback (Norwood), Beth Grant (Helen), Hawthorne James (Sam), Carlos Carrasco (Ortiz), David Kriegel (Terry), Natsuko Ohama (Mrs Kamino), Daniel Villarreal (Ray), Jacquie Gleave (Panicking Passenger), Margaret Medina (Robin), Jordan Lund (Bagwell)

When a madman plants a bomb on a Los Angeles bus, primed to go off if its speed varies from 50 miles per hour, and demands $37 million ransom, a policeman saves the passengers and the day.

Utterly implausible, suspenseful and immensely exciting, and directed at a breakneck pace by former cinematographer De Bont, who makes sure it lives up to its title and sees to it

that viewers never need to move their brains out of neutral to enjoy it. Bullock bravely drives the bus and looks cute, Reeves strips to his singlet, looks cute and is Action Man made flesh, and Hopper hams it up fit to bust. It may not be 'Art' but it *is* a perfect popcorn movie.

'It's wall-to-wall with action, stunts, special effects and excitement. We've seen this done before, but seldom so well, or at such a high pitch of energy.'
Chicago Sun-Times

'This is pure entertainment of the first order.'
Film Review

SPELLBOUND
(US 1945)

pc Selznick International. p David O Selznick. d Alfred Hitchcock. w Ben Hecht. adap Angus McPhail, from the novel *The House of Dr Edwardes* by Francis Beeding. ph George Barnes. B&W. ed William Ziegler. ad James Basevi, John Ewing. sfx Jack Cosgrove. m Miklos Rosza. dream sequence Salvador Dali. psychiatric cons May E Romm. 111 mins

Cast: Ingrid Bergman (Dr Constance Peterson), Gregory Peck (John Ballantine), Jean Acker (The Directress), Rhonda Fleming (Mary Carmichael), Donald Curtis (Harry), John Emery (Dr Fleurot), Leo G Carroll (Dr Murchison), Norman Lloyd (Garmes), Michael Chekhov (Professor), Steven Geray (Dr Graff), Paul Harvey (Dr Hanish)

An amnesiac doctor subconsciously

SPEED

believes he is a murderer until a woman psychiatrist helps to 'cure' him and expose the real killer.

Hitchcock deploys just about every stylistic and narrative trick at his considerable command (including a fascinating but largely irrelevant dream sequence designed by Salvador Dali and shot by William Cameron Menzies, who asked that his contribution should be anonymous) but fails to create much in the way of genuine suspense or credibility. The result is a thin piece of pretentious paperback psychiatry decked out with excellent cinematography and an Oscar-winning score, and suffering from, among other demerits, a dull leading man and a matching script, and in Ingrid Bergman, one of the least credible cinema psychoanalysts since Boris Karloff in *The Secret Life of Walter Mitty*.

'It's just another manhunt picture wrapped up in pseudo-psychoanalyis,' said Hitchcock in 1966, 'The whole thing's too complicated, and I found the explanations towards the end very confusing.'

'The picture has its periods of suspense of which Hitchcock is the master ... but for all that it's not vintage Hitchcock. One feels that it is Hitchcock versus producer David Selznick and script writer Ben Hecht with Hitchcock often losing out to his opponents.'
Reynolds News

'There is in *Spellbound* not one trace of kindliness, gentless, tenderness or passion. The players are icy puppets acting out Mr Hitchcock's pleasures as if they were in a dream ... go to see *Spellbound* but wear your winter woolies.'
Daily Express

THE SPLIT
(US 1968)
pc MGM. A Spectrum Production. p Robert Chartoff, Irwin Winkler. d Gordon Flemyng. w Robert Sabaroff, from the novel *The Seventh* by Richard Stark. ph Burnett Guffey. Colour. Panavision. ed Rita Roland. ad Urie McCleary, George W Davis. m Quincy Jones. songs *The Split, It's Just A Game, Love* by Quincy Jones, Ernie Shelby, *A Good Woman's Love* by Quincy Jones, Sheb Wooley. 90 mins

Cast: Jim Brown (McClain), Diahann Carroll (Ellie McClain), Ernest Borgnine (Bert Clinger), Gene Hackman (Lt Walter Brill), Julie Harris (Gladys), Jack Klugman (Harry Kifka), Warren Oates (Marty Gough), James Whitmore (Herb Sutro), Donald Sutherland (Dave Negli), Joyce James (Jennifer)

After a man and his female accomplice successfully steal $500,000 from the Los Angeles Coliseum during a big football game, things go disastrously wrong.

Slick but forgettable crime caper with better acting than it deserves.

'A tense crime story, this has a plot with an original twist and a tough set of villains. Palatable red meat fare for all.'
Kine Weekly

SPOORLOOS
(NETHERLANDS/FRANCE 1988)
(GB, US: THE VANISHING)
pc Golden Egg Film/Ingrid Productions. For MGS Film. p Anne Lordon, George Sluizer. d, George Sluizer. w Tom Krabbé, from his novel *The Golden Egg*. adap George Sluizer. ph Toni Kuhn. Colour. ed George Sluizer, Lin Friedman. ad Santiago Isodro Pin, Cor Spijk. m Henry Vrientien. 106 mins

Cast: Bernard-Pierre Donnadieu (Raymond Lemorne), Gene Bervoets (Rex Hoffman), Johanna Ter Steege (Saskia Wagter), Gwen Eckhaus (Lieneke), Bernadette Le Saché (Simone Lemorne), Tania Latarjet (Denise), Lucille Glenn (Gabrielle), Roger Souza (Manager), Pierre Forget (Farmer Laurent), Didier Rousset (TV Journalist), Carole Appéré (Cashier)

Three years after his girlfriend mysteriously vanishes from a filling station in France, a man is approached by a stranger who claims to have kidnapped her.

A supremely terrifying suspenser with a truly nightmarish ending. Sluizer plays on audience fears with a skill and sadism Hitchcock would have envied, and never puts a frame wrong. His dire 1993 Hollywood remake rarely put a frame right.
'A constantly bewildering and surprising thriller, chillingly unsensationalist and expertly constructed, far more effective in its everyday creepiness than such comparable Hollywood products as *Frantic*.'
Monthly Film Bulletin.

THE SPY IN BLACK
(GB 1939) (US: U-BOAT 29)
pc Harefield. Presented by Alexander Korda. d Michael Powell. w Emeric

Pressburger. adap Roland Pertwee, from the novel by J Storer Cloustin. ph Bernard Brown. B&W. pd Vincent Korda. ad Frederick Pusey. sup ed William Hornbeck. ed Hugh Stewart. m Miklos Rosza. 82 mins

Cast: Conrad Veidt (Capt. Hardt), Valerie Hobson (The Schooolmistress), Sebastian Shaw (Lt Ashington), Marius Goring (Lt Schuster), June Duprez (Anne Burnett), Athole Stewart (Rev. Matthews), Angnes Langhlin (Mrs Matthews), Helen Haye (Mrs Sedley), Cyril Raymond (Rev. Harris), Hay Petrie (Engineer), Grant Sutherland (Bob Bratt), Torin Thatcher (Submarine Officer)

In 1917 a German submarine captain is sent to the Orkneys to contact a German agent who is posing as a schoolmistress, but the British Secret Service replace her with the wife of a British Navy officer.

Taut direction make the most of the intriguing situations and strong leads.

'It has its gripping moments. There are episodes of keen suspense … the climax is excitingly staged and thrilling.'
CEA Film Report

THE SPY WHO CAME IN FROM THE COLD
(GB 1965)

pc Salem. p, d Martin Ritt. w Paul Dehn, Guy Trosper, from the novel by John le Carré. ph Oswald Morris. B&W. ed Anthony Harvey. pd Tambi Larsen. ad Edward Marshall. m Sol Kaplan. 112 mins

Cast: Richard Burton (Alec Leamas), Claire Bloom (Nan Perry), Oskar Werner (Fiedler), Peter Van Eyck (Hans-Dieter Mundt), Sam Wanamaker (Peters), George Voskovec (East German Defence Attorney), Rupert Davies (Smiley), Cyril Cusack (Control), Michael Hordern (Ashe), Robert Hardy (Carlton), Bernard Lee (Patmore), Walter Gotell (Holten), Beatric Lehmann (President of the Tribunal)

SPOORLOOS

A dismissed British agent becomes an alcoholic and is recruited by the Communists in what turns out to be a complex scheme to discredit an East German spy.

Well-made, relentlessly gloomy spy thriller designed to show the downside of the espionage business, as opposed to the glamour, girls and gimmicks of the world of James Bond.

Excellent acting all round. Burton, giving probably his best, least mannered performance, was nominated for the Best Actor Academy Award (losing it to Lee Marvin for *Cat Ballou*), and Cyril Cusack gives an exemplary demonstration of clever underplaying.

'Right from the start *The Spy Who Came in From The Cold* hits a wonder-fully rhythmic stride that let's you know you're in for a narrative that is going to excite an audience but isn't going to get excited itself.'
The Sunday Telegraph

'I suppose you might find the whole affair reasonably gripping – although I can't guarantee that you won't come out feeling that somehow it has just missed being something more than that.'
The Guardian

THE SPY WHO LOVED ME

(GB 1977)
pc Eon Productions. p Albert R Broccoli. assoc p William P Cartlidge. d Lewis Gilbert. 2nd unit d Ernest Day, John Glen. w Christopher Wood, Richard Maibaum, from the novel by Ian Fleming. ph Claude Renoir. underwater ph Lamar Boren. ski sequence ph, sup Willy Bogner. sfx ph

Alan Maley. Colour. Panavision. ed John Glen. pd Ken Adam. ad Peter Lamont. sfx Derek Meddings, John Evans. action arr Bob Simmons. ski jump performed by Rick Sylvester. m Marvin Hamlisch. song *Nobody Does It Better* by Marvin Hamlisch, Carole Bayer Sager, sung by Carly Simon. titles Maurice Binder. 125 mins

Cast: Roger Moore (James Bond), Barbara Bach (Major Anya Amasoca), Curt Jurgens (Stromberg), Richard Kiel (Jaws), Caroline Munro (Naomi), Walter Gotell (Gen. Gogol), Geoffrey Keen (Minister of Defence), Bernard Lee ('M'), Lois Maxwell (Miss Moneypenny), George Baker (Capt. Benson), Michael Billington (Sergei), Olga Bisera (Felicca), Desmond Llewellyn ('Q'), Edward De Souza (Sheikh Hosein), Vernond Dobtcheff (Max Kalba), Valerie Leon (Hotel Receptionist), Sydney Tafler (Liparus Captain), Nadim Sawala (Fekkesh)

James Bond defeats a megalomaniac who 'kidnaps' British and Russian submarines as part of his scheme to create a new undersea civilization.

Where would the world be without Bond to save it? The tenth film in the series abandons any connections (apart from the title and the name of the hero) with Ian Fleming and becomes an all-action comic-strip with little pretence of reality.

Moore (and his stuntman) fill the invincible superhero role perfectly, there is a splendid pre-credits ski jump, and while Curt Jurgens is the ostensible villain of the piece, he is rather lacklustre. There is compensation, however, in Richard

Kiel's 'Jaws', a man-mountain with lethal metal teeth and the indestructibility of a cartoon character.

While the action is as exciting as ever, the longueurs are more frequent.

'The plot barely matters. There are some fairly scrumptious intermittent maidens,, a splendid running gag with a 7' 2" heavy named Jaws, the usual battery of technical gee whizzery ... but in the end I grew weary of the pyrotechnics; a case of licensed to overkill?'
The Guardian

'It is the best Bond film so far. The sexiest, the fastest-moving and cer-tainly the most witty.'
The Sun

'The film – bearing no relation to its nominal source – seems to do nothing more than anthologise its forerunners, and comes out looking, for all the expensive hardware and location shooting, like a Saturday serial risen grandiloquently above its station.'
Monthly Film Bulletin

THE SQUEAKER

(GB 1937) (US: MURDER ON DIAMOND ROW)
pc Denham Productions. p Alexander Korda. d William K Howard. w Edward O Berkman, Bryan Wallace, from the novel by Edgar Wallace. ph Georges Périnal. B&W. sup ed Jack Dennis. ed Russell Lloyd. ad Vincent Korda. m Miklos Rosza. songs William Kernell, Edward O Berkman. 77 mins

Cast: Edmund Lowe (Insp. Barrabal), Sebastian Shaw (Frank Sutton), Ann

Todd (Carol Stedman), Tamara Desni (Tamara), Robert Newton (Larry Graeme), Allan Jeayes (Insp. Elford), Alastair Sim (Joshua Collie), Stewart Rome (Supt. Marshall), Mabel Terry-Lewis (Mrs Steedman), Gordon McLeod (Mr Field)

A Scotland Yard inspector goes undercover to unmask a notorious jewel fence, The Squeaker, who betrays criminals who cross him to the police.

Wallace's sturdy melodrama is sturdily transposed to the screen, and while the identity of the villain hardly comes as a surprise, tension and atmosphere are well maintained by Howard. (Wallace directed the 1930 film.)

'The play is well constructed, the dialogue is good and the acting all round is first rate. Romantic interest and comedy relief round off the entertainment.'
CEA Film Report

THE SQUEEZE
(GB 1977)
pc Martinat Productions. For WB. p Stanley O'Toole. d Michael Apted. w Leon Griffiths, from the novel by David Craig. ph Dennis Lewiston. Colour. ed John Shirley. ad William McCrow. stunt arr David Brandon. m David Hentchel. 107 mins

Cast: Stacy Keach (Jim Naboth), David Hemmings (Keith), Edward Fox (Foreman), Stephen Boyd (Vic),

THE SQUEAKER

THE ST VALENTINE DAY'S MASSACRE

Carol White (Jill), Freddie Starr (Teddy), Hilary Gleason (Barbara), Rod Beacham (Dr Jenkins), Stewart Harwood (Des), Alan Ford (Taff), Roy Marsden (Barry), Leon Greene (Commissionaire)

An alcoholic former policeman rescues his wife and daughter from kidnappers.

Crisp editing and fast direction help compensate for poorly-characterized protagonists. Unfamiliar London locations help, too.

'A British gangland movie determined to be quite as tough, bloody, violent, squalid and ugly as any Hollywood model. It succeeds.'
Evening Standard

ST IVES
(US 1975)
pc WB. A Kohner-Beckerman-Canter production. p Pancho Kohner, Stanley Kanter. d J Lee Thompson. w Barry Beckerman, from the novel *The Procane Chronicle* by Oliver Bleeck. ph Lucien Ballard. Colour. ed Michael F Anderson. pd Philip M

Jefferies. sfx Gene Griggs. m Lalo Schifrin. 94 mins

Cast: Charles Bronson (Raymond St Ives), John Houseman (Abner Procane), Jacqueline Bisset (Janet Whistler), Maximilian Schell (Dr John Constable), Elisha Cook Jr (Eddie the Bellboy), Burr De Benning (Officer Frann), Harry Guardino (Det. Beal), Harris Yulin (Det. Oliver), Dick O'Neill (Hesh), Daniel J Travanti (Johnny Parisi), Michael Lerner (Michael Green), Jeff Goldblum (Hood)

STAGE FRIGHT

A former crime reporter turned novelist is enmeshed in mystery and murder when he agrees to deliver a ransom for a wealthy recluse.

Slickly over-directed by Thompson, but muddled and not very interesting.

'*St Ives* merely confirms a point: eliminate gratuitous, offensive and overdone violence from a dull and plodding film story, and all you've got left is a dull and plodding film.'
Variety

THE ST VALENTINE DAY'S MASSACRE

(US 1967)

pc Los Altos/20th Century Fox. p, d Roger Corman. assoc p Paul Rapp. w Howard Browne. ph Milton Krasner. sfx ph L B Abbott, Art Cruikshank, Emil Kosa Jr. Colour. Panavision. ed William B Murphy. ad Jack Martin Smith, Philip Jefferies. md Lionel Newman. m Fred Steiner. 100 mins

Cast: Jason Robards (Al Capone), George Segal (Peter Gusenberg), Ralph Meeker (Bugs Moran), Jean Hale (Myrtle), Clint Ritchie (Jack McGurn), Frank Silvera (Sorello), Michele Guayini (Patsy Lelordo), Joseph Campanella (Weinshank), Richard Bakalyan (Scalisi), David Canary (Frank Gusenberg), Bruce Dern (May), Harold J Stone (Frank Nitti), Kurt Kreuger (James Clark), John Agar (Dion O'Banion), Jack Nicholson (Gino), Leo Gordon (James Morton)

Bitter rivalry between gangs led by Al Capone and Bugs Moran culminates in the bloody assassination of seven of Moran's men in a Chicago garage on

St Valentine's Day, 1929.

Corman doesn't let a large (for him) budget get in the way of his usual vigorous brand of film-making. The subject is well served by to-the-point semi-documentary-style direction, impeccably-staged action, evocative period recreation and almost uniformly apt casting. Segal, in particular, is first-rate, but Robards is a less-than-credible Capone. Corman's only film shot on a large studio lot.

'It's a cool, violent film, romantic in a disciplined, disenchanted way about its battling gangsters.'
The Spectator

'A well made reconstruction of the boot-leg 1930's and can be recommended to those who enjoy a particularly gruesome thriller.'
The People

'Almost every scene in the film can be corroborated by evidence that it really happened or could be deduced to have happened from available records.'
Roger Corman

STAGE FRIGHT
(GB 1950)
pc ABPC. p, d Alfred Hitchcock. w Whitfield Cook, Alma Reville, James Bridie, Ranald MacDougall, from the stories *Man Running* & *Outrun the Constable* by Selwyn Jepson. ph Wilkie Cooper. B&W. ed Edward Jarvis. ad Terence Verity. m Leighton Lucas. 111 mins

Cast: Marlene Dietrich (Charlotte Inwood), Jane Wyman (Eve Gill), Michael Wilding (Smith), Richard Todd (Jonathan Penrose), Alastair Sim (The

Commodore), Kay Walsh (Nellie Good), Sybil Thorndike (Mrs Gill), Miles Malleson (Mr Fortescue), Andre Morell (Insp. Byard), Hector MacGregor (Freddie Williams), Joyce Grenfell ('Lovely Ducks')

A murder suspect goes on the run while his girlfriend takes a job as a maid with the famous actress he claims committed the crime to try and clear him.

Slow to start, and not all of the casting works – Dietrich and Wilding do little more than fill their roles and much of the pleasure comes from Wyman's bright performance and the reliable comedy playing of stalwarts Sim, Walsh and Malleson in minor roles. Still, even non-vintage Hitchcock is better than a dry throat.

'*Stage Fright* has its quota of thrills, complicated twists, and unexpected turns. It also abounds in humour, the last due to a very witty script of which the talented cast takes every advantage.'
Picture Show

STATE SECRET
(GB 1950) (US: THE GREAT MANHUNT)
pc London Films. p Frank Lander, Sidney Gilliat. d, w Sidney Gilliat, from the novel *Appointment with Fear* by Roy Huggins. ph Robert Krasker, John Wilcox. B&W. ed Thelma Myers. ad Wilfrid Shingleton. m William Alwyn. Vosnian language created by Georgina Shield. 104 mins

Cast: Douglas Fairbanks Jr (Dr John Marlowe), Glynis Johns (Lisa), Jack Hawkins (Col. Galcon), Herbert Lom

(Karl Theodor), Walter Rilla (Gen. Niva), Karel Stepanek (Dr Revo), Carl Jaffe (Janovik Prada), Gerard Heinz (Bendel), Hans Moser (Sigrist), Gerik Schelderup (Bartorek), Guido Lorraine (Lt Pracht), Anton Diffring (Policeman) Peter Illing (Chaco), Olga Lowe (Baba)

An American surgeon is brought from London to operate on the head of a totalitarian European state. When his patient dies, he makes a run for it with the secret police on his trail, determined to silence him.

Crisp, witty and bright chase thriller tangily spiced with sly comedy, with its own highly-convincing Vosnian language and boasting top-flight performances from Hawkins as a police chief with a ghoulish sense of humour and Lom with yet another of his fully-realized shifty-foreigner characterizations.

'Extremely well dialogued, brilliantly satirical, with excellently contrived and varied background, the film reflects credit on the producers, Launder and Gilliat.'
Picturegoer

'An intelligent picture built around an interesting and original situation.'
CEA Film Report

STILETTO
(US 1969)
pc Harold Robbins Company. exec p Joseph E Levine. p Norman Rosemont. d Bernard Kowalski. w A J Russell, from the novel by Harold Robbins. ph Jack Priestley. Colour. ed Frank Mazzola. ad Jan Scott. m Sid Ramin. 99 mins

Cast: Alex Cord (Count Cesare

Cardinali), Britt Ekland (Illeana),
Barbara McNair (Ahn Dessje), Patrick
O'Neal (Baker), Joseph Wiseman
(Emilio Matteo), John Dehner (DA
Simpson), Titos Vandis (Tonio),
Edouardo Ciannelli (Don Andrea),
Roy Scheider (Bennett), Lincoln
Kilpatrick (Hannibal Smith), Luis
Martinez (Vanicola)

A wealthy playboy racing driver who
doubles as a Mafia executioner is
marked for death himself when he
decides to quit.

Tedious in every department, and
guaranteed to do more damage to the
image of the Mafia than a dozen
congressional anti-organized crime
Committees. But at least it perfectly
matches the tone and quality of the
source material.

'Incomprehensible Mafia rubbish …
even those in search of kicks are likely
to be battered insensible by the dullness of it all.'
Evening Standard

STILL OF THE NIGHT
(US 1982)
pc MGM/UA. p Arlene Donovan,
assoc p Wolfgang Glattes, Kenneth
Utt. d, w Robert Benton. st David
Newman, Robert Benton. ph Nestor
Almendros. add ph Joe Coffee. optical
fx J Kleiser. Colour. ed Jerry
Greenberg, Bill Pankow. pd Mel
Bourne. ad Michael Molly. m John
Kander. electronic m Jonathan Elias.
titles Henry Wolf. 91 mins

Cast: Roy Scheider (Sam Rice), Meryl
Streep (Brooke Reynolds), Jessica
Tandy (Grace Rice), Joe Grifasi
Joseph Vitucci), Sara Botsford (Gail

Phillips), Josef Sommer (George
Bynum), Rikki Borge (Heather
Wilson), Irving Metzman (Murray
Gordon), Larry Joshua (Mugger),
Raymond Hoxie (Mr Harris), Tom
Norton (Auctioneer), Hyon Cho
(Mr Chong)

A psychiatrist who falls for the mistress
of a murdered man who was his
patient starts to suspect that she may
be the killer.

Remember *Marnie? Vertigo? Rear
Window? I Confess? Rebecca?* Benton
clearly does, but his homage to
Hitchcock is poorly-written,
derivately-directed and fatally lacking
suspense or interest. More fromage
than homage.

'The film cheats me rather cheaply.
Deluding me into excitement without

troubling to create an illusion – or
even a convincing plot … meant as
pure enteratinment, acceptable purely
as television, the film really just
manipulates. It needs to see its
psychiatrist.'
The Observer

THE STONE KILLER
(US 1973)
pc De Laurentiis Productions. p, d
Michael Winner. w Gerald Wilson,
from the novel *A Complete State of
Death* by John Gardner. ph Richard
Moore. Colour. sup ed Frederick
Wilson. ad Ward Preston. m Roy
Budd. 96 mins

Cast: Charles Bronson (Det. Lou
Torrey), Martin Balsam (Vescari),
Ralph Waite (Mathews), David
Sheiner (Guido Lorenz), Norman Fell

THE STONE KILLER

(Les Daniels), Eddie Firestone (George Armitage), Walter Burke (JD), David Moody (Gus Lipper), Charles Tyner (Psychiatrist), Paul Koslo (Al Langley), Stuart Margolin (Lawrence), John Ritter (Hart), Byron Morrow (LA Police Chief), Jack Colvin (Lionel Jumper), Frank Campanella (Calabriese)

A police officer uncovers a plot by a Mafia godfather to use a private army of Vietnam veterans to avenge a 42-year-old gangland massacre.

Slick, bloody, violent and mindless, with Winner's facile, faceless direction pointing to his true metier – as a director of television commercials. Bronson is stone-faced, as always, but who could blame him in the face of such intractable material?

'Stupid, sordid stuff ... a potboiler that oozes the weary devices and clichés of the genre.'
TV Guide

STRAIGHT ON TILL MORNING

(GB 1972)
pc Hammer. exec p Michael Carreras.
p Roy Skeggs. d Peter Collinson. w Michael Peacock. ph Brian Probyn. Colour. ed Alan Patillo. ad Scott McGregor. m Roland Shaw. title song Annie Ross, John Peacock. 96 mins

Cast: Rita Tushingham (Brenda Thompson), Shane Briant (Peter), Tom Bell (Jimmy Lindsay), Annie Ross (Liza), Katya Wyeth (Carolina), James Bolam (Joey), Claire Kelly (Margo Thompson), Harold Berens (Mr Harris), John Clive (Newsagent), Tommy Godfrey, Lola Willard (Customers)

STRANGERS ON A TRAIN

A plain girl comes from Liverpool to London, where she becomes romantically involved with a psychotic serial killer.

Degrading, tediously derivative and predictable from the first to the last frame, with lame performances and dreadful direction.

'An interesting development thematically from the usual run of commercially exploited themes on lone women trembling in outward terror by the implicit desire to be raped.'
Films and Filming

STRANGERS ON A TRAIN
(US 1951)

pc WB. p, d Alfred Hitchcock. w Raymond Chandler, Czenzi Ormonde. adap Whitfield Cook, from the novel by Patricia Hitchcock. ph Robert Burks. B&W. ed William H Ziegler. ad Ted Haworth. sfx H F Koenekamp. md Ray Heindorf. m Dimitri Tiomkin. 101 mins

Cast: Farley Granger (Guy Haines), Ruth Roman (Anne Morton), Robert Walker (Bruno Antony), Leo G Carroll (Senator Morton), Patricia Hitchcock (Barbara Morton), Laura Elliott (Miriam), Marion Lorne (Mrs Anthony), Jonathan Hale (Mr Anthony), Howard St John (Capt. Turley), John Brown (Prof. Collins), Norma Varden (Mrs Cunningham), Robert Gist (Hennessey), John Doucette (Hammond)

A psychopath proposes to 'swap' murders with a tennis star he meets on a train and kill the star's recalcitrant wife in exchange for the slaying of his repressive father. When his wife is killed, the star realizes that he is expected to keep his side of the 'bargain'.

Remarkable, supremely suspenseful exercise in guilt and tension, with Hitchcock at his best and (not always the case) obviously held by his material. He creates classic sequences – notably a fairground murder seen reflected in the lenses of a pair of dropped spectacles, and the death of the psychopath on an out-of-control carousel. Walker's portrayal of the carefree, crazy killer is probably his best, and even succeeds in arousing a measure of sympathy for the character.

'To be stretched by Mr Hitchcock on the rack of his own particular brand of suspense is torture at its most exquisite.'
Sunday Chronicle

'An admirable thriller, restrained, amusing, clever with just the right quota of Hitchcock.'
The Spectator

'I still think *Strangers on a Train* is the best thing Hitchcock has done for a good many years.'
The Sunday Times

SUDDEN FEAR
(US 1952)

pc RKO/Joseph Kaufman Productions. p Joseph Kaufman. d David Miller. 2nd unit d Ralph Hoge. w Lenore Coffee, Robert Smith, from the novel by Edna Sherry. ph Charles Lang Jr. B&W. ed Leon Barsha. ad Boris Leven. m Elmer Bernstein. 110 mins

Cast: Joan Crawford (Myra Hudson), Jack Palance (Lester Blaine), Gloria Grahame (Irene Neves), Bruce Bennett (Steve Kearney), Virginia Huston (Ann), Touch (later Mike) Connors (Junior Kearney)

A wealthy woman playwright marries an actor who plans to kill her.

High-temperature suspenser that is far too long for its over-complex story. Fortunately, Palance's confident performance helps dilute Crawford's usual larger-than-life histrionics.

'It is essentially a routine chiller, replete with more or less clever gimmicks.'
Variety

SUDDENLY
(US 1954)

pc Libra. p Robert Bassler. d Lewis Allen. w Richard Sale. ph Charles G Clarke. B&W. ed John F Schreyer. ad Frank Sylos. m David Raksin. 77 mins

Cast: Frank Sinatra (John Baron), Sterling Hayden (Tod Shaw), James Gleason (Pop Benson), Nancy Gates (Ellen Benson), Willis Bouchey (Dan Carney), Kim Charney (Midge Benson), James Lilburn (Jud Hobson), Paul Frees (Benny Conklin), Christopher Dark (Bart Wheeler), Paul Wexler (Slim Adams)

A hired killer posing as an FBI security agent takes a small-town family hostage and prepares to assassinate the US President as he alights from his special train.

Sinatra's first 'assassination' thriller (see *The Manchurian Candidate*) is well produced, doesn't outstay its relatively short running time and generates effective tension given the fact that the ultimate outcome is never in doubt.

SUDDENLY

s in some respects novel and unusual
or, although revolving on the familiar
theme of a gangster who terrorizes a
household, it has some clever twists
and maintains both interest and
excitement throughout.'

CEA Film Report

SUNBURN

(GB/US 1979)

pc Hemdale/Bind Films. A Tuesday
Films Production. exec p John
Quested, Derek Dawson, Jay
Bernstein. assoc p David Korda. d
Richard C Sarafian. 2nd unit d Paul
Baxley. w John Daly, Stephen Oliver,
James Booth, from the novel *The Bind*
by Stanley Ellin. ph Alex Phillips Jr.
underwater ph Ramon Bravo. Colour.
d Geoff Foot. pd Ted Tester. ad
Augustin Ituarte. sfx Laurencio
Cordero, Jesus Deran. sc Paul Baxley.
m John Cameron. 98 mins

Cast: Farrah Fawcett-Majors (Ellis
Morgan), Charles Grodin (Jake
Dekker), Art Carney (Al Marcus), Joan
Collins (Nera), William Daniels
(Crawford), John Hillerman (Webb),
Eleanor Parker (Mrs Thoren), Keenan
Wynn (Mark Elmes), Robin Clarke
(Karl Thoren), Jack Kruschen (Gela),
Seymour Cassel (Dobbs)

An unorthodox insurance investigator
hires a model to pose as his wife when
goes to Acapulco to inquire into a
massive fraud.

Sloppy in all departments, with
everyone over-acting like crazy to try
and compensate for the inane plot and
stupid dialogue – apart, that is, from
Fawcett-Majors, who doesn't even try
to act. Perfect therapy for insomniacs.

It is the sort of predictable non-

sense they show as inflight movies
aboard jumbos.'

Evening Standard

SUSPICION

(US 1941)

pc RKO. p, d Alfred Hitchcock. w
Samson Raphaelson, Joan Harrison,
Alma Reville, from the novel *Before the
Fact* by Francis Iles. ph Harry
Stradling. B&W. ed William Hamilton.
ad Van Nest Polglase. sfx Vernon L
Walker. m Franz Waxman. 99 mins

Cast: Cary Grant (Johnnie Aysgarth),
Joan Fontaine (Lina McLaidlaw),
Cedric Hardwicke (Gen. McLaidlaw),
Nigel Bruce (Beaky), Dame May
Whitty (Mrs McLaidlaw), Isabel Jeans
(Mrs Newsham), Heather Angel
(Ethel), Ariol Lee (Isobel Sedbusk),
Reginald Sheffield (Reggie Wetherby),
Leo G Carroll (Capt. Melbeck)

A woman starts to believe her playboy
husband is planning to kill her.

Moderately suspenseful, though
not vintage Hitchcock, badly
compromised by an imposed 'happy
ending', variously attributed to the
studio's belief that Grant was too
valuable a box-office property to
play a villain, and to Hitchcock's
own insistence on altering the
original premise of the source novel,
in which the putative killer turned
out to be innocent.

The Academy Award-nominated
musical score, atmospheric
cinematography, some typical
Hitchcock touches, notably a light
placed inside the glass to accentuate
the drink Grant is carrying up to his
wife, and Fontaine's performance, for
which she won the Oscar, are major

assets. Grant is not. Nominated for
the Best Picture Academy Award.

'One must remark that the ending is
not up to Mr Hitchcock's usual
style, and the general atmosphere of
the picture is far less genuine that
he previously hs wrought. But still
he has managed to bring through a
tense and exciting tale, a psychological thriller which is packed with lively suspense and a picture that
entertains you from beginning to –
well, almost the end.'

The New York Times

SWEENEY!

(GB 1976)

pc Euston Films. exec p Lloyd
Shirley, George Taylor. p Ted Childs.
d David Wickes. w Ronald Graham,
from the television series *The Sweeney*
created by Ian Kennedy Martin. ph
Dusty Miller. 2nd unit ph Norman
Langley. Colour. ed Chris Burt. ad
Bill Alexander. sfx Arthur Beavis. m
Denis King. 89 mins

Cast: John Thaw (Regan), Dennis
Waterman (Carter), Barry Foster
(McQueen), Ian Bannen (Baker),
Colin Welland (Chadwick), Diane
Keen (Bianca), Michael Coles
(Johnson), Joe Melia (Brent), Brian
Glover (Mac), Lynda Bellingham
(Janice), Morris Perry (Flying Squad
Commander), Nick Brimble
(Burtonshaw)

Scotland Yard's Flying Squad – the
Sweeney – investigates the death of a
high-class prostitute and uncovers
blackmail and corruption in
high places.

Violent, well-plotted and one of

the relatively few television spin-offs to hold its own as a cinema feature, thanks to sturdy performances from a good (if second-league) cast, well-used London locations, no-nonsense direction and crisp editing.

'Pace, in fact, is the key element in *Sweeney!*, since one of its major assets is that it finds thoroughly British equivalents of many of the traditional American *clichés* without pandering to any other market than the home one.'
Films and Filming

THE TALL TARGET
(US 1951)

pc MGM. p Richard Goldstone. d
Anthony Mann. w George Worthing
Yates, Art Cohn. st George Worthing
Yates, Geoffrey Homes. ph Paul Vogel.
B&W. ed Newell P Kimlin. ad Cedric
Gibbons, Eddie Imazu. 78 mins

Cast: Dick Powell (John Kennedy),
Paula Raymond (Ginny Beaufort),
Adolphe Menjou (Caleb Jeffers),
Marshall Thompson (Lance Beaufort),
Richard Rober (Lt Coulter), Will Geer
(Homer Crowley), Ruby Dee (Rachel),
Victor Kilian (John K Gannon),
Florence Bates (Mrs Alsop), Katherine
Warren (Mrs Gibbons), Leif Erickson
(Stranger), Peter Brocco (Fernandina),
Will Wright (Thomas I Ogden), Regis
Toomey (Tim Reilly), Leslie Kimmel
(Abraham Lincoln)

A police officer saves Abraham Lincoln
from assassination on the train
carrying him to his inauguration in
Washington in 1861.

Clever and holding suspenser
which makes excellent use of confined
settings to underscore the tension,
lifted above its essentially second-
feature origins by sharp direction and a
welcome lack of pretension.

'The film converts this intriguing piece
of history into ingenious and colourful
"whodunit" ... I found it quite exciting.'
Picturegoer

THE TATTERED DRESS
(US 1957)

pc Universal-International. p Albert
Zugsmith. d Jack Arnold. w George
Zuckerman. ph Carl E Guthrie. B&W.
Scope. ed Edward Curtiss. ad

Alexander Golitzen, Bill Newberry. m
Frank Skinner. 93 mins

Cast: Jeff Chandler (James Blane),
Jeanne Crain (Diane Blane), Jack
Carson (Nick Hoak), Gail Russell
(Carol Morrow), Elaine Stewart
(Charleen Heston), George Tobias
(Billy Giles), Edward Andrews (Lester
Rawlings), Philip Reed (Michael
Reston), Edward C Platt (Ralph
Adams), Paul Birch (Frank Mitchell),
Alexander Lockwood (Paul Vernon),
Edwin Jerome (Judge), William
Schallert (Court Clerk)

A lawyer defends a society couple on a
murder charge, secures an acquittal,
and is then framed by a vindictive
sheriff and put on trial for bribing a
juror.

Competent Universal
programmer with holding direction,
a fair measure of thrills and suspense,
and excellent contributions from
Chandler and Carson.

'*The Tattered Dress* is out of the slick
fiction hopper ... Arnold's direction
and the technical aspects are as
slick as the script.'
Variety

THE TECKMAN MYSTERY
(GB 1954)

pc London Films. A Corona Film
Production. p Josef Somlo. d Wendy
Toye. w Francis Durbridge, James
Matthews, from the BBC television
serial by Francis Durbridge. ph Jack
Hildyard. B&W. ed Albert Rule. ad
William Kellner. m Clifton Parker.
90 mins

Cast: Margaret Leighton (Helen), John

Justin (Philip Chance), Meier Tzelniker (John Rice), Michael Medwin (Martin Teckman), Roland Culver (Harris), George Coulouris (Gavin), Jane Wenham (Ruth), Duncan Lamont (Hilton), Raymond Huntley (Miller), Harry Locke (Leonard)

An author writing the biography of a dead test pilot finds his subject is still alive and is menaced by foreign agents.

Unpretentious, with plenty of suspects and a script and direction that keep it moving to a good climax, although regularly-occurring cliffhangers betray its television serial origins.

'The plot is intriguing and is so ingeniously developed that many are likely to be kept guessing and completely misled as to the identity of the criminal ... fast-moving, enjoyable entertainment of its kind.'
CEA Film report

TELEFON
(US 1977)
pc MGM. p James B Harris. d Don Siegel. w Peter Hyams, Stirling Silliphant, from the novel by Walter Wager. ph Michael Butler. Colour. ed Douglas Stewart. pd Ted Haworth. ad William F O'Brien. sfx Joe Day. m Lalo Schiffrin. 103 mins

Cast: Charles Bronson (Grigori Borzov), Lee Remick (Barbara), Donald Pleasence (Nicolai Dalchimsky), Tyne Daly (Dorothy Putterman), Alan Badel (Col. Malchenko), Patrick Magee (Gen. Strelsky), Sheree North (Marie Wills), Frank Marth (Harley Sandburg), Helen Page Camp (Emma Stark), Roy Jenson (Doug Stark), Jacqueline Scott

(Mrs Hassler), John Mitchum (Harry Bascom)

A KGB agent is sent to the US to eliminate a Soviet fanatic who has activated a network of hypnotized saboteurs planted in America at the height of the Cold War.

One more nail in the coffin of those still dedicated to proving Siegel was a consistent *auteur* and not simply, like most film-makers, at the mercy of his material. Here, faced with an improbable script and Bronson in what appears to be a state of dramatic rigor mortis, Siegel sinks without trace.

'While the film is busy, it is also dull and ridiculous.'
Cue

THEY CALL ME MISTER TIBBS!
(US 1970)
pc Mirisch Productions. exec p Walter Mirisch. p Herbert Hirschman. d Gordon Douglas. w Alan R Trustman, James R Webb, based on the character created by John Ball. st Alan R Trustman. ph Gerald Finnerman. Colour. ed Bud Molin. ad Addison F Hehr. m Quincy Jones. 108 mins

Cast: Sidney Poitier (Virgil Tibbs), Martin Landau (Rev. Logan Sharpe), Barbara McNair (Valerie Tibbs), Anthony Zerbe (Rice Weedon), Jeff Corey (Capt. Marden), David Sheiner (Herbert Kenner), Juano Hernandez (Mealie), Norma Crane (Marge Garfield), Edward Asner (Woody Garfield), Ted Gehring (Sgt Deutsch), Beverly Todd (Puff), Gary Walberg (Medical Examiner)

Lieutenant Virgil Tibbs investigates the murder of a girl in San Francisco.

Routine and colourless. Its few feeble resonances derive from Poitier's reprise of the character of Virgil Tibbs he created in 1968's *In the Heat of the Night* (q.v.)

'It is about as well done as the average episode of *Hawaii Five-0* but at least twice as long. Who wants to move away from the box for that?'
The Guardian

THIEF
(US 1981) (GB: VIOLENT STREETS)
pc Michael Mann Company/Caan Productions. exec p, d, w Michael Mann, from the novel *The Home Invaders* by Frank Hohimer. assoc p Richard Brams. ph Donald Thorin. add ph Don Cahill. Colour. ed Dov Hoenig. pd Mel Bourne. ad Mary Dodson, Michael Molly. sfx Russell Hessey. sc Walter Scott. m Tangerine Dream. add m Craig Safan. 123 mins

Cast: James Caan (Frank), Tuesday Weld (Jessie), Willie Nelson (Okla), James Belushi (Barry), Robert Prosky (Leo), Tom Signorelli (Attaglia), Denni Farina (Carl), Nick Nickeas (Nick), John Santucci (Urizzi), Gavin McFadyen (Boresko), Chuck Adamson (Ancell), Sam Cirone (Martello)

A safe-breaker takes on a dangerous assignment for a gangster and seeks revenge when he is double-crossed.

Well-photographed and edited, and rather more stylishly directed than the subject can stand. It is stronger on the minutiae of criminal activity than on characterization.

Powerful entertainment which lives up to its British title but doesn't open any doors to the criminal mind that have not been opened before.'
Screen International

THE THIEF WHO CAME TO DINNER
(US 1973)

pc Tandem. p, d Bud Yorkin. assoc p D Michael Moore. w Walter Hill, from the novel by Terence L Smith. ph Philip Lathrop. Colour. ed John C Horger. pd Polly Platt. m Henry Mancini. 105 mins

Cast: Ryan O'Neal (Webster McGee), Jacqueline Bisset (Laura Keaton), Warren Oates (Dave Reilly), Jill Clayburgh (Jackie), Charles Cioffi (Henderling), Ned Beatty (Deams), Austin Pendleton (Zuchovsky), Charles Morfogen (Rivera), Gregory Sierra (Dynamite), Michael Murphy (Ted), John Hillerman (Lasker)

A computer expert throws up his job to become a jewel thief.

Tired crime caper with better-than-it-deserves performances by Oates and, especially, Clayburgh in the small but vivid role of O'Neal's ex-wife. But if nature *really* abhors a vacuum, what is blander-than-bleached-bread O'Neal doing in the leading role?

'The thrills and the comedy both seem rather *déjà vu*.'
Financial Times

THIEVES LIKE US
(US 1973)

pc United Artists. A Jerry Blick-George Litto production. exec p George Litto. p Jerry Blick. assoc p Jerry Eggenweiler. d Robert Altman. w Calder Willingham, Joan Tewkesbury, Robert Altman, from the novel by Edward Anderson. ph Jean Bofferry. Colour. ed Lou Lombardo. 123 mins

Cast: Keith Carradine (Bowie Bowers), Shelley Duvall (Keechie), John Schuck ('Chicamaw' Elmo Mobley), Bert Remsen ('T-Dub' T W Masefield), Louise Fletcher (Mattie), Ann Latham (Lula), Tom Skerritt (Dee Mobley), Al Scott (Capt. Summers), John Roper (Jasbo), Mary Waits (Noel), Rodney Lee Jr (James Mattingly), William Watters (Alvin)

A young killer and three hardened lifers escape from a Mississippi prison farm at the height of the Depression and return to a life of crime.

Altman's over-long, hardly necessary remake of *They Live By Night* (1948) is strong on period detail but outstays its welcome by at least two reels. Compensations come from the fine acting of Carradine, Schuck and Duvall.

'An exceptional film, one mostly devoid of clutter, auteurist mannerism, and other auteur chic.'
Daily Variety

'A puzzling, unsatisfactory but not unstylish film, it would seem to be attempting some feat of alienation – and succeeding, I would say, but not quite as intended.'
The Daily Telegraph

THE THIN MAN
(US 1934)

pc MGM. p Hunt Stromberg. d W S Van Dyke. w Albert Hackett, Francis Goodrich, from the novel by Dashiell Hammett. ph James Wong Howe. B&W. ed Robert J Kern. ad Cedric Gibbons. m William Axt. 93 mins

Cast: William Powell (Nick Charles), Myrna Loy (Nora Charles), Maureen O'Sullivan (Dorothy Wynant), Nat Pendleton (Lt Guild), Minna Gombell (Mimi Wynant), Porter Hall (McCauley), Henry Wadsworth (Andrew), William Henry (Gilbert), Harold Huber (Nunheim), Cesar Romero (Chris Jorgenson), Natalie Moorehead (Julia Wolf), Edward Brophy (Joe Morelli), Edward Ellis (Clyde Wynant, 'The Thin Man')

Husband-and-wife amateur sleuths solve the disappearance of an eccentric inventor.

Fast-moving, funny, entertaining blend of comedy and thrills, smartly shot by Van Dyke in a brisk two weeks. Powell and Loy blithely ignored the miseries of the Depression in favour of unconcerned high living, and their wisecracking, carefree and credible relationship (many believed, wrongly, that they were married off-screen as well) struck a chord with critics and public alike. Along with their scene-stealing terrier, Asta, they played Nick and Nora Charles in a further five films. Only *After the Thin Man* (1936) recaptured the unforced high spirits of the original.

Peter Lawford and Phyllis Kirk starred in the bland 1957–58 television series which ran for 78 episodes and, in 1978, Robert Wagner and Stefanie Powers reprised the formula, compete with a clever dog, in the television series *Hart To Hart*, which, however, made no mention of its creative debt to *The Thin Man*.

THE THIRD MAN

On the whole it was thoroughly well conceived and carried out – a strange mixture of excitement, quips and hard-boiled (but clear and touching) sentiment. It is a good movie and should not be missed.'
The New Republic

Brilliantly put over by expert direction and an outstanding cast. Story clever, dialogue smart and humour sophisticated and popular.'
Cine Weekly

THE THIRD DAY
(US 1965)

pc WB. p, d Jack Smight. w Burton Wohl, Robert Presnell Jr, from the novel by Joseph Hayes. ph Robert Surtees. Colour. Panavision. ed Stefan Arnsten. ad Edward Carrere. m Percy Faith. song *Love Me Now* by Percy Faith, Jay Livingston, Ray Evans. 119 mins

Cast: George Peppard (Steve Mallory), Elizabeth Ashley (Alexandria), Roddy McDowall (Oliver Parsons), Arthur O'Connell (Dr Wheeler), Mona Washbourne (Catherine), Herbert Marshall (Austin), Robert Webber (Dom Guardiano), Charles Drake (Lawrence Conway), Sally Kellerman (Holly Mitchell), Arte Johnson (Lester Aldrich), Bill Walker (Logan), Vincent Gardenia (Preston)

A man suffering from amnesia after a car accident learns he is facing a charge of murder.

Glossy, interestingly cast and, while hardly original, consistently maintains interest and tension, due in large measure to Smight's stylish direction.

'The director and the scriptwriters ... produce a fine set of alarms and keep the suspense tingling tantalizingly until the end.'
Daily Cinema

THE THIRD MAN
(GB 1949)

pc London Film Productions/British Lion/David) Selznick. exec p Alexander Korda. p, d Carol Reed. assoc p Hugh Perceval. w Graham Greene. ph Robert Krasker. add ph John Wilcox, Stan Pavey. B&W. ed Oswald Hafenrichter. ad Vincent Korda, Joseph Bato, John Hawkesworth. assoc ad Ferdinand Bellin, James Sawyer. m Anton Karas. 104 mins

Cast: Joseph Cotten (Holly Martin), Orson Welles (Harry Lime), Alida Valli (Anna Schmidt), Trevor Howard (Maj. Calloway), Paul Hoerbiger (Porter), Ernst Deutsch (Baron Kurtz), Eric Ponto (Dr Winkel), Siegfried Breuer (Popescu), Bernard Lee (Sgt Paine), Geoffrey Keen (British Policeman), Wilfrid Hyde-White (Crabbin), Hedwig Bleibtrai (Anna's 'Old Woman'), Annie Rosar (Porter's Wife), Paul Hardtmuth (Hall Porter), Harbut Helbek (Hansl)

An American pulp writer comes to post-World War Two Vienna to look up an old friend and is told he has been killed, but he subsequently finds him alive and running a black market racket in diluted penicillin.

A justified classic, whose taut Graham Greene screenplay is given full value by Reed's acute, firmly-controlled direction of both actors (Welles, for once, underplays) and narrative, by

his use of unusual camera angles to underscore the mounting atmosphere of unease, complemented by Krasker's moody Oscar-winning cinematography and Anton Karas's haunting zither score.

The relatively simple storyline makes a vivid background for the depiction of a ruined city in which evil and corruption are a norm. The meeting of Cotten and Welles in a deserted fairground and the climactic chase through the sewers still deservedly compel attention.

Ironically, Harry Lime reappeared, no longer venal or corrupt but suitably sanitized for the small screen and transformed into a standard heroic crimefighter, played by Michael Rennie in the 1959–61 television series *The Third Man*.

'The expert timing, the building of each little pattern of suspense, the sharp relief of ordinary happenings played against the widening web of extraordinary evil are anything but run of the mill.'
Time and Tide

'Crammed with cinematic plums that could do the early Hitchcock proud.'
Time

'Reed has never before elaborated his style so desperately, nor used so many tricks in the presentation of a film ... his whole trick-laden film is itself a trick, and often a very brilliant one, with moments that I suspect will long be quoted as classic touches. It is imperatively a film to see, and will add to the reputations of its players.'
The Observer

THE THIRD VOICE
(US 1959)

pc 20th Century Fox. p Maury Dexter, Hubert Cornfield. d, w Hubert Cornfield, from the novel *All the Way* by Charles Williams. ph Ernest Haller. B&W. Scope. ed John A Bushelman. ad John Mansbridge. m Johnny Mandel. 79 mins

Cast: Edmond O'Brien (The Man), Laraine Day (Marian Forbes), Julie London (Corey Scott), Ralph Brooks (Harris Chapman), Henry Delgado (Desk Clerk, Palacio Hotel), André Oropeza (Desk Clerk, Miramar Hotel), Olga San Juan (Blonde Prostitute), George Trevino (Capt. Campos), Roque Ybarra (First Fisherman), Ruben Mareno (Second Fisherman)

A woman murders her industrialist lover and hires a man to impersonate him in lucrative business dealings, only to have the scheme founder when the imposter attempts a double-cross.

Complex, gripping and cleverly plotted, with a satisfying denouement, although the direction is derivative of better film-makers.

'The master, Alfred Hitchcock, couldn't have done better. It's a thriller that compels attention from the arresting credits to the alarming fade-out.'
Picturegoer

THE THIRTY-NINE STEPS
(GB 1935)

pc Gaumont British. p Michael Balcon. assoc p Ivor Montagu. d Alfred Hitchcock. w Alma Reville, Charles Bennett, from the novel by John Buchan. add dial Ian Hay. ph Bernard Knowles. B&W. ed Derek N Twist. ad

Otto Werndorff, Albert Juillon. md Louis Levy. m Hubert Bath, Jack Beaver. 81 mins

Cast: Robert Donat (Richard Hannay), Madeleine Carroll (Pamela), Lucie Mannheim (Miss Smith/Annabella), Godfrey Tearle (Prof. Jordan), Peggy Ashcroft (Crofter's Wfe), John Laurie (Crofter), Helen Haye (Mrs Jordan), Frank Cellier (Sheriff), Wylie Watson (Mr Memory), Gus MacNaughton, Jerry Verno (Commercial Tavellers), Peggy Simpson (Maid)

An innocent man suspected of the murder of a British agent goes on the run from the police and foreign agents and heads for Scotland.

One of Hitchcock's most thoroughly entertaining thrillers. At the time he said: 'I am out to give the public good, healthy, mental shake-ups. Civilization has become so screening and sheltering that we cannot experience sufficient thrills at first hand. Therefore, to prevent ourbecoming sluggish and jellified, we have to experience them artificially.'

Suspense, action and humour are ideally blended, the pace is fast and rarely flags, and the screenplay is engagingly adult for the time, no more so than when Donat and Carroll are forced to spend a night together while handcuffed to each other. The classic sequences – the discovery of a corpse by a maid, whose scream merges into the whistle of an express train which, inevitably, has subsequently been much imitated by lesser film-makers, Donat's escape from a train on the Forth Bridge and his escape from a political meeting by posing as a platform

speaker – still work splendidly.

Twice remade, in 1959 and 1978 (both q.v.), this is the definitive version.

'The producer [sic] Alfred Hitchcock has approached the original plot from a "tongue-in-cheek" angle without harm to atmosphere and scores freely all along the line with his brilliant and unorthodox treatment.'
Kine Weekly

'When a picture is as good as *The Thirty-Nine Steps*, it is almost super-fluous to detail its individual virtues ... it will be simpler and less selfish, I think, to include everything in the one recommendation, go to *The Thirty-Nine Steps* and find it all out for yourselves.'
The Observer

'It's melodrama and at times far-fetched and improbable, but the story twists and spins artfully from one high-powered sequence to another while the entertainment holds like steel cable from start to finish ... criticism is cancelled in pleasure.'
Variety

THE THIRTY-NINE STEPS
(GB 1959)

pc A Betty E Box-Ralph Thomas Production. p Betty E Box. d Ralph Thomas. w Frank Harvey, from the novel by John Buchan. ph Ernest Steward. Colour. ed Alfred Roome. ad Maurice Carter. m Clifton Parker. 93 mins

Cast: Kenneth More (Richard Hannay), Tania Elg (Fisher), Barry Jones (Prof. Logan), James Hayter

Mr Memory), Michael Goodliffe
Brown), Duncan Lamont
Kennedy), Brenda De Banzie (Nellie
Lumsden), Reginald Beckwith
Lumsden), Faith Brook (Nanny),
ameson Clark (McDougal), Andrew
Cruikshank (Sheriff), Leslie Dwyer
Milkman), Betty Henderson (Mrs
McDougal), Joan Hickson (Miss
Dobson), Sidney James (Perce), Brian
Oulton (Mr Pringle)

man is framed for the murder of a
py and pursued by the police and
oreign agents.

Tepid and redundant remake with
slack screenplay and even slacker
irection. The wit and sophistication
f the orginal (1935, q.v.) are
orely missed.

'It should all have been wildly exciting.
But since Kenneth More seems to
ake the whole thing as seriously as a
rep school paper chase, the tension
emains low throughout.'
Reynolds News

THE THIRTY-NINE STEPS
(GB 1978)

pc Norfolk International. exec p James
Kenelm Clarke. p Greg Smith. assoc p
Frank Bevis. d Don Sharp. w Michael
Robson, from the novel by John
Buchan. ph John Coquillon. add ph
Harry Waxman, Jimmy Bawden.
Colour. ed Eric Boyd-Perkins. pd
Harry Pottle. asst ad Peter Childs, Jack
Notman. sfx Ron Ballanger. m Ed
Welch. 102 mins

Cast: Robert Powell (Richard
Hannay), David Warner (Edmund
Appleton), Eric Porter (Insp. Lomas),
Karen Dotrice (Alexandra Mackenzie),
John Mills (Col. Scudder), George
Baker (Sir Walter Bullivant), Ronald
Pickup (Bayliss), Donald Pickering
(Marshall), Timothy West (Porton),
Andrew Keir (Lord Rohan), Miles
Anderson (David Hamilton), Robert
Flemyng (Magistrate), William Squire
(Harkness), Paul McDowell (McLean),
John Welsh (Lord Belthane)

A man is framed for the murder in
1914 and, pursued by the police and
foreign spies, foils a plot to assassinate
the Greek Prime Minister in London.

The screenplay is reasonably
faithful to Buchan, but the film lacks
the wit of Hitchcock's classic.
Nevertheless, Sharp's zestful direction
goes a long way towards disguising
both the lacunae in the narrative and
the low budget, Powell is a spirited
hero, and the climax ('borrowed'
from the 1936 Will Hay comedy *My
Learned Friend*) with Powell hanging
from the face of Big Ben is an
entertaining cliffhanger.

'Send not to ask for whom Big Ben
eventually tolls – it's not for Alfred
Hitchcock.'
Evening Standard

'In short, a curate's egg but an enjoyable one.'
Financial Times

THIS GUN FOR HIRE
(US 1942)

pc Paramount. p Richard M
Blumenthal. d Frank Tuttle. w Albert
Maltz, W R Burnett, from the novel *A
Gun For Sale* by Graham Greene. ph
John Seitz. B&W. ed Archie Marshek.
ad Hans Dreier. m Frank Loesser,
Jacques Press. 80 mins

Cast: Alan Ladd (Philip Raven),
Veronica Lake (Ellen Graham), Robert
Preston (Michael Crane), Laird Cregar
(Willard Gates), Tully Marshall (Alvin
Brewster), Mikhail Rasumny (Slukey),
Marc Lawrence (Tommy), Pamela
Blake (Annie), Harry Shannon
(Flaherty), Frank Ferguson (Albert
Baker), Yvonne De Carlo (Showgirl)

A professional killer seeking revenge
for a double-cross becomes involved
with fifth-columnists selling poison gas
to Japan and with a nightclub singer.

Ladd's minimalist acting and
passive persona admirably suited his
unsmiling gunman role in this brisk,
unpretentious thriller, and he became a
star in the first of his frequent forties
teamings with Lake. Greene's novel was
efficiently Americanized and pacily
directed with excellent
cinematography.

'Comes pretty high in the melodrama
class. It is exciting and ingenious without losing the directness of its plot,
fast moving without disturbing the
neat dove-tailing of its parts.'
The Sunday Times

THE THOMAS CROWN AFFAIR
(US 1968)

pc Mirisch/Simkoe/Solar. p, d Norman
Jewison. assoc p, sup ed Hal Ashby. w
Alan R Trustman. ph Haskell Wexler.
Colour. Panavision, ed Ralph Winters,
Byron Brandt. ad Robert Boyle.
multiple screen sequences Pablo Ferro
Films. m Michel Legrand. song *The
Windmills Of Your Mind* by Michel
Legrand, Alan & Marilyn Bergman.
102 mins

Cast: Steve McQueen (Thomas

Crown), Faye Dunaway (Vicky Anderson), Paul Burke (Eddy Malone), Jack Weston (Erwin Weaver), Yaphet Kotto (Carl), Todd Martin (Benjy), Sam Melville (Dave), Addison Powell (Abe), Sidney Armus (Arnie), John Shank (Curley), Allen Emerson (Don), Harry Cooper (Ernie), Biff McGuire (Sandy), Gordon Pinsent (Jamie McDonald), Carol Corbett (Miss Sullivan)

A property tycoon pulls off an audacious bank robbery and matches wits with the female insurance investigator who comes after him.

Flashy, empty-headed sixties chic which is so self-consciously clever that it hurts, with Jewison fatally mistaking elaborately-mannered optical effects and 'creative' editing for storytelling. The dialogue is witless, the leads are dull and far too self-admiring, and only the attractive cinematography really impresses. The unexceptional Academy Award-winning song *The Windmills Of Your Mind* is more memorable than the film.

'This stylish thriller should do well in most situations.'
Kine Weekly

THREE DAYS OF THE CONDOR
(US 1975)
pc Wildwood Enterprises. For Dino De Laurentiis Inc and Paramount. p Stanley Schneider. d Sydney Pollack. w Lorenzo Semple Jr, David Rayfiel, from the novel *Six Days of the Condor* by James Grady. ph Owen Roizman. Colour. Panavision. sup ed Frederic Steinkamp. ed Don Guidice. pd Stephen Grimes. ad Gene Rudolph. sfx Augie Lohman. m Dave Grusin. titles Phil Norman. 117 mins

Cast: Robert Redford (Joe Turner), Faye Dunaway (Kathy), Cliff Robertson (Higgins), Max Von Sydow (Joubert), John Houseman (Mr Wabash), Addison Powell (Atwood), Walter McGinn (Barber), Tina Chen (Janice), Michael Kane (Wicks), Don McHenry (Dr Lappe), Michael Miller (Fowler), Patrick Gorman (Martin), Jess Osuna (Mitchell), Dino Narizzano (Thomas)

A CIA analyst uncovers an assassination plot within The Company and is marked for murder.

Pollack's rather too-careful direction does a good job of building tension and keeps the story moving, but signally fails to generate much interest in either Redford or, particularly, Dunaway, who both give uncharismatic and flabby performances. Ultimately, a lot less than meets the eye. For once, though, Hollywood steers clear of hyperbole, cutting the source novel's *Six Days of the Condor* to a mere three.

'*Three Days of the Condor*, a reasonably entertaining espionage picture, is mainly noteworthy for enshrining most of the Redford clichés to date.'
Rolling Stone

THUNDERBALL
(GB 1965)
pc Eon. p Kevin McClory. d Terence Young. action sequence d Bob Simmons. underwater d Ricou Browning. w Richard Maibaum, John Hopkins, from an original screenplay by Jack Whittingham, Kevin McClory & Ian Fleming & from the novel by Ian Fleming. ph Ted Moore. underwater ph Lamar Boren. Colour. Panavision. ed Peter Hunt, pd Ken Adams. ad Peter Murton. sfx John Stears. m John Barry. title song John Barry, Don Black, sung by Tom Jones. titles Maurice Binder. 130 mins

Cast: Sean Connery (James Bond), Claudine Auger (Domino), Adolfo Celi (Largo), Luciana Paluzzi (Fiona), Rik Van Nutter (Felix Leiter), Bernard Lee ('M'), Lois Maxwell (Miss Moneypenny), Martine Beswick (Paula), Guy Doleman (Count Lippe), Molly Peters (Patricia), Desmond Llewellyn ('Q'), Roland Culver (Foreign Secretary), Earl Cameron (Pinder), Paul Stassino (Palazzi), Rose Alba (Mme Boitier), Philip Locke (Vargas), Edward Underdown (Air Vice-Marshal), Michael Brennan (Jannie), Reginald Beckwith (Kenniston)

Bond saves the day when SPECTRE hijacks two nuclear weapons and holds the West to ransom.

A change of producer (Kevin McClory owned the rights to an original screenplay part-authored by Ian Fleming from his own book) makes the fourth film in the series rather less satisfactory than its predecessors. Over-long, it too often tends to sideline Connery and instead concentrate on action and on gadgets, which, as usual, are ingenious but increasingly improbable. While the climactic underwater battle is impressively staged and photographed it goes on far too long and tension evaporates.

Thunderball was a huge money-spinner, though, and was remade by Connery in 1983 as *Never Say Never Again.*

Thunderball spreads a treasure of wish-fulfilling fantasy over a nickel's worth of plot.'
Time

'Stripped of all the gimmicks, the girls and the geiger counters, *Thunderball* is a skilfully photographed, expertly designed, well produced underwater Western. DIVE IN.'
Daily Mirror

THUNDERBOLT AND LIGHTFOOT
(US 1974)

pc Malpaso Company. p Robert Daley. d, w Michael Cimino. ph Frank Stanley. Colour. Panavision. ed Ferris Webster. ad Tambi Larsen. sfx Sass Bedig. sc Buddy Van Horn. special action sequences Carey Loftin. m Dee Barton. 115 mins

Cast: Clint Eastwood (John 'Thunderbolt' Doherty), Jeff Bridges (Lightfoot), George Kennedy (Red Leary), Geoffrey Lewis (Goody), Catherine Bach (Melody), Gary Busey (Curly), Jack Dodson (Vault Manager), Burton Gilliam (Welder), Roy Jenson (Dunlop), Vic Tayback (Mario), Claudia Lennear (Secretary), Dub Taylor (Gas Station Attendant), Gregory Walcott (Used Car Salesman)

A criminal on the run from his former accomplices achieves a rapprochment and, with a young drifter, they execute a daring robbery.

Amiable but somewhat unfocused crime thriller which gets by pleasantly on the personalities and performances of Eastwood and Academy Award nominee Bridges. Cimino's directorial debut.

'Cimino paces the film so comfortably that there are no real lulls in its two hours of running time – not a common achievement these days.'
Films and Filming

TIGER BAY
(GB 1959)

pc A Julian Wintle-Leslie Parkyn Production. p John Hawkesworth. d J Lee Thompson. w John Hawkesworth, Shelley Smith. ph Eric Cross. B&W. ed Sidney Hayers. ad Edward Carrick. m Laurie Johnson. 105 mins

Cast: Horst Bucholz (Korchinsky), John Mills (Supt Graham), Hayley Mills (Gillie), Yvonne Mitchell (Anya), Megs Jenkins (Mrs Phillips), Anthony Dawson (Barbclay), George Selway (Det. Sgt Harvey), George Pastell (Captain), Shari (Christine), Meredith Edwards (Constable Williams), Paul Stassino (First Officer), Marne Maitland (Dr Das)

An 11-year-old girl who witnesses a murder in Cardiff is subsequently kidnapped by the killer.

An engaging, scene-stealing screen debut by Hayley Mills (whose real-life father John hands her the film on a plate) decorates a tense, well-characterized suspenser with workmanlike direction and effective location filming.

'A clear-cut thriller emerges, quickly take shape and keeping quick tempo throughout, tempered with sentiment but all for the better since this highlights the toughness of the action.'
CEA Film Report

TIGHT SPOT
(US 1955)

pc Columbia. p Lewis J Rachmil. d Phil Karlson. w William Bowers, from the play *Dead Pigeon* by Leonard Kantor. ph Burnett Guffey. B&W. ed Viola Lawrence. ad Carl Anderson. m George Duning. 97 mins

Cast: Ginger Rogers (Sherry Conley), Edward G Robinson (Lloyd Hallett), Brian Keith (Vince Striker), Lucy Marlow (Prison Girl), Lorne Greene (Benjamin Costain), Katherine Anderson (Mrs Willoughby), Allen Nourse (Marvin Rickles), Peter Leeds (Fred Packer), Doye O'Dell (Mississippi Mac), Frank Gerstle (Jim Hornsby), Robert Shield (Carlyle), Kathryn Grant (Honeymooner)

A US government attorney tries to persuade a female prisoner to give evidence against her former gangster lover.

Skilful direction, snappy dialogue and a surprisingly good performance by Rogers turn the none-too-original story into a well above-average genre movie. Robinson, strangely, plays the attorney, not the gangster.

'In most respects a satisfying thriller, demonstrating what can be accomplished within a conventional, even time-worn, plot framework with good craftsmanship and a little artistry.'
Monthly Film Bulletin

TIME BOMB
(GB 1952) (US: TERROR ON A TRAIN)

pc MGM. p Richard Goldstone. d Ted Tetzlaff. w Ken Bennett. ph Frederick A Young. B&W. ed Frank

Clarke. ad Alfred Junge. m John Addison. 72 mins

Cast: Glenn Ford (Peter Lyncort), Anne Vernon (Janine Lyncort), Maurice Denham (Mr Warrilow), Harcourt Williams (Vicar), Victor Maddern (Saboteur), Harrold Warrender (Sir Evelyn Jordan), John Horsley (Constable Charles Barton), Campbell Singer (Insp. Branson), Bill Fraser (Constable Reed)

A Canadian engineer volunteers to defuse a time bomb placed on a train carrying navy mines.

Crisp and unpretentious second feature with strong contributions from Ford and Denham.

'This is one of those unpretentious films that pack into a short footage more entertainment than many a much boosted and star-spangled "super".'
Picturegoer

TO CATCH A THIEF

(US 1955)
pc Paramount. p, d Alfred Hitchcock. 2nd unit d Herbert Coleman. w John Michael Hayes, from the novel by David Dodge. ph Robert Burks. 2nd unit ph Wallace Kelley. process ph Farciot Edouart. Colour. VistaVision. ed George Tomasini. ad Hal Pereira, Joseph MacMillan Johnson, Sam Comer, Arthur Kram. sfx John P Fulton. m Lynn Murray. 97 mins

Cast: Cary Grant (John Robie), Grace Kelly (Frances Stevens), Jessie Royce Landis (Mrs Stevens), John Williams (H H Hughson), Charles Vanel (Bertani), Brigitte Auber (Danielle),

Jean Martinelli (Foussard), Georgette Anys (Germaine), Roland Lesaffre (Claude), Jean Hebey (Mercier), Rene Blanchard (Lepic)

A former cat burglar living on the French Riviera comes out of retirement to track down the perpetrator of a series of thefts bearing his trademark.

Glossy but uninvolving misfire that seems longer than it is, more interesting for its picture-postcard Riviera backgrounds than for what takes place in front of them. Low on thrills, long in longueur, with Hitchcock apparently unaware that Kelly, while pretty, is pretty inadequate too, and Grant seems disinterested in the proceedings.

'Boring? Hitchcock? It's incredible, but almost true. Quite obviously the maestro of the chills-and-thrills technique has been blinded by two pale gold beauties: the scenery of the French Riviera and Grace Kelly. All right, so they're both nice to look at. But when Hitchcock concentrates on them – as he does so often through the film – the plot certainly goes for six.'
Picturegoer

'The mystery carries little real suspense.'
CEA Film Report

TOPAZ

(US 1969)
pc Universal. p, d Alfred Hitchcock. assoc p Herbert Coleman. w Samuel Taylor, from the novel by Leon Uris. ph Jack Hildyard. sfx ph Albert Whitlock. ph cons Hal Mohr. Colour. ed William H Ziegler. pd Henry Bumstead. m Maurice Jarre. 125 mins

Cast: John Forsythe (Michael Nordstrom) Frederick Stafford (André Devereaux), Dany Robin (Nicole Devereaux), John Vernon (Rico Parra), Karin Dor (Juanita de Cordoba), Michel Piccoli (Jacques Granville), Philippe Noiret (Henri Jarre), Roscoe Lee Browne (Philippe Dubois), Per-Axel Arosenius (Kusenov), John Forsythe (Michael Nordstrom), Claude Jade (Michele Picard), Michel Subor (François Picard)

A French agent works with a US Intelligence operative to uncover a spy ring involving high-level French officials who are working for the Soviet Union.

The only point of interest in Hitchcock's lumbering, lifeless and dull dinosaur is that – no mean achievement – it is even more tedious than the novel on which it is based, with a second-league cast giving third-league performances. If, as claimed, it is partly based on fact, then espionage must be more depressingly downbeat than many 'realistic' movies would have us believe. Definitely late Hitchcock, although in this case 'late' serves as a synonym for 'dead'.

'In fact, the manner is surprisingly uncertain for Hitchcock, who appears to be hovering between the glamour of James Bond and the elusive realities of spies who stay out in the cold. If perchance he is looking for something to imitate, all he needs to do is to re-run *Foreign Correspondent*, *Notorious*, the 1956 version of *The Man Who Knew too Much* and *North by Northwest*.'
Films and Filming

ORN CURTAIN

(US 1966)

pc Universal. p, d Alfred Hitchcock. w
Brian Moore. ph John F Warren.
Colour. ed Bud Hoffman. pd Hein
Heckroth. ad Frank Arrigo. m John
Addison. 128 mins

Cast: Paul Newman (Michael
Armstrong), Julie Andrews (Sarah
Sherman), Lila Kedrova (Countess
Kushinska), Hansjörg Felmy (Heinrich
Gerhard), Tamara Toumanova
Ballerina). Wolfgang Kieling (Herman
Gromek), Günter Strack (Prof. Karl
Manfred), Ludwig Donath (Prof.
Gustav Lindt), David Opatoshu (Mr
Jacobi), Gisela Fischer (Dr Koska),
Mort Mills (Farmer), Carolyn Conwell
Farmer's Wife), Arthur Gould-Porter
Freddy)

When a top American nuclear scientist
defects to East Germany his fiancee
tags along, and it turns out his
'treachery' is only a ploy.

Badly miscast leads hardly help –
Newman seems surly and is hardly
convincing, and Andrews tries hard
but fails to shed her *Mary Poppins*
image in the largely embarrassing love
scenes –and matters are not advanced
by a sophomoric screenplay, frequently
visible studio-bound settings, and lurid
over-acting by Kedrova that would
embarrass an amateur production.
Even Hitchcock's set-piece – Newman's
attempt to kill an East German
security policeman – which was
designed to show how difficult it is to
dispose of someone in real (as opposed
to reel) life, is so over-long and drawn-
out that it raises more laughs than
chills. A major disappointment: barely
Hitchcock, barely bearable.

'There is a distracted air about much
of the film – as if the master were not
really paying attention to what he was
doing. Therefore our emotional involvement never grows to the point where
it overrules rational disbelief and
blocks out those flaws of logic which
should not be noticed until we emerge
into the daylight.'
Life Magazine

TOUCH OF EVIL

(US 1958)

pc Universal-International. p Albert
Zugsmith. d Orson Welles.
(uncredited) Harry Keller. w Orson
Welles, from the novel *Badge of Evil* by
Whit Masterson. ph Russell Metty.
B&W. ed Virgil W Vogel, Aaron Stell.
ad Alexander Golitzen, Robert
Clatworthy. m Henry Mancini.
93/108 mins

Cast: Charlton Heston (Ramon
Miguel 'Mike' Vargas), Janet Leigh
(Susan Vargas), Orson Welles (Hank
Quinlan), Joseph Calleia (Pete
Menzies), Akim Tamiroff ('Uncle' Joe
Grandi), Joanna Moore (Marcia
Linnekar), Ray Collins (Adair), Dennis
Weaver (Motel Clerk), Valentin De
Varga (Pancho), Mort Mills
(Schwartz), Victor Milan (Manuelo
Sanchez), Lalo Rios (Risto), Michael
Sargent (Pretty Boy), Phil Harvey
(Blaine), Joi Lansing (Blonde), guest
stars: Marlene Dietrich, Zsa Zsa
Gabor, Mercedes McCambridge,
Joseph Cotten, Keenan Wynn.

The corrupt police chief of a Mexico
border town frames the American wife
of a honeymooning Mexican narcotics
investigator for murder.

Nothing succeeds like excess, and

Welles's return to major studio film-
making is dramatically overwrought
and visually riveting. Its fluid
camerawork — memorably the brilliant
long tracking cum crane shot that
opens the film — and often baroque
camera angles disguise a tortuous,
often unfathomable storyline which,
refuting the layers of myth and legend
attached to the film, is not a great deal
clearer when the film is shown at its
original 108-minute length, rather
than the cut-down version in which it
was released in 1958.

Heston plays a Mexican as
Charlton Heston with a moustache,
leaving the supporting performances
to catch the eye, notably Dietrich as a
cigar-smoking madam and Tamiroff's
rank underworld figure. Welles's
performance is as overbloated as his
epicene appearance: clearly the
director was unable to control the star.

A fascinating example of a huge
but fatally undisciplined talent
struggling, not always successfully, to
succeed within the constraints of a
Hollywood system that gave him
Albert Zugsmith as producer, better
known for such classic contributions
to world cinema as *Sex Kittens Go To
College* and *Teacher was a Sexpot.*

'Clarity is in no respect its outstanding feature; on the contrary, it is
vague and confusing and the man-in-
the-street might well regard it as
obscure if not incomprehensible. This
is all the more regrettable as there
are scenes of arresting individual
drama, no lack of effective characterization and a well-knit climax which,
however, comes too late to save the
dramatic day.'
CEA Film Report

TRUE ROMANCE

Welles' direction, opulently imagina-ive in detail, action, and colour, successfully conceals most of the important plot lines during the first half of the film ... after such a spendthrift outpouring of talent it is rather sad to feel that most of it has been squandered.'
Monthly Film Bulletin

TOWN ON TRIAL

(GB 1956)

pc Marksman Films. p Maxwell Setton. assoc p William Weedon. d John Guillermin. w Ken Hughes, Robert Westerby. ph Basil Emmott. B&W. ed Max Benedict. ad John Elphick. m Tristram Cary. 96 mins

Cast: John Mills (Supt Mike Halloran), Charles Coburn (Dr Fenner), Barbara Bates (Elizabeth Fenner), Derek Farr (Mark Roper), Alec McCowen (Peter Crowley), Elizabeth Seal (Fiona Dixon), Geoffrey Keen (Mr Dixon), Margaretta Scott (Mrs Dixon), Fay Compton (Mrs Crowley), Magda Miller (Molly Stevens)

A policeman investigating murder in a an English country town is faced with a plethora of suspects.

Unpretentious and not overly unbalanced by its two imported American leads, with consistent suspense and a good sense of place and character.

I've heard it said that the British don't know how to make screen thrillers. Here's one which can make rings around a dozen Hollywood offerings.'
News of the World

TREAD SOFTLY STRANGER

(GB 1958)

pc Alderdale. A Geirge Minter Production. p Denis O'Dell. d Gordon Parry. w George Minter, Denis O'Dell, from the play by Jack Popplewell. ph Douglas Slocombe. B&W. ed Anthony Harvey. ad Elven Webb. m Tristram Cary. 90 mins

Cast: Diana Dors (Calico), George Baker (Johnny Mansell), Terence Morgan (Dave Mansell), Patrick Allen (Paddy Ryan), Jane Griffiths (Sylvia), Joseph Tomelty (Old Ryan), Thomas Heathcote (Sgt Lamb), Russell Napier (Potter), Norman MacOwan (Danny), Maureen Delaney (Mrs Finnegan), Chris Fay (Eric Downs)

A man on the run from race-track creditors goes to the north of England, where his embezzler brother and flashy mistress involve him in a payroll robbery that ends in murder.

Truly dreadful, compounded of paper-thin characterization, trite dialogue, appalling acting, unnoticeable direction and unintentional parody that adds to its risibility. Ripe rubbish.

'It has been insensitively treated as full, purple melodrama, painfully remi-niscent of some of those twenty-year-old British movies we see on TV – and then wish we hadn't.'
Picturegoer

TRUE ROMANCE

(US 1993)

pc Morgan Creek Productions/Davis Film. exec p James G Robinson, Gary Barber, Bob Weinstein, Harvey Weinstein, Stanley Margolis. p Bill Unger, Steve Perry, Samuel Hadida. co-p Don Edmonds, James W Skotchdopole. assoc p Lisa Cogswell, Spencer Franklin, Gregory S Manson. d Tony Scott. w Quentin Tarantino. ph Jeffrey L Kimball. Colour. Panavision. ed Michael Tronick, Christian Wagner. sc Charles Picerni. m Hans Zimmer. add m Mark Mancina, John Van Togneren. 119 mins

Cast: Christian Slater (Clarence Worley), Patricia Arquette (Alabama Whitman), Dennis Hopper (Clifford Worley), Gary Oldman (Drexl Spivey), Christopher Walken (Vincenzo Coccotti), Brad Pitt (Floyd), Val Kilmer (Mentor), Bronson Pinchot (Elliot Bitzer), Samuel L Jackson (Big Don), Michael Rappaport (Dick Ritchie), Saul Rubinek (Lee Donowitz), Chris Penn (Nick Dimes), Tom Sizemore (Cody Nicholson)

A (relatively) innocent couple are pursued by hoods and the police after they accidentally steal a fortune in cocaine.

Scott does a supremely stylish razzle-dazzle job of direction, but cinematic skill and sleight of hand cannot disguise the emptiness of the derivative and trashy screenplay. (This was Tarantino's first finished screenplay, written before *Reservoir Dogs*.)

'The true romance on display here is between scriptwriter Quentin Tarantino and a litany of great B-movies. The film is as full of as many homages – or rip-offs, depending on how generous you are – as star cameos.'
Sight and Sound

TWISTED NERVE

'Preposterous plotting and graphic violence ultimately prove an audience turnoff ... cinematic references are rife, but the story's downfall can be credited in part to the writers wholehearted embrace of both the best and worst of the noir canon.'
Variety

TWISTED NERVE

(GB 1968)
pc Charter Films. exec p Roy Boultin. p George W George, Frank Granat. d Roy Boulting. w Leo Marks, Roy Boulting, from a story by Roger Marshall, based on an idea by Roger Marshall & Jeremy Scott. ph Harry Waxman. Colour. ed Martin Charles. ad Albert Witherick. m Bernard Herrmann. titles Morton Lewis. 118 mins

Cast: Hayley Mills (Phyllis Harper), Hywel Bennettt (Martin Durnley), Billie Whitelaw (Joan Harper), Phyllis Calvert (Enid Durnley), Frank Finlay (Henry Durnley), Barry Foster (Gerry Henderson), Salmaan Peer (Shahis Kadir), Gretchen Franklin (Clarkie), Christian Roberts (Philip Harvey), Thorley Walters (Sir John Forrester), Timothy West (Supt Dakin), Russell Napier (Prof Fuller)

Under stress, a psychotic young man slips into the character of 'George', who has the mind of a six-year-old. When he becomes involved with a young student, he draws her into his murderous plans against his step-father and mother.
 Repugnant in all respects, and particularly in its fanciful link between psychosis and Down's syndrome, it tries to emulate *Psycho* in particular

and Hitchcock in general, and simply emerges as distasteful trash.

'A crudely sensationalist thriller.'
Monthly Film Bulletin

'Undoubtedly *Twisted Nerve* is one of the mosr nerve jangling shockers we've seen for a long time ... definitely not for the squeamish.'
Photoplay

TWO-MINUTE WARNING

(US 1976)
pc Filmways. For Universal. p Edward S Feldman. d Larry Peerce. w Edward Hume, from the novel by George LaFountaine. ph Gerald Hirschfeld. sfx ph Albert Whitlock. optical fx Universal Title. Colour. Panavision. ed Eve Newman, Walter Hannemann. ad Herman A Blumenthal. sp weapons fx Art Brewer. sc Glen Wilder. m Charles Fox. US national anthem sung by Merv Griffin. 115 mins

Cast: Charlton Heston (Capt. Pete Holly), John Cassavetes (Sgt Chris Hutton), Martin Balsam (Sam McKeever), Beau Bridges (Mike Ramsay), Marilyn Hassett (Lucy), David Janssen (Steve), Jack Klugman (Stu Sandman), Gena Rowlands (Janet), Walter Pidgeon (Pickpocket), Brock Peters (Paul), David Groh (Al), Mitchell Ryan (Priest), Pamela Bellwood (Peggy Ramsay), Allan Miller (Mr Green)

A Los Angeles police captain and a SWAT team leader try to stop a sniper firing at the crowd in a packed football stadium.
 Utterly predictable suspenser whose major interest comes from

trying to guess which clichéd character the sniper will shoot next. Heston's flat performance is as mechanical as the slick but uninspired, by-numbers direction.

'Peerce's technical skill and all these stars unfortunately don't add any sense to the script, which leads from the ominous to the disastrous with little intelligence along the way. There are a few weakly suspenseful twinges, but *Warning* is finally as pointless as its own violence.'
Christian Science Monitor

UNDER SIEGE

(US 1992)

pc WB. exec p J F Lawton, Gary Goldstein. p Arnon Milchan, Steven Seagal, Steven Reuther. co-p Jack H Bernstein, Peter MacGregor-Scott. d Andrew Davis. 2nd unit d Conrad Palmisano. w J F Lawton. ph Frank Tidy. 2nd unit ph Gary Holt. aerial ph Frank Holgate. Colour. ed Robert A Ferretti, Dennis Virkler, Don Brochu, Dov Hoenig. pd Bill Kenney. ad Bill Hiney. sfx co-ord Thomas L Fisher. sc Conrad E Palmisano, Jeff Dashnaw. m Gary Chang. 102 mins

Cast: Steven Seagal (Casey Ryback), Tommy Lee Jones (William Strannix), Gary Busey (Commander Krill), Erika Eleniak (Jordan Tate), Patrick O'Neal (Capt. Adams), Damian Chapa (Tackman), Troy Evans (Granger), David McKnight (Flicker), Lee Minton (Cue Ball), Glenn Morshower (Ensign Taylor), Bernie Casey (Commander Harris), Colm Meaney (Daumer), Nick Mancuso (Breaker), Dale A Dy (Capt. Garza), Leo Alexander (Lt Smart)

The terrorists who seize a US battleship intending to sell its nuclear warheads for $100 million are brought down by a disgraced former Navy SEAL turned ship's cook.

Die Hard at sea, with Seagal, whose frozen-faced expression makes Buster Keaton seem hyper-animated, striking a highly-successful blow for all-action, no-brain action thrillers in a blaze of bone-snapping mayhem, gunplay and nuclear-sized explosions uncontaminated by logic or credible characterization, although writer J F Lawton deserves some kind of perverse award for introducing topless former *Playboy* Miss July 1989, Erika Eleniak, into the macho proceedings.

Undoubtedly entertaining, high-gloss hokum.

'Despite a Bond-style emphasis on gadgetry and hardware, the feeling here is not of a lightweight, comic-strip action picture, but of a laughably po-faced adventure yarn.'
Sight and Sound

UNDER SIEGE 2: DARK TERRITORY

(US 1995)

pc WB/Regency Enterprises. exec p Gary Goldstein, Jeffrey Neuman, Martin Wiley. p Steven Seagal, Steve Perry, Arnon Milchan. co-p Julius R Nasso. assoc p Edward McDonnell, Dan Romero, Doug Metzger. d Geoff Murphy. 2nd unit d, sc Dick Ziker. w Richard Hatem, Matt Reeves, based on characters created by J F Lawton. ph Robbie Greenberg. 2nd unit ph Michael Gershman. add ph Alexander Witt, Rick Bota. sfx ph Richard Yuricich. aerial ph Frank Holgate, Don Morgan. Colour. ed Michael Tronic. pd Albert Brenner. ad Carol Wood. sfx co-ord Dale L Martin. m Basil Poledouris. song *After The Train Has Gone* by Steven Seagal, Todd Smallwood. 99 mins

Cast: Steven Seagal (Casey Ryback), Eric Bogosian (Dane), Everett McGill (Penn), Katheriune Heigl (Sarah Ryback), Morris Chestnut (Bobby Zachs), Peter Green, Patrick Kilpatrick, Scitt Sowers (Mercenaries), Alifi (Female Mercenary), Andy Romano (Admiral Bates), Brenda Bakke (Gilder), Jonathan Banks (Scotty), Sandra Taylor (Kelly), Nick Mancuso (Breaker), Royce D Applegate (Ryback's Cook), David Gianpoulos (David Trilling), Dale A Dye (Col. Darza)

UNDER SIEGE

A former US Navy SEAL turned chef foils a renegade scientist who has hijacked a passenger train for use as a moving base from which he can take control of a space satellite and eradicate a huge slice of the USA.

Low-credibility, high-excitement, crowd-pleasing action extravaganza, whose podgy one-man-army hero reprises his stone-faced character from *Under Siege* (1992, q.v.), says little but does much, leaving what little acting is required to villain Bogosian, who does more than enough for a cast of thousands. Characterization is stunted, the stunts are stunning.

'It isn't as good as the original *Under Siege*, but it moves quickly, has great stunts and special effects, and is a lot of fun.'
Chicago Sun-Times

UNDERWORLD USA

(US 1961)
pc Globe Enterprises. p, d, w Samuel Fuller. ph Hal Mohr. B&W. ed Jerome Thoms. ad Robert Peterson. m Harry Sukman. 98 mins

Cast: Cliff Robertson (Tolly Devlin), Dolores Dorn (Cuddles), Beatrice Kay (Sandy), Paul Dubov (Gela), Robert Emhardt (Conners), Larry Gates (Driscoll), Richard Rust (Gus), Gerald Milton (Guther), Allan Gruener (Smith), David Kent (Tolly, aged 12), Sally Mills (Connie), Peter Brocco (Vic Farrar)

A slum boy grows up to be a criminal, and determines to avenge his father's murder which he witnessed as a child.

Fast-moving, shallow and covers familiar ground very competently. The editing is exemplary, Emhardt scores as a venal mob leader, and while it doesn't actually prove Fuller's claim to *auteur* status, it does not detract from it either.

'A slick gangster melodrama made to order for filmgoers who prefer screen fare explosive and uncomplicated.'
Variety

THE UNGUARDED MOMENT

(US 1956)

pc Universal-International. p Gordon Kay. d Harry Keller. w Herb Meadow, Larry Marcus. st Rosalind Russell, Larry Marcus. ph William Daniels. Colour. ed Edward Curtiss. ad Alexander Golitzen, Alfred Sweeney. m Herman Stein. 95 mins

Cast: Esther Williams (Lois Conway), George Nader (Harry Graham), Edward Andrews (Mr Bennett), John Saxon (Leonard Bennett), Les Tremayne (Mr Pendleton), Jack Albertson (Prof), Dani Crayne (Josie Warren), John Wilder (Sandy), Edward Platt (Attorney Briggs), Robert Williams (Detective)

A high-school teacher is the recipient of unwelcome advances from a pupil whose father then conducts a vendetta against her.

Contrived but suspenseful. Particularly notable for a rare non-aquatic (and quite good) performance by Williams.

'There are many exciting situations and a thrilling climax. Smoothly directed and admirably acted.'
CEA Film Report

UNION STATION

(US 1950)

pc Paramount. p Jules Schermer. d Rudolph Maté. w Sydney Boehm. st Thomas Walsh. ph Daniel L Fapp. process ph Farciot Edouart. B&W. ed Ellsworth Hoagland. ad Hans Dreier, Eal Hedrick. m Irving Talbot. 80 mins

Cast: William Holden (Lt William Calhoun), Nancy Olson (Joyce Willecombe), Barry Fitzgerald (Insp. Donnelly), Lyle Bettger (Joe Beacom), Jan Sterling (Marge Wrighter), Allene Roberts (Lorna Murcall), Herbert Heyes (Henry Murcall), Don Dunning (Gus Hadder), Fred Graff (Vince Marley), James Seay (Det. Shattuck), Parley Baer (Gottschalk), Byron Foulger (Horace)

A police inspector and a railway policeman join forces when a millionaire's blind daughter is kidnapped.

Well-used backgrounds of Chicago's crowded Union Station, brisk direction and taut editing add impact, although the details of the police procedure have dated.

'Almost all the action takes place in and about the station and this concentration of scene, together with a sacrifice of character and occasionally of plausibility in the plot, to the demands of speed, make an exciting film.'
Monthly Film Bulletin

AN UNSUITABLE JOB FOR A WOMAN

(GB 1981)

pc Boy's Company. For Goldcrest International. In association with the National Film Finance Corporation. exec p Don Boyd. p Michael Relph, Peter McKay. assoc p David A Barber, Corinne Carter. d Christopher Petit. w Elizabeth McKay, Brian Scobie, Christopher Petit, from the novel by P D James. ph Martin Schäffer. Colour. ed Nick Audlsey. pd Anton Furst. ad John Beard. m Chas Jankel, Philip Bagenal, Peter Van-Hooke. 94 mins

Cast: Billie Whitelaw (Elizabeth Leaming), Pippa Guard (Cordelia Gray), Paul Freeman (James Callender), Dominic Guard (Andrew Lunn), Elizabeth Spriggs (Mrs Marklan), David Horovitch (Sgt Maskell), Bernadette Short (Temp), Dawn Archibald (Isobel), Alex Guard (Mark Callender)

A woman left in charge of a detective agency when her partner commits suicide is hired to investigate the suicide of the son of a rich man, and ends up targeted for murder.

A rigor mortis-inducing blend of tediousness and pretentiousness, with film-critic turned film-maker Petit apparently confusing poor lighting with *film noir*. An unsuitable film for watching.

'A darker picture ... I have never seen. While it may have added to the eerie atmosphere, it would have done better to shed some more light on a thick plot.'
The Daily Telegraph

THE UNTOUCHABLES

(US 1987)

pc Paramount. p Art Linson. assoc p Ray Hartwick. d Brian De Palma. w David Mamet, suggested by the television series, based on the works by Oscar Fraley with Eliot Ness & Paul Tobsky. ph Stephen H Burum. Colour. Panavision. ed Jerry Greenberg, Bill Pankow, Ray Hubley. ad William a Elliott. visual cons Patritzia von Brandenstein. sc Garry Hymes. m Ennio Morricone. cos Marilyn Vance-Straker. 120 mins

Cast: Kevin Costner (Eliot Ness), Sean Connery (Jim Malone), Robert De

THE UNTOUCHABLES

Niro (Al Capone), Charles Martin Smith (Oscar Wallace), Andy Garcia (George Stone), Richard Bradford (Mike), Jack Kehoe (Payne), Billy Drago (Frank Nitti), Patricia Clarkson (Ness's Wife), Vito D'Ambrosio (Bow-tie Driver), Steven Goldstein (Scoop), Peter Aylward (Lt Anderson), Don Harvey (Preseuski)

In Chicago in 1930, US Treasury Bureau Special Agent Eliot Ness forms an elite squad to put an end to Al Capone's violent operations.

Lavishly-mounted, surprisingly unmemorable gangster melodrama that resembles a throwback to thirties genre pictures, with added colour, blood and violence. Connery finally won an Oscar for his forceful playing of a veteran street cop, De Niro put on weight but hardly put his heart into his hammy portrayal of Capone, and Costner's nice-guy blandness worked well in the role.

De Palma's direction is solid but, like De Niro, has a tendency to go over the top. However, there are some potent scenes, and notably his homage to (or depending on your point of view, imitation of) Eisenstein's celebrated 1925 *Battleship Potemkin* Odessa Steps sequence in the station ambush works remarkably well. De Niro replaced originally-cast British character actor Bob Hoskins, whose pain was presumably eased by payment of his entire fee.

'Both this and *Scarface* are largely allegories about power, about America, as if De Palma had switched the self-reflecting games of his "Hitchcock" pictures for a different kind of self-reflection.'
Monthly Film Bulletin

'De Palma's *Untouchables*, like the TV series that inspired it, depends more on clichés than on artistic invention.'
Chicago Sun-Times

THE USUAL SUSPECTS

(US 1995)

pc Polygram/Spelling Films International present A Blue Parrott/Bad Hat Harry Production/Rosco Film GmbH. exec p Robert Jones, Hans Brockman, François Duplat, Art Horan. p Bryan Singer, Michael McDonnell. d Bryan Singer. w Christopher McQuarrie. ph Newton Thomas Sigel. add ph Bruce Douglas Johnson. 2nd unit ph Scott Sakamoto, Eric Goldstein. Colour. ed John Ottman. sc Gary Jensen. 2nd unit sc Ethan Jensen. m John Ottman. 105 mins

Cast: Stephen Baldwin (Michael McManus), Gabriel Byrne (Dean Keaton), Benicio Del Toro (Fred Fenster), Kevin Pollack (Todd Hockney), Kevin Spacey (Roger 'Verbal' Kint), Chazz Palminteri (Dave Kujan), Pete Postlethwaite (Koabayashi), Suzy Amis (Edie Finneran), Giancarlo Esposito (Jack Baer), Dan Hedaya (Jeff Rabin), Paul Bartel (Smuggler), Christine Estabrook (Dr Walters), Carl Bressler (Saul Berg), Philip Simon (Fortier), Jack Shearer (Renault)

Five criminals who meet on a police line-up are recruited for a $3 million heist which goes spectacularly wrong.

An ingenious screenplay with more twists than an anaconda suffering from strychnine poisoning. Vivid characters matched by ideal casting, including Oscar-winner Spacey, fine performances and stylish direction brilliantly reinvent the *noir* thriller on a mere $6 million budget. The story and its execution are so rich that knowledge of the clever climactic twist does not mar the pleasure of subsequent viewings.

One of the finest thrillers of the decade.

'The measure of the success of *The Usual Suspects* is not that it takes you in, but that you it makes you want to be taken in by it. It implicates you in your own duping.'
The Boston Globe

'Give *The Usual Suspects* credit for uniqueness. Director Singer and writer Christopher McQuarrie clearly aren't dummies, and they've taken time to construct a puzzle that holds up under scrutiny.'
San Francicso Chronicle

'The movie is sensational, a modern-day noir about petty crime, a mythic gangster, loyalty, going straight and double crosses. This movie has everything but Humphrey Bogart, and I'm sure he's sorry he was unavailable.'
San Francisco Examiner

'Dark, tortuous and richly atmospheric, *The Usual Suspects* is the most satisfyingly close-textured thriller for years.'
Sight and Sound

VERTIGO

(US 1958)

pc Alfred J Hitchcock Productions. p, d Alfred Hitchcock. assoc p Herbert Coleman. w Alec Coppel, Samuel Taylor, from the novel *D'Entre les Morts* by Pierre Boileau & Thomas Narcejac. ph Robert Burks. Colour. VistaVision. ed George Tomasini. ad Hal Pereira, Henry Bumstead. sfx John P Fulton. special sequence design John Ferren. m Bernard Herrmann. titles Saul Bass. 126 mins

Cast: James Stewart (John 'Scottie' Ferguson), Kim Novak (Madeleine/Judy), Barbara Bel Geddes (Midge), Henry Jones (Coroner), Tom Helmore (Gavin Elster), Raymond Bailey (Doctor), Ellen Corby (Manageress), Konstantin Shayne (Pop Leibel), Lee Patrick (Mistaken Identity), Paul Bryar (Capt. Hansen)

A San Francisco policeman who suffers from vertigo resigns after his acrophobia causes the death of a colleague. Later, shadowing a friend's neurotic wife with whom he falls in love, his fear of heights prevents him from saving her when she throws herself from a bell tower. Then, after a breakdown, he meets her double and is sucked into a bizarre murder plot.

Over-complex, over-leisurely, over-reliant on coincidence, and ultimately offering rather less than meets the eye, but Hitchcock skilfully creates suspension of disbelief, although, almost inevitably, even he fails to coax a believable performance out of Novak, who is a dead dramatic weight in two roles. Stewart is left to carry the film and largely succeeds, giving, in particular, the scenes in which he attempts to refashion the 'double' of his dead love into a new living simulacrum considerable depth and power. Probably the most interesting use of San Francisco locations until *Bullitt* (q.v.) a decade later.

Vertigo is claimed by some to be Hitchcock's masterpiece but does not really reward multiple viewings, since the artificial plot contrivances and Novak's numbing inadequacies tend to become increasingly irksome. Inevitably over-analysed, and as inevitably overrated.

'There is plenty of his old suspense thrill technique in *Vertigo*, the sharp kick-in-the-belly Hitchcock stuff of old.'
Sunday Express

'The production is slick, the performances are good, and San Francisco, the scene of the action, never looked prettier.'
Newsweek

'Pursues its theme of false identity with such plodding persistence that by the time the climactic cat is let out of the bag, the audience has long since had kittens.'
Saturday Review

'It is with some relief that the audience can finally watch Mr Hitchcock, like some benevolently successful conjuror, step in to lift the tension by explaining how it has all been done.'
Times Educational Supplement

VICE SQUAD

(US 1953) (GB: THE GIRL IN ROOM 13)

pc Sequoia Pictures. p Jules Levy,

VERTIGO

Arthur Gardner. d Arnold Laven. w
Lawrence Roman, from the novel
Harness Bull by Leslie T White. ph
Joseph C Biroc. B&W. ed Arthur H
Nadel. ad Carroll Clark. m Herschel
Burke Gilbert. 88 mins

Cast: Edward G Robinson (Capt.
Barnaby), Paulette Goddard (Mona), K
T Stevens (Ginny), Porter Hall (Jack
Hartrampf), Adam Williams (Marty
Kusalich), Edward Binns (Al Barkis),
Lee Van Cleef (Pete), Jay Adler

(Frankie), Joan Vohs (Vickie), Dan
Riss (Lt Imlay), Mary Ellen Kay
(Carol)

During a routine day a police captain
brings a cop killer to book.

Remember *Detective Story*? This
lacklustre piece does, but the formula
doesn't work twice.

'This film never departs from the
pedestrian and the predictable.'
Monthly Film Bulletin

THE VICIOUS CIRCLE
(GB 1957)
pc Romulus. A Beaconsfield
Production. p Peter Rogers. d Gerald
Thomas. w Francis Durbridge, from
his television serial *The Brass
Candlestick*. ph Otto Heller. B&W. ed
Peter Boita. ad Jack Stevens. m Stanley
Black. 84 mins

Cast: John Mills (Dr John Latimer),
Noelle Middleton (Laura James),
Derek Farr (Ken Palmer), Roland

Culver (Det. Insp. Dane), Wilfrid Hyde White (Robert Brady), Mervyn Johns (Dr Kimber), Lionel Jeffries (Geoffrey Windsor), Rene Ray (Mrs Ambler), Lisa Daniely (Freida Veldon)

A doctor who is suspected of murder finally discovers the police are using him as bait to trap an international criminal.

Flaccid and mediocre, all too clearly showing the joins from its television serial orgins.

'Very ordinary entertainment, with little that is fresh or outstanding in its treatment, but which nevertheless offers a certain amount of interest in the working out of its over-complicated and top-heavy with incident story.'
CEA Film Report

VILLAIN
(GB 1971)
pc Anglo-EMI. A Kastner/Ladd/Kanter Picture. exec p Elliott Kastner. p Alan Ladd Jr, Jay Kanter. d Michael Tuchner. w Dick Clement, Ian La Fresnais. adap Al Lettieri, from the novel *The Burden of Proof* by James Barlow. ph Christopher Challis. Colour. Panavision. ed Ralph Sheldon. ad Maurice Carter. m Jonathan Hodge. 98 mins

Cast: Richard Burton (Vic Dakin), Ian McShane (Wolfe Lissner), Nigel Davenport (Bob Matthews), Donald Sinden (Gerald Draycott), Fiona Lewis (Venitia), T P McKenna (Frank Fletcher), Joss Ackland (Edgar Lowis), Cathleen Nesbitt (Mrs Dakin), Elizabeth Knight (Patti), Colin Welland (Tom Binney), Tony Selby (Duncan), John Hallam (Terry), Del

Henney (Webb), James Cossins (Brown), Clive Francis (Vivian)

A mother-fixated, homosexual East End gangster has trouble with his former boyfriend and even more trouble with the police.

White Heat (1949, q.v.) reworked, but where the original had Cagney, this repellent, gratuitously sadistic thriller has to make do with Burton, who mistakes a great deal of acting for good acting.

Apart from the star, it is interestingly cast and competently acted, but signally fails to reach the level of the Hollywood exemplars towards which it strives.

'A tense but ugly film written and played ... in the sawn-off style of TV crime drama but studded with more first rate character studies than TV can usually accommodate.'
Daily Mail

VIOLENT SATURDAY
(US 1955)
pc 20th Century Fox. p Buddy Adler. d Richard Fleischer. w Sydney Boehm, from the novel by William L Heath. ph Charles G Clarke. Colour. CinemaScope. ed Louis Loeffler. ad Lyle Wheeler, George W Davis. m Hugo Friedhofer. 91 mins

Cast: Victor Mature (Shelley Martin), Richard Egan (Boyd), Stephen McNally (Harper), Virginia Leith (Linda), Lee Marvin (Dill), Tommy Noonan (Harry Reeves), Margaret Hayes (Emily Fairchild), J Carroll Naish (Chapman), Sylvia Sidney (Elsie Braden), Ernest Borgnine (Stadt), Brad Dexter (Clayton), Dorothy Patrick

(Helen), Billy Chapin (Steve Martin)

Three criminals stage a brutal bank hold-up in a small midwestern town, and their actions catalyse the townspeople.

Routine, with pretensions towards significant character analysis of both robbers and townspeople, although director Richard Fleischer is more at ease with storytelling than with psychology. Marvin and Borgnine create the only three-dimensional characters.

'A big, rough, savvy sort of pell-meller, perhaps the best thing of its crude kind that Hollywood has offered in 1955.'
Time

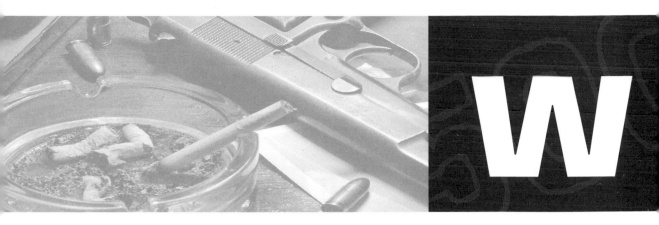

W
(US 1973)
pc Bing Crosby Productions. exec p Charles A Pratt. p Mel Ferrer. d Richard Quine. w Gerald Di Pego, James Kelly. st Ronald Shusett, James Kelly. ph Gerry Hirschfeld. Colour. ed Gene Milford. ad Cary Odell. m Johnny Mandel. 95 mins

Cast: Twiggy (Katie Lewis), Michael Witney (Ben Lewis), Eugene Roche (Charles Jasper), Dirk Benedict (William Caulder), John Vernon (Arnie Felson), Michael Conrad (Lt Whitfield), Alfred Ryder (Investigator), Carmen Zapata (Betty), Dave Morick (Paul), Ken Lynch (Guard), Peter Walker (Prison Official)

A psychopath terrorizes his ex-wife and her second husband.

Uncertain in tone and over-directed, its leading lady tries hard but is embarrassingly out of her dramatic depth.

'Looks like low-budget telly-filler-fodder, including establishing shots of terrain (designed to show you what you are missing after a commercial break) and violence carefully matched to late-night settee taste.'
The Observer

WAIT UNTIL DARK
(US 1967)
pc WB/Seven Arts. p Mel Ferrer. d Terence Young. w Robert Carrington, Jane Howard Carrington, from the play by Frederick Knott. ph Charles Lang. Colour. ed Gene Milford. ad George Jenkins. m Henry Mancini. title song lyrics by Jay Livingston, Ray Evans. 108 mins

Cast: Audrey Hepburn (Susy Hendrix), Alan Arkin (Roat), Richard Crenna (Mike Talman), Effrem Zimbalist Jr (Sam Hendrix), Jack Weston (Carlino), Samantha Jones (Lisa), Julie Herrod (Gloria), Frank O'Brien (Shatner)

Three hoodlums searching for a doll stuffed with heroin terrorize a blind woman in her apartment.

While never entirely managing to disguise its single-set stage origins, Young achieves a sweaty measure of claustrophobia and suspense, and stages at least one memorable shock when, in an effect that has now become a cliché, an apparently dead person turns out to be alive and leaps at the heroine. But the play's *coup de théâtre*, when the totally dark stage was suddenly flooded with the light from an opened refrigerator, is, unfortunately, muffed. Hepburn is rather more credible than usual, and Arkin is genuinely chilling.

'When you find yourself screaming advice to a movie heroine in peril, you know you're seeing one hell of a scary movie.'
Playboy

'Sometimes a tiresome play suffers a sea-change on its way to the screen and turns into something thoroughly enjoyable. Not so, unfortunately, Frederick Knott's last long-running stage thriller. Indeed, it has hardly been changed at all ... all the arguments against the play still hold good of the film, starting with its glaring improbability and the extreme wastefulness of the means in relation to the end.'
The Times

WARNING SHOT
(US 1966)
pc Bob Banner Associates. p, d Buzz

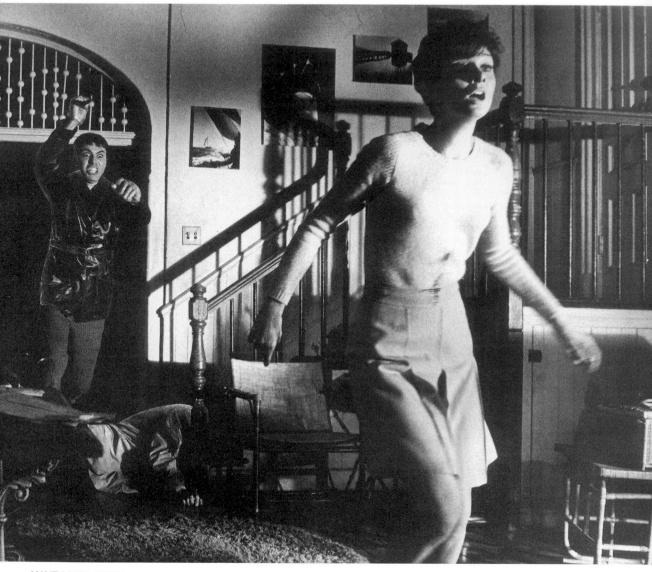

WAIT UNTIL DARK

Kulik. assoc p Tom Egan. w Mann Rubin, from the novel *711 – Officer Needs Help* by Whit Masterson. ph Joseph Biroc. optical sfx Paul K Lerpae. Colour. ed Archie Marshek. ad Hal Pereira, Roland Anderson. m Jerry Goldsmith. 100 mins

Cast: David Janssen (Sgt Tom Valens), Ed Begley (Capt. Klodin), Keenan Wynn (Sgt Musso), Sam Wanamaker (Frank Sanderman), Lilian Gish (Alice Willows), Stefanie Powers (Liz Thayer), Eleanor Parker (Mrs Ruston), George Grizzard (Walt Cody), George Sanders (Calvin York), Steve Allen (Perry Knowland), Carroll O'Connor (Paul Jerez), Joan Collins (Joanie Valens), Walter Pidgeon (Orville Armes), John Garfield Jr (Police Surgeon), Vito Scotti (Designer)

A Los Angeles policeman has to try and clear himself when the sex killer he shoots turns out to be a respected doctor.

Fast-paced throwback to forties thrillers, with a strong and interesting cameo cast, enjoyably laconic dialogue and competent direction.

'A very timely police drama, in which fine production, direction and

performances overcome a sometimes-flawed script ... pic has the immediacy of contemporary headlines about police brutality, irresponsibility, etc.'
Variety

WHERE THE SIDEWALK ENDS

(US 1950)
pc 20th Century Fox. p, d Otto Preminger. w Ben Hecht. adap Victor Trivas, Frank P Rosenberg, Robert E Hunt, from the novel *Night Cry* by William L Stuart. ph Joseph La Shelle. B&W. ed Louis Loeffler. ad Lyle Wheeler, J Russell Spencer. sfx Fred Sersen. md Lionel Newman. m Cyril Mockridge. 95 mins

Cast: Dana Andrews (Mark Dixon), Gene Tierney (Morgant Taylor), Gary Merrill (Scalise), Bert Freed (Klein), Tom Tully (Jiggs Taylor), Karl Malden (Lt Thomas), Ruth Donnelly (Martha), Craig Stevens (Ken Paine), Robert Simon (Insp. Foley), Harry Von Zell (Ted Morrison), Don Appell (Willie), Neville Brand (Steve), Grace Mills (Mrs Tribaum), Lou Krugman (Mike Williams)

A brutal police officer who accidentally kills a suspect during interrorgation tries to pass the death off as a gangland killing.

Routine, stolid, and unconvincing to boot.

'A competent but not very exciting murder story.'
Sunday Dispatch

WHILE THE CITY SLEEPS

(US 1956)
pc RKO. p Bert Friedlob. d Fritz Lang. w Casey Robinson, from the novel *The Bloody Spur* by Charles Einstein. ph Ernest Laszlo. B&W. ed Gene Fowler Jr. ad Carroll Clark. m Herschel Burke Gilbert. 100 mins

Cast: Dana Andrews (Ed Mobley), Ida Lupino (Mildred Donner), Sally Forrest (Nancy Liggett), George Sanders (Mark Loving), Thomas Mitchell (John Griffith), Rhonda Fleming (Dorothy Kyne), Vincent Price (Walter Kyne), Howard Duff (Lt Kaufman), James Craig (Harry Kritzer), John Barrymore Jr (Robert Manners), Robert Warwick (Amos Kyne), Vladimir Sokoloff (George Pilski), Mae Marsh (Mrs Manners), Ralph Peters (Meade)

The new playboy owner of a press empire offers a top job to the journalist who scoops the story of a psychopathic killer terrorizing the city.

Enjoyable combination of thriller, newspaper melodrama and back-stabbing office politics, zestfully acted and inventively directed by Lang, who resolutely ignores the coincidences, implausibilities and lacunae in the plot in favour of getting on with the primary job of storytelling.

'The realistic and sophisticated dialogue is the kind more often encountered in the freer framework of a play than in films. An excellent cast and good direction keep the threads of the plot at an entertaining level throughout.'
Library Journal

WHITE HEAT

(US 1949)
pc WB. p Louis F Eedman. d Raoul Walsh. w Ivan Goff, Ben Roberts. st Virginia Kellog. ph Sid Hickok. B&W. ed Owen Marks. ad Edward Carrere. sfx Roy Davidson, H F Koenekamp. m Max Steiner. 114 mins

Cast: James Cagney (Cody Jarrett), Virginia Mayo (Verna Jarrett), Edmond O'Brien (Hank Fallon/Vic Pardo), Margaret Wycherly (Ma Jarrett), Steve Cochran (Big Ed Somers), John Archer (Philip Evans), Wally Cassell (Cotton Valetti), Fred Clark (Daniel Winston), Ford Rainey (Zuckie Hommell), Fred Coby (Happy Taylor), Paul Guilfoyle (Parker), Robert Osterloh (Tommy Ryley)

A psychopathic, mother-fixated gangster breaks out of jail and embarks on a crime spree which is ended by the undercover policeman who infiltrates his gang.

Cagney, returning with heady relish to the genre that brought him stardom, created one of his most memorable screen hoodlums, whose amoral sadism and unregenerate evil overlaid with a remarkably overt (for the period) Oedipal fixation dominates a vivid, slightly old-fashioned thriller, recalling the heyday of the gangster film a decade earlier. In effect, Cagney's Cody Jarrett is the last dinosaur. His triumphant 'Made it, Ma! Top of the world!', shouted just before his fiery end on the summit of an exploding gas tank, is a classic, subsequently much-parodied sequence, and an effective climax to brutal and violent proceedings directed with driving, no-nonsense vigour by Walsh, a veteran like Cagney and, like him, essentially a throwback to an earlier, more direct cinema age. (Migraine sufferers may derive some minor

WHITE HEAT

comfort from the fact that blinding headaches are offered as a partial excuse for Cagney's antisocial behaviour, although it would be an unwise defence to offer recurrent headaches as justification for real-life, as opposed to reel-life, crime.)

Virginia Kellogg received an Academy Award nomination for her original story.

'Tense and grimly unleasant, this streamlined essay in hoodlum depravity is a good example of the sort of film which Hollywood does so well.'
Time and Tide

'A wild and exciting mixture of mayhem and madness.'
Life Magazine

'The director has seen to it that the audience never has time to lose interest in the record of murder, and the screenwriters have seen to it that death and savagery dominate the tale.'
The Sunday Times

WHITE LIGHTNING
(US 1973)
pc UA. A Levy-Gardner-Laven Production. p Arthur Gardner, Jules V Levy. d Joseph Sargent. 2nd unit d Hal Needham. w William Norton. ph Edward Rosson. 2nd unit ph Jack Williams. Colour. ed George

THE WINDOW

Nicholson. sfx Cliff Wenger. sfx
ph/titles Westheimer Company. m
Charles Bernstein. 101 mins

Cast: Burt Reynolds (Gator
McKlusky), Jennifer Billingsley (Lou),
Ned Beatty (Sheriff Connors), Bo
Hopkins (Roy Boone), Matt Clark
(Dude Watson), Louise Latham
(Martha Culpepper), Diane Ladd
(Maggie), R G Armstrong (Big Bear),
Conlan Carter (Deputy), Dabbs Greer

(Pa McKlusky), John Steadman
(Skeeter)

A moonshiner is released from jail to
help Treasury agents bring the corrupt
Arkansas sheriff who murdered his
brother to justice.

Pacy and painless, with plenty of
action and some briskly-staged car
chases. Reynolds reprised his character
and made his directorial debut in the
1976 sequel *Gator*.

'A highly professional piece of work,
swift and suspenseful, with a good
sense of time, place and ominous
atmosphere.'
Los Angeles Times

THE WHOLE TRUTH
(GB 1958)
pc Romulus. p Jack Clayton. d John
Guillermin. w Jonathan Latimer, from
the play by Philip Mackie. ph Wilkie
Cooper. B&W. ed Gerry Hambling. ad

THE WINDOW

Tony Masters. m Mischa Spoliansky. 85 mins

Cast: Stewart Granger (Max Poulton), Donna Reed (Carol Poulton), George Sanders (Carliss), Gianna Maria Canale (Gina Bertini), Michael Shillo (Insp. Simon), Richard Molinas (Gilbert), Peter Dyneley (Willy Reichel), John Van Eyssen (Archer), Philip Vickers (Jack Leslie)

A film producer is framed for the murder of an actress.

Implausible timewaster – and the actors behave as though they know it.

'Hardly worth the while of its star cast.'
Picturegoer

THE WINDOW
(US 1949)
pc RKO. p Frederic Ullman Jr. d Ted Tetzlaff. w Mel Dinelli, from the novelette *The Boy Cried Murder* by Cornell Woolrich. ph William Steiner. Colour. ed Frederick Knudson. ad Walter E Cornell, Sam Corso. sfx Russell a Cully. m Roy Webb. 73 mins

Cast: Barbara Hale (Mrs Woodry), Bobbie Driscoll (Tommy), Arthur Kennedy (Mr Woodry), Paul Stewart (Joe Kellerton), Ruth Roman (Mrs Kellerton), Anthony Ross ((Ross), Richard Benedict (Drunken Sailor), Jim Nolan (Stranger on Street), Ken Terrell (Man), Lee Kass (Reporter), Lee Phelps, Eric Mack, Charles Flynn, Budd Fine, Carl Faulkner, Lloyd Dawson, Carl Saxe (Policemen), Tex Swan (Milkman)

A young boy who is an inveterate storyteller witnesses a murder and almost loses his life because neither his parents nor the police will believe him.

Twelve-year-old Driscoll won a special Academy Award as Outstanding Juvenile Actor for this vivid suspenser, which, voted best mystery film of the year by the Mystery Writers of America, benefits from taut, unpretentious direction and the sharply-characterized, paranoia-prone 'boy-who-cried-wolf' screenplay. A minor low-budget classic.

'It is a show that can be highly recommended and it is a piece of suspense entertainment seldom equalled.'
Variety

WITNESS
(US 1985)
pc Paramount. p Edward S Feldman. co-p David Bombyk. assoc p Wendy Weir. d Peter Weir. w Earl W Wallace, William Keley. st William Kelley, Pamela Wallace, Earl W Wallace. ph John Seale. 2nd unit ph Chuck Clifton. Colour. ed Thom Noble. pd Stan Jolley. m Maurice Jarre. sfx John R Elliot. 112 mins

Cast: Harrison Ford (John Book), Kelly McGillis (Rachel Lapp), Josef Sommer (Paul Schaeffer), Lukas Haas (Samuel Lapp), Jan Rubes (Eli Lapp), Alexander Godunov (Daniel Hochleitner), Danny Glover (McFee), Brent Jennings (Carter), Patti LuPone (Elaine), Angus McInnes (Fergie), Frederick Rolf (Stoltzfus), Viggo Mortensen (Moses Hochleitner), Ed Crowley (Sheriff)

A policeman and a young Amish boy who witnesses a murder in Philadelphia hide out in the Amish community where the cop falls for a young woman – but the killers come after them.

A palpable hit, well-deserved by Australian film-maker Weir, who, in his American directorial debut, expertly blends suspense and romance against the interesting, well-realized Amish background, and elicits fine performances from his principals. Oscar-winning editing sets the pace.

'A remarkable film – both an exciting thriller and a beautifully directed meditation on violence.'
New York Magazine

WITNESS FOR THE PROSECUTION
(US 1957)
pc Theme Pictures. An Edward Small Presentation. p Arthur Hornblow Jr. d Billy Wilder. w Billy Wilder, Harry Kurnitz. adap Larry Marcus, from the play by Agatha Christie. ph Russell Harlan. B&W. ed Daniel Mandell. ad Alexander Trauner. m Matty Malneck. song *I May Never Go Home Any More* by Ralph Arthur Roberts, Jack Brooks. 116 mins

Cast: Tyrone Power (Leonard Vole), Marlene Dietrich (Christine Vole), Charles Laughton (Sir Wilfrid Roberts), Elsa Lanchester (Miss Plimsoll), John Williams (Brogan-Moore), Henry Daniell (Mayhew), Ian Wolfe (Carter), Una O'Connor (Janet Mackenzie), Torin Thatcher (Mr Meyers), Francis Compton (Judge), Norma Varden (Mrs French), Philip Tonge (Insp. Hearne), Ruta Lee (Diana), Molly Roden (Miss McHugh), J Pat O'Malley (Shorts Salesman)

An eminent Queen's Counsel undertaking the apparently hopeless defence of a murderer is thoroughly taken in.

Wilder adds wit to Christie and delivers an engrossing, plot-heavy whodunnit decorated with Laughton's engagingly over-the-top performance as a defence lawyer, apparently based on Sir Winston Churchill but without the latter's reticence.

He and Lanchester (delightful as his much put-upon nurse) are first-rate and were both Academy Award-nominated, as were Wilder and the film. Power, however, looks unwell and uneasy and is lacklustre, while Dietrich ranges from bad to risible.

'The whole story, in fact, is fair to good Christie, with interest focused not on character or plausibility but on the mechanics and turns of the plot. This kind of subject offers no great opportunities to the director, other than to keep the plot machinery going firmly and to sustain court-room suspense. Billy Wilder efficiently manages both.'
Monthly Film Bulletin

WOMAN IN HIDING
(US 1949)

pc Universal-International. p Michael Kraike. d Michael Gordon. w Oscar Saul, from the *Saturday Evening Post* serial *Fugitive From Terror* by James R Webb. ph William Daniels. B&W. ed Milton Carruth. ad Bernard Herzbrun, Robert Clatworthy. m Frank Skinner. 92 mins

Cast: Ida Lupino (Deborah Chandler Clark), Howard Duff (Keith Ramsey), Stephen McNally (Selden Clark), John

Litel (John Chandler), Taylor Holmes (Lucius Maury), Irving Bacon (Link), Don Beddoe (Fat Salesman), Joe Besser (Salesman), Peggy Castle (Waitress)

A woman survives an attempt by her husband to kill her in a faked car accident, and has to keep one jump ahead of him while trying to prove his guilt.

Lupino and Duff's first screen teaming is competent, with pace and tension but little style.

'It's action all the way and well-planned action at that. Although basically just a thriller, it has intelligence in its construction.'
Picturegoer

THE WOMAN IN THE WINDOW
(US 1944)

pc International Picture. p, w Nunnally Johnson, from the novel *Off Guard* by J H Wallis. d Fritz Lang. ph Milton Krasner. B&W. sup ed Paul Weatherwax. ed Marjorie Johnson, Gene Fowler Jr. ad Duncan Cramer. sfx Vernon L Walker. m Arthur Lange. 99 mins

Cast: Edward G Robinson (Richard Wanley), Joan Bennett (Alice Reed), Raymond Massey (Frank Lalor), Edmund Breon (Dr Barkstane), Dan Duryea (Heidt), Thomas E Jackson (Insp. Jackson), Arthur Loft (Mazard), Dorothy Peterson (Mrs Wanley), Frank Dawson (Steward), Carol Cameron (Elsie), Bobby (Robert) Blake (Dickie), Arthur Space (Capt. Kennedy), Alec Craig (Garageman)

A professor becomes involved with a

beautiful woman in New York and is drawn into murder and blackmail while his wife and family are on vacation.

Involving *film noir*, with Lang rather less self-consciously clever than usual, although his badly misjudged cop-out ending – the drama is revealed to be a dream – fatally undercuts its impact. Robinson is impressive, Duryea is superb as a blackmailer.

'A chilling study in crime. It belongs to the same brutal school of murder films as *Double Indemnity* in that you see the murder committed near the beginning of the film, and the plot is less concerned with mystery (practically no mystery at all) than with suspense ... the whole film, mainly because of its fine photography, effective cutting, and Fritz Lang direction, is like a bad dream.'
The Commonweal

WOMAN OF STRAW
(GB 1964)

pc Novus. A Michael Relph and Basil Dearden Production. p Michael Relph. d Basil Dearden. w Robert Muller, Stanley Mann, Michael Relph, from the novel by Catherine Arley. ph Otto Heller. Colour. ed John D Gutheridge. pd Ken Adam. ad Peter Murton. m Muir Matheson. title song Norman Percival. 117 mins

Cast: Gina Lollobrigida (Maria), Sean Connery (Anthony Richmond), Ralph Richardson (Charles Richmond), Johnny Sekka (Thomas), Lawrence Hardy (Baines), Danny Daniels (Fenton), A J Brown (Third Executive), Peter Madden (Yacht Captain), Alexander Knox (Lomer),

Edward Underdown (First Executive), George Curzon (Second Executive), Andre Morell (Judge)

A nurse and her lover, the nephew of a millionaire, plan to kill his wheelchair-bound uncle, but their scheme misfires.

Handsomely-produced, with expensive settings, a thin story and even more emaciated performances.

'I can't see *Woman of Straw* as anything more than an elaborate, moody psychological drama-cum-thriller, show to get under way and unexcitingly but capably made with a luxury budget to compensate for the absence of low-cost ingenuity.'
Films and Filming

WORLD FOR RANSOM

(US 1953)
pc Allied Artists. p Robert Aldrich, Bernard Tabakin. d Robert Aldrich. w Lindsay Hardy. ph Joseph Biroc. B&W. ed Michael Luciano. ad William Glasgow. m Frank DeVol. song *Too Soon* by Walter Samuels. 82 mins

Cast: Dan Duryea (Mike Callahan), Gene Lockhart (Alexis Pederas), Patric Knowles (Julian March), Reginald Denny (Major Bone), Nigel Bruce (Governeor Coutts), Marian Carr (Frennessey March), Douglas Dumbrille (Insp. McCollum), Keye Luke (Wong), Arthur Shields (Sean O'Connor)

An adventurer is caught up in a scheme to kidnap a nuclear scientist in Singapore.

A confused, television-inspired (by Duryea's series *China Smith*) film with

a palsied grip and few thrills. The sole surprise is the involvement of Aldrich.

'It will get by as a supporter.'
Variety

THE WRONG MAN

(US 1956)
pc WB. p, d Alfred Hitchcock. assoc p Herbert Coleman. w Maxwell Anderson, Angus McPhail, from *The True Story of Christopher Emmanuel Balastrero* by Maxwell Anderson. ph Robert Burks. B&W. ed George Thomasini. ad Paul Sylbert, William L Kuehl. m Bernard Herrmann. 105 mins

Cast: Henry Fonda (Manny Balastrero), Vera Miles (Rose Balestrero), Anthony Quayle (O'Connor), Harold J Stone (Lt Bowers), Esther Minciotti (Manny's Mother), Charles Cooper (Det. Matthews), John Heldabrand (Tomasini), Doreen Lang (Mrs James), Laurinda Barrett (Constance Willis), Norma Connolly (Betty Todd), Nehemiah Persoff (Gene Conforti), Lola D'Annunzio (Olga Conforti), Dayton Lummis (Judge Groat), Werner Klemperer (Dr Banay)

A New York musician is wrongly identified as a hold-up man, and his ordeal at the hands of the law drives his wife into an insane asylum before the real perpetrator is apprehended.

Resolutely downbeat, fact-based case history, whose detailed depiction of police procedure and obvious good intentions do not compensate for the overall tedium of an aberrant Hitchcock offering that stylistically resembles a sincere but ininspired television true-life

docudrama with its heart – but little else – in the right place.

'It seems ungrateful to be disappointed but to me the film achieves dullness without conviction. I like my factual films to be less theatrical. I like my Hitchcock to be more Hitchcock.'
The Observer

YEAR OF THE DRAGON
(US 1985)

pc Dino De Laurentiis Corporation. for MGM/UA. p Dino De Laurentiis. d Michael Cimino. w Oliver Stone, Michael Cimino, from the book by Robert Daley. ph Alex Thompson. 2nd unit ph Francis Grumman. Colour. ed Françoise Bonnot. pd Wolf Kroeger. ad Vicki Paul. sfx co-ord Jeff Jarvis. m David Mansfield. 136 mins

Cast: Mickey Rourke (Capt. Stanley White), John Lone (Go Joey Tai), Ariane (Tracy Tzu), Leonard Termo (Angelo Rizzo), Ray Barry (Louis Bukowski), Caroline Kava (Connie White), Eddie Jones (William McKenna), Joey Chin (Ronnie Chang), Victor Wong (Harry Yung), K Dock Yip (Milton Bin), Pao Han Lin (Fred Hung), Mark Hamner (Commissioner Sullivan), Dennis Dun (Herbert Kwong), Fabia Drake (Nun)

A New York policeman who is a Vietnam veteran and hates Orientals is assigned to rid Chinatown of violent youth gangs, and clashes with a young crimelord.

Violent, vigorous and lavishly-produced, but badly over-inflated and ultimately routine.

'Never as important as director Michael Cimino thinks it is, but there's a fair amount of solid action and gunplay.'
Variety

THE YELLOW BALLOON
(GB 1952)

pc ABPC. A Marble Arch Production. p Victor Skutezky. d J Lee Thompson. w Anne Burnaby, J Lee Thompson. ph Gilbert Taylor. B&W. ed Richard Best. ad Robert Jones. m Philip Green. 80 mins

Cast: Andrew Ray (Frankie), Kathleen Ryan (Em), Kenneth More (Ted), William Sylvester (Len), Bernard Lee (Police Constable Chapman), Stephen Fenemore (Ron), Marjorie Rhodes (Mrs Stokes), Elliott Makeham (Pawnbroker), Veronica Hurst (Sunday School Teacher), Hy Hazell (Mary), Sandra Dorne (Iris), Campbell Singer (Potter), Peter Jones (Spiv), Sidney James (Barrow Boy)

A petty criminal convinces a young boy that he has murdered a friend, and forces him to help commit a robbery.

Minor suspenser with good cinematography. Ray gives an attractive performance as the youngster under pressure.

'Melodramatic, but nevertheless convincing; it moves fairly swiftly and works up to a tense and exciting, if horrifying climax.'
CEA Film Report

YELLOW DOG
(GB 1973)

pc Akari Productions. p, d Terence Donovan. assoc p David Barber. w Shinobu Hashimoto, from an idea by Terence Donovan. translated from the Japanese by Prof. Alan Turney. add dial John Bird. ph David Watkin. Colour. Panavision. ed Fergus McDonnell. pd Roger Burridge. ad Bernard Spencer. sfx Nick Alder. m Ron Grainer. 101 mins

Cast: Jiry Tamiya (Kimura), Robert

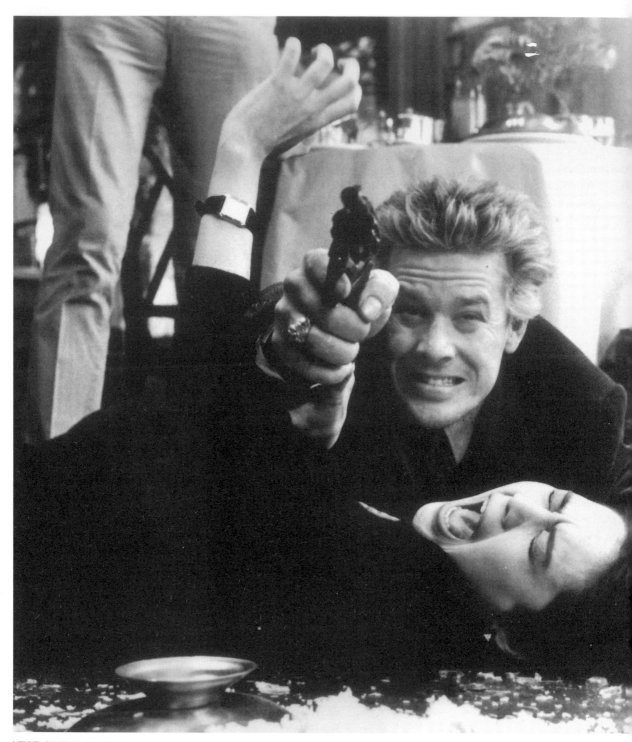

YEAR OF THE DRAGON

Hardy (Alexander), Carolyn Seymour (Delia), Joseph O'Conor (Dover), Hilary Tindall (Helen), Jonathan Newth (Tim), Keith Drinkel (Eric), Madge Ryan (Della's Mother), Gay Singleton (Della 2), Angela Thorne (Jenny Alexander), Annabel Lord (Paulie Alexander), Geoffrey Lumsden (Sir William Renfrew), Harold Innocent (Marceau), Belinda Carroll (Miss Henderson), Jerome Willis (Hawk Curtis)

A Japanese secret agent comes to London to protect a mysterious scientist.

Perversely enjoyable comedy-thriller whose bizarre plot ranges between opacity and near-incoherence and is decorated in high-camp style by debuting director Donovan. Odd but endearing.

It is quite fortuitous that Oriental cinema has enjoyed such a boom since *Yellow Dog* went into production. However, it may well be that that happy coincidence will introduce the film to an audience that might otherwise have shied away. Certainly this brave little curio deserves all the support it gets.'
Films Illustrated

YOU CAN'T GET AWAY WITH MURDER
(US 1939)

pc First National/WB. assoc p Samuel Bischoff. d Lewis Seiler. w Robert Buckner, Don Ryan, Kenneth Gamet, from the play *Chalked Out* by Warden Lewis E Rawes & Jonathan Finn. ph Sol Polito. B&W. ed James Gibbon. ad Hugh Reticker. m Heinz Roemheld. 78 mins

Cast: Humphrey Bogart (Frank Wilson), Billy Halop (Johnnie Stone), Gale Page (Madge Stone), John Litel (Attorney Carey), Henry Travers (Pop), Harvey Stephens (Fred Burke), Harold Huber (Scappa), Joe Sawyer (Red), Joseph Downing (Smitty), George E Stone (Toad), Joseph King (Principal Keeper), Joseph Crehan (Warden), Herbert Rawlinson (District Attorney). Frank Faylen (Spieler)

A small-time hoodlum introduces a young man to a life of crime.

Routine B-feature, with Bogart wearing the same suit he wore in similar programmers and giving a similar performance. Well enough done, but hardly worth it.

'Though it contains nothing new, it is all done with a grim realism that carries conviction ... see it, if you like strong stuff.'
Film Weekly

YOU ONLY LIVE TWICE
(GB 1967)

pc Eon/Danjaq. p Harry Saltzman, Albert R Broccoli. d Lewis Gilbert. 2nd unit d, ed Peter Hunt. action sequences d Bob Simmons. w Roald Dahl. add st material Harry Jack Bloom, from the novel by Ian Fleming. ph Freddie Young. 2nd unit ph Bob Huke. aerial ph John Jordan. underwater ph Lamar Boren. Colour. Panavision. pd Ken Adam. ad Harry Pottle. sfx John Stears. m John Barry. title song John Barry, Leslie Bricusse, sung by Nancy Sinatra. titles Maurice Binder. 116 mins

Cast: Sean Connery (James Bond), Akiko Wakabayashi (Aki), Tetsuro Tamba (Tiker Tanaka), Mia Hama (Kissy Suzuki), Teru Shimada (Osatu), Karin Dor (Helga Brandt), Bernard Lee ('M'), Lois Maxwell (Miss Moneypenny), Desmond Llewellyn ('Q'), Charles Gray (Henderson), Tsai Chin (Chinese Girl), Donald Pleasence (Blofeld), Alexander Knox (US President), Robert Hutton (Presidential Aide), Burt Kwouk (SPECTRE 3), Michael Chow (SPECTRE 4)

SPECTRE snatches an American space capsule from its orbit and dangerous tension builds between the US and the Soviet Union, until Bond saves the day.

Connery's fifth outing as 007 shows him in complete command of the role – and vice versa. But despite the usual lavish production design and stunning sets, plethora of amazing gadgets (including a do-it-yourself helicopter kit), well-orchestrated mayhem and well-used Japanese locations, the proceedings have a feeling of *déjà vu* – by now the Bond formula had been adopted and adapted by many other moviemakers and the originality had been replaced by familiarity.

'He is the victim of the same misfortune that befell Frankenstein – there have been so many flamboyant imitations that the original looks like a copy.'
Time

'Represents the ultimate triumph of gadgetry. Plot twists are devised simply to use the gadgets.'
Village Voice

YOUNG AND INNOCENT

'Really no better and no worse than its predecessors, the fifth James Bond is rather less enjoyable mainly because the formula has become so completely mechanical (and Bond himself so predictably indestructible) without any compensation in other directions.'
Monthly Film Bulletin

'*Young and Innocent* may be superficial – but it is enjoyable enough to repay a second visit.'
The Spectator

YOUNG AND INNOCENT
(GB 1937)
pc Gainsborough-Gaumont British. p Edward Black. d Alfred Hitchcock. w Charles Bennett, from the novel *A Shilling for Candles* by Josephine Tey. ph Bernard Knowles. B&W. ed Charles Frend. ad Alfred Junge. md Louis Levy. 84 mins

Cast: Derrick de Marney (Robert Tidall), Nova Pilmeam (Erica), Percy Marmont (Col. Burgoyne), Edward Rigby (Old Will), Mary Clare (Erica's Aunt), John Longden (Kent), George Curzon (Roy), Basil Radford (Uncle Basil), Pamela Carme (Christine Clay), George Merritt (Miller), J H Roberts (Solicitor), Jerry Verno (Truck Driver), H F Maltby (Court Sergeant), Torin Thatcher (Dosshouse Owner), John Miller (Court Constable)

A man is falsely accused of murder, escapes from the police, and sets out to clear himself with the help of a young woman.

Fast-moving minor Hitchcock comedy-thriller with just about enough of his trademark 'touches' – notably the long crane shot that tracks across a crowded ballroom to end in a dramatic close-up of the killer's twitching eyelid – to compensate for lack of depth and a lightweight cast.

THE MAGNIFICENT 25 B-FEATURES

In the sadly long-dead heyday of cinema, when television broadcasts were still relatively infrequent (but as intellect-eroding as they are today), moviegoers were treated to two films for the price of one, and the bottom half of the regulation double bill could be a treasure trove of unsung second features that were sometimes unexpectedly more entertaining than the expensive 'big' films people had actually paid to see.

Quite a few major directors cut their celluloid teeth on B-features, giving pleasure to many at the time, and even more pleasure to those later generations of *cinéastes* and movie buffs who, armed with hindsight, found themes, signals and felicities in these early works that might well have surprised their creators, who rightly believed at the time that they were simply earning quick bucks making quick movies whose sole purpose was to serve as a cheap support for A-features, and which were never intended for major critical scrutiny. They weren't *all* good. Indeed, some B-features were so terrible that their only destiny – unhappily too often fulfilled – is as time-wasting fodder on late-night television.

It has been claimed that nobody actually sets out to make a bad movie. Perhaps. Hopefully, the good, bad and indifferent B-features that follow prove the point, though, to be honest, it is a very close-run thing. The one attribute they have in common (apart from patently low budgets) is that they were not intended to be seen as single features.

Remember that when you watch them now.

ABY FACE NELSON

(US 1957)

c A Fryman-ZS Production. p Al
Zimbalist. d Don Siegel. w Irving
Schulman, Daniel Mainwaring. ph
Hal Mohr. B&W. m Van Alexander.
85 mins

Cast: Mickey Rooney (Lester
Gillis/Baby Face Nelson), Carolyn
Jones (Sue), Cedric Hardwicke (Doc
Saunders), Chris Dark (Jerry) Ted de
Corsia (Rocca), Leo Gordon (John
Dillinger), Dan Terranova (Miller),
Emile Meyer (Mac), Anthony Caruso
(Hamilton), Jack Elam (Fatso), John
Hoyt (Parker)

Violent biopic of the thirties gangster.
Made fast (some 16 days) and
cheap (circa $170,000), this is an
action-packed and enjoyably amoral
genre piece in which psychology and
motivation are subordinated to the
demands of fast-moving exploitation.
Rooney clearly relishes his role, and
Siegel's direction makes the most of the
occasionally unbelievable.

'This film," intones a March of Times
voice, "was made as a tribute to the
FBI." And if you believe that one, my
friends, you'll believe anything. As a
piece of film-making Baby-Face Nelson
is hard, fast and efficient. As a social
document, it is utterly corrupt.'
Evening Standard

THE BONNIE PARKER STORY

(US 1958)

c AIP. exec p James H Nicholson,
Samuel Z Arkoff. p, w Stanley
Shpetner. d William Witney. ph Jack
Marta. B&W. sfx Thol Simionson. m
Ronald Stein. 81 mins

Cast: Dorothy Provine (Bonnie
Parker), Jack Hogan (Guy Darrow),
Richard Bakalyan (Duke Jefferson),
Joseph Turkel (Chuck Darrow),
William Stevens (Paul), Ken Lynch
(Restaurant Manager), Douglas
Kennedy (Tom Steel), Joel Colin
(Bobby), Patti Huston (Chuck's Girl),
Vince Williams (Narrator)

When her bank robber husband is
jailed for life, Bonnie Parker takes up
with two small-time crooks and
embarks on a life of violent lawlessness.

Low-budget, luridly fictionalized
biopic of the thirties public enemy,
more vigorous than memorable,
although Dorothy Provine is rather
better as Bonnie Parker than Faye
Dunaway in the overrated 1967
Bonnie and Clyde (q.v.).

'Sheer brutality is the keynote of its
entertainment value and its poor
moral tone merits an "X" label.'
CEA Film Report

BULLDOG DRUMMOND'S
REVENGE

(US 1937)

pc Paramount. d Louis King. w Edward
T Lowe, from the novel *The Return of
Bulldog Drummond* by 'Sapper' (rn H C
McNeile) ph Harry Fishbeck. B&W. ad
Hans Dreier, Robert O'Dell. m Boris
Morros. 60 mins

Cast: John Barrymore (Col. Neilson),
John Howard (Hugh 'Bulldog'
Drummond), Louise Campbell (Phyllis
Clavering), Reginald Denny (Algy
Longworth), E E Clive (Tenny), Frank
Puglia (Draven Neigais), Nydia Westman
(Gwen Longworth), Robert Glecker
(Hardcastle), Lucien Littlefield (Smith)

BABY FACE NELSON

Drummond and Col. Neilson of Scotland Yard go after the transvestite who steals the formula for a new explosive.

The second of Paramount's seven Bulldog Drummond second features is par for the course, with fast-moving action and a suitably short running time, but the comic relief provided by Denny and Clive is rather more entertaining than the thrills.

'Far fetched yarn and the situations are hard to swallow ... an acceptable proposition for other than sophisticated patrons.'
CEA Film Report

THE BONNIE PARKER STORY

THE CASE OF THE LUCKY LEGS

(US 1935)

pc WB. p sup Henry Blanke. d Archie L Mayo. w Brown Holmes, Ben Markson. adap Edward Chodorov, from the story by Erle Stanley Gardner. ph Tony Gaudio. B&W. ed James Gibbon. 76 mins

Cast: Warren William (Perry Mason), Genevieve Tobin (Della Street), Patricia Ellis (Margie Clune), Lyle Talbot (Dr Doray), Allen Jenkins (Spudsy), Barton MacLane (Bissonette), Peggy Shannon (Thelma Hall), Porter Hall (Bradbury), Anita Kerry (Eva Lamont)

Lawyer-sleuth Perry Mason solves the murder of the promoter of a 'Lucky Legs' contest.

The third (of four) outings by Williams as Gardner's lawyer-sleuth combines humour and thrills, although Mason tends to behave more like a flip celluloid private eye than a lawyer.

'Smart handling in the direction of this mystery yarn, otherwise would not be above ordinary. Slick writing also sets it up as pretty smart entertainment.'
Variety

CITY OF FEAR

(US 1958)

pc Orbit. p Leon Chooluck. d Irving Lerner. w Steven Ritch, Robert Dillon. ph Lucien Ballard. B&W. ed Robert Lawrence. ad Jack Poplin. m Jerry Goldsmith. 75 mins

Cast: Vince Edwards (Vince Ryker), John Archer (Lt Mark Richards), Patricia Blair (June), Steven Ritch (D Wallace), Kelly Thorsden (Johnson), Lyle Talbot (Chief Jensen), Joseph Mell (Crown), Cathy Browne (Jeanne Sherwood Price (Hallon)

An escaped convict is hunted by police, who need to stop him before he can open the deadly canister containing radioactive cobalt 60 he is carrying.

Providing you accept the artificial premise, brisk direction, well-shot locations and effective suspense go a long way towards disguising its obvio low-budget second-feature origins and aspirations.

'Parts of it are good – above its class – and while parts are also not s good, it is never a dull picture and it occasionally gripping.'
Variety

CRIME IN THE STREETS

(US 1956)

pc Allied Artists. A Lindbrook Production. p Vincent M Fennelly. d Donald Siegel. w Reginald Rose, from his television play. ph Sam Leavitt. B&W. ad Serge Krizman. m Franz Waxman. 91 mins

Cast: James Whitmore (Ben Wagner) John Cassavetes (Frankie Dane), Sal Mineo (Baby Gioia), Mark Rydell (Lou Macklin), Virginia Gregg (Mrs Dane), Peter Votrian (Richie Dane), Will Kuluva (Mr Gioia), Malcolm Atterbury (Mr McAllister), Denise Alexander (Maria Gioia), Dan Terranova (Blockbuster)

A social worker prevents murder by rival street gangs.

What worked well enough on television emerges as a well-intentioned bore, not helped by Siegel's surprisingly tedious direction. The actors try hard, though.

'A programme filler and a mighty dreary one at that.'
Variety

CRIME WAVE

(US 1953) (GB: THE CITY IS DARK)

pc WB. p Bryan Foy. d André de Toth. w Crane Wilbur. st John and Ward Hawkins. adap Bernard Gordon, Richard Wormser. ph Bert Glennon. B&W. ad Stanley Fleischer. m David Buttolph. 73 mins

Cast: Sterling Hayden (Det. Sgt Sims), Gene Nelson (Steve Lacy), Phyllis Kirk (Ellen), Ted de Corsia ('Doc' Penny), Charles Buchinsky (later Charles Bronson) (Hastings), Jay Novello ('Dr' Otto Hesler), James Bell (Daniel O'Keefe), Dub Taylor (Gus Snider), Gayle Kellogg (Kelly)

A paroled ex-convict attempts to go straight but is implicated in a bank robbery and murder.

Minor programmer, well-directed and written, with effective use of Los Angeles locations and good police procedural detail.

'A well-portrayed, exciting and gripping film.'
Picture Show

CRY BABY KILLER

(US 1958)

pc Allied Artists. A Roger Corman Production. p David Kramarsky, David March. d Justus Addis. w Leo Gordon, Melvin Levy. st Leo Gordon. ph Floyd Crosby. B&W. ad Don Ament. m Gerald Fried. song Dick Kallman. 62 mins

Cast: Harry Lauter (Porter), Jack Nicholson (Jimmy), Carolyn Mitchell (Carole), Brett Halsey (Manny), Lynn Cartwright (Julie), Ralph Reed (Joey), John Shay (Gannon), Barbara Knudson (Mrs Maxton), Jordan Whitfield (Sam), Leo Gordon (Bystander)

A juvenile delinquent panics when he believes he has killed two youths, and holes up in a storeroom with three hostages.

Routine, mercifully short, teen-oriented suspenser with a soft centre, notable only for Nicholson's inauspicious film debut.

'As entertainment it is a fill in for the masses, but it is arguably the type of picture the average British audience – certainly family audience – could well do without.'
CEA Film Report

DILLINGER

(US 1945)

pc Monogram. p Maurice King, Franklin King. d Max Nossek. dial d Leon Charles. tech d Herman King. w Philip Yordan. ph Jackson Rose. B&W. m Dimitri Tiomkin. 74 mins

Cast: Lawrence Tierney (John Dillinger), Edmund Lowe (Specs), Anne Jeffreys (Helen), Eduardo Cianelli (Hugh), Marc Lawrence (Doc), Elisha Cook Jr (Kirk), Ralph Lewis (Tony), Ludwig Stossel (Otto), Else Janssen (Mrs Otto), Lou Lubin (Walter), Hugh Prosser, Dewey Robinson (Guards)

Fictionalized, inaccurate biopic of gangster John Dillinger, culminating in his death in 1934, shot down in front of Chicago's Biograph Theatre after seeing *Manhattan Melodrama*.

Probably the best film from Poverty Row producers Monogram, but still stilted, tedious, ill-directed and padded out with stock footage, including a robbery from 1937's You Only Live Twice. However, its dire warning against promiscuous filmgoing is impeccable. The film is partially redeemed by an effective, career-best portrayal by Tierney, who went on to give the best performance 47 years later in Reservoir Dogs (q.v.). Improbably, Philip Yordan's leaden screenplay was Oscar-nominated. Dillinger was banned in Chicago.

'Somehow, the pic smacks of the same intensity imparted to gangland pictures of the '30s, when such films seemed the box-office rage. But in 1945, Dillinger, as most such pix, seems passé.'
Variety

FINGER MAN

(US 1955)

pc Allied Artists. A Lindsley Parsons Production. p Lindsley Parsons. d Harold Schuster. w Warren Douglas. st Morris Lipsius, John Lardner. ph William Sickner. B&W. ed Maurice Wright. ad William Ross. m Paul Dunlap. 81 mins

Cast: Frank Lovejoy (Casey Martin), Forrest Tucker (Dutch Becker), Peggie Castle (Gladys Baker), Timothy Carey (Louis Terpe), John Cliff (Cooper), William Leicester (Rogers), Glen Gordon (Carlos Armour), John Close (Walters), Hugh Sanders (Mr Burns), Evelynne Eaton (Lucille), Charles Maxwell (Amory), Lewis Charles (Lefty Stern), Ben Girdlestone (Poser with Pizza)

A three-time loser agrees to infiltrate a gang to gain evidence against a racketeer rather than go to jail.

Unpretentious direction makes the most of a familiar crime story and elicits vivid supporting performances from Carey and Eaton.

'Effectively characterized and well acted, holds the interest throughout.'
CEA Film Report

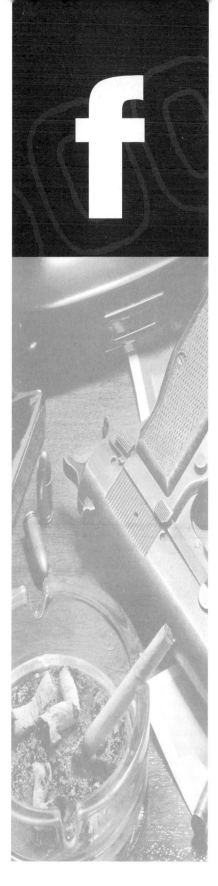

GANG WAR

(US 1958)

pc Regal Films. p Harold E Knox. d Gene Fowler Jr. w Louis Vittes, from the novel *The Hoods Take Over* by Ovid Demaris. ph John M Nickolaus. B&W. Scope. ed Frank Baldridge. ad John Mansbridge. m Paul Dunlap. 75 mins

Cast: Charles Bronson (Alan Avery), Kent Taylor (Bryce Barker), Jennifer Holden (Maries), John Doucette (Maxie Matthews), Gloria Henry (Edie Avery), Gloria Grey (Marsha Brown), Barney Phillips (Sam Johnson), Ralph Manza (Axe Duncan), George Eldridge (Sgt Ernie Tucker), Whit Bissell (Mark)

A schoolteacher testifies in a gangland murder and, when his pregnant wife is murdered, seeks vengeance against the gangster who ordered her death.

Efficient B-feature with Bronson flexing his acting muscles to some effect in a role that almost exactly mirrors his 1974 success *Death Wish* (q.v.).

'A bang-bang opus with more than enough excitement for a second-feature life.'
Variety

THE GIRL IN BLACK STOCKINGS

(US 1957)

pc Bel-Air. exec p Aubrey Schenck. d Howard W Koch. w Richard Landau, from the story *Wanton Murder* by Peter Godfrey. ph William Margulies. B&W. ed John F Schreyer. m Les Baxter. 73 mins

Cast: Lex Barker (David Hewson), Anne Bancroft (Beth), Mamie Van Doren (Harriet Ames), John Dehner (Sheriff Holmes), Ron Randell (Edmond Perry), Marie Windsor (Juli Perry), Gene O'Donnell (Felton), John Holland (Norman Grant), Diana Vandervlis (Louise Miles), Stuart Whitman (Prentiss)

Brutal murders are committed at a chic resort hotel in Utah.

Slickly-scripted, low-budget murder mystery (transposing the original story from South Africa to the US), and well-directed, with competent acting and a good climactic twist.

'Sound and useful-length entertainment for double billing. Here's a whodunit with all the angles the fans like plenty of suspects and plot twists.'
Daily Film Renter

THE GREAT ST LOUIS BANK ROBBERY

(US 1958)

pc Charles Guggenheim and Associates Inc. p Charles Guggenheim. assoc p, w Richard T Heffron. d Charles Guggenheim, John Stix. ph Victor Duncan. B&W. ed Warren Adams. m Bernardo Segall. song *Night Train* by Bernardo Segall, Peter Ude. guitar ballads/singer Jim Symington. 86 mins

Cast: Steve McQueen (George Fowler), David Clarke (Gino), Graham Denton (John Egan), Molly McCarthy (Ann), James Dukas (Willie)

Criminals plan to rob a bank in St Louis.

Minor fact-based crime caper whose deficiencies in plot and execution are partly redeemed by atmospheric location cinematography and semi-documentary style direction. McQueen's first film to bill him as 'Steve', not 'Steven'.

Inept handling of events leading up to the holdup in closing reels will hold booking to smaller program situations.'
Variety

THE HOUR OF 13
(GB 1952)
pc MGM p Hayes Goetz. d Harold French. w Leon Gordon, Howard Emmett Rogers, from a novel by Philip MacDonald. ph Guy Green. B&W. ed Robert Watts, Raymond Poulton. ad Alfred Junge. m John Addison. 78 mins

Cast: Peter Lawford (Nicholas Revel), Dawn Addams (Jane Frensham), Roland Culver (Connor), Derek Bond (Sir Christopher Lenhurst), Leslie Dwyer (Ernie Perker), Michael Horden (Sir Hubert Frensham), Colin Gordon (MacStreet), Heather Thatcher (Mrs Chumley Orr), Jack McNaughton (Ford), Fabia Drake (Lady Embridge)

A society thief turns detective to clear himself when he is suspected of being the maniac who stabbed ten policemen in Edwardian London.

Passable, studio-bound second-feature whodunnit with rather more atmosphere than conviction and Lawford overdoing the Raffles-like charm. A remake of 1934's *The Mystery of Mr X.*

This murder melodrama has at least a fresh approach and some good acting.'
Picturegoer

THE HUMAN JUNGLE
(US 1954)
pc Allied Artists. p Hayes Goetz. assoc p Marvin Mirisch. d Joe Newman. w William Sackheim, Daniel Fuchs. st William Sackheim. ph Ellis Carter. B&W. sup cd Lester Sansom. ed Samuel Fields. ad Dave Milton. m Hans Salter. 82 mins

Cast: Gary Merrill (Capt. Danforth) Jan Sterling ((Mary), Paula Raymond (Pat Danforth), Emile Meyer (Rowan), Regis Toomey (Geddes), Lamont Johnson (Lannigan), Chuck Connors (Swados), James Westerfield (Capt. Harrison), Pat Waltz (Strauss), George Wallace (O'Neil), Chubby Johnson (Greenie)

A police captain put in charge of a notoriously crime-ridden city precinct gambles his career on solving a murder.

A holding police procedural whose taut direction and competent performances improve on the routine storyline.

'A brutal and laconic essay in crime-breaking. And not all the brutalities are justified. Though it doesn't probe deep into moral issues, where the film prods, it often hits home.'
Picturegoer

I, MOBSTER

(US 1958)

pc Edward L Alperson. p Roger Corman, Gene Corman. d Roger Corman. w Steve Fisher, from the novel by Joseph Hilton Smith. ph Floyd Crosby. B&W. ed William B Murphy. ad Daniel Haller. m Gerald Fried, Edward L Alperson Jr. songs Edward L Alperson Jr, Jerry Winn. 82 mins

Cast: Steve Cochran (Joe Sante), Lita Milan (Teresa Porter), Robert Strauss (Black Frankie), Celia Lovsky (Mrs Sante), Lili St Cyr (Herself), John Brinkley (Ernie Porter), Yvette Vickers (The Blonde), Jeri Southern (Herself), Grant Withers (Paul Moran), Robert Shayne (Senator), John Mylong (Mr Sante)

A hoodlum testifying at the Senate Rackets Hearing recalls his criminal life.

A standard story of a slum kid who grows up to be a gangster benefits from Corman's no-nonsense direction and Cochran's forceful characterization.

'A well turned-out melodrama ... under Roger Corman's knowhow direction action unfolds smoothly and swiftly.'
Variety

'It was made on my customary low budget.'
Roger Corman

KILL ME TOMORROW

(GB 1957)

pc Delta Films. p Francis Searle. d
Terence Fisher. w Robert Falconer,
Manning O'Brien. ph Geoffrey
Faithfull. B&W. ed Ann Chegwidden.
ad Bernard Robinson. m Temple
Abady. 80 mins

Cast: Pat O'Brien (Bart Crosbie), Lois
Maxwell (Jill Brook), George
Coulouris (Heinz Webber), Robert
Brown (Steve), Ronald Adam (Brook),
Richard Pasco (Dr Fisher), Wensley
Pithey (Insp. Lane), Peter Swannick
(Harrison), April Olrich (Bella
Braganza), Freddie Mills (Waxy),
Tommy Steele (Himself)

An alcoholic reporter takes the
blame for the murder of his editor
in exchange for money to pay for a
life-saving operation for his young son.

Archetypal British B-picture
directed with well-paced efficiency by
Fisher, his last routine assignment
before becoming one of the major
post-war horror movie-makers. Steele's
film debut.

'Neat and praiseworthy.'
Picture Show

KILL ME TOMORROW

LOOPHOLE

(US 1954)

pc Allied Artists. A Lindsley Parsons Production. p Lindsley Parsons. d Harold Schuster. w Warren Douglas, from an unpublished story by George Bricker & Dwight V Babcock. ph William Sickner. B&W. ed Ace Herman. ad David Milton. sfx E J Frank. m Paul Dunlap. 79 mins

Cast: Barry Sullivan (Mike Donovan), Charles McGraw (Gus Slavin), Dorothy Malone (Ruthie Donovan), Don Haggerty (Neil Sanford), Mary Beth Hughes (Vera), Don Beddoe (Herman Tate), Dayton Lummis (Mr Starling), Gillian Schuster (Little Girl), Joanne Jordan (Georgia), John Eldredge (Mr Temple), Richard Reeves (Peter Mazurki), Lawrence Galkoff (Engineer)

A chief cashier suspected of embezzlement after a bank robbery is made to resign and is hounded by an insurance investigator.

Well-used Los Angeles and Malibu locations add dimension to a tautly-directed suspenser that makes good use of its running time.

'This story is arrestingly told and cleverly developed with the result that it grips the interest.'
CEA Film Report

MACHINE GUN KELLY

(US 1958)

pc AIP/James H Nicholson, Samuel Z Arkoff. d Roger Corman. w R Wright Campbell. ph Floyd Crosby. B&W. ed Ronald Sinclair. ad Dan Haller. m Gerald Fried. 80 mins

Cast: Charles Bronson (Machine Gun Kelly), Susan Cabot (Flo), Morey Amsterdam (Fandango), Wally Campo (Maize), Bob Griffin (Vita), Barboura Morris (Lynn), Richard Devon (Apple), Connie Gilchrist (Ma), Ted Thorp (Teddy), Mitzi McCall (Harriet), Frank De Kova (Harry), Larry Thor (Drummond)

A former bootlegger turned gunman and bank robber is goaded by his mistress into becoming a kidnapper, which leads to his downfall.

More a variation on a theme than a serious attempt at a biopic, it packs plenty of excitement into its relatively short running time, and is kept moving by Corman's brisk direction and a strong performance from Bronson in his first starring role.

'The pace of the action is so fast as to be almost frantic and the acting is more than adequate to the occasion – particularly by the two principals. But this apart, the film is in all other respects highly unpleasant.'
Monthly Film Bulletin

MURDER IS MY BEAT

(US 1955)

pc Allied Artists. p, w Aubrey Wisberg. st Aubrey Wisberg, Martin Field. assoc p Isle Kahn. d Edgar J Ulmer. ph Harold E Wellman. B&W. ed Fred R Feitshans. ad David Milton. m Al Glasser. 77 mins

Cast: Paul Langton (Patrick), Barbara Payton (Eden), Robert Shayne (Rawley), Selena Royle (Mrs Abbott), Roy Gordon (Abbott), Tracey Roberts (Patsy), Kate McKenna (Landlady), Henry A Harvey Sr (Attendant), Jay Adler (Bartender)

A detective escorts a nightclub singer convicted of murder to jail, and on the way they discover the real killer.

Below-average B-picture, indifferently directed and another large nail in the coffin of Ulmer's claim to major *auteur* status.

'It's a shoddily-made melodrama ... the entire affair can be chalked off as a waste of negative.'
Variety

MY NAME IS JULIA ROSS

(US 1945)

pc Columbia. p Wallace MacDonald. d Joseph H Lewis. w Muriel Roy Bolton, from the novel *The Woman in Red* by Anthony Gilbert. ph Burnett Guffey. B&W. ed James Sweeney. ad Jerome Pycha Jr. m Mischa Bakaleinikoff. 64 mins

Cast: Nina Foch (Julia Ross), Dame May Whitty (Mrs Hughes), George Macready (Ralph Hughes), Roland Varno (Dennis Bruce), Anita Bolster (Sparkes), Doris Lloyd (Mrs Mackie), Leonard Mudie (Peters), Joy Harrington (Bertha), Queenie Leonard (Alice), Harry Hays Morgan (Robinson) Ottola Nesmith (Mrs Robinson), Olaf Hytten (Rev. Lewis), Evan Thomas (Dr Keller)

A young girl who accepts a job as a resident secretary is forced to impersonate an heiress.

Tense, reeking with atmosphere and

making every minute of its short running time count. Not quite the seminal *film noir* claimed by those wishing to transform Joseph J Lewis from above-average B-film director to pantheon *auteur*, but very well directed, excellently acted by a superior cast and moodily photographed by Burnett Guffey.

'All round, a likeable, unpretentious, generally successful attempt to turn good trash into decently artful entertainment.'
The Nation

RIOT IN CELL BLOCK 11
(US 1954)

pc Allied Artists. A Walter Wanger Production. p Walter Wanger. d Don Siegel. w Richard Collins. ph Russell Harlan. B&W. ed Bruce P Pierce. ad David Milton. m Herschel Burke Gilbert. 80 mins

Cast: Neville Brand (Dunn), Emile Meyer (The Warden), Frank Faylen (Haskel), Leo Gordon (Carnie), Robert Osterloh (The Colonel), Paul Frees (Monroe), Don Keefer (Newspaperman), Alvy Moore (Gator), Dabbs Greer (Schuyler), Whit Bissell (Snader), James Anderson (Acton), Carleton Young (Capt. Barrett), William Schallert (Reporter), Roy Glenn (Delmar)

Three convicts hold guards hostage in a large American state prison and insist their demands be discussed in the presence of the press.

Hard-edged and suspenseful, benefiting from well-used Folsom Prison locations and the taut direction of Don Siegel in the days before he

became aware of his cult *auteur* status. The central performances of Brand and Meyer are compelling, and the movie argues its case for prison reform cogently and with justifiable anger, and mostly without resorting to facile melodrama.

'It is a frightening picture charged with terror and shocks, but I came away deeply impressed.'
News of the World

'A tough, believable account of what happens when convicts are pushed around too much ... a movie of almost unrelenting violence, but the uproar finds its justification in their purpose: the correction of abuses in penal establishments.'
The New Yorker

THE SNORKEL
(GB 1958)

pc Hammer. p Michael Carreras. d Guy Green. w Peter Myers, Jimmy Sangster, from the original story by Anthony Dawson. ph Jack Asher. B&W. sup ed James Needs. ed Bill Lenny. ad John Stoll. md John Hollingsworth. 90 mins

Cast: Peter Van Eyck (Jacques Duval), Betta St John (Jean), Mandy Miller (Candy), Gregoire Aslan (The Inspector), William Franklyn (Wilson), Henry Vidon (The Gardener), Marie Burke (Daily Woman), Irene Prador (Frenchwoman), Robert Rietty (Station Sergeant), Armand Guinle (Waiter)

A man devises what he believes is the perfect murder of his wife, but is exposed by his step-daughter.

The writers come up with an original, if improbable, method of murder, and then run out of inspiration. So do the actors and director.

'The picture misses fire to a large extent because of loose ends and highly improbable incidents; can any murderer have been so careless as to leave his prime clue lying around for anyone, including a spaniel, to find?'
CEA Film Report

WITNESS TO MURDER

(US 1954)

pc Chester Erskine Productions. p, w Chester Erskine. d Roy Rowland. ph John Alton. B&W. ed Robert Swink. ad William Ferrari. m Herschel Burke Gilbert. song Herschel Burke Gilbert, Sylvia Fine. 81 mins

Cast: Barbara Stanwyck (Cheryl Draper), George Sanders (Albert Richter), Gary Merrill (Lawrence Matthews), Jesse White (Eddie Vincent), Harry Shannon (Capt. Donelly), Claire Carleton (The Blonde), Lewis Martin (Psychiatrist), Dick Elliott (Apartment Manager), Harry Tyler (Charlie), Juanita Moore (Woman)

A killer almost succeeds in having a woman murder witness declared insane.

Short, briskly-directed, with above-average suspense.

'Thrilling crime entertainment with excellent performances from stars and supporting cast.'
Picture Show

Index

Cinematographer Index

Composer Index

INDEX

ABBREVIATIONS

ABBREVIATIONS

The abbreviations for the
credit lists are as follows:

ad	art director
adap	adaptation
add	additional
adv	adviser
arr	arranger
assoc	associate
asst	assistant
B&W	black and white
chor	choreography
co-ord	co-ordinator
co-p	co-producer
cons	consultant
cos	costumes
d	director
dial	dialogue
ed	editor
exec p	executive producer
fx	effects
m	music
m-u	make-up
md	music director
p	producer/production
pc	production company
pd	production designer
ph	photographer/photography
rn	real name
sc	screenplay
sfx	special effects
st	screen treatment
sup	supervising/supervisor
tech	technical
w	writer